JOURNEY

OF

Love

A PRIDE AND PREJUDICE VARIATION

BRENDA J. WEBB

Journey of Love – A Pemberley Tale is a work of fiction. All characters are either from the author's imagination, or from Jane Austen's novel, Pride and Prejudice. At no point in this body of work has Artificial Intelligence (AI) been employed to write it.

Cover design and formatting by Roseanna White

DEDICATION

I dedicate this book to those who helped me create this story. My friend and editor, Debbie Styne, who worked on chapters one through twenty-six and whose expertise and encouragement are invaluable.

To Barbara Cornthwaite, who graciously stepped in to edit chapters twenty-seven through thirty-two when Debbie had to drop out.

My betas: Kathryn Begley, Janet Foster, Terri Merz and Wendy Delzell, who do everything within their power to make the story error free. Also, I would like to thank Debbie Fortin for cold reading the story.

Lastly, I dedicate it to those of you who read my books and promote them by word of mouth and review. Without your help and support, I would not be writing.

Thank you all for being a part of my team.

OTHER BOOKS BY BRENDA J. WEBB

Fitzwilliam Darcy - An Honourable Man

Mr. Darcy's Forbidden Love

Darcy and Elizabeth – A Most Unlikely Couple

Darcy and Elizabeth – A Promise Kept

Passages – A Pemberley Tale

Taking Another Chance

Proof of Love – A Pemberley Tale

The Appearance of Goodness

*"Being deeply loved by someone gives you strength,
while loving someone deeply gives you courage."
~ Lao Tzu*

Chapter 1

Weymouth
Willowbend Hall

Taking advantage of the gazebo he had had constructed on the secluded beach below his estate to provide relief from the unrelenting sun, William smiled at the scene playing out before him. Had he not just finished riding over the entire estate with Mr. Danvers, his steward, he would have been on the sand with his family. Instead, when a maid brought a pitcher of lemonade down from the manor just as he arrived, Elizabeth had insisted he rest in the shade and enjoy a glass whilst he watched their son play in the sand and she took their daughter for a walk.

A barefoot Elizabeth walked two-year-old Anne Elizabeth Darcy several yards down the beach, bending over the girl, holding her hands to keep the child upright in the soft, wet sand at the edge of the water. Suddenly, a wave washed over their feet, making them laugh. A miniature of her mother with dark eyes and hair and with Elizabeth's small stature, Anne had trouble navigating the sand with her short legs. She was clearly enjoying herself, though, for with every step she took, she looked up and smiled.

Elizabeth had tied up the skirt of her thin, yellow-striped, muslin gown to keep the hem from getting soaked, providing William with an excellent view of her shapely calves. This, and the sight of the woman he loved guiding his child, was so pleasing that William's heart swelled with pride.

As he watched, a small white terrier raced down the beach and circled the two, barking furiously, before returning to where William's eldest child Bennet Fitzwilliam George Darcy, sat busily building a fort in the sand several yards in front of the gazebo. Clancy had fallen in love with Ben, as the heir to Pemberley was called, the instant the child was born, and had assumed the role of his protector. After Anne was born, the dog had added her to his watch, which meant that, at times like this, he found it frustrating to guard both his charges.

As William glanced back to Ben, who was filling yet another bucket with sand, he wondered if his son realised his creation would soon end up a victim of the tides. Just as this thought came to mind, a familiar voice interrupted his reverie.

"Oh, to live the life of the idle rich!"

Recognising the voice, William tried not to smile as he spoke without turning. "What are you doing here, Cousin?"

"Is that any way to welcome your favourite relation?" Colonel Richard Fitzwilliam questioned, feigning offence by bringing his hand to his heart.

William stood as Richard began up the steps of the gazebo, and they embraced, slapping each other on the back, as was their wont when they had been apart for any length of time.

"I did not mean to imply you were not welcome. I am simply surprised to see you arrive so late in our stay," William replied.

Looking to where Ben was playing and seeing that all was well, he walked over to pour a glass of lemonade for his cousin. As he held it out to Richard, he added, "We leave for London in the morning. Of course, you are welcome to stay on here for as long as you like."

"Alas, I cannot. I was sent to Exeter by General Lassiter, and I must report back to him straightaway," Richard replied, doffing his hat and coat, and drinking half the glass of lemonade before sitting down. "It was only upon leaving Exeter that I recalled you mentioned you might be at Willowbend about this time. It was then I decided I could make this my stop for the night."

"I am pleased that you did; you can ride back to London with us."

"I shall not refuse such a generous offer. A soft seat beats a saddle any day!" Finishing his lemonade and setting the empty glass on the table, he waved a hand across the scenic view. "I am glad you were not forced to sell this estate; the view is magnificent."

"I am pleased as well. Many of my favourite memories of Mother are rooted in this place, not to mention that Elizabeth fell in love with it the first time she saw it. However, it is still a bit of a struggle to manage both estates and the townhouse."

"I thought you had recovered the funds Uncle George wasted."

"Most, but not everything; however, by concentrating on increasing the number of animals raised for profit, converting more pastures to crops, and investing in the stocks your father suggested, I have been able to increase our assets substantially in the last few years."

"I never doubted you would," Richard replied. "Tell me. Have you heard from Georgiana? Is she ready to toss that dandy aside and come back home?"

Reflecting on Georgiana's new husband, Viscount Hayworth of Berkley Hall in Southampton, William answered forlornly, "She is not. Still, there was something strange about her last letter, though I could not determine exactly what. Elizabeth swears she saw no difference, but I was left with the impression that something has changed since the viscount's father insisted she and Hayworth visit the family's estate in Armagh."

"Now, Darcy, do not go borrowing trouble. I know you were not in favour of her marrying at nineteen ... neither was I; however, seeing that she did not wish to follow society's dictates and come out, she was right to accept the hand of Viscount Hayworth. His reputation for being honest and sensible does him credit, and he will inherit Berkley Hall upon his father's death. Even Mother was jubilant when he made Poppet an offer."

William bristled. "I am not borrowing trouble! I just happen to know my sister well enough to notice when the tone of her letters has changed."

"I apologise," Richard said. "I did not mean to make light of your intuition. Let us hope all is well at—" He went silent. Then, after a while, he said, "I do not recall the name of their estate in Ireland."

"Ballyneen; Ballyneen Castle actually, though Georgiana says the castle was destroyed centuries ago."

"Now that is an Irish name if ever I heard one! One would think I could remember that." Closing his eyes, Richard took a deep breath. "Being here is like stepping into a different world. One breath of ocean air and my mental clarity is restored."

"I could not agree more."

A noise from Ben's direction caught Richard's attention. "I swear that boy looks exactly like you did when you were his age. There is no way you could deny he is yours."

"Not that I would want to deny him," William replied wryly, "but I wonder at your ability to recall what I looked like at the age of four."

"You forget I am four years older, so I remember quite well."

At that instant, Ben noticed his cousin. Jumping to his feet, he rushed towards him with Clancy on his heels. As he ran up the steps, he exclaimed excitedly, "Cousin Richard, did you bring me the cannon?"

"Now, Son," William said, "is that how you are supposed to greet your cousin? What have we discussed regarding manners?"

Properly chastised, Ben dropped his head. "I am sorry, Papa." Then addressing Richard, he performed a quick bow and held out a very sandy hand. "It is good to see you again, Cousin Richard. I pray this visit finds you well."

Richard winked at William, stood and bowed slightly before grasping the hand and shaking it. "It is good to see you again, Master Ben. I am very well indeed. Thank you for asking. How are you faring?"

"I am well, too."

Nodding towards the fort, Richard said, "I see you took my advice and asked Mrs. Beatty to find you a bucket. In my experience, old buckets construct the best sandcastles."

"It is not a castle," Ben asserted. "It is a fort!"

"Of course," Richard said, restraining a smile. "Only girls build castles."

"And I am not a girl!" Ben stated firmly. Then, glancing back at his handiwork just as a particularly high wave threatened to sweep it away, he added, "I believe next time I should build my fort farther from the water."

"Good thinking!" Richard declared. "Now, you asked about the cannon. As luck would have it, this trip took me right past the very shop where I first saw it."

Richard reached into his coat pocket and brought out something wrapped in paper. As he held it out, Ben eagerly took it and ripped away the paper to find the replica of a cannon and a separate piece consisting of three cannon balls in a stack. Also included was one of the painted soldiers Richard had been gifting Ben since he was old enough to sit up.

"Thank you!" Ben exclaimed, reaching up to bestow a hug on his favourite cousin. "I must add them to my fort!" Instantly, he and Clancy rushed down the steps towards his creation.

"He enjoys playing soldier," William observed. "Perhaps one day he will enlist in His Majesty's service."

"Not as long as I live."

"I was only teasing, Darcy. Do not take everything I say so seriously." Then Richard squinted, looking around. "Where are your lovely wife and daughter? Mrs. Keagan said the entire family was down here."

"Elizabeth and Anne are walking along the beach," William said, nodding towards two figures barely discernible in the distance. "She is helping Anne to walk in the sand and probably has lost track of how far she has gone. I should go fetch her." As William started down the gazebo steps, he said, "If you watch Ben, I shall go after Elizabeth."

"Having been in the saddle all morning, I shall be glad to sit comfortably for a while." Sinking down on the sand next to the fort, he allowed Clancy to jump into his lap as he asked, "Would you like your old cousin to keep you company, Ben?"

"I would! And will you tell me another story about fighting the French?"

"Nothing too gory," William warned under his breath. "The last time you told him one of your tales he had night terrors for months. Elizabeth will not be pleased if that happens again."

"Warning duly noted," Richard answered just as quietly.

As William began to walk away, he heard his cousin say, "Ben, did I tell you about the time I had to milk a cow in the middle of a battlefield?"

Unable to hold back a chuckle, William hurried towards his wife and daughter.

Elizabeth sat in the sand holding Anne in her lap, who was occupied playing with several coral-coloured seashells that had washed up on the beach. Suddenly she looked up to see William striding towards them. Stripped down to his breeches and an untucked shirt that billowed in the wind, he looked so handsome that her breath caught. His valet had been left behind at Pemberley, so his hair was longer than usual and was being tossed about by the wind. Elizabeth cared not a jot, for she was delighted when his hair was long enough to grasp during their lovemaking.

Suddenly, Anne saw her father and held up both arms, crying, "Papa!"

Scooping his daughter from her mother's lap, William kissed her forehead before placing her in the crook of his arm and holding out a hand to Elizabeth. "Richard has arrived and plans to stay the night. I persuaded him to ride back to London with us tomorrow."

"How fortunate," Elizabeth said, placing the shells in a bag and allowing William to assist her to her feet as she brushed sand from the back of her gown. "No one can entertain Ben like Richard, and that will prove useful on our journey."

"I warned him to keep the tales he spins less gruesome."

Elizabeth stood on tiptoes to give her husband a kiss. "You think of everything, sweetheart."

Suddenly, Anne held out a hand, wiggling her fingers as though she wanted something. "Mine!" she declared.

From the bag Elizabeth pulled out a seashell and handed it to her. Instantly, Anne clasped it to her chest.

William laughed. "I fear our daughter has reached the age when she may no longer want to share her possessions with her brother."

"She will just have to learn that she cannot always get her way," Elizabeth replied. "I will need your help to see that she does."

As they walked towards the gazebo, William answered, "I have no idea what you mean, dearest."

"Do not feign innocence with me, Fitzwilliam Darcy," Elizabeth said, giving his arm a playful pinch. "Anne has you under her spell."

"Is that my fault? She looks so much like you that when she fixes me with those big, brown eyes, I forget what I meant to chastise her about in the first place."

Elizabeth laughed, threading her arm through his and laying her head against him. "I will not allow you to use Anne's resemblance to me as an excuse not to discipline her. After all, Ben is the image of you, and we both make him behave. Just think of it this way: when Anne is old enough to notice boys, you will want her to listen to your advice, will you not?"

"Of course."

"Then you must make certain she listens to you now. Otherwise, when more challenging issues arise—and they will—she may not listen."

"As usual, you are correct. I shall strive to do better."

"I knew I could rely on you, my love."

Dinner that evening

Conversation at the table had been as entertaining as ever, with Richard recounting the latest misfortunes he suffered simply because he chose to serve king and country.

William wiped tears from his eyes from laughing so heartily. "Please, Cousin, no more until we have finished eating, or I may choke."

Proud that he had made his reticent cousin laugh, Richard was ready to oblige as the last course was brought into the room. "I shall be as quiet as a mouse."

As soon as the footmen left the room, the housekeeper, Mrs. Keagan, slipped quietly inside with an alarmed look on her face.

"Sir, I hate to interrupt your dinner, but this express was just delivered, and the rider was instructed to wait for a reply." With that, she held out a letter.

William's expression darkened, and his eyes sought Elizabeth's. Taking the missive and breaking the seal, he began to read silently.

"Whatever news it contains, I wish to hear it," Elizabeth declared at length.

Knowing his wife would not be deterred, William sighed heavily. "It is from Lord Matlock. He writes—"

"Is it Mother?" Richard interrupted, his voice full of concern.

"No. It is our cousin, Anne. She has taken a turn for the worst and is not expected to live. Your father has left for Rosings and asks me to come directly there. He believes that if I arrive in time to attend the funeral, it may help to heal the breach in my relationship with Aunt Catherine. He also mentioned that he wrote to you, though he has no idea if his letter will find you in time."

"We can travel directly to Rosings from here ... that is, if you intend to go," Richard said.

"I do," William replied. "But what about your orders?"

"Seeing that it is a family crisis, the general will understand if I am a day or two late." Intentionally avoiding looking at Elizabeth, he added, "However, I feel I must warn you that our aunt will not welcome Elizabeth or the children at Rosings. I do not wish to bring up old offences but when I was last in Kent I called on Rosings to see Anne. Whilst I was there, our aunt raged that you had accelerated Anne's decline by refusing to marry her. She also reiterated that she had no intention of ever accepting Elizabeth as your wife."

William hissed, "Then she will not accept our children, either!"

A comforting hand came to rest on his arm. "Dearest, you must honour your uncle's request. He will understand that you are trying to avoid discord. The children and I can always stay at Grassley Manor whilst you stay at Rosings. After all, women cannot attend funerals."

Lord Grassley, a lifelong friend of Lord and Lady Matlock, owned the estate that abutted Rosings on the north. He and his wife had always been kind to Fitzwilliam and Elizabeth, inviting them for tea whenever they were in London at the same time.

Instantly, Elizabeth's suggestion was rejected. "I will not stay under the same roof with someone who hates you or our children," William declared.

"Neither will I," Richard agreed. "We will *all* stay at Grassley Manor. From there we can attend the funeral, offer our condolences and then leave."

"I think that would be better, that is, if Lord Grassley does not mind. I would like to pay my respects to Anne. I loved her as a cousin, no matter what Aunt Catherine thinks."

"Then it is settled," Elizabeth said. "We shall go to Kent instead of London."

That night

After dinner William talked with Richard far longer than he had planned, so when he entered the bedroom he shared with Elizabeth, he expected to find her asleep. That was not the case, however, for their bed was empty.

Glancing to the balcony, he saw her standing at the railing. A strong wind, signifying that a storm was moving in, blew her pale-blue silk nightgown and her glossy, dark hair in every direction. She looked so beautiful that his body reacted as it always had at the sight of her dressed so enticingly.

For a moment he considered if making love to Elizabeth the same day he learned his cousin was dying would be disrespectful. Then he recalled the last conversation he had had with Anne.

"Do not let Mother's tirades confound you, Fitzwilliam. Because of my health, I have never entertained thoughts of marriage. Moreover, had I wished to marry, you would not be my choice." She had smiled wryly. "While I love you, I could not see myself as your wife. Besides, you need someone who can give you many children, and I cannot." Her frail hand had reached to grasp his. "Marry someone you love, and fill Pemberley with children. Name one of the girls after me, and I shall be content."

Undressing quickly, William grabbed his black silk robe from where it hung inside the wardrobe and hurried towards Elizabeth, donning the garment as he walked. Slipping quietly behind her, he wound his arms around her slim frame, and buried his face in the softness of her shoulder. She turned into his embrace and their lips met in a kiss that rapidly grew passionate. He had not tied the belt to his robe, and when it fell open, his nakedness prompted Elizabeth to disrobe as well. As her nightgown floated to the balcony floor, he shrugged the robe off his shoulders, and their bodies melded into one.

Breaking the embrace, William picked Elizabeth up and carried her into the bedroom. Gently placing her on the satin sheets, he joined her and began placing hot, impassioned kisses over every inch of her silky skin. Soft gasps and moans let William know when she was ready, and they soon joined without either uttering a word. Normally a gentle lover, this time his thrusts soon became demanding. Elizabeth lifted her hips in response, and it seemed only moments before each reached satisfaction.

Spent, William whispered hoarsely, "What you do to me, Elizabeth! After all these years, I still desire you so much that sometimes I lose all control. Forgive me."

"Have you ever known me to complain?" she asked, smiling as he shook his head. "That is because I love it when you lose control." Another passionate kiss followed.

The Darcys were very sleepy the next morning.

Chapter 2

Kent
Grassley Manor
Three days later

Fortunately for the Darcy party, by the time they alighted from their coach the lord and lady of the manor were descending the front steps to greet them.

"Fitzwilliam, my boy," Lord Grassley said, shaking William's hand the instant he was out of the coach. "Dorothea and I had a feeling you and Mrs. Darcy would arrive today. Your uncle was here only yesterday, and he mentioned that he expected you, and perhaps Richard, to return for Anne's funeral. Moreover, he was quite adamant that you would not stay at Rosings."

As William was helping Elizabeth from the coach, he asked, "Anne has passed away?"

"Please excuse my blunder! I forgot that because you were travelling, you had no way of knowing. Yes, she has died."

By now Richard was standing beside William, so Lord Grassley addressed them both. "You have our deepest sympathy on the loss of your cousin."

"We appreciate your kindness," Richard replied as William nodded.

"Despite not being in her company as often as we would have liked, Anne was dear to our hearts," William added.

"No one familiar with you, or Richard, doubts that," Lord Grassley replied. Then he turned to Elizabeth and bowed. "Welcome to Grassley Manor, Mrs. Darcy."

Elizabeth dropped a curtsey. "Thank you, sir. I pray we are not imposing by coming without an invitation."

"Nonsense!" Lady Grassley interrupted. She took Elizabeth's hand. "We are pleased that you felt you could come."

As they walked away, Lord Grassley focused anew on Richard. "It is good to see you again, Colonel, though I regret the circumstances that brought you here."

"As do I," Richard said. "You mentioned my father. Dare I hope that he is staying here?"

"I tried to convince him to stay—one can only imagine how unstable Lady Catherine's mind is at this point—but he said he must try to tolerate her company for Anne's sake." He looked as though he was lost in a memory before adding, "Miss de Bourgh's death is a sad end to a life that held so much promise. I remember the day she was born."

"Yes. Unfortunately, her life was filled with so much sadness," Richard stated.

Whilst the men conversed, Lady Grassley hurried to speak to Bennet who had been helped to the ground by Florence, Elizabeth's maid, the only servant included in this trip.

Suddenly shy, the boy tried to hide behind his mother's skirts when Lady Grassley asked, "How are you, Master Bennet?"

Prompted to come forward by his mother, he performed a smart bow and said, "I am very well, thank you."

Lady Grassley gushed, "What fine manners!"

Elizabeth beamed as their hostess next turned her attention to Anne, who was now in Florence's arms. Gently patting the child's dark curls, she murmured, "How lovely you are! The image of your mother."

Being wary of strangers, Anne reached out for Elizabeth, and her proud mother took her. This left Florence to take Bennet's hand as they began to follow their hostess up the steps.

Upon reaching the portico, Lady Grassley stopped to say, "I understand why you would not wish to stay at Rosings. Though I feel sympathy for Catherine—after all, no parent should ever bury their child—that woman has always been hard to stomach, much less admire. I told Horace that at least now poor Anne is out from under her tyrannical thumb."

By then the men had caught up, and hearing her last words, Lord Grassley said, "Now, Dorothea, pray remember Catherine is their aunt, after all."

"We are not shocked by your opinion," Richard replied. "Darcy and I have been the recipients of her ire all our lives, and we are well aware of how insensitive she can be."

"Still, in light of recent events, perhaps we should extend her more compassion," Lord Grassley suggested.

"Humph!" Lady Grassley said. "I shall see how she treats Fitzwilliam before I give her the benefit of any of my sympathy."

After dinner

Once the men retired to the smoking room, Lord Grassley brought up the subject of his godson. "I must ask, Fitzwilliam, have you seen Gregory of late? I declare I have seen very little of him in the last six months."

Gregory Wright had married William's neighbour at Parkleigh Manor, Lady Emma, shortly after her father's death. Though the union seemed to come completely out of the blue, they appeared to be well matched, and over time, the matter of Emma's former cruelty towards Elizabeth had largely been forgotten—at least by Elizabeth. As for William, he was not as prone to forgive an attack on his wife. Still, when Emma died giving birth to her first child, Jonathan, the following year, both he and Elizabeth were saddened by her death, and as Jonathan grew older, he had become a frequent playmate of Bennet's.

"Elizabeth and I were discussing him several days ago. We wondered why he had not brought Jonathan over to play with Bennet as was his usual habit, but then she recalled he mentioned taking the child to Brighton to enjoy the sea air, seeing that he is subject to coughs and colds."

Lord Grassley held his chin, slowly stroking a thumb across it. "That is what we were told. Dorothea and I hoped to see Gregory and Jonathan as they travelled to Brighton or on their return, but I suppose he could have been too busy to stop."

"Might he attend the funeral?" Richard asked. "As I recall, after Darcy married Elizabeth, Wright became the object of my aunt's scheme to find a husband for Anne ... at least until she learned he had not inherited a fortune when his father died."

"Most likely Gregory will not hear of the funeral in time to attend. After all, the notice was put in the paper only this morning. In any case, the next time you see him, Fitzwilliam, will you tell him I need to speak with him?"

"I shall be happy to oblige," William replied.

The next day

The funeral was less grandiose than William had imagined it would be. In truth, other than a myriad of flowers and numerous attendees from amongst Rosings' tenants and surrounding neighbours, it was no grander than the funeral of someone of a lower station.

In view of the fact that the vicar at Hunsford had just been dismissed by his sister, Lord Matlock had arranged for the vicar of nearby Leesburg to conduct the funeral, and although that man did the best he could under the circumstances, the fact that he was not familiar with Anne made all his accolades ring hollow. After the service was over, Lord Matlock waited alongside William and Richard to follow the procession to the cemetery.

"I would like you both to join me at Rosings after Anne is laid to rest," Lord Matlock said. "Food has been prepared, and I hope my sister will take your presence there as a sign that you seek family accord, Fitzwilliam. Moreover, Catherine seems much more subdued than I expected. I think the loss of her only child may have mellowed her."

"I shall join you and do my best to be civil," William said, "but I warn you that the second she disparages my wife or children I will leave."

"I would not expect anything less. And though I feel sorry for my sister, I will not allow sympathy to cloud my judgement. I will rebuke her should she become uncivil."

At Rosings
A drawing room

Luncheon had been a subdued affair, for Lady Catherine had sent word that she would not be joining them, as she had no appetite. She did ask that once they had finished eating, they move to the front drawing room to await her. Having acquiesced, now all three men sat in silence, wondering what Lady Catherine might say.

Suddenly the door flew open, slamming against the wall as the grande dame entered the room. If she had appeared humble to Lord Matlock before Anne's funeral, the scowl on her face made it obvious that the *real* Lady Catherine had returned. As she crossed the room and walked straight to an imposing, throne-like chair in front of the hearth, a loud thump from her cane marked every step. Once seated, she silently studied each of them for so long a time that Lord Matlock felt it necessary to break the uncomfortable silence.

"We are here, Catherine, because we all wish to convey our deepest sympathy in the loss of dear Anne."

"Humph!" Lady Catherine grunted. "I think you are here to learn which of you will inherit Rosings upon my death."

Glancing to William, whose hands quickly formed fists, Lord Matlock's eyes pleaded for him to keep silent. Seeing William nod curtly, Lord Matlock continued. "That is not the case at all. Fitzwilliam has his own holdings to consider and does not need the added burden of Rosings. Moreover, I plan to turn over our grandmother's estate in Derbyshire to Richard when he retires from His Majesty's service, and he is already working with the steward to improve it. As for me, I have more than enough. So you see, your supposition is completely untrue."

"Nonsense! Rosings is worth two of Pemberley, and I dare say, half again more than Matlock! Furthermore, our grandmother's estate will never provide a decent living!" She cut her eyes to William. "Insofar as Fitzwilliam decided to marry that little tart against my—"

Instantly William was on his feet. "Not another word! I came to promote peace, Aunt, but I see that you had rather behave in your usual insufferable manner. Know this: My wife and my children are more precious to me than gold and worth more than anything you could offer. Never think for one minute that I care what happens to Rosings now or after your death."

With that William exited the room, slamming the door behind him.

Richard stood. "I have nothing more to add to what my cousin said. I agree with Darcy entirely. Goodbye, Aunt."

After Richard left, Lord Matlock addressed his sister. "You have always been a cruel, vindictive person, Catherine. For years, I attributed that to the fact that you were spoiled by our parents and then by Lewis.

Still, as the head of this family, I do not intend to tolerate your hateful rhetoric towards Darcy or his wife any longer. Elizabeth is a wonderful wife and mother, and I am sorry I ever harboured any reservations about her worthiness. I only wish I had secured a woman with her character for Leighton instead of that harridan Eleanor favoured. Still, what is done is done." Then, coming to his feet, he declared, "Until you apologise to Fitzwilliam, your portion of our family's jointly held bonds, stocks and income from rents will be deposited in an account that you will not have access to until I am convinced you have had a change of heart."

"If you think your threats will change my mind, you are badly mistaken! You have no say over the holdings Lewis left me, and they are enough to keep Rosings in the style to which I am accustomed."

"I fear, dear sister, you are badly mistaken. As I review Rosings' ledgers each year, I find that our family funds are what keeps this estate afloat."

"I do not believe you!"

"Believe me or not, it is true. Moreover, you never had any justification for badgering our nephew to marry Anne. According to your own physician, with her frail constitution Anne could never have borne children, and Fitzwilliam needed an heir."

Lady Catherine stood, slamming her cane on the floor. "Cease with these lies and get off of my property!"

"Gladly," Lord Matlock said resignedly. Once he reached the door, he hesitated and turned to add, "It was mentioned more than once by those attending the funeral that Anne is better off because she is no longer suffering from her maladies. I could not agree more, but for an entirely different reason. How horrible it must have been living with your unrelenting hatred."

As he went through the door, closing it behind him, something crashed into the other side. He was still shaking his head when the butler came running in his direction.

"Please send a footman to my room to fetch my trunk and send word to my driver to ready the coach," he ordered. "I shall be leaving as soon as may be."

Mere minutes after Lord Matlock's coach cleared the drive, an un-marked carriage pulled to a stop in front of Rosings Park. A tall, blond gentleman climbed out of the vehicle, then stopped to look up at the imposing facade before he approached the front door.

After being allowed entrance into the house, Gregory Wright wait-ed in the foyer whilst a maid went upstairs to give his card to the lady of the house. As he studied the costly painted ceiling several stories above, he recalled with regret how his own failings had given Rosings' mistress control of his life.

I cannot believe I let my foolishness get me into this predicament.

A second later, Lady Catherine appeared at the top of the grand staircase. She glared at him for a time before beginning down the stairs. Her cane tapped out a rhythm with each step until she reached the marble foyer. "Follow me!"

She walked in the direction of the study where they had met the first time. After they had settled into chairs on either side of a large desk, a maid hurried in with a tray of tea and set it on the end of the desk. Lady Catherine dismissed her with a wave of her hand. And, as the door closed, she barked, "You are late, Mr. Wright!"

"I … I was trying to avoid encountering Lord Matlock. I waited until his coach left before approaching the house."

"I am not speaking of today! You were supposed to be here a week ago."

"When I reached the village of Crossley, I heard talk of your daugh-ter's precarious state and thought it best not to come right away, know-ing that if she passed, Fitzwilliam and other members of your family would most likely descend on Rosings. That is why I lodged at the inn there." When she did not answer, he added, "Allow me to offer my condolences on Miss de Bourgh's passing."

"I need no condolences, Mr. Wright. I need help to make her tor-mentors pay!" Lady Catherine shouted like a madwoman. Then, all of a sudden, she seemed to recover her senses. "Have you studied the information I sent to you?"

"I did; however, I do not understand how you purchased a dis-tillery in Belfast using my name, or why you would want to."

"It was simple enough to accomplish. I forged your signature and had my solicitor buy the distillery as your representative. Moreover, I kept the manager and the employees on to run the business long enough to draw my nephew into accepting your offer to become part owner before he learns it is a losing proposition."

"A losing proposition?"

"Yes. You see, the distillery's main products are made from apples—ciders, vinegars, and such. For the time being, I am one of the few who know a blight has attacked the orchards that supply the distillery and that it will likely spread over all of Ireland. Not many in or outside Belfast are aware of this because the newspapers have been ordered to keep silent to protect local merchants and banks. Presently, they are secretly buying apples from Scotland, which cost much more, and shipping them to the port at Larne. There, they are picked up using the same wagons as before and delivered to the distillery just as they have always been. News of the blight will leak out eventually, but hopefully, not before you have convinced my nephew to invest in what *was* once a profitable enterprise."

"Darcy is very cautious with money—"

"He has had to be because his father squandered so much on that harlot he married after my sister died. And, I happen to know Fitzwilliam still has very little cash on hand."

"That is why I think it will be impossible for me to accomplish what you propose, seeing that he is aware I have made disastrous decisions regarding Parkleigh Manor in the past. It was only with his assistance I was able to turn a small profit last year."

"A profit you immediately gambled away!"

Wright lied. "That is not true; the profits were used to pay my *old* gambling debts."

"I am not certain I believe that. In any case, I assume you never told my nephew about your new debt?"

"No."

"I thought not. Fitzwilliam is not the type to help a man who gambles." She sniffed derisively, took a deep breath, and let it go loudly. "But my nephew seems to pity you because you lost your wife and that makes you the perfect choice to carry out my scheme. Therefore, I bought your debts, so he will not know how irresponsible you have been."

"I would like to know which banker informed you they were about to foreclose on my loan."

"Why should I divulge the name of my spy?" she retorted. "Just be glad I saw fit to purchase your debts to keep the bank from foreclosing."

"You are too optimistic about my ability to influence Darcy."

"I am seldom wrong in my opinions, and I believe if you tell him you spent every penny you made last year to purchase this distillery, only to discover you will lose it all if the equipment is not repaired, he will feel obligated to help you once more."

"Our agreement was that I would spy on Darcy, not dupe him into a losing endeavour. Moreover, why would you want him to fail when he is your sister's child?"

"His betrayal of my daughter crushed Anne's spirit! She would still be alive if Fitzwilliam had married her instead of that chit from Hertfordshire." As Wright looked on in stunned silence, she added, "I now own all your debts, even the gambling ones. If you do not wish me to assume ownership of Parkleigh Manor, simply repay me."

"You know very well I cannot at this time. I am, however, working on increasing Parkleigh Manor's crop yields and—"

"You have not the slightest idea how to run an estate successfully!"

"I know that! It is only because Darcy schooled me in crop rotations that I was able to make a profit last year, but he will keep advising me." Wright stood and began to pace. "Please do not ask this of me. After Emma died, he became a mentor to me without being asked and then became a friend. I do not wish to do him harm."

"Spare me your sentimentality. If you keep to your present attitude, I shall force you and your son to vacate Parkleigh Manor and survive off the kindness of Lord Grassley." She laughed mercilessly. "Oh, I forgot! You already owe him a fortune, too, and do not wish him to learn of your latest debts."

"It seems you leave me no recourse."

"I wonder that it took you so long to come to that conclusion." Lady Catherine pulled open a drawer and brought out a folder. "Here are the papers concerning the distillery that you will present to my nephew. Memorise them until you can repeat them by heart and practice assuming a pathetic face. I am counting on your performance to convince Fitzwilliam to come to your rescue again. And do not drag your feet! There is not much time until the whole of Ireland will know of the apple blight."

"How much time do I have?"

"I want you to approach him as soon as he returns to London. Make your plea and leave him the reports to study. Say you wish him to go over them before coming to a decision and that you will call when he returns to Derbyshire. Let me know what he decides as soon as you know."

Grassley Manor
That evening at dinner

In view of the fact that Lord Matlock had vacated Rosings Park, there was one more guest for dinner that evening. As was her wont, Lady Grassley said exactly what was on her mind.

"I am not surprised Lady Catherine acted like a tyrant, despite her daughter's death. Far be it from her to let Anne's death temper her attitude. Regardless, we are pleased to have you with us again, Edward."

"Now, Dorothea—" Lord Grassley began before being interrupted by Lord Matlock.

"Let her say what she will, Horace. Eleanor and I have known you and Dorothea since before Catherine married Lewis. Through the years, you have taken us in whenever my sister got angry and asked us to leave Rosings. That practically makes you a part of our family, and I know you will not be shocked by anything I may say, either."

"I hate family disputes!" Lord Grassley declared. "Lord knows Dorothea and I have endured enough of them in our own family, what with my sister trying to manipulate me into leaving Grassley Manor to her second son in my will. That scoundrel would bankrupt the estate before my body got cold. Besides, I intend for Dorothea to stay here unless and until she wishes to live elsewhere." He reached to pat his wife's hand. "There will be no dowager's house for my Dorothea."

Elizabeth caught William's eye, and they shared a smile.

"I hope Catherine comes to her senses soon," Lord Matlock said, "else she may find herself unable to meet the estate's salaries by the end of this year. She has far too many servants. I should have forced her to eliminate half of them after reviewing the accounts last year. I tried to raise the subject, but she bristled at the mention of conserving funds."

"She has always bristled at anything you had to say regarding Rosings," Richard declared.

"You are correct, Son," Lord Matlock said. "I should have done what I felt needed doing and just let her complain."

"By the way," Lord Grassley said, "I looked for my godson at the funeral, but I did not see him. Did any of you happen to?"

As evidenced by the silence, no one else had either.

"Strange. I felt certain he would come back through Kent on his way north. Even if he did not know about Anne's death, one would think he would stop by to see his godfather."

"I have learned that most young people nowadays have no manners," Lord Matlock replied. Then glancing about the table, he added, "Present company excepted."

In the silence that followed, Lady Grassley turned to Elizabeth. "I hope you do not mind if I retire after dinner. I am too tired to exhibit my poor skills at the pianoforte tonight, and I trust you can do a much better job of it."

Elizabeth smiled apologetically. "I fear that Ben's asking you one question after another, whilst Anne insisted on sitting in your lap, has contributed to your fatigue."

"I enjoyed every minute of it," her hostess said, patting her hand. "It was delightful having children in the house again."

"In truth," Elizabeth said. "I was about to beg off playing, too. I wish to retire early because we will leave tomorrow."

"Retire without hesitation, ladies," Lord Grassley said. "Whilst we men shall miss the entertainment, we understand your need to rest."

As Lady Grassley and Elizabeth stood to take their leave, their husbands came around the table to bid them goodnight. William's desire was to escort Elizabeth to the bedroom they shared so he could kiss her thoroughly before she retired, but he could not. Instead, he whispered, "I love you," and kissed her hand before watching her depart the room with their hostess.

"Well, gentlemen," Lord Grassley said after the ladies had gone, "if you will follow me, we shall solve all the world's problems over cigars and port."

"I should be happy if we could merely solve *my* problems with Catherine," Lord Matlock said with a laugh.

"Let us limit ourselves to those things we have a chance of conquering!" Lord Grassley declared, guffawing.

As their host led the way out of the room, William lagged behind the others, trying to think of a good excuse to retire early, too.

Chapter 3

Armagh, Ireland
Ballyneen Castle

Evening shadows were creeping across the grounds of Ballyneen Castle as Georgiana, Viscountess Hayworth, leaned against the balcony railing trying to identify the riders in the distance. Unwittingly rising on her toes, she began to pray that one was her husband, because she had not seen him all day. In truth, she had seen very little of Matthew after their arrival at his family estate two months previously. That was when he had suddenly changed from the most considerate man in the world to one preoccupied and distant. His daily routine had changed as well. Whereas he once enjoyed making love to her before the day started, he now rose and left the house before she awoke. Moreover, he was absent the better part of each day, leaving her to wander about the grounds and the manor house either alone or in the company of his aunt, Lady Mary.

Lady Mary was a petite, silver-haired matron of approximately three and sixty. She had resided at Ballyneen since her husband's death years before, having moved from her previous home in Dublin at her brother's request. Matthew's father, Lord Camden, had wished to have someone he trusted residing at Ballyneen because he rarely visited the place, and his childless sister fit the role of overseer perfectly. Not only was she knowledgeable about estate matters, having helped her husband run their estate just outside Dublin, but she could be decisive and strong-willed when necessary. In fact, given the small income it provided, Lord Camden figured she had run Ballyneen as well as any steward could have and at little cost to him.

Georgiana had been greatly disappointed upon her arrival to learn that Ballyneen Castle was not actually a castle but a grey-block manor that had not been updated in years—and neither had its furnishings.

All that remained of the castle that had once stood guard over the estate were s few stone walls and a crumbling tower in a field several hundred yards behind the stables, and its appearance served only to remind Georgiana of her own crumbling marriage.

She had recently found the courage to ask Matthew if she had done something to upset him, and now she recalled the argument that had followed.

"Why would you say such a thing?" he had demanded.

"I ... I cannot think of another reason for you to have changed so completely since we came to Armagh. No! I am mistaken! You began to change when we were still in Southampton—after your father decided you should bring me here."

"You are talking nonsense, Georgiana! I have not changed! It is merely that there is much to do if I am to accomplish the repairs Father wants finished before we return to Southampton."

"I was told we would only be here a short time, but with all the projects you have scheduled, we could be here a year. I am beginning to think we have been exiled."

"There you go again speaking nonsense! The estate is in much worse shape than Father realised. Most likely because my aunt had little funds to repair what was here. If you would only have some patience, it would make our lives so much easier."

"How can I be patient when I hardly see you? You are gone when I wake, and many times I am asleep when you return. In fact, you do not even bother to sleep in my bed anymore."

Looking chastised, Matthew had pulled her into his arms and rested his head atop hers. "I do not wish to wake you, that is all."

She started to cry. "I wish you would wake me. At least then I would know you actually miss me, too."

Matthew had slept in her bed that night, which was weeks ago, but the next day he had returned to his routine. Georgiana knew he was being truthful about the plethora of repairs needed; still, she could not help feeling there was something else amiss—something her husband either could not or would not talk about.

As she watched the riders, they turned their horses towards a thicket. Georgiana sighed and settled back on her heels. *If it is Matthew, he is certainly not headed in this direction.*

Walking back into her bedroom, she slumped down in one of the plush, upholstered chairs and brought her feet up to rest on the matching footstool. Soon she would be summoned to dinner—another meal she would likely share with only Matthew's aunt. Lady Mary always made excuses for her nephew's absences, which irritated Georgiana almost as much as her husband's behaviour.

Though she had no objection to his aunt's company—after all, it was better than being entirely alone—Georgiana was so disillusioned with her relationship with Matthew that she had finally written to her brother and asked him to come to Ireland. If anyone could get to the truth regarding her husband's perplexing behaviour, it was Fitzwilliam, and Georgiana preferred knowing the truth to dealing with the horrible thoughts that assailed her whenever she lay in her bed alone.

Suddenly, a knock on the door broke through her reverie. "Come!" she called.

A maid opened the door and bobbed a curtsey. "The countess asked me to say that dinner is ready, ma'am!"

"Thank you. Tell her I will be right down."

London
Darcy House

They had not been long at their London house when William excused himself, saying he wished to look through the mail that had accumulated on the desk in his study during their absence. Though normally mail was forwarded from London to Pemberley, he had instructed Mrs. Barnes to hold all the mail until they came through Town on their way back to Derbyshire.

Ben and Anne had fallen asleep in the coach on the journey from Kent to London, and both were now well-rested and wide awake. Whilst it was easy to distract the baby with the toys in the nursery, Bennet was old enough to want to be with his father. Consequently, the minute William mentioned heading to his study, his son said, "Papa, may I help you open the mail?"

It was impossible for William to say no. "Of course you may."

Picking up his son, he placed him on his shoulders, causing Elizabeth to caution, "He is getting too big for you to carry him about like that."

"He is not too big yet!" William declared as he ducked under the doorframe and into the hall.

The last thing Elizabeth heard was Ben urging his father to run and the sound of footsteps galloping down the hall. Content, she went into her bedroom to steal a nap.

The study

Ben had fallen asleep in William's lap by the time he reached the last of the letters that had completely covered the top of his desk. As he gingerly broke the seal on the next missive, trying not to jostle Ben, there was a knock on the door.

"Come!" he said as quietly as possible.

Ben stirred but did not wake as the door opened, and Mr. Barnes stepped inside. Seeing the boy asleep in his father's lap, Barnes said softly, "Excuse me for interrupting, sir, but there is someone waiting on the portico to see you."

"Now? I thought the knocker was off the door."

"It is, but he kept knocking so I felt I must ask him to leave. When I explained that you were not in, he argued that you were. Then, after I explained that you were not receiving visitors today, he insisted you *would* see him."

"Who is it?"

"It is your neighbour from Derbyshire, Mr. Wright."

As William debated whether to receive the intruder, the butler ventured, "Would it help if I took Master Bennet to the nursery to finish his nap?"

"It would," William replied. He stood with his sleeping child and gingerly handed him to the butler. "Take Ben up the back stairs, and I will see to Wright."

As William walked towards the foyer, he reflected on how hard he had worked to keep Gregory Wright from losing Parkleigh Manor. Wrought with grief and left with the responsibility of a motherless child, Wright had begun drinking heavily and letting the estate go to ruin. After the steward of Parkleigh Manor mentioned the dilemma to his own steward, William had taken Wright under his wing and was able to convince him to stop drinking. Then he worked with Wright to halt the downward spiral into which the estate was falling. In time, he had given the reins of Parkleigh back to Wright and, to William's knowledge, he was doing quite well.

As William opened the front door, Gregory Wright walked straight into the foyer without invitation. He looked anxious and began speaking animatedly.

"I apologise for coming when the knocker was off the door, Darcy, but I really must see you."

"I have only a few minutes to spare, so let us remove to my study where we will not be disturbed."

As they walked in that direction, Wright added, "I hope Mrs. Darcy and the children are well."

"They are. And Jonathan? How is he faring?"

"Jonathan is doing very well, I thank you."

Suddenly the housekeeper came around a corner. "Mrs. Barnes, I could use a fresh cup of tea. Would you have a pot sent to my study and, if there are any left, some of those ginger biscuits?"

"Of course," she replied, bobbing a curtsey before hurrying towards the kitchen.

Not long afterwards, William and his neighbour were settled in chairs on opposite sides of his desk, and Wright began to speak.

"I truly hate to bother you, but—" Wright's head dropped, and he began to run his fingers through his hair nervously. "You have been such a good friend, and you have done so much for me already that I hesitate to ask more of you."

"Surely, it cannot be as bad as all that." William's concern rose, and he leaned forward. "Tell me why you are here."

"Six months ago, I heard from a close friend that a distillery in Belfast was for sale at a bargain price. He had looked into buying it himself and had in his possession all the information regarding the business going back as far as five years. For centuries, it has produced hard cider, brandy and vinegar, as well as other products derived from apples; however, last year the owner died. His death prompted his widow to put the business on the market."

Suddenly there was a knock on the door, and Wright went silent. "Come!" William called.

A maid entered carrying a tray with a pot of tea and biscuits, and she set it on the end of the desk. William dismissed her, asking that she shut the door on her way out. Once the door clicked shut, he began to pour the tea.

"Sugar and cream?"

"Just cream, thank you," Wright replied.

As William slid the cup towards his guest, he said, "Pray, continue." Then, taking a biscuit from the plate, he sat down with his own cup of tea and began to eat.

"The price was so low that my friend thought I might wish to take advantage of the sale." Suddenly, Wright looked sheepish. "I had mentioned to him that I was having money troubles, you see."

"Who is this friend? And if it is such a bargain, why did he not purchase it?"

Prepared for William's questions, Wright had invented a name and a story about this fictious friend. "Robert Hedges. I have known him since I was at university. He imports goods from the Indies, and he needed to replace one of his ships instead of buying the distillery. In any case, I had my solicitor go over the records Robert provided, and the solicitor assured me the business was a viable company at a good price. Therefore, I sunk all my profits from last year's crops into it as a down-payment."

"You spent two thousand pounds without a word to me? I thought we agreed you would consult me before making any major expenditures."

Wright tried to look repentant. "I thought I had struck a sound bargain and ... and that you would be pleased."

"Pleased that you bought a distillery when you know nothing about running one?"

"The manager agreed to stay on and run it."

"If two thousand pounds is the down-payment, how much more do you owe?"

"Seven thousand pounds." At William's scowl, he quickly added, "but I can pay a thousand pounds a year against the balance until I own it outright."

William stared at him silently, and under his gaze Wright seemed to wither. Finally, William spoke. "It seems you have worked out the details to your satisfaction, so why are you here?"

"I ... I encountered a problem straight off."

William's frown deepened as he leaned forward to place the pen he had been using into the ink stand. "I cannot say I am surprised."

Wright hurried to explain. "For the first time in the history of the distillery, a wheel broke and locked the main press. Unfortunately, I learned that wheels of that type are not ready-made. It will take anywhere from five to six thousand pounds to have another one created, though I was assured they could have the distillery operational in four months if I ordered it soon."

"And, inasmuch as every farthing you had went towards the deposit, you cannot afford the repairs," William stated calmly.

"I know now how reckless this makes me appear, but I had hoped to impress you with my resourcefulness. As it turned out, I stand to lose everything if I cannot repair the press."

"So, you are here to ask me to be your banker."

"Not my banker—my partner. I cannot think of anyone else with whom I would want to be in business."

"I do not wish to be in the distillery business."

"But if you could just see your way to repairing the press, I would gladly give you half ownership without expecting you to participate in running it. And I will pay you back for the wheel as soon as the distillery has the funds."

"I have just now made substantial progress in replenishing Pemberley's reserves. Why would I gamble on an enterprise I know absolutely nothing about—especially one where I will owe the balance of the loan, should you default?"

"I understand! Truly, I do!" Wright declared, pulling an envelope from inside his coat and placing it on the desk. "Allow me to leave the distillery records with you. Study them at your leisure, and you will see that the business will prove very valuable to the right owners."

William stood, setting his empty cup on the desk. "My instinct is to refuse you straight out; however, I will take time to look over the accounts between now and when I return to Pemberley."

"That is all I ask," Wright said.

"By the way, Lord Grassley asked me to tell you that he wishes to speak with you soon."

"I intended to call on him when we returned from Brighton, but Jonathan did not feel well, so instead we came straight to London. As it turned out, he was merely worn out from our travels. I shall write to

Lord Grassley and explain." Then he offered a wan smile to William. "When do you plan to return to Pemberley?"

"God willing, we leave in three days."

"I shall call on you when next we are both in Derbyshire. Hopefully, by then the reports will have convinced you that the distillery is a good investment."

"I would advise you not to be optimistic."

Gregory Wright forced a smile. "Knowing what I do, I cannot help but be."

That evening
The billiard room

Richard had accepted William's invitation to dine at Darcy House, and when Elizabeth announced after dinner that she was retiring early, he and his cousin removed to the billiard room.

As William was lining up his first shot, Richard said, "Father is still fuming at how ugly our aunt was to everyone after Anne's funeral ... especially to you."

"Lady Catherine's anger cannot affect me. I have no problem living the rest of my life without her company."

"Neither do I," Richard said, as William missed the shot. "I suppose, though, that at some point, you or I will have to oversee Rosings. After all, Father is not in good health, and Leighton swears he will never manage it."

Mention of Richard's older brother prompted William to ask, "How is Leighton? When last your father mentioned him, he said your brother was not drinking nearly as heavily as he had in the past."

Richard sighed. "If this is true, and I am not around Leighton enough to verify it, I would attribute it to the fact that his wife is at her family's estate in Shropshire and has been for the last six months."

"I take it he and Lady Susan are still at odds."

Richard lined up his first shot. "Nothing has changed in that regard."

"A shame. I cannot fathom being married to someone I do not love. Elizabeth and I are so alike that we finish each other's sentences."

As Richard made the shot, he chuckled, "I have noticed."

Sombrely, William addressed Richard. "I pray, Cousin, that you find the ideal woman and experience as much happiness in marriage as I have with Elizabeth."

Richard chuckled mirthlessly as he made two more shots, then missed the next. "I suggest that you keep praying, then, for I am having as much luck in that quarter as I am with this game."

"You can count on my prayers and Elizabeth's," William replied, preparing to take his shot. "By the way, you have not remarked on what I shared earlier."

"About Wright, you mean? I almost brought it up at dinner, but I recalled that you said Elizabeth does not know about it yet."

Sinking three balls in succession before missing the next, William replied, "I wished to study the information about the distillery in more depth before telling her. Elizabeth has enough on her mind with the children."

"I understand. Seeing that you asked my opinion, however, I will have to say that I think it would be unwise to help Wright out of this predicament, especially because he brought it on himself by ignoring his promise to consult with you before any major expenditures. Wright is a grown man, and you are not his guardian angel. Let him sink or swim on his own."

"If it were not for Jonathan, I would without giving it a second thought."

"Jonathan will learn soon enough that his father is a dullard. It is not your place to prop up Gregory Wright, and especially not for thousands of pounds."

William shook his head slowly. "I know you are right. Only—"

"I can see where this is heading, Darcy, and I do not like it."

"Please do not say anything to your father until after I have reached a decision."

"I will abide by your wishes, but I assure you that Father will be livid if you bail Wright out. He still occasionally mentions how Pemberley was almost ruined by the time Uncle George died and how much he admires you for bringing her back to viability."

"I do not wish to disappoint him. Still —"

"Still, you have a heart bigger than Derbyshire," Richard interrupted, "and you cannot stand to watch a friend fail."

William crimsoned. "I am not the saint you make me out to be."

"I shall not argue the point, for you will not listen. Just promise me one thing."

"If I can."

"Promise me that you will not make a decision regarding the distillery without first giving me another chance to dissuade you."

William chuckled. "I promise."

"Good!" Richard's next stroke took several balls out of play. He stood, grinning, before taking his next shot. "What was it we wagered? A pound?"

"I do not recall that we were playing for anything other than bragging rights," William replied.

"Why is it that when I am ahead, you never recall betting on the game?"

"I imagine because you do the same when I am ahead."

"Sarcasm does not become you, Cousin," Richard said as he sank the rest of the balls on the table. "It does not become you in the least!"

Chapter 4

Pemberley
Three weeks later

As William entered the sitting room of their suite, he noticed his wife on the balcony. Going through his bedroom, he joined her.

Elizabeth, sitting on a chaise, looked up at his approach and smiled. "There you are! I was looking for you earlier, and, unless I was greatly mistaken, you were not in the house."

"You are correct, my dear," William said, bending down to brush a kiss across her lips. "I was at the stables looking over the pony for Ben. Mr. Langley delivered her just this morning. She is dark gold with white socks and mane."

"I worry that Ben is too much like you to have a pony now."

"What do you mean?"

"Do not take offence, sweetheart. I only wish to point out that he knows no fear. I worry he may get hurt trying to ride like his father."

William brought her hand to his mouth for a kiss. "Do not worry. I intend to teach him how to ride safely. Besides, the pony is only fourteen hands, and, should he fall off, it is not that far to the ground. In addition, I had a saddle made specially for him that should help him keep his seat."

"I should like to see the pony."

"We could walk down to the stables after tea, if you would like."

"I would, and that will be an excellent time in view of the fact that the children will be taking a nap. I had rather Ben not see the pony until we decide it is time. Once he has, I fear neither of us will have any peace until he is allowed to ride."

William laughed. "Are you saying he also inherited my impatience?"

"I do not think you are an impatient man," Elizabeth said. Then, she smiled teasingly. "Except in regard to one thing."

The twinkle in her eyes ignited a fire inside him that William could not ignore. Glancing towards the open door to her bedroom, he tilted his head in that direction. "Tea will not be served for another hour."

Instantly on her feet, Elizabeth stood on tiptoes and brought her hands to his chest. Sliding them up until she buried her fingers in the long hair at the nape of his neck, she gave him a sound kiss before settling back on her heels, saying, "I feared you might not take the hint!"

After walking down to the stables to examine Ben's pony, Elizabeth and William returned to the house to find that the post had been delivered. Crossing the foyer to a mahogany table where a silver salver was stacked high with letters, William began shuffling through them.

He held one out to her. "This is for you."

Elizabeth took the missive and looked at the return address. "It is from Jane."

"This one is from Georgiana."

"That is odd. I thought you received a letter from her the day before we left London."

"I did, but it was very brief." William's expression grew more anxious the longer he stared at his sister's handwriting. "I have felt for some time that something is amiss, and getting another letter so soon makes me uneasy."

Elizabeth reached out to take his hand, giving it a loving squeeze. "What say you to returning to our sitting room and reading Georgiana's letter together?"

Forcing a smile he did not feel, William nodded.

The sitting room

Elizabeth paced the room as she read Georgiana's letter a second time. "I cannot believe Viscount Hayworth's feelings would change so quickly." Recalling the tall, handsome man with light brown hair and dark blue eyes who had swept her sister off her feet, she added, "He seemed besotted with Georgiana when they married. What could possibly alter a love that strong in such a short period of time?"

"I can think of several things!" William said, rising to his feet. "None of which is acceptable. If that cad thinks he can treat my sister as though she is of no consequence, he had best think again! She can always come back home to us."

Elizabeth wrapped her arms around him. "Calm yourself, darling. You must keep your wits about you, or you will be of no use to your sister."

"You are right," William conceded as he embraced her, "but it will not be easy. Frankly, I do not see any alternative but to travel to Armagh and speak to Hayworth myself insofar as Georgiana has confronted him, and he denies anything is wrong."

"The children and I will accompany you."

William shook his head. "That would be a difficult journey with Anne so small. I can make the trip much faster if I go alone. Moreover, it will give me a chance to inspect the distillery Wright bought in Belfast after I meet with Hayworth. I would like to believe he has not squandered his money."

"I still cannot believe Mr. Wright acted without consulting you."

"Neither can I."

William had informed Elizabeth of their neighbour's purchase, though he had omitted Wright's offer to make him part owner and the five to six thousand pounds needed for a new wheel. Though Wright was pressing him for an answer, William was in no rush to decide; however, he was almost certain he was going to reject the offer and the loan. In addition, he felt there was no need to tell Elizabeth unless he changed his mind.

"Most likely I can have a look at the distillery on my way back from Armagh and still sail home the same day."

Elizabeth offered William a slight smile, hoping it hid her growing uneasiness. As of this morning, her courses were almost two weeks late. "How long will it take to travel there and back?"

"From here to Liverpool will take a day and a half. Once there, I shall have to locate a ship sailing to Belfast. Depending on the weather, the trip could take anywhere from two to three days, and I understand Armagh is a little over a day's journey from Belfast." William tightened his embrace. "I cannot bear the thought of leaving you and the children for a day, much less for weeks."

Elizabeth swallowed hard. "Do not worry, my love. All will be well here at Pemberley, and I know you will not rest until you learn what is wrong at Ballyneen."

William buried his face in her silky locks, taking a deep breath of the lavender scent there. "I have no idea what I would do if you were not in my life, Elizabeth. You are the very air I breathe."

"I feel the same about you, sweetheart, but please do not speak of either of us being without the other. God brought us together, and we must trust Him to keep each of us whilst we are separated by circumstances such as these."

William kissed her tenderly, then pulled back to say, "You are a very wise woman, Mrs. Darcy."

Elizabeth smiled. "I do recall you saying that once or twice, Mr. Darcy."

William laughed. "I have not said it nearly enough! You are an extremely intelligent woman, Elizabeth, and I love you with all my heart, body and soul. I always will." He followed this declaration with another passionate kiss.

Elizabeth laid her head against his chest. "Oh, darling, please do not be gone any longer than is absolutely necessary. The children will be lost without you." Left unsaid was that she would be as well.

"You may rely on it, my love."

Armagh, Ireland
Flannery's Inn

Being the nearest town to Ballyneen, Viscount Hayworth visited Armagh each day in hopes that his informant would arrive from England with news about his sister. Only eight weeks after his wedding to Georgiana, though she was not yet one and twenty, Aileen had eloped with their father's steward, Mr. Gable.

His father, Lord Camden, was determined to find her and to return her to Berkley Hall before the gossips of the *ton* discovered what had occurred. Consequently, he had forbidden Matthew to tell Georgiana what had happened, instead ordering them to leave immediately for the family estate in Ireland whilst telling friends that Aileen had travelled to Ireland with them. It was explained to Georgiana that the purpose of the trip was to allow her husband to evaluate the property and make any repairs necessary because Lord Camden wished to sell it.

Matthew felt great guilt—not only for keeping secrets from his wife, but because he felt he should have seen the debacle with Gable coming and intervened. Aileen had been indulged by their mother and completely ignored by their father. When Lady Camden died, it was a harder blow for his sister than for him, for it had ignited a struggle between father and daughter over her future. Lord Camden demanded that Aileen accept an offer from Viscount Bateman, the son of a life-long friend. Aileen maintained that she loathed the man, and that led to an impasse which resulted in the elopement.

As days turned into weeks, Matthew had thought the likelihood of finding his sister and bringing her home with no one the wiser was highly unlikely. Not wishing to rely entirely on letters from his father, who was half out of his mind with rage, Matthew had hired a retired Bow Street Runner, Robert Osgood, to search for the couple and report directly to him. In spite of all that, he had a niggling feeling that even if Aileen was found, she might not listen to him, either.

It broke his heart to think of his sister being lost to him and to see Georgiana so tortured, but Matthew knew that if he were in his wife's company for any length of time, it would be impossible to keep his sister's dilemma undisclosed. And, whilst he blamed his father for swearing him to secrecy, in truth, he wondered how Georgiana would react to the news that Aileen had ruined not only her reputation but their good name. After all, his wife was still an innocent in so many ways and embodied all that was good and decent in his life. Despite her shyness, Georgiana had striven to be accepted by Southampton's society for his sake and had been successful ... up to now.

With these thoughts swirling in his head, Matthew had not noticed that a post coach had stopped across the street and a stranger had alighted from it. It was not until the man entered the inn and stopped to contemplate who was there that Matthew took notice of him. At length, the neatly dressed man crossed to where he sat at a table next to a window.

Removing his hat, he said, "Excuse me, sir. Would you, by chance, be Viscount Hayworth?"

Clearly not Mr. Osgood, Matthew's brows knit in question with his reply. "I am."

The man looked relieved. "My uncle, Robert Osgood, asked that I meet you in his stead. I carry a letter from him with news."

"And you are?"

"Bert Atkins, sir. Uncle Robert would have come himself, but he has just caught up with Arthur Gable and thinks it best to keep an eye on him—his words, not mine."

"I was expecting your uncle to keep my case confidential."

"I would never repeat the details of any of my uncle's cases. In fact, he is presently training me to be his assistant so that I may take over the business when he retires. So you see, I am well aware that confidentiality is paramount in this type of work."

"My agreement with Mr. Osgood was that after he had located my sister, he would meet me here. Then I would accompany him to where she is presently. He assured me that he could find her quickly! This whole exercise will be futile if he cannot keep his word."

Mr. Atkins reached inside his coat and brought out a letter. "I believe this will answer any questions you may have."

As Matthew took the letter, Mr. Atkins added, "I need to arrange for a room, for I intend to stay the night. Once you are done reading, should you wish to reply, I have paper, pen and ink in a case in my trunk. You are welcome to use my room for that purpose if you wish."

"Thank you. I will meet you in your room shortly."

Once he was alone again, Matthew opened the letter. Noting that it was dated about a week earlier, he began to read.

> *Viscount Hayworth,*
>
> *Forgive me for not meeting you as planned. I assure you that my nephew, who is acting in my stead, can be trusted to work on your case.*
>
> *It has taken much longer to find your sister than I anticipated. Only in the last two days have I managed to find Mr. Gable enjoying the gambling dens in Bath, though I saw no trace of your sister.*
>
> *Unfortunately, before I could ascertain if she was with him, Gable stole away during the night. Inspecting the room afterwards, I found it unoccupied. Moreover, the innkeeper could not say for certain that a woman was with him. All he recalled is that Gable asked about a post coach to Liverpool. Naturally, I am on my way there.*
>
> *In my opinion it would not be wise for you to come until I*

can determine if your sister is with him. I will send more information once I reach Liverpool.

Yours truly,
Robert Osgood

Though Matthew wished more than anything for the matter to be over, he had no choice but to wait until Mr. Osgood was certain of Aileen's location. His plan was to leave Georgiana at Ballyneen under the guise of having business to conduct in Dublin, then he would return to England to confront his sister. Placing the letter in his coat pocket, Matthew rose and crossed to the desk to enquire about Mr. Atkins' room number.

As he started up the stairs to Atkins' room, his mind flew to Georgiana and what she might be doing at that moment. He hoped that when he returned to Ballyneen, she would still be angry with him, for that meant she would be in her room sulking and not bombarding him with questions he could not answer.

Incapable of dwelling on such depressing thoughts any further, Mathew quickly concluded his business with Mr. Atkins and left the inn. As he crossed the street towards his carriage, he noticed a millinery shop window filled with colourful parasols and decided to buy Georgiana a gift that he could present to her before he left to confront his sister.

Leaving only minutes later, carrying one of the parasols and a white shawl embroidered with flowers, he climbed into the carriage and ordered his driver to return to Ballyneen ... only at a snail's pace.

Pemberley
A day later

As Colonel Fitzwilliam entered the front door of Pemberley, he noticed numerous maids going up and down the grand staircase in a great hurry. The butler was nowhere in sight, so the footman who always attended the door began to collect his hat and gloves whilst he waited.

"Thank you, Sanders," Richard said.

Before the footman could reply, Mr. Walker rushed into the foyer looking very flustered. "Colonel Fitzwilliam, I was not expecting you!"

"I did not have time to alert anyone," Richard answered as still another maid passed carrying an armful of folded clothes. "Is my presence a problem?"

"Oh, no, sir!" Walker assured him. "Mr. Darcy is not expected to leave until tomorrow."

"He is leaving again? Where on earth is he off to now?"

"He is preparing to visit Miss Darcy—excuse me, I meant to say Lady Hayworth."

"Is he now?" Richard answered dryly. "Where might my cousin be at present?"

"If I am not mistaken, he is still in his suite. Would you like me to announce you?"

"No, thank you, Walker. I would rather announce myself, as always."

"As you wish, sir."

As Richard proceeded up the staircase, the elderly butler could not help but smile at his audacity. Then, noticing that he was in the way of yet another maid, he returned to his office.

The master bedroom

Having entered the suite through the shared sitting room because that door was open, Richard watched from the doorway as Darcy's valet, Adams, packed his trunk. He had always been fond of Adams, for, like himself, the valet was not afraid to contradict his cousin when he thought he should. Suddenly, Adams turned to pick up a stack of clothes on the bed and spied him.

"Colonel Fitzwilliam!" he exclaimed. "Mr. Darcy did not mention you were expected today."

"That is because he did not know I was coming," Richard said wryly. "I enjoy surprising my cousin by dropping in unexpectedly, but in this case, I had no choice. My orders changed so quickly there was no time to alert anyone."

"Regardless, Mr. Darcy is always glad to see you, sir."

"Come now, Adams! We both know there are times Darcy considers my impromptu visits a pain in the arse."

"Only when you give him advice that he does not wish to hear," Adams stated dryly. "I know that feeling only too well."

"That is what I like about you, Adams. You are brutally honest at all times."

"I try, sir."

"Now, can you tell me where I might find my elusive cousin? Walker said he was in here." Richard turned in a circle. "Is he hiding under the bed?"

"He just went into Mrs. Darcy's bedroom. Do you want me to inform him of your arrival?"

"I would not dare have you interrupt their ... their ... whatever! But when you do see him, inform him that I am here. Meanwhile, I shall be in my room changing clothes and after that, in the billiard's room."

"It will be my pleasure."

The billiard room
An hour and a half later

Just as William walked in the room, Richard made a shot that began sinking one ball after another until he had dispatched four in a row. Only then did he acknowledge his cousin.

"Darcy, I am pleased that you finally found time to join me."

"Do not be sarcastic, Richard. I came as soon as Adams informed me you had arrived."

"Yes, well, Adams did tell me that you were in Mrs. Darcy's bedroom so—"

"You may tease me about many things, Richard, but not about my relationship with my wife."

"Seeing that you are a married man, that leaves very little to tease you about then." As William began to object, Richard raised a hand to silence him. "I was only trying to goad you. I know that once a man marries, his relationship with his wife is sacrosanct, so do not get up in arms."

"Since you managed to talk yourself out of that *faux pas*, may I ask why you are here? It was my understanding that you were assigned to General Lassiter in Cornwall until he was finished training new recruits."

"I was. However, I am so trustworthy the general asked me to escort his wife and children back to their estate in Yorkshire. Having done that, I am presently on my way to London. I assumed it could not hurt to stop here for a day or so."

"You know you are always welcome."

"And, as usual, I am grateful for your hospitality." Then a quizzical expression crossed Richard's face. "There is something I would like to know, however."

"And that is?"

"From the number of clothes Adams is packing in your trunk, you must be planning to embark on a long trip. May I ask where you are headed, when you will leave and when you were planning to tell me?"

"I sent you a letter soon after I had decided. That was only two days ago. Most likely the letter will be awaiting you when you reach London."

"I see."

"To answer your questions, I am off to visit Georgiana, and I leave the day after tomorrow." Seeing Richard's brows knit yet again, he added, "You do recall me saying I thought there was something Georgiana was not telling me in her letters?" At Richard's nod, he continued. "I received one this week, and in it she emphasised that she is miserable and—"

"I knew that dandy could not be trusted!" Richard exclaimed, his face turning red. "I shall ask for the leave I have accumulated and accompany you!"

"That will not be necessary. Thus far, Georgiana's complaints are vague. She did mention that she sees little of Hayworth. Apparently, he leaves at dawn and stays away all day. She fears there is another woman, but I hope to ascertain that is not the case. In any event, I plan to get to the root of the problem and, if necessary, have words with Hayworth. Meanwhile, you can best serve me by promising to keep watch over Elizabeth and the children whilst I am away."

"I shall be happy to oblige. I have enough influence to request assignment to London once I reach there. An express from Mrs. Darcy requesting my help will see me at Pemberley in mere days."

"I felt certain I could rely on you." William said, clasping Richard's shoulder.

"Always," Richard replied. Quickly he added, "You have no idea how relieved I am that you are not travelling to Ireland on behalf of Mr. Wright."

"I hate to disappoint you, but I do plan to visit the distillery Wright purchased in Belfast whilst I am in Ireland. Not with the intention of becoming his partner, mind you, or of lending him any money. I would just like to see for myself if he has bought a pig in a poke."

"With your kind heart, it would be best if you did not know for certain."

"Duly noted," William said. Then he smiled. "Now, did you come in here to play billiards, or is there something else you wish to argue about?"

"I thought I was allowed to do both."

Chapter 5

Pemberley
Two days later

Richard had already returned to London when the day arrived for William to depart for Liverpool. It was with a heavy heart that he and Elizabeth entered the nursery that morning so he could bid the children farewell.

Anne, of course, was too young to understand, so instead of trying to explain, William picked her up and placed kisses all over her face before hugging the child as though he would never let her go. Growing emotional at the thought of how much Anne might change before he saw her again, he whispered into her soft, dark curls, "Papa loves you very much, sweetheart."

"Papa!" Anne parroted and was rewarded with yet another kiss.

Whilst holding her, he stooped to speak to his son, who watched him with wide eyes full of interest. "Come here, Ben."

Bennet rushed to William, who wrapped his other arm around the boy. "I received a letter from your Aunt Georgiana, and she has asked for my help in a matter of great importance. This means I must leave today to travel to her new home in Ireland."

Bennet's brows furrowed. "Is Ireland a long way from here?"

"It is not too far."

"Then may I go with you?"

"Your mother and I feel it best that I go alone. It will make the journey much faster if I do."

Tears filled Ben's eyes and his bottom lip began to tremble. "I ... I do not want you to go, Papa."

William swallowed against the lump forming in his throat. "I do not wish to leave you either, Son; however, your aunt will be very sad if I refuse her plea for help."

"Suddenly, Ben brightened a bit. "Why not ask Aunt Georgiana to come here!"

49

"That is a good idea, but unfortunately, it is not possible at this time."

Ben's expression grew sad again, and he dropped his head.

"Sometimes we must act promptly when our family has need of us, even if it is inconvenient. Do you understand?"

"I ... I think so."

"Good. Now, I have something very important to ask of you."

Ben look confused. "Me, Papa?"

"Yes. I need someone I can trust to take care of Anne and your mother whilst I am away. Do you think you can do that for me?"

A sombre expression crossed his son's face, and he stood as tall as possible. "Yes, sir."

At that, William embraced both children tightly, kissing the tops of their heads as he murmured, "I could not have asked for better children. I love you both more than you will ever know."

Though barely able to move, Ben murmured against his chest, "I love you, too."

This prompted Anne, who had been struggling to break free of his grasp, to say, "Too!"

Elizabeth had been trying not to cry, lest seeing her upset would affect the children, but Anne's pronouncement sent her scurrying from the room to compose herself.

As the time came for William's departure, he and Elizabeth descended the grand staircase hand in hand, crossed the foyer and walked onto the portico, followed closely by Mr. Walker and Mrs. Reynolds. The footmen, who had been seeing to the coach and loading trunks, were now standing stiffly at attention along the steps.

In spite of the fact that they had made love that morning and had said goodbye in the privacy of their bedroom, William found it difficult to leave. Still, he hoped to make Elizabeth smile before he left.

Taking her in his arms, he murmured quietly, "This will be the first time we have been apart for more than a day since you were kidnapped, and I brought you back to Pemberley."

"I ... I am very aware of that," Elizabeth replied, blinking back tears.

BRENDA J. WEBB

"Do you recall the last trip of any consequence I ventured on without you?"

"It was when Mr. Sturgis was injured. You and Richard travelled to Weymouth."

"And do you recall how I bid you goodbye on that occasion?"

Elizabeth smiled through tear-filled eyes. "How could I ever forget?"

"Well, inasmuch as we must part for God only knows how long, I believe it only fitting that I repeat the words you found so unforgettable," William said cheekily.

Employing the same exaggerated Scottish burr, and as poorly rendered as the first time, William began to recite the poem by Robert Burns.[1]

And fare thee weel, my only luve!
And fare thee weel, a while!
And I will come again, my luve,
Tho' it ware ten thousand mile!

Though Elizabeth was unable to hold back a smile whilst he quoted the poem, once William had finished, an expression of anguish swiftly replaced it.

"Never think, Mr. Darcy, that I have grown so fond of that verse—" Elizabeth's voice broke, and she struggled to continue, "so ... so fond that I long to hear it repeated. The truth is, I had rather never hear it again."

Instantly somber, William looked longingly at the woman he loved more than life. Running fingertips softly down the side of Elizabeth's face, he said, "I feel the same way, my love."

The kiss that followed this declaration was ardent, and Mr. Walker found it necessary to glower at the servants who began stealing glances at the couple. The footmen quickly came to attention, however, as William began to guide Elizabeth down the steps. At the coach, the door was opened and the steps let down as William addressed the butler and housekeeper.

"I have asked Richard to watch over Elizabeth and the children

---

[1] **Robert Burns** *(25 January 1759 – 21 July 1796), also known as the Bard of Ayrshire, Ploughman Poet and various other names and epithets, was a Scottish poet and lyricist.*

whilst I am away. I shall return as soon as possible, but I cannot say when that may be. Do not hesitate to call on the colonel should something arise that you feel you cannot manage."

As Mr. Walker and Mrs. Reynolds nodded in acknowledgement, he addressed Elizabeth. "I asked the vicar and Mrs. Green to visit more often whilst I am in Ireland." Close to tears, Elizabeth could only nod. "And I asked God to watch over you and the children and to keep you safe until I return."

"I have prayed the same for you. I love you with all my heart, William."

William leaned in to brush a final soft kiss across her lips before entering the coach. "And I love you with all of mine."

Elizabeth stayed rooted to the spot as the coach began around the circle drive, waving until it disappeared into the distance. Then, taking a deep breath, she pasted on a faux smile and walked past the servants as she headed straight to her bedroom. Once in there, she fell on the bed and wept as though her heart would break.

Parkleigh Manor
The study

Sitting behind the desk that had once belonged to Emma's late father, Gregory Wright could not help but recall all that had happened since he first sat there shortly after marrying Lord Waterston's daughter.

Lady Emma was one of the most beautiful women he had ever seen, and Gregory had fallen in love with her immediately. He had been flabbergasted when she paid him particular attention at the Blaylock's ball, for as a penniless heir to a small estate mired in debt, his future depended on marrying a wealthy woman or scratching out a living practicing law. Although he had passed his exams to become a solicitor, he had never practiced as one. Instead, he had survived off the generosity of his godfather, Lord Grassley, who had always indulged him. Subsequently, most members of the *ton* thought him of no value when it came to making matches for their marriageable daughters.

Luckily, not only had Emma fallen in love with him, but he learned shortly thereafter that she was the sole heir of her ailing father. His death paved the way for a short courtship and impetuous marriage. He had paid little attention when his own father had talked of estate matters, but Emma had assisted her father in managing Parkleigh Manor for years, and she had tutored him in the basics until her untimely death. Wright's brows knit at the remembrance of Jonathan's birth and his beloved wife's death.

How could a day filled with such happiness contain so much heartache?

Emma's death had almost been his downfall. Drinking and gambling helped to take his mind off his pain, and for a time he did both with great enthusiasm. Then his steward had confided in Fitzwilliam Darcy's steward the toll his dissolute ways were taking on Parkleigh Manor. He was certain that if not for the intervention of Darcy—an intervention he resented at first—he and Jonathan would have ended up on the streets.

Without hesitation, Darcy had stepped in as a mentor, helping him to get sober, quit gambling and make crucial decisions regarding the estate. Over time, he had managed to crawl out of despair, and it had only been in the last six months that he felt he could take a chance on gambling again. Unfortunately, his luck had not changed, and now he had accumulated more debts—something he had not confessed to Darcy yet.

Recalling what that man's evil aunt was asking of him, Gregory dropped his head in his hands. *If only I had listened to you, Darcy, and never gambled again!*

The letter he received from that harridan yesterday beckoned from its place on the desk. Picking it up, he read it again.

> *Mr. Wright,*
>
> *I am most seriously displeased that you have not kept in touch as I instructed. I assure you that I mean to have satisfaction.*
>
> *I will give you a fortnight to reply to this letter before I begin foreclosure on Parkleigh Manor to satisfy your debts.*
>
> *C. de Bourgh*

Having no alternative, Wright retrieved paper from a drawer and selected a pen from the ink stand. Dipping pen in ink, he began composing a reply.

> *Madam,*
>
> *I regret to inform you that thus far I have not been successful*

in convincing your nephew to become a partner in the distillery or to loan me funds for a new wheel. If it is any consolation, Darcy did say he has not made up his mind.

I can also report that he just left on a trip to Armagh, Ireland to see his sister. Whilst in Belfast, he plans to stop and examine the distillery— which may not work to our advantage.

I sent a note to the manager as soon as I knew Darcy was going, warning the man not to mention the apple blight and to speak favourably about the business to Darcy should he follow through on his plans.

I think you will agree that, for the time being, there is nothing to be done but to await his return to England.

Yours truly,
Gregory Wright

Once he had finished, Wright sealed the letter and rang for a footman. He intended to have it taken into Lambton and posted straightaway, hoping to placate Lady Catherine until Darcy returned from Ireland. After that, should her nephew not take the bait, he had no idea what course he would take.

Pemberley
Elizabeth's sitting room

As soon as a maid showed Judith Green into the room, Elizabeth rose and rushed to embrace her. Since their earliest acquaintance, Mrs. Green had been more to Elizabeth than merely the vicar's wife. She had become a second mother, and after Bennet and Anne were born, another grandmother to her children.

"Mimi," she cried, addressing Judith by the name Bennet had bestowed upon her when he first began to talk. "I have missed you."

When at last Mrs. Green pulled back from their embrace to look at her, Elizabeth pasted on a smile. Her friend was not fooled.

"You do not have to pretend for me, my dear. I know your heart is broken, for mine would be if James had just left for Ireland."

Trying to stay strong, Elizabeth closed her eyes as she shook her head slowly side to side.

"I fear that while William is away, I cannot be a competent mistress of Pemberley! Whenever he is gone—even if only at a neighbouring estate—my heart goes with him, and there is a huge, empty space inside me that aches horribly until he returns." She dropped her face into her hands. "For heaven's sake, I have two children for whom I must be strong. Still, each time I remember that he will not return tonight—" She began to weep. "Forgive me."

Pulling Elizabeth into her arms, Judith rocked her side to side, patting her back gently. "Oh, my dear, there is nothing to forgive. When one is deeply in love with their spouse, there is no magical point when suddenly you feel sufficient to carry on without them. My James teaches that is how God designed us—once we marry, each of us becomes half of a whole. So, you see, there is no reason to think badly of yourself when it is all God's design."

After Elizabeth had composed herself, Mrs. Green continued. "You may count on us if you need anything whilst our dear boy is away. As I told Fitzwilliam, it is no punishment to spend more time with you and the children. Come to think of it, where are Anne and Bennet?"

"They are napping, though it is about time they woke. When we have no company, William and I let them have tea with us as we are trying to teach them manners. Would you stay and have tea with the children and me?" Then Elizabeth smiled. "I fear I should warn you, though, that Anne has not taken to minding her manners as well as Ben. Do not be surprised if she attempts to stand in her chair to reach the biscuits."

"I would love to stay, and whilst we are having tea, perhaps you can tell me more about the area of Ireland where Georgiana is living. I had a cousin that moved to Belfast years ago."

"I know very little about Armagh, but I can tell you what my sister writes."

Just then, the children's nanny entered the sitting room door. "The children are ready for tea, ma'am. Where do you wish to have it today?"

"On the terrace, please."

Armagh, Ireland
Ballyneen
A bedroom

Lord Hayworth's ploy to avoid his wife by staying away from Ballyneen much of each day was put to an end when he suffered a twisted ankle after falling from his horse. His other injuries—a bruised shoulder, a broken finger and a wrenched knee—forced him to remain in bed until the local physician, Mr. Quinn, pronounced him well enough to resume activities. Thus far, Matthew had managed to avoid Georgiana by feigning sleep whenever she came in to see him.

Today, however, Georgiana managed to slip into his room earlier than usual, moving so quietly that she was beside the bed before he realised it. Emboldened by weeks of worry and anguish, she said curtly, "At last I have caught you awake."

"I ... I am," Matthew stammered, trying to think how best to handle the situation. Despite the fact that he had been awake for hours, he rubbed his eyes, hoping she would assume he had just stirred. "I feel as though I have been in this bed for months. Have I been insensible long?"

"I have not seen you awake from the time when you were carried into the house two days ago, though your aunt and Mrs. Murphy both say they have spoken to you since then."

"The draught Mr. Quinn prescribed must put me to sleep."

"Is it the draught, or are you merely feigning sleep to avoid having a conversation with me?"

"How could you say such a thing, especially when I lie here injured?"

"I am truly sorry you were hurt, but I have *every* right to say that and more. Since we set out on this horrible journey, you have paid scant attention to me. It is as though the man I fell in love with—the one who won my heart with his sweet devotion—has been replaced by a stranger."

Pulling a handkerchief from the pocket of her gown, Georgiana dabbed at her eyes. "In truth, I feel I have been betrayed and abandoned."

Knowing every word was true, Matthew reached out with his good hand, saying, "Come to me, sweetheart."

"No. You will only act like the man I married for a short while before resuming your uncaring attitude."

Matthew closed his eyes. "Dearest, there are matters— schemes if you will—at work that you know nothing about, and I am not at liberty to disclose them. Once I am able, I promise I will explain all."

"Not at liberty!" Georgiana cried, taking a step back. "I have seriously considered asking my brother to come and take me home to Pemberley, and you are *not at liberty*? If you wish me to continue as your wife, I suggest that you explain everything to me this instant!"

Realising he had no choice, Matthew confessed everything that had transpired after his sister ran off with the steward, including his father's demand that he tell no one and spirit her away to Ireland. Georgiana was so astonished at what she heard that as Matthew continued to speak, her legs grew weak and she sank down on the edge of the bed.

Once he had finished explaining, his wife's face had lost all colour; however, it was her unblinking stare that made him the most uneasy. "Sweetheart? Would a glass of brandy help? Shall I have one brought to you?"

Georgiana ignored his questions. "Am I to understand that Aileen has not been seen since leaving Berkley Hall with the steward on the 20th of February?"

"So I have been told."

Her eyes dropped to the handkerchief she was busily twisting through her fingers. "My poor, poor sister," she said. Then she began to cry in earnest.

Leaning forward, Matthew cupped her cheek. "I am so very sorry, my darling. I should have defied Father and taken you into my confidence straight away, but I cannot blame him alone. I feared how you would react to news of the scandal. Once my sister's recklessness is known throughout Southampton, we may be shunned by those who welcomed you only a few months ago, and any hope of being received by proper society in London may be lost forever."

"You cannot possibly think I would be more concerned with the *ton's* approval than knowing my sister could be lost to us forever."

Taking her hand, Matthew brought it to his lips for a gentle kiss. "Forgive me. I should have known you would react with kindness. Your caring nature is one of the reasons I fell in love with you."

"Yes! You *should* have known," Georgiana stated angrily. "In addition to being disappointed in you, I am disappointed that your father would press Aileen to marry someone she loathed. My brother would never have forced me to wed any man."

"Your brother is not of my father's generation. Things were done differently in his day. His marriage to Mother was arranged, and whilst they learned to care for one another, it was certainly no love match. He simply does not understand why Aileen did not realise that he was doing what he thought was best for her. Father may be inflexible, but his purpose was to ensure Aileen's future by placing her under the protection of an honourable man with a settlement that would assure her future. Can you not see his point of view?"

Reluctantly, Georgiana nodded. "If only they had had a better relationship, one where they could talk to each other, this might never have happened."

"Those are my thoughts exactly."

"So, all we can do is wait to hear from Mr. Osgood?"

"For now, I am afraid so," Matthew said. "However, there is something I must do." Lifting her chin so that he could look into her eyes, he said, "I must do everything in my power to earn your forgiveness. God knows that I do not deserve it, but I long for our relationship to return to what it was before this happened. Do you think you can forgive me?"

Captured by the pleading eyes of the man she loved, Georgiana could no longer stay angry. "If you promise never to keep a secret from me again, I will forgive you."

With his uninjured hand, Matthew lay his hand on his heart. "I promise, sweetheart."

Georgiana leaned in, offering her husband a soft kiss as proof of her forgiveness. When Matthew tried to deepen the kiss, however, she broke away.

Standing, she said, "I shall speak to Cook and have her prepare each of us a tray so that we may breakfast together."

"But, darling, we do not have to eat right now!" Matthew implored. "Lie down here beside me."

"Mr. Quinn left specific instructions that you are to lie completely still until you heal, and I intend to see that you do!"

Matthew was bereft. Watching as she headed towards the door, he cried, "Please, wait, Georgiana!"

Smiling mischievously, Georgiana closed the door behind her before looking up to see Lady Mary coming down the hall.

"Is my nephew awake?"

"He has just now fallen asleep. I had rather you call on him later."

As Georgiana walked in the direction of the grand staircase, that matron's brows knit. Hayworth's wife had never spoken to her in such an authoritative fashion. Dismissing it as an anomaly, Lady Mary continued towards her suite.

Chapter 6

Liverpool
Three days later

The evening William arrived, he took a room at Crown Inn and enquired about buying passage on a ship to Ireland. After being given the name of a reputable freight company that shipped passengers as well as goods between Liverpool and Belfast, he left his room early the next morning to find the establishment and purchase a ticket.

William found the street in front of the docks a far cry from the clean, shop-lined St. George Street where the inn was located. In fact, though he was only a short distance from the inn, it was as though he was in an entirely different world—one with shabby buildings where freight and trash covered the pavement, forcing both men and rats to take to the middle of the street. Not only did he have to thread his way through all manner of carts filled with goods, but also a seedy assortment of sweaty labourers and ne're-do-wells who looked ready to relieve him of his wallet.

The scene reminded William of a night spent on the docks of London when, if not for Richard, he might have been kidnapped or killed. That recollection prompted him to be certain he was not being followed. He had just done so when he happened upon the building he was looking for: Watson's Freight Services. Opening the door, William walked straight to a counter where a neatly dressed gentleman was busily shuffling through papers.

The man looked up. "May I help you?"

"Are you the proprietor?"

"Aye. Thomas Watson at your service."

"Mr. Watson, I wish to purchase passage on a ship to Belfast. I understand you have ships that sail there frequently."

"We do. The *Endeavour* will be back in port tomorrow and will leave again for Belfast three days afterwards. A passage is five pounds."

William reached into his coat to retrieve the necessary funds. Placing them on the counter, he said, "I assume the passage includes meals?"

"It does, and we serve good food, if I say so myself. The cook on that ship once cooked for His Majesty's navy," the man replied. "You are allowed only one trunk unless you wish to pay for extra luggage."

"That will be sufficient for my needs."

Sliding a paper across the counter, the ship owner said, "Write your name and address and whom to contact in case something should happen to you." Seeing William's brows knit, he added, "Nothing will happen. We run a tight ship, but the council governing passengers on board ships requires us to have a manifest on file."

Nodding, William wrote down his name, address, and Elizabeth as the person to contact. Once finished, the man took the paper and reached under the counter for a ticket. After stamping it in red ink, he held it out.

"This is your ticket, Mr. Darcy. I suggest you guard it carefully. Some of the rounders who infest the docks pinch them to sell for less than full price."

William nodded. "Be here no later than seven in the morning four days from today."

As William was leaving the building, a man entering almost ran into him. Suspecting a pickpocket, he backed up and waved him past; however, as he watched the stranger approach the counter and enquire about two passages to Belfast, he realised there was something familiar about the fellow. Certain he had seen him before, William presumed that in view of the fact they would be on the same ship, he would have an opportunity to discover where and when later. Exiting the building, he headed towards the inn.

Once reaching St. George Street again, William noticed a sign approximately one hundred feet away—Rundell and Bridge, Goldsmiths and Jewellers.[2] Recognising the name of the same trusted jewellers he patronised in London, on an impulse he decided to purchase a small gift for Elizabeth and have it delivered to Pemberley.

As he entered the well-appointed shop, an overhead bell rang, alert-

---

[2] ***Rundell and Bridge.*** *One of the most influential of a new breed of jewellers in the Regency era was Rundell and Bridge, jewellers to the crown. Their London store was located at 32 Ludgate Hill, a continuation of Fleet Street. For purposes of this story, I added a branch of the store in Liverpool.*

ing the manager, and a tall, slender, silver-haired gentleman instantly walked through a curtained door. William recognised him as Mr. Rundell, the owner of the Bond Street store.

"Mr. Darcy! I did not expect to see you here!"

"I could say the same for you, Mr. Rundell. I had no idea you had a shop in Liverpool."

"We have only been here a few months. We hope this location will thrive like our shop in London. If it does, my son Benson will manage it, and I will return to London." He smiled. "I am too old to give up all the amusements London has to offer, so when Benson asked about establishing a shop here, I insisted that should it be a success, he manage it."

"I dare say Liverpool has a way to go before it can compete with London's diversions."

"My point exactly! Now, may I enquire how Mrs. Darcy and the children are faring? I believe the last time I saw your wife was when she purchased a silver rattle from our London shop. If memory serves, it was for your daughter, Anne."

"You have an excellent memory, sir. I had no idea it had been that long since my wife was in your shop. Anne is presently a year and eight months old."

"Time passes far too quickly. Now, did you come in with something particular in mind?"

"Yes. Mrs. Darcy admires the tortoiseshell hair combs that seem to be the latest fashion. Do you perhaps have any?"

"We certainly do!"

Mr. Rundell walked over to a counter, opened it, and brought out a tray of tortoiseshell combs—some plain and others featuring gold inlay, diamonds, or pearls. Knowing that Elizabeth would prefer the unadorned combs, he inspected those first before choosing a pair. Then, he chose another pair adorned with pearls that matched a necklace he had gifted her.

"These will do nicely. Could you ship them directly to Mrs. Darcy at Pemberley and charge my account?"

"I would be delighted to handle that." The man took two blank cards from under the counter. "Please write the directions where they should be shipped on one card and on the other any sentiments you wish to include with the gift."

William complied and was soon on his way.

Back in his room, William sat down to compose a letter to Elizabeth, something he had promised he would do upon reaching Liverpool. He considered hinting in the letter that she should look for a package but decided he had rather the combs come as a complete surprise.

Reaching inside his coat, he removed the watch his father had presented him on his twentieth birthday and opened the case. The likeness of Elizabeth that resided inside it made his heart begin to ache. Leaving it open, he set the watch down on the desk so he could look at her whilst he wrote.

> *My darling wife,*
>
> *I am trusting God that this letter finds you and the children in good health. I made Liverpool late yesterday, and other than being tired from the journey, I am well.*
>
> *I took a room at the Crown Inn, which reminds me of the hotel by the same name where we stayed when we were in Brighton last year. Unfortunately, the inn is much smaller than that hotel. Still, the linens are clean and the food is edible, so I have no complaints.*
>
> *Today I purchased passage on a ship called the Endeavour. It is owned by Watson's Freight Services, whose main purpose, as evidenced by the name, is to transport goods between here and Ireland, though they do transport passengers when space is available. I leave in four days and will write again before I leave.*
>
> *I miss you and the children terribly. I feel as though I am lost in a wilderness without a compass. You are my first thought each morning and my last each night. Pray with me that this trip will conclude quickly.*
>
> *I love you so very much, Elizabeth, that I am finding it much more difficult than I ever imagined to be parted from you. Kiss the children and tell them I love and miss them.*
>
> *Your loving husband,*
> *William*

After bringing her image to his lips for a kiss, he closed the watch and put it back inside his coat. Folding and sealing the letter, he went downstairs to have the proprietor send it by an express courier for he knew Elizabeth would worry until she heard from him..

The Crown Inn
Three days later

If William had not kept to his room the majority of the time he waited for the ship to Belfast to arrive, he might have encountered Matthew's sister, Lady Aileen, who was staying at the same inn under an assumed name. Arthur Gable, her father's former steward, had registered Aileen as his sister, Barbara, whom he proclaimed to all who listened, was visiting from Bath. Afterwards, at her request, he left to find lodging elsewhere. Gable found it odd that someone who cared so little about her reputation thought it in poor taste to pretend they were married and insisted on having separate accommodations until they actually wed.

Unbeknownst to her, being in separate inns suited Gable just fine, for he had no intentions of marrying Lady Aileen, much less taking her to Ireland. His plan was to sell the jewellery she brought with her when they fled Berkley Hall and take his true love, Jenny Russell, to Ireland instead. Jenny, a woman he had known since childhood, worked at a run-down pub her uncle managed in the poorest section of Liverpool and resided in one of the rooms above the pub, which was where Gable planned to stay.

Inasmuch as he had convinced Aileen the ship was not leaving for another week instead of the next day, his present task consisted of convincing her that he must sell the rest of her jewellery right away. Gable was not worried, however, for thus far she had believed all his lies.

The town was awake and lively by the time Arthur Gable knocked on Lady Aileen's door at the Crown Inn. When she opened it, he smiled and walked inside.

"I thought we would break our fast together in the dining room downstairs. This inn has the reputation of serving the best food in Liverpool, and I wish to know if that is true."

Aileen turned to consider her appearance in the mirror over the dresser. Running her hands over her wrinkled skirt, she asked, "Do I look presentable? Without a maid it is impossible to look appropriate." Without waiting for an answer, she patted at her hair before donning a hat. "Thank goodness for bonnets. At least I can disguise my unruly hair."

"Do not fret about your appearance, my dear," Gable said. "Your natural beauty puts other women to shame."

As they proceeded into the hall, she smiled up at the handsome, brown-haired philanderer. "You flatter me, Arthur, but I need flattery just now. I have been so downhearted, and I do not think I shall recover until we arrive in Ireland and are wed. Perhaps, if my brother is at Ballyneen as you had heard, he will be willing to give me away."

Gable thought her ideas so foolish that he could not repress a taunt. "Why do you think your brother would welcome you? After all, his name was ruined when we left Southampton together."

"Must you always think in terms of the worst results?"

"It is merely that I do not want you to get your hopes up, my dear. If you ask me, your brother is too much like your father—not the type to forgive and forget."

"You are wrong! My brother loves me. He may not agree with my actions, but I know he will not be unkind."

Without letting her see, Gable rolled his eyes. "You may be right, darling. You know him better than I do."

"I *am* right."

By then they had reached the dining room, where a waiter escorted them to a table.

Whilst they ate, the former steward brought up the subject of selling the balance of her jewellery. He was not surprised to be met with resistance.

"How could we have already spent what you received for my bracelets?"

"You forget, dearest. We left Berkley Hall in such a rush that you insisted on purchasing shoes and other necessities in Bath. We had to pay for our lodgings there and for the tickets to Birmingham and then to Liverpool, not to mention lodging and food along the way. Moreover, after I was told each passenger on the ship is allowed only one trunk, I knew the small one you brought would never suffice. I purchased the largest trunk available for you and it was not inexpensive."

"I have seen no such trunk."

"It is so large that I left it in the room where I am presently. I shall have it brought here when it is time for us to leave."

"Still, it would seem—"

"My dear Aileen, you must consider also that you are staying in one of the most expensive rooms available and enjoying the finest food and wine. When we leave, we may not be able to cover the bill with what little funds we have on hand." He reached for her hand and brought it to his lips for a kiss. "Besides, in my judgement, we will get far more for the jewellery in this thriving port city than in grimy, industrial Belfast."

"I ... I suppose you are right."

"Then, let us retrieve the jewels. They are still hidden in the lining of your trunk, are they not?"

"They are."

"Good. Once we have them, I will head straight to a jeweller I passed just down the street and see what he will offer. In the event he does not make a fair offer, we can always sell only what is necessary to get us to Belfast and hold the balance to sell later."

"That seems sensible."

Gable smiled. "I am glad you agree."

As soon as their meal was finished, they were on their way to Aileen's room to retrieve the jewels.

Armagh, Ireland
Ballyneen

In the days after Georgiana confronted her husband, things had improved dramatically. Other than the fact that he still suffered from his injuries, which prevented reconciling in the manner both desired, it was as though their estrangement had never happened.

Because Matthew was still confined to his bed or a chaise, Georgiana sat with him each day, playing cards, or reading aloud from books he chose. Today when refreshments were brought up for tea, Georgiana set aside the book she had been reading, in preparation to pour. Once she had, Matthew brought up a subject she had hoped to avoid.

"Dearest, you have not mentioned hearing from Fitzwilliam or Elizabeth in ages. Surely they still correspond with you."

Georgiana had refused to dwell on why she had not heard from her brother after she sent him the letter lamenting the state of her marriage. Not responding to her letter was totally out of character for Fitzwilliam, and Matthew's question forced her to consider that he might not have replied because he was on his way.

She stopped whilst the teapot was in mid-air. "I fear I may have stirred up a hornet's nest."

Matthew's brows knit. "Whatever do you mean?"

She set the teapot back down on the table. "I ... I was so miserable ... and you were acting so strangely ... that I—"

Matthew held out his hand, and she clasped it. As he pulled her towards the chaise, he said, "You had every right to be upset, sweetheart. Just tell me."

"I felt I had no choice, so I wrote to Fitzwilliam, pouring out all my frustrations and suspicions."

"Suspicions?"

"Since you were home so little, it occurred to me that you might have a mistress." She looked down. "I was crushed, and there was no one else I could turn to but Brother. I was too ashamed to confide in Elizabeth."

Closing his eyes, Matthew rubbed his tightening forehead with his fingers. "I can understand why you might think that. However wrong your assumption, it was entirely my fault for being absent so often. When did you send the letter?"

"About two weeks ago."

"And he has not written?"

"No."

Matthew patted the chaise. "Sit down, darling."

Once Georgiana was sitting beside him, he framed her face with his hands and kissed her soundly. "If Fitzwilliam does come, I shall just have to face him like a man. He will be livid at how I have conducted myself. I would be if I were he."

"I am so relieved that, if he does come, he will find that we are no longer at odds."

Matthew chuckled. "No more relieved than I."

"You are not afraid of William, are you?"

"Any sane man would be. Fitzwilliam Darcy knows no fear where his family's wellbeing is concerned."

"Is that not how it should be?"

"Yes," Matthew said. At Georgiana's smile, he added, "Now that we have that settled, what would you say if, after enjoying our tea, I asked you to join me for a nap? I will rest better with you lying beside me."

"I will, as long as you promise to rest. You know Mr. Quinn says your shoulder is not completely healed, and we cannot resume relations until it is."

Matthew crossed his fingers. "I promise."

Chapter 7

Liverpool
The Crown Inn
The next day

As the noon hour approached, it became clear to Lady Aileen that her fiancé was not going to return. Gable had always arrived early to escort her to the dining room in order for her to break her fast. Today, of all days, his presence was especially important, because she was to learn how much he had gotten for the remainder of her jewellery.

More than once since leaving Berkley Hall, it had crossed her mind that perhaps she should not trust Gable implicitly, but she had brushed those qualms aside. Now, heart beating like a drum, Aileen took several deep breaths to calm herself as she began searching her reticule for any coins she might have overlooked. She found a single shilling. The only other thing of value she possessed was a diamond and emerald ring, a present from her mother that she had hidden from Gable.

Removing it from the hidden pocket in her reticule, she slid it onto her finger. As Aileen gazed at it, her heart ached with the realisation that it, too, must be sold. She prayed it would bring enough to pay any charges she might have accrued at the inn, purchase a passage on a ship to Ireland, and a coach to Ballyneen Castle. Then, if the rumours she had heard in Bath were true, and her father had sent Matthew and Georgiana to Ireland, she could reunite with them.

Deciding she must speak to the inn's clerk to find out if Mr. Gable had paid anything towards her bill, she glanced at her reflection in the mirror. The realisation that she looked defeated brought tears to her eyes. Instantly, something her mother had always said came to mind.

Even if your heart is breaking, Aileen, never let any man see you cry. If you do, they will have the advantage.

Willing the tears that had pooled to dissipate, Aileen pasted a faux smile on her face and went downstairs.

After learning that Mr. Gable had paid nothing towards the bill, Aileen exited the inn. Once on the pavement, she stopped to look in both directions in hope of spotting the jewellery shop Arthur had mentioned. Spying the *Rundell and Bridges* sign, she ignored the stares of those stunned to see a woman walking down St. George Street unescorted and headed in that direction. She had gone no more than a hundred feet, however, when a man of dubious character came out of nowhere to walk alongside her. As he did, he murmured untoward suggestions, causing Aileen to crimson with humiliation. She was about to cry out for help, when a well-dressed gentleman suddenly came upon them from the rear. Pushing the villain out of the way, he stepped between them.

"Leave my sister alone, you blackguard!" the stranger demanded.

Startled, the beast disappeared into a nearby park, leaving her rescuer to say, "Please forgive me for the intrusion, ma'am, but I could tell the man was frightening you."

Still shaken, Aileen stammered, "I ... I am grateful that you did, Mr.—"

Tipping his hat, the gentleman smiled. "Stevens. Noel Stevens of Houghton Park, in Leicester."

"Lady Davidson of Berkley Hall in Southampton."

"It is none of my business, Lady Davidson, but I fear it is unsafe for any woman to be without an escort in this area—much less a gentlewoman such as yourself."

Aileen's eyes dropped to study her feet. Having no one else to confide in, she decided to take a chance and confess at least part of the truth to the man who had come to her aid. "Unfortunately, I have found myself deserted by my fiancé and in debt to the local inn. I hope to sell a piece of jewellery to pay my bill and purchase passage on a ship to Ireland."

The man smiled. "Might you have family in Ireland? I have cousins in Dungannon,"

"Actually, my family owns a small estate in Armagh."

"What a coincidence!" the man said enthusiastically. "Dungannon is just north of Armagh. I came to Liverpool to book a ship to Belfast and have just learned that the ship I hoped to sail on left port this morning. It is not supposed to return for five or six days, so I am on my way to the docks to learn if another vessel might be leaving sooner."

"It is my understanding that Watson's Freight Service has a ship leaving for Belfast soon."

"I fear you are mistaken, my lady, for that ship sailed this morning."

In an effort not to cry, Aileen took a deep breath and let it go slowly. "My fiancé and I were supposed to sail on that ship together. Apparently, the departure date he gave me was also a lie."

"I am truly sorry," Mr. Stevens replied. Then, his face lit up. "Why not accompany me to the docks? If there are other ships heading to Belfast soon, we may both be fortunate enough to purchase a passage."

"I appreciate your kind offer very much," Aileen replied, surreptitiously glancing towards the jewellery shop, "but first I must sell my ring. Would you be willing to wait until I have done so?"

"I shall do better than that," Mr. Stevens said, holding out an arm. "I shall be happy to escort you to the shop."

Silverhill Shipping Company

Located not 300 feet down the docks from Watson's Freight Service was a company of a different sort. Silverhill Shipping Company was owned by John Silverhill, known as Cap'n Silver to his crew of former sailors and privateers. Though not a handsome man, Silverhill dressed expensively, which made him appear more a gentleman than a crusty sea captain. Tall and lean with grey hair, his most distinguishing feature was sky-blue eyes that contrasted vividly against a deep-brown, weathered complexion—the result of too many years in the sun.

At one time a promising midshipman in His Majesty's navy, Silverhill had become cynical after being passed over for a ship far too many times, even after he had passed the test to become a lieutenant. Without a ship, he would never be more than a midshipman; thus, when a merchant with ships transporting goods to and from the West Indies gave him the chance to captain a ship, Silverhill resigned from the navy and took the position. Upon that merchant's death, he had saved enough coin to purchase one of his vessels and start his own shipping company using the contacts he had made.

His company soon earned a reputation for fast, efficient service between Liverpool, Scotland, and Ireland. Still, after years in business, the wealth Silverhill craved eluded him. It was about that time that he was approached by another former navy midshipman named David Grubbs with an offer he could not refuse.

David Grubbs owned ships, too, and for years he had been stealing merchandise from those who used his services, including the navy. He took the goods to his private island off the southern end of the Isle of Man, storing them in caves there until the search for the missing goods diminished. Then he transported the items to Scotland or Ireland and sold them.

Grubbs' island, known as the Calf of Man, was home to Windemere Manor, an estate that once belonged to an eccentric great-uncle he had never met and knew little about until notified after the man's death that he was his heir. Upon visiting the island, Grubbs discovered a once magnificent house badly in need of repairs. Built centuries before, it and a herd of indigenous sheep were being cared for by servants whose ancestors had inhabited the island for centuries.

Going over his uncle's ledgers, Grubbs soon learned the main source of revenue in his uncle's lifetime came from a fleet of fishing vessels, which explained the magnificent docks on the east side of the island. Though only two of the four ships moored there were seaworthy, Grubbs hired a friend to sail one whilst he captained the other and began a freight hauling service. Through the years, it had transformed into a lucrative plundering organisation.

Liverpool's docks had expanded so rapidly, however, that in a short while, Grubbs was unable to keep up with the quantity of merchandise his men stole. In need of a warehouse to store the goods until a ship could pick them up, Grubbs had approached Silverhill about becoming his partner. It had taken little effort to persuade him, and theirs had proved the ideal alliance until Grubbs died less than a year later when his ship sank during a storm.

Grubbs' death had left Silverhill short on men and ships. That, and the fact that the navy had sent more investigators to Liverpool to discover where their shipments were going astray, not only made Silverhill nervous, but had severely reduced his income.

In the meantime, Grubbs' young widow, Cecile, who still resided on the island with her young child, had no idea that her husband and Silverhill were thieves, and she had begun asking questions about her portion of the company. Silverhill, acting the part of a concerned friend, insisted she let him worry about the business until her mourning period was over, but now that the money was dwindling fast and the navy was closing in, he felt pressured to act. Certain that if he could persuade Cecile to marry him before she learned the truth, it would buy her silence, he had begun a campaign to win her heart. Nonetheless, thus far all his efforts to charm her had proven unsuccessful.

Presently, Silverhill had more pressing problems on his mind. The night before, his men had intercepted two wagon loads of leather goods on the outskirts of Liverpool that were bound for the navy's new garrison. The ship required to transport them to the island had not returned to port, and the warehouse was full to overflowing. Pondering where else he might hide the goods before the local constable conducted his usual search of the warehouse district, voices raised in anger demanded his attention. Irritated at the interruption, Silverhill tossed his pen on the desk, rose, and hurried down the stairs to the warehouse, which was on the same level as the road running behind all the buildings.

Opening the door, he was stunned to see a well-dressed couple being held at gunpoint by two of his employees. Before he could ask, one dockhand offered, "They be spying on us, Cap'n Silver."

"Aye, they be hiding behind the pallets what we *picked up* last night," the other man added, clearly referencing the shipment they had pinched from the navy.

"I can assure you that we were not spying on you, or anyone else, for that matter," Mr. Stevens stated more calmly than he felt. "The sign on the front door said the office was closed. When we heard voices coming from amongst the merchandise stacked on the pavement, we went through them in hope of finding someone to ask about purchasing a passage to Ireland."

"Who might you be?" Silverhill demanded.

"Noel Stevens ... of Houghton Park in Leicester," Stevens stuttered. Motioning to Aileen, he said, "This is my ... my fiancée, Lady Davidson of Berkley Hall in Southampton."

Silverhill did not trust them, but he was willing to act civilly until he had the answers he wanted. "Where are you headed to in Ireland?"

Though shocked by her companion's claims of familiarity, Aileen went along with the charade, interjecting, "Belfast! My sister is to be married in three days, and we hoped to arrive in time for her wedding."

"It seems you waited until the last minute," Silverhill stated doubtfully.

Aileen swallowed hard and presented the man with a faux smile as Stevens said, "We only learned of the wedding a few days ago."

"I wonder at you coming to my business. Ask anyone in Liverpool, and they will tell you that Silverhill Shipping does not carry passengers."

Having long since realised they were in danger, Mr. Stevens was eager to give the captain a reason to keep them alive.

"I have always found that money opens doors, and we were willing to sail on any vessel that could take us there quickly."

Silverhill's first thought had been to rob the intruders and then dispose of them. The mention of money, however, gave rise to another idea. If this couple had rich families willing to pay well for their safe return, that might prove profitable enough to allow him to start over in another country.

"How much money are we talking about?"

"I ... I was told a passage costs roughly five pounds," Mr. Stevens replied.

"Come now, Stevens. We both know we are no longer talking about passages to Ireland." Seeing Steven's expression grow more anxious, Silverhill was encouraged to add. "To be truthful, I was pondering having you and the lady taken out to sea and tossed overboard, so I suggest you give me a reason not to."

Swallowing hard, Noel Stevens decided to exaggerate his wealth. "In addition to owning Houghton Park, I inherited my grandmother's estate in Wales when she died—Whistledown Farm. Have you heard of it?" When Silverhill showed no reaction, he continued. "I also own property in Dungannon, Ireland. As I mentioned, Lady Davidson's home is Berkley Hall in Southampton. Her father, Lord Camden, is one of the wealthiest men in England, if not in all Ireland. I am certain our relations would be glad to assure our safe return."

Cradling his chin with one hand, the captain slowly ran his thumb across his lips. "I hope you are telling the truth, sir, for I aim to investigate your claims. If you are lying, you will be killed outright. If, however, you are telling the truth and your relations are willing to pay a nice sum for your return, I will negotiate with them for your lives."

Turning to his men, Silverhill ordered, "Take them to my quarters and tie them up. Assign a trustworthy person to watch them day and night. Then move those pallets into the cellar. The cesspool should keep the investigators out of there until I can decide where to take them."

"Aye, aye, Cap'n."

Pemberley

As she had done each day since William left for Ireland, Elizabeth went through the motions of living, but it was as though in a fog, as she forced herself to concentrate during meetings with Mrs. Reynolds regarding household matters and discussions with the steward concerning the estate. She had experienced this same confusion during the first few months of pregnancy with Bennet and later Anne, which served to bolster her belief that she was with child again.

Wanting the servants to recognise that Pemberley would continue as it always had, even with William away for a time, Elizabeth tried to act as though nothing had changed. If she were pregnant and the staff found out, they would begin to coddle her, as they had in the past. Like it or not, she was in charge until William returned, and she intended to be a force to be reckoned with if anyone tried to usurp her authority. With this occupying her thoughts, the only time of late Elizabeth completely relaxed was when she was with her children.

Now, sitting under a tall tree in the garden in the huge white swing William had specially built so the entire family could sit together, she tried to hold her laughter in check as she watched Bennet playing with Clancy. With each throw of the ball, her son's frustration grew because the little dog insisted on running in increasingly larger circles around the yard before returning to him with the prize.

Seeing Bennet's scowl in response to Clancy's antics sent a fresh pain through Elizabeth's heart. He looked so much like his father when he frowned that she was reminded of the letter she received the day before—the one now tucked inside the bodice of her gown.

William had always known what to say to make her fall more deeply in love with him, and the words in this missive were no exception.

Placing a hand over her heart, she closed her eyes and tried to recall all he had written.

"Mama?"

Elizabeth's eyes flew open. Her son was standing before her looking so sombre that she forced a smile. "Yes, Ben."

"Are you thinking of Papa?"

"Yes, I was, but how could you tell?"

"Because you look sad just like you did last night when you read Papa's letter to Anne and me."

"Did I?" Quickly assuming a cheery air, Elizabeth pulled Bennet into her lap and placed a kiss atop his head. "Fortunately, I have you and Anne here to keep my spirits up."

"If I tell you something, will you promise not to tell Papa?"

Pulling back to look into his light blue eyes that were identical to William's, she replied, "You can always tell me your secrets, and I will keep them."

Ben took a deep breath and let it go loudly. "Sometimes I miss Papa so much that I cry before I go to sleep."

"Would you believe that I do, too?"

"You do?"

"Yes. Sometimes even grown men and women cry when they miss someone they love."

As Ben seemed to consider that, Elizabeth added, "Never be afraid to talk with me or your father about your feelings. We love you and will do all in our power to help you to feel better. Remember, we cannot help you if we do not know that you are sad. Do you understand?"

"Yes, Mama."

Suddenly, both noticed a man walking towards them across the lawn. In his arms he held a boy of approximately three years of age. Their arrival sent Bennet flying out of Elizabeth's lap to stand straight as a soldier next to the swing.

Recognising who it was, Elizabeth rose to greet their neighbour. "Mr. Wright, with your new beard I did not recognise you at first!"

Gregory Wright removed his hat and dipped his head in acknowledgement. "I hope it does not make me look so different as to be unrecognisable."

"Of course not. What is more, I am pleased that you answered my plea to bring Jonathan here to play with Bennet. I think it will be a good diversion for them both."

"Thank you for the invitation, Mrs. Darcy. Jonathan always enjoys playing with Bennet. He talks about it for days afterwards."

Suddenly, Clancy ran up with the ball in his mouth and dropped it in front of Bennet, who picked it up and tossed it towards the goldfish pond in the centre of the garden. Clancy ran after the ball with Bennet right on his heels, prompting Mr. Wright to set his son on his feet to catch up with his friend.

The goldfish pond, fashioned entirely from river rocks, employed larger, flat rocks around the rim as a bench, and today a fleet of brightly painted, wooden boats sat upon it, waiting to be set afloat. Seeing the boats, both boys quickly abandoned the ball, with each grabbing a boat and placing it in the water.

Wright glanced at Elizabeth. "I imagine it has been very hard on Ben with his father away."

"It has been hard on us all," Elizabeth replied, as she shaded her eyes to watch the children.

Wright took the opportunity to study Elizabeth surreptitiously. After Emma died, Elizabeth had encouraged him not to leave Jonathan's care entirely to a nanny but to get to know his child by assuming at least some of his care. She had also made herself available to answer any question he had and, as a result, he was almost as well-versed regarding children as Fitzwilliam, whom he had always admired for his affectionate relationship with his children.

Though Elizabeth was the total opposite of his late wife in appearance and personality, Wright had halfway fallen in love with her by the time his son was a year old. Not only was she vivacious, as well as beautiful, but he found it increasingly hard not to let his feelings get in the way of their friendship. He was also well aware that the Darcys were a love match and that should his feelings become known, he would not be welcome in their company. Still, with Darcy away, it was easy to imagine a life where she was his wife and Jonathan's mother.

Suddenly, Elizabeth turned to catch him staring. "Please do not think you must wait the whole afternoon. You may attend to your business and return for your son later."

Wright was about to say he had no pressing business when Mrs. Green walked up carrying Anne. "I hope I am not intruding. Mrs.

Reynolds was showing me through the house when we came across Anne's nanny near the terrace. She was bringing the baby to you, so I offered to carry her the rest of the way."

"You could never be an intrusion!" Elizabeth replied.

Anne reached for Elizabeth, who took the girl. Kissing her daughter's forehead, she sat down in the swing with Anne in her lap. Patting the place next to her, she said, "Come! Sit beside us, Mimi."

"Mrs. Green," Mr. Wright acknowledged at last. "How are you and the vicar faring?"

"We are well, thank you. My husband called at Parkleigh Manor, but your butler said you were not available. He wished to say we have missed you at Sunday services and to inquire if you had been ill."

"I fear I have only been very busy of late. I intend to return to attending services soon, though."

"I dare say that all the congregants will be glad to hear it," Mrs. Green replied sincerely.

Recognising that any chance to be alone with Elizabeth had been lost, Wright said, "I shall leave Jonathan in your capable hands, Mrs. Darcy, and return for him late this afternoon, if that is agreeable."

"Of course," Elizabeth replied.

After performing a crisp bow, Wright walked away. He had not gotten completely out of sight before Mrs. Green leaned closer to Elizabeth to whisper, "I do not understand that man in the least."

"Whatever do you mean?"

"James and I have tried several times to facilitate introductions between him and several eligible ladies who have settled in the neighbourhood and who are attending our church. Two of them have titles, wealth, and connections, but Gregory Wright has not shown the least bit of interest in either of them."

"Perhaps he is still mourning Emma and is simply not ready to move forward."

"Marrying again is not all about *his* needs; that child needs a mother."

"Has he met Lord Albany's daughter?" Elizabeth asked. "She is quite young, but she has a sweet spirit about her. Moreover, she is very pretty."

"Lady Alice was one of those we recommended, but I heard that Mr. Wright completely ignored her at Lady Romstead's ball."

Elizabeth laughed. "I am certain he will marry again when he meets the right woman."

"I fear that Jonathan may be grown before that happens," the vicar's wife said, sighing. "And children brought up motherless, or fatherless, always seem to attract the wrong people when they look for a mate. Mark my words. I have seen it too many times—men who are looking for their mothers and girls looking to replace their fathers instead of seeking wives or husbands."

"Well, we shall pray he will meet the perfect woman. One who will make him a good wife and Jonathan a loving mother."

Judith Green broke into a grin. "I am the vicar's wife. I should have said that."

Laughing, Elizabeth squeezed her hand. "It matters not which of us said it, as long as both of us agree."

"Amen to that!"

Chapter 8

Aboard the *Endeavour*

Immediately upon boarding the ship that was to take him to Ireland, William was greeted by the captain, Harold Beacham, who began introducing William to the other passengers, most of whom had preceded him onboard.

Turning to an older, well-dressed man of approximately five and fifty, Beacham said, "Lord Chelsey, allow me to introduce Fitzwilliam Darcy of Pemberley in Derbyshire." To William he said, "Lord Chelsey is master of Chelsey Manor in Sussex. He and his lovely wife are on their honeymoon."

Lord Chelsey acknowledged William before reaching for the hand of a woman who looked no more than two and twenty. Pulling her to his side, he smiled broadly, proudly proclaiming, "Mr. Darcy, may I present my wife, Lady Chelsey."

"I am pleased to meet you, Lady Chelsey," William replied, hoping his face did not reflect his thoughts.

Then Captain Beacham motioned to three men standing directly to his right. "Lord Douglas is from Edinburgh, as is his nephew, Lord Erskine, and his cousin, Lord Loudin." To them he said, "Gentlemen, Fitzwilliam Darcy of Pemberley in Derbyshire."

Whilst they acknowledged each other with bows, two more passengers came aboard, a man and a woman. As the captain went to greet them, William recognised the man as the one he had seen at Watson's Freight office. Upon seeing him again, William suddenly recalled where they had met before—at Georgiana's wedding. At the time, Mr. Gable was the steward for Viscount Hayworth's father, Lord Camden, and was so well thought of that Camden had invited him to the ceremony.

The captain brought Gable and the woman forwards to be introduced, but before he could say anything, William remarked, "Mr. Gable, it is good to see you again."

Gable's eyes darted about anxiously, and he seemed at a loss for words.

"We met at my sister's wedding at Pemberley last December," William added, hoping to prod his memory.

"I ... I remember," Gable murmured at last. "A pleasure to see you again, Mr. Darcy." Then, without introducing his companion, he turned to her. "Come, my dear. I will escort you to our cabin."

As the two walked away, Captain Beacham quietly murmured, "How odd! Not only does it appear that Mr. Gable does not wish to renew your acquaintance, apparently he does not care to introduce his wife to you or the other passengers."

William shrugged. "At least his attitude relieves me of any obligation to converse with him during our trip."

The captain laughed heartily. "An excellent observation, sir."

"Ladies and gentlemen," Beacham said loudly, "please locate your cabins and make certain all of your luggage is onboard. We sail shortly, and after we have left the docks, it will be too late to complain that something is missing. Your meals will be served in your cabins. If you think of any questions, please do not hesitate to ask them of whoever delivers your dinner tray. If they cannot answer, they will pass the question along to me, and I shall address it with you personally. For now, please go below and get acquainted with your accommodations."

As he watched the captain head towards the bow of the ship, William lost sight of him after he passed several large pallets strapped to the deck. Having never cared for travel in a ship's belly, William took one last look at a perfectly blue sky before going below deck to locate his cabin.

It did not take long for William to find the cabin assigned to him. It was not very large, but it contained two small beds and had a narrow water closet in the corner of the back wall. The remainder of that wall featured a waist-high countertop with drawers that went all the way to the floor underneath it. A good-sized mirror hung over the countertop, whilst a pitcher of water and a wash bowl rested in specially made openings in the counter. Opening the drawers, William discovered towels, a heavy blanket and two unused candles.

Spying his trunk on the floor, he picked it up and laid it on a bed. After unlocking it, he began to shuffle through the contents, removing a robe and a comfortable pair of slippers. These he placed on the corner of the opposite bed. Then, removing his coat, he hung it on a hook on the wall, sat down on the bed and began removing his boots.

William had never slept well the few times he was apart from Elizabeth, and this trip proved no exception. Consequently, the last few days had been more exhausting than he had thought possible. So, unable to resist, he lay back on the unencumbered bed and closed his eyes. Thinking only to rest a short while, he was soon lulled to sleep by the gentle sway of the ship.

Ballyneen Castle

With her marriage to Matthew restored to its former felicity, Georgiana found living at Ballyneen was not as tedious as before. Her husband now went out of his way to spend time with her, showing her the finer aspects of the estate, as well as the advantageous features of the neighbouring town of Armagh. This day they were on their way to Demesne Palace,[3] south of Armagh, to tour the buildings open to the public, including the observatory which both longed to see, and to picnic on the grounds before returning home.

As Georgiana admired the view from the window of the carriage, she noted everything might have been perfect, were it not for the fact she had still not heard from her brother. Deciding perhaps the letter pouring out her disappointment with Matthew might have gone astray, she had sent another speaking of her current contentment. She hoped it might assure Fitzwilliam of her present happiness.

"Georgiana."

When she did not react, Matthew repeated her name a little louder. When that got no reply, he placed two fingers under her chin and gently turned her to face him.

"What are you doing?" Georgiana asked, chuckling.

"Attempting to get your attention," he said with an indulgent smile.

"I am sorry. I was wool-gathering."

---

[3] ***Demesne Palace*** *– Also known as the Archbishop's Palace is a landmark Neo-Classical building located on 300 acres just south of the centre of the city. The building served as primary residence of the Church of Ireland Archbishops of Armagh for over two hundred years, from 1770 to 1975 https://en.wikipedia.org/wiki/Archbishop%27s_Palace,_Armagh*

"I believe you were thinking of your brother and why he has not replied to your letters."

Georgiana's expression proved that he had touched on the truth. "You know me so well, darling. It is as though you can read my mind."

Teasingly, Matthew pressed two fingers to his forehead and closed his eyes. "This very second you are thinking 'how did I manage to marry such a handsome, intelligent fellow?'"

Georgiana laughed. "I was entirely wrong! You have no idea what is on my mind!"

"Oh? Then suppose you share with me what you are thinking right this second."

Her expression grew sombre. "I was thinking how fortunate I am to have married the man I love when so many of my friends were forced to marry someone their parents chose."

Grasping his wife's hand, Matthew brought it to his lips for a kiss. "And at this very moment, I am thinking how fortunate I am to have found a rose amongst all the thorns my father had singled out as my potential bride."

"You never mentioned your father was involved in selecting your wife!"

"I suppose I felt it not worth revisiting after I met you. Father had his ideas and thank goodness, Lady Matlock had hers. It was she who convinced Father that he should include you on the list."

"My aunt was also insistent I meet you," Georgiana said. "From the beginning, she contended that we were formed for one another and, mercifully, she was proved correct. I can never thank her enough for convincing me to consider you and convincing Brother to listen to reason."

"Listen to reason? Was Darcy opposed to our courtship?"

"At the time, he was not in favour of *anyone* courting me. He thought me too young. Surely you were aware of that when you asked his permission."

Matthew tilted his head. "Now that you mention it, he was not very pleasant when I spoke to him the first time. Still, because of Lady Matlock's counsel, I thought that was merely Fitzwilliam's normal disposition."

Georgiana laughed. "What was my aunt's advice?"

"As I recall, she said I should not take offence if your brother acted surly. I was to stay calm, smile and be civil, no matter how argumentative he might become."

"My poor brother!" Georgiana declared. "He had such a bad reputation, merely because he was overprotective of me. Otherwise, he could be as charming as anyone else."

Now it was Matthew's turn to laugh. "I fear you have him confused with your cousin the colonel."

"I have not!" Georgiana said, slapping Matthew's arm playfully.

"If it is a fight you want, Lady Hayworth," Matthew said, "then a fight you shall have."

He began tickling Georgiana, letting go when the finger he had previously broken began to complain. Unable to resist, he leaned in and kissed her fervently. This kiss erased all Georgiana's desire to fight, and soon her arms were free to wrap around his neck. Turning Georgiana so that he could pull her onto his lap, Matthew was deepening the kiss when their driver called, "Demesne Palace straight ahead, m'lord!"

Instantly, the spell was broken. Georgiana slid off Matthew's lap to resume her place beside him. Grabbing her bonnet from the opposite seat, she placed it on her head and tied the ribbons under her chin.

"Do I look presentable?"

He smiled adoringly. "Perhaps I am not the one to ask. You always look perfect to me, sweetheart."

"You flatterer!" Georgiana said, giving his hand a squeeze.

Looking out the window, she caught sight of the elaborate gate Matthew said would mark the entrance to the grounds. "The gate is so beautiful that I cannot imagine how marvellous the rest will be. I once read about the observatory of Demesne Palace in a book from my brother's library, and the author described it in glowing terms."

"I share your enthusiasm," Matthew replied. "Whilst at Oxford, I became friends with a student who was just as interested in astronomy. As it turned out, Charles Whitaker is a distant cousin of Baron Rokeby,[4] the man who had the palace and the observatory constructed when he became Archbishop of Armagh. In fact, I would not be surprised if

---

[4] **Richard Robinson** (1708 – 10 October 1794), Archbishop of Armagh (1765 to 1794) created **Baron Rokeby** (1777), constructed The Archbishop's Palace as part of a project to revitalise the old city upon his succeeding to the See of Armagh. https://en.wikipedia.org/wiki/Richard_Robinson,_1st_Baron_Rokeby

we should meet Charles whilst we are here, for by the time we graduated, his goal was to work for the observatory".

"That would be delightful, would it not?"

"It would."

As the carriage came to a stop in front of a stately building, a footman climbed down to open the door. Matthew stepped to the ground and turned to hand Georgiana out.

"Come, Lady Hayworth. Let us see what discoveries await us."

Aboard the *Endeavour*
Later that evening

William was awakened by a knock on the door. Opening his eyes, he was disoriented until he recalled where he was. Sitting up, he placed his feet on the floor and looked about. If not for an almost burnt candle in a sconce on the wall, the room would have been completely dark. Shaking off his drowsiness, William stood and unlocked the door. Immediately a tray was shoved into his hands.

"Your dinner, sir!" a wizened-looking man declared and vanished before William could thank him.

Recollecting the captain said meals would be served in their rooms, William took the tray over to the extra bed and set it there; then, he looked through the drawers of the chest to locate the candles he had seen earlier. Once he found them, he exchanged a new candle for the one on the wall. Now that he could see, he turned his attention back to his dinner tray.

Sitting down on the bed beside it, William removed the cover to examine what the cook had prepared for dinner. The fare included a large bowl of beef stew, two slices of bread, butter, an apple tart and a tankard of ale. The food smelled appetizing, and being hungry, William began to eat. One drink of the ale, however, proved too unpleasant for his taste, so he poured the rest out a porthole and retrieved the bottle of wine he had secreted in his trunk.

William had planned to walk around the deck after eating dinner, thus he had donned his coat and his boots again; however, shortly before he finished eating, his entire body felt too heavy to stand, let alone walk. He lay back down on his bed and was insensible in a while.

No sooner had the man who delivered the dinner trays returned to the galley, than a short, burly man motioned for him to come forwards. "Were you able to get all the passengers to take a tray, Jake?"

"I was."

"Excellent! Mark my words, what we pinch from old Lord Chelsey alone should make us wealthy. I was told he brought three trunks on-board, one of 'em just to hold the jewels he gave to that young wife of his!" Drago laughed, then sobered almost as quickly. Looking about to make certain they were not being observed by the crew who were eating in the adjoining dining room, he continued, "Now, we wait on the laudanum to do its job."

"What if it does not work?"

"It will! I slipped enough in the ale to put a horse to sleep. Once they are asleep, we'll grab the captain's keys and rifle through the passenger cabins. Afterwards, the jollyboat[5] and the tide will take us and our riches to Man."[6]

"I hope you know what you're talking about," Jake replied. "I don't fancy rowing that far against the tide."

"Trust me! I know me seas and me tides!"

"Maybe so, but once the captain discovers what we done, he might decide to sail to Man after us."

"Not when a storm is brewing straight ahead. By the time the crew recovers from the laudanum, they should be right in the thick of it. Once through the storm, they'll be closer to Ireland than to Man, so it stands to reason they'll report the theft in Belfast after they land."

"I still have a bad feeling about this, Drago. We ain't done it this way before."

"Like I told you. It'll be best if we ain't stuck in Ireland. My friend Artie's aboard a ship docked at the port of Peel this very minute. It sails the day after tomorrow to

---

[5] **Jollyboat:** *a small ship's boat, used for a variety of purposes. It was clinker-built, propelled by oars, and was normally hoisted on a davit at the stern of the ship where it could be released easily and quickly in the case of an emergency.*

[6] **The Isle of Man** - *The Isle of Man (Manx: Mannin also Manx: Ellan Vannin), sometimes referred to simply as Man is a self-governing British Crown dependency in the Irish Sea between Great Britain and Ireland. https://en.wikipedia.org/wiki/Isle_of_Man*

Dunbarton, and he swears he can get us hired on before it leaves. Once we reach Scotland, the law will never find us!"

"I guess you're right," Jake said begrudgingly.

"I am. Just keep to our plan, and we will be wealthy men before this day is over."

Pemberley

Having been Mr. Darcy's valet for many years, Adams had developed intuition regarding his employer, and even before William departed for Ireland, he could not dismiss the feeling that some disaster awaited the master on this trip. Adams had suggested several times that he accompany William; however, each time he was informed that there was no need. Though Adams did not know the particulars of Pemberley's finances, he was aware that the former mistress, Lady Henrietta, had depleted the coffers before George Darcy's death and assumed the need for economy was one of the reasons he was left behind.

Unable to ignore the dread that washed over him when he awoke from yet another disturbing dream, Adams decided to return to William's dressing room to finish working on a greatcoat that had several seams in need of re-stitching and two buttons missing. Adams had long since learned that the mirrored walls of the dressing room amplified candlelight enough to allow him to mend without the benefit of daylight, and he welcomed the chance to keep his mind occupied until he felt sleepy once more.

As most servants were already in their beds and loathing the use of the servant's corridor, Adams took the grand staircase and walked down the hall where the family rooms were located. As he passed Mrs. Darcy's bedroom, he was not surprised to see a faint light under the door. Though the master was not often away, whenever he was Mrs. Darcy remained awake late into the night, pacing the balcony connecting their bedrooms and quietly murmuring prayers. Adams knew this for a fact because he had chanced upon her several times, though he had never made his presence known.

Upon entering the master's dressing room, he used the candlestick he had brought to light more candles. Then, retrieving his mending bag, he slipped the greatcoat off the back of a chair and sat down with it across his lap. Before he began to sew, however, the dressing room door creaked open, and a small head peeked inside.

"Papa?"

"No, Master Bennet. It is me, Adams."

Upon hearing the familiar voice, Bennet rushed into the room. "I ... I saw the light just before the door closed, and I thought Papa might have returned."

"I imagine it will be at least a fortnight before he does," Adams replied. Seeing the disappointment in Bennet's eyes, he changed the subject. "How did you manage to escape your nanny?"

"She is not *my* nanny," Bennet protested. "She is Anne's!"

"Still, Mrs. Cummings keeps watch over you both, does she not?" When Bennet nodded, he added, "I imagine she will raise quite a commotion if she discovers you are not in bed."

"She never knows when I am not in my bed."

"Oh? Do you often tramp about Pemberley at night?"

Bennet shook his head vehemently. "I do not like the dark."

"Then what brought you here at this hour?"

Bennet looked down as though considering whether to confess. He looked so much like his father whilst deliberating that Adams found himself smiling. Placing a comforting hand on the child's small shoulder, he said, "I will not tell anyone."

With wide-eyed innocence, Bennet said, "I hoped to find one of Papa's shirts so that—"

When he hesitated, Adams said, "Go on."

"I thought I might sleep better if I had something that smelled like Papa."

A large lump-filled Adams' throat, and he worked hard to swallow in order to reply. "Let me see what I can do." Standing, he added, "Wait right here."

At Bennet's nod, he took the candlestick and entered William's bedroom. Heading straight to the dresser, he opened a drawer and pulled out a shirt. From the tray atop the dresser, he removed the stopper from a bottle of sandalwood cologne and splashed several drops on the shirt's collar. When he was satisfied, he returned to the dressing room.

"Do you think this will suffice?" Adams asked, holding it out to the boy.

Bennet brought the shirt to his nose and, after taking a deep breath, smiled. "It will. Thank you, Mr. Adams."

"You are most welcome, Master Bennet. Now, I strongly suggest you return to your bed."

"Would you ... would you walk me back to my room?" Bennet asked hesitantly.

"I should be happy to, lad."

Thus, holding the hand of the boy he considered a grandchild, Adams walked Bennet back to his bed. After he returned to William's dressing room, he made a mental note to inform Mrs. Darcy about how the shirt ended up in Bennet's bed, lest the maids confiscate and wash it.

Adams trusted Mrs. Darcy not to reveal to Bennet that he had shared his secret.

Chapter 9

Aboard the *Endeavour*

The steady rain of the afternoon had transformed into a deluge coming down in sheets so impenetrable that Jake could not see more than a few feet ahead. Looking to the sea below, he finally spied the jollyboat when it was lifted by a huge wave before plunging into the depths once again. Because of the sway of the ship and the slickness of the deck, he was having difficulty keeping his footing.

He had last seen Drago when he returned with a bag full of cash and jewels from Lord Chelsey's cabin. After adding that to the loot in the jollyboat, they had made the decision to lower the boat to the sea because the winds were growing progressively stronger. It was at that point that Jake had argued for abandoning the ship straightaway.

"We got enough!" he had cried. "I say we settle for what we have!"

"I won't leave without the chest in the captain's office!" Drago had shouted over the howl of the wind. "It has the salaries for everyone onboard."

As he awaited Drago's return, Jake recalled the gold watch he had pinched from Mr. Darcy and patted his pocket where it now resided. He had not placed it in the trunk with the other valuables, for he intended to keep the watch as part of his portion of the spoils. Hoping that seeing it again might take his mind off the present danger, he pulled it from his pocket to admire it. At that precise moment, a noise caught his attention, and he looked up to see a man coming towards him through the storm.

"It's about time!" Jake announced. Too late, he realised it was not Drago.

Fitzwilliam Darcy grabbed the watch with his left hand, placing it inside his coat, whilst at the same time striking Jake with a right hook with such force that the thief dropped to his knees. As Jake scrambled to stand, another right hook sent him flying to the deck on his back. Just as Jake feared he was going to die, Drago appeared from out of nowhere. Watching him raise a wooden belaying pin[7] high overhead, Jake winced as Drago struck Mr. Darcy with it, causing him to fall towards the side of the ship.

At that moment, the ship dipped in that direction, and he and Drago watched helplessly as their victim flipped over the rail and landed in the jollyboat below. The impact freed the ropes securing the boat to the ship, and though Jake tried to grab one, he was not successful.

Watching the jollyboat quickly vanish into the distance, Jake cried, "Look what you did! Most of what we stole is in that boat, and now we ain't got no way to leave the ship!"

"Shut up!" Drago hissed. After a moment of silence, he cried, "I know! We'll wake the others to help us get through the storm. When they discover they was robbed, and realise Mr. Darcy is missing, they will assume he was the thief."

"Even I would not believe that!" Jake moaned.

"They will have no choice!" Drago cried angrily. "Now, follow me!"

Once back in the kitchen, Drago began making coffee, which prompted Jake to ask, "What're you doing? We ain't got time for coffee."

"It's not for us, you fool! Given the amount of laudanum I poured in the ale, the crew may be out for hours. We're going to ply them with coffee until they can think straight."

"Do you reckon the coffee will work fast enough?"

"I don't know, but what choice do we have?" Whilst he worked, Drago addressed their situation. "At least with the cash and spoils we have left, we can live at ease whilst planning our next heist."

"What if Captain Beacham decides to search the ship even after learning Mr. Darcy and the jollyboat are gone? Where can we hide the loot?"

"One time, I hid jewels in a bag under the garbage in the kitchen pail. It worked then, and it will work now," Drago said. "The trick is not to let nobody handle the garbage save us."

---

[7] *A belaying pin is a solid metal or wooden device used on traditionally rigged sailing vessels to secure lines of running rigging. Belaying pins are or were used as improvised weapons and means of discipline on both military and civilian ships. https://en.wikipedia. org/wiki/Belaying_pin*

Suddenly, as the ship pitched to one side, the porthole in the kitchen was blown out by the storm. The winds that roared through the breach almost drowned out Jake's voice as he cried, "Hurry up with that coffee or it will be too late for any of us!"

Pemberley

To Elizabeth's delight, whilst she, the children and their maids were in the garden, Colonel Fitzwilliam suddenly appeared. He was halfway up the gravel path that led from the stables to the house when Ben saw him and, running in that direction, cried, "Cousin Richard!"

Elizabeth was sitting in the swing holding Anne, who, upon seeing Bennet dart towards their cousin, squirmed to be put down. Setting her daughter on her feet, Elizabeth watched as Anne headed towards Richard as fast as she could whilst managing to keep her balance.

He was carrying both children in his arms when he reached Elizabeth. "Richard! We were not expecting you!"

"I was not expecting to be here, either. On the spur of the moment, General Lassiter decided that he needed a dispatch delivered to his counterpart in the navy at Liverpool and that I was just the man to take it. Because I promised Darcy that I would look in on you and the children whenever I could, I asked if I might detour through Derbyshire, and having known George Darcy well, the general was kind enough to oblige."

"We are always pleased to have you, no matter the reason."

Setting the children on their feet, Richard squatted down to pull two miniature sailboats from his pocket and hand them to Ben. "Help your sister sail hers."

"Thank you, Cousin Richard!" Ben cried, throwing his arms around Richard's neck for a hug before taking Anne's hand and leading her towards the goldfish pond.

"Will you sit with me?" Elizabeth asked, waving towards the swing. "I find I can watch the children very well from here."

"You do not trust the maids?" Richard said, smirking as he tilted his head towards the women shadowing the children.

"Quite the opposite; however, they are my children, and I feel it my duty to keep watch over them, too." After Richard sat down, Elizabeth added, "You do realise that you are spoiling them, especially Ben. He thinks you are supposed to bring him a toy every time he sees you."

"Who else do I have to spoil?" Richard asked playfully. "Besides, they are young for such a short period of time."

Taking a longing look at her children, Elizabeth said wistfully, "Far too short a period."

"Have you heard from my fearless cousin of late? In the last letter I received from you, he had just arrived in Liverpool."

"I received a letter only hours ago which was very short, though he included these lovely combs to make up for not writing a longer one," Elizabeth replied, laughing as she touched the tortoiseshell combs in her hair.

"Darcy chose well. They complement your hair."

"Thank you. William wrote that he was about to board the ship to Ireland and would write again once he arrived in Belfast."

"What was the name of the ship on which he sailed? I do not recall."

"The *Endeavour*."

"A fine name for a vessel."

Suddenly a man on horseback came riding towards them from the direction of the front of the house. As he got closer, Richard recognised the Darcys' neighbour, Gregory Wright, and stiffened.

⁓

Nearing the couple, Wright recognised the man sitting with Elizabeth as Darcy's cousin and swore under his breath. He had hoped to speak with her unhindered, and once again his plans were thwarted.

"Mrs. Darcy ... Colonel Fitzwilliam," he said, presenting a faux smile as he dismounted and bowed. "How long has it been since we were in each other's company, Colonel? A year? Longer? In any event, it is a pleasure to see you again."

"Wright," Richard responded as he stood to shake hands. Ignoring the intruder's questions, he added, "I am surprised to see you here now. Darcy is away, or were you not aware of that?"

"Mr. Wright is fully aware that my husband is away, for he has been bringing Jonathan over to play with Bennet since Fitzwilliam left," Elizabeth explained innocently.

Richard made a spectacle of looking about, quipping frostily, "Jonathan is here? Correct me if I am wrong, but I do not see him."

Wright coughed self-consciously, stammering, "I ... he ... Jonathan has a cold. That is the purpose of my visit ... to inform Eliz—err, Mrs. Darcy that that is why I had not come earlier."

"How thoughtful of you to come in person instead of sending a servant," Richard mocked.

"Yes ... well, I have accomplished what I set out to do, so I will take my leave," Wright stated. Remounting his stallion in one smooth move, he brought his riding whip to his hat in a salute before disappearing as speedily as he had come.

Silently, Richard kept an eye on Wright until he was completely out of sight. When he turned to sit down, he found Elizabeth biting her lip to stifle a laugh. Feigning innocence, he asked, "What?"

Letting go a peal of laughter, Elizabeth said, "If I did not know better, I would think you were poised to call him out."

"I cannot help it. I do not like the man, nor do I trust him!"

"I hope that you know my only interest in Mr. Wright is in having him bring Jonathan over to play with Bennet."

"Your motives were never in question, but you never know what a man like that has on his mind. Just be conscious that you are a very lovely woman, and Wright may have hidden motives in coming here when Darcy is away."

"I will keep that in mind," Elizabeth said, pursing her lips to keep from smiling. "Now that that is settled, I do hope you are planning to stay the night."

"You should know by now that I never turn down an opportunity to stay at Pemberley. You have the best food and accommodations in all of England."

"I dearly love Pemberley, but surely in all your travels you have experienced food and lodging more spectacular than what we have to offer."

Richard's hand flew to his heart. "You wound me, madam. As a colonel in His Majesty's army, I would never lie about matters of such importance."

Elizabeth grinned. "Thank you."

"For what?"

"For always making me smile when I am at my lowest. With William absent . . ." Elizabeth's voice caught, and she looked away.

Hoping to lift her spirits, Richard teased, "What can I say? I am simply a fount of cheerfulness."

Suddenly Bennet was rushing towards them, sopping wet, with Anne following as fast as her short little legs could carry her. The maids who trailed them both were trying to stifle their laughter.

Upon reaching Elizabeth, Bennet cried breathlessly, "Mama, please make Anne behave! Just because her boat is not as fast as mine, she pushed me into the water."

Trying not to smile as an equally out of breath Anne caught up to them, Elizabeth asked, "Anne, did you push your brother into the pond?" Anne nodded vigorously. "That was not very kind of you."

Anne's usually angelic face scrunched in fury. "Ben mean!"

"I am not!" Bennet shouted.

"I know, Son," Elizabeth whispered quietly to him before addressing Anne. "Do you think Ben is mean because his boat always beats your boat?"

There was more silent nodding, so Elizabeth drew Anne into her lap. Kissing the top of her head, she said, "I will wager that very soon your boat will be faster than your brother's, and you will win a race. Am I right, Ben?"

She could tell Bennet was weighing her words, for his brow furrowed just like his father's did whenever he contemplated anything. At length, Ben conceded. "I think her boat will win next time, Mama."

Ruffling her son's hair, Elizabeth pulled him into her arms for a kiss. "I am very proud of you. Now, go and change clothes."

"Do I have to, Mama? I will only get wet again."

"He is right, you know," Richard interjected. "Why not let him finish playing? A little water will not hurt him."

"I suppose both of you are right," Elizabeth said.

The second she turned him loose, Bennet said, "Do you want to try again, Anne?"

Nodding, Anne slid off Elizabeth's lap, and in no time at all, both were back at the pond.

Richard, who had been watching silently said, "You amaze me with how effortlessly you teach your children to be kind to one another. My brother and I hated each other when we were children." Then, he guffawed. "Come to think of it, we still do."

"Surely you do not mean that."

Richard's expression turned wistful as he stared at some point in the distance. "I fear the part about him hating me is true. After Leighton was forced to marry that harridan, Lady Susan, he is not only angry with me, but angry with the world."

"Have you considered how difficult it must be for him? I cannot imagine being married to someone you do not love with all your heart and soul."

Richard smiled. "You and Darcy have completely spoilt my theory of what constitutes the perfect marriage. Before he married you, I was determined to marry the first filthy rich woman who made me an offer. Now, I am determined to marry the first filthy rich woman I love who makes me an offer."

"You are incorrigible!" Elizabeth said, laughing.

"So, I have been told!"

Parkleigh Manor

Upon returning home, Gregory Wright went straight to his study to peruse the correspondence that, according to the butler, had arrived during his absence. He was disheartened to find another letter from Lady Catherine atop the stack. Fearing what she might ask of him now, he debated tossing it away. In the end, however, he knew he had no choice, so he broke the seal.

> *Mr. Wright,*
>
> *I assume you are in contact with that trollop Darcy married in order to ascertain where my nephew is along his journey. Do you know if he has reached Ireland?*
>
> *In the event that whilst in Belfast he learns the distillery is bankrupt, we must concoct an explanation for your offering of a partnership. Therefore, it follows that I must know when he is scheduled to return. To that end, I propose we meet at my townhouse in London in a sennight.*
>
> *I expect a prompt reply.*
>
> *C. de Bourgh*

Wright frowned. Thus far all he knew about Darcy's journey was what little he had coaxed from Elizabeth whenever they talked, and, of late, he had not been able to speak with her privately because of her many visitors. That realisation brought to mind Colonel Fitzwilliam, someone he loathed.

Examining why he felt that way, Wright realised it was because the colonel always managed to make him feel inferior. Soundly rejecting the idea that he might be, Wright was pulling a sheet of paper from the drawer of his desk to reply to Darcy's detestable aunt when another thought came to mind.

With any luck Lady Catherine will perish in a carriage accident on the way to Town, and Darcy and I will both be free of her interference.

Liverpool
Captain Silverhill's quarters
The next morning

Being imprisoned in the captain's quarters had its advantages, for the rooms housed far fewer mice than the warehouse and, thus far, the food had been edible; however, last night they had been bound hand and foot, and it was taking its toll on Noel Stevens and Lady Aileen. For what seemed like days instead of hours, they had lain on a mattress in a room with boards nailed across the windows so they could not see out. The only consolation was that their captors had not yet blindfold-ed or gagged them.

"Do you think it morning already?" Lady Aileen asked at length.

"If my stomach is any indication, it is," Mr. Stevens replied cheek-ily. "I hope they remember to feed us."

Aileen smiled. It was not lost on her that her fellow prisoner had been doing all in his power to keep up her spirits. And it was not the first time she considered how different it would have been had Arthur Gable been captured with her instead. In comparing the two men, Arthur had come up lacking; therefore, she was about to thank Mr. Stevens for his helpfulness when the clank of the latch announced the door was about to open.

Two men walked in—one carrying a tray of food, whilst the other wielded a pistol. The one with the pistol kept watch even as the other man set the tray on a small table and walked over to cut the ropes binding their hands and feet. As Noel and Aileen rubbed their aching wrists, the man who had cut them loose spoke.

"Eat up me lord and lady, for today ye be going sailing."

Worried that the captain had decided to toss them into the sea, Noel said, "I thought we were to be held here for ransom."

"Cap'n says he will hold you on the island."

"The island?" Aileen repeated. "What island?"

"Ne'er mind what island, Miss. Just thank yer lucky stars you've not been marked for death." With that the man motioned towards the tray. "You got half an hour to eat before I return."

After he exited the room, the one with the pistol backed out and slammed the door. The sound of a lock being secured announced they were alone once again.

"We had best eat, Lady Aileen," Stevens said as he stood. "God only knows when we will have the chance again."

"Inasmuch as we will likely be close friends before this ordeal is over, I propose that we dispense with the formalities," Aileen replied. "From now on I shall call you Noel and you may call me Aileen."

Stevens smiled, "That is very sensible."

As she turned to place her feet on the floor, he rushed to steady her. "Allow me to assist. Rise slowly or you may faint."

After each was seated in one of the wooden chairs next to the table, Stevens removed the lid from the tray. Upon seeing scrambled eggs, sausages, and bread with butter, he sighed in relief. "The captain would not feed us this well if he was intending to kill us."

Lady Aileen looked down. "I ... I fear my father may not wish to ransom me."

"Surely you cannot mean that."

"Tis true," Aileen replied tearfully.

"If that be the case, please know that my relations will be glad to pay the ransom for you as well."

Though she had meant to keep her past a secret, Noel's generosity compelled Aileen to confess how she had ended up in Liverpool all alone.

After she had finished, she added, "I feel better knowing that you are aware of my foolishness. Perhaps now you will understand why we cannot remain friends once we are liberated."

Noel reached out to clasp her hand. "Nothing you have said makes me think less of you. I have long believed that women are not chattel to be traded by their fathers or guardians to men they do not wish to marry."

Aileen smiled wanly. "Unfortunately, you are not in the majority."

"I may not be, but I am hopeful such things will change in the future." He reached for a piece of bread and began to butter it. "Now, try not to dwell on what happened in the past. We will need all our faculties to see us through this predicament, so let us eat heartily whilst we can and then focus on devising a plan of escape."

Aileen nodded and began to eat as well.

Chapter 10

The crew of the *Endeavour* had consumed too much laudanum to be roused by any amount of coffee, and without a full crew to man the ship, it sank halfway between the Isle of Man and Ireland. All onboard lost their lives.

What would forever be referred to as "the storm of the century" not only took down the *Endeavour*, but a ship named *The Pearl of Lancaster* and a freighter, the *Edward Blaine*, were also lost on that fateful night.

The *Endeavour's* fate would not be confirmed until days later when rumour had it that debris from that ship began washing up on shore—including a plank from a deck chair with the ship's name on it. It was at that point that those awaiting its arrival at Watson's Freight office in Belfast knew for certain the *Endeavour* had not survived the storm.

Calf of Man
Windemere Manor

As Cecile Grubbs broke her fast on the terrace of her late husband's estate, the vicious storm of the night before seemed only a figment of her imagination. Though she had lived on the island for several years, she still found the weather's propensity to change almost instantly unnerving. Even as she savoured the view of a now tranquil sea, the remnants of small tree limbs and leaves strewn across the terrace gave evidence of why she had spent most of the night worrying for her safety. Still, weathered as it was, the stone house had stood strong ... just as it had for the last two centuries, and she clung to the fact that there was little reason to believe it would not stand for another.

Whenever she occupied the terrace, Cecile was thankful that the manor sat perched on a hill. The east side of the island—the one with water deep enough for ships to dock—dropped straight off into the sea, whilst this side, the west side, wound slowly down to the water. From this height, she had a good view of the long stretch of pebbled beach where her family had often enjoyed picnicking and wading in the water. As usual, wonderful memories sprang to mind; however, they were quickly joined by the realisation that she must come to a decision soon regarding her future.

Glancing at her husband's namesake, her two-year-old son, David, whilst he sat playing at her feet, Cecile pondered for what seemed the hundredth time what she ought to do. It was obvious that John Silverhill wanted to marry her, though she had no intention of agreeing to that. Moreover, she feared what his reaction would be once she refused him, for he was a man used to giving orders and being obeyed.

Now that her husband was dead, half the shipping company belonged to her—at least that is what his will stipulated; however, Cecile had no doubt that Silverhill would not continue to pay her half the profits because she was unable to take David's place as captain of a ship. In addition, should she wish to sell her half, she had no idea how much it was worth or if Silverhill would accept a new partner.

In truth, she had never so much as managed an estate, having gone from her father's protection to her husband's after her brother's marriage forced her from the only home she had ever known and into the arms of a man she would never before have considered. She had learned to care for David after their marriage, but he was much older and more crass than the men she had known as a gentleman's daughter.

She chuckled mirthlessly. *A gentleman's daughter … how far removed I am from that life now.*

Exasperated at the complexity of her situation, Cecile tossed what was left of the scone she had been eating to the birds and watched as they fought over the crumbs. Picking up the tray holding the teapot and empty dishes, she said, "Come, David," and turned to go inside.

Reaching for the latch, she noticed yet again that the paint was peeling on the wood trim around the door—not only there, but on the shutters. It was obvious that the once magnificent structure needed repairs, but there were no funds for that. Sighing, Cecile opened the door and looked back to see if her child had risen. Occupied with a toy horse his father had once brought back from Liverpool, David was paying her no mind. She was about to admonish him, when the sight of a servant hurrying up the path from the beach caught her eye. From the look on his face, it appeared Daniel had seen a ghost.

Five and twenty, with the mind of a child of about ten, Daniel had grown up on the estate as his parents, Patrick and Mary Kelly, had served Windemere Manor for thirty years as butler and housekeeper. Over the years, as fewer and fewer servants stayed on at Windemere, he had been given charge of all the livestock and doing whatever jobs he was capable of handling. If Cecile found any fault with the man, it was that he spoke very little and sometimes it was difficult getting information out of him.

Once he reached the terrace, Daniel bent over, placing both hands on his knees as he gasped for breath. Then, he rasped, "Man in boat on beach!"

Seeing that the island was too far removed from the Isle of Man to be accessible by anything but a ship, she wondered at Daniel's use of the word boat. "A man in a boat?" Cecile repeated.

Daniel nodded. "Hurry! He is hurt!"

"Mrs. Kelly!" Cecile shouted into the house. A short time later, the housekeeper appeared in the doorway. "Daniel said a boat has washed up on the beach with a man aboard. I am going down to have a look. Please take David with you and have Mr. Kelly follow me with two footmen."

"Yes, ma'am."

By the time Cecile turned around, Daniel was already halfway down the path to the beach.

"Wait, Daniel!" she called as she hurried after him.

Following those carrying the occupant of the boat up the hill to the house, Cecile could not help pondering what might have transpired for a man to be in a boat on the open sea with a large gash on his head marring his handsome features. From his clothes, it was obvious that he was a gentleman; however, a quick search of his person revealed nothing to indicate who he was. With no way of knowing the answer to that unless he survived, as she followed the others, Cecile vowed to do whatever she could to see that he did.

After the footmen had gently lowered the man into a bed in one of the guest rooms, Cecile sat down on the bed beside him. Placing a hand on his brow, she grew alarmed at how hot he felt.

"Where is Mrs. Kelly?"

"I am here," the housekeeper announced, hurrying into the room. Always prepared to take charge in emergencies, she barked orders to the two maids who followed her. "Bring towels, more sheets, my bag of medicine and the hot water boiling on the stove!"

As the maids rushed off, Mrs. Kelly stated, "With the injury to his head, it may be kinder to cut that shirt off."

"Do what you think is best," Cecile replied, standing and stepping aside. "He looks about my husband's size. I shall find some of David's clothes and see if they fit him."

On the east side of the island

After the ship was secured to the dock, Captain Silverhill glanced to the hills where a small house and a row of colourful cabins sat gleaming in the sun. Unused, except by his crew when they stayed on the island, he was pleased that from the sea the area appeared more of an outpost for tourists than a hideaway for thieves.

It never crossed his mind that Cecile might discover what happened on this side of the island. David Grubbs had explained that he kept his wife completely in the dark regarding his shipping business and had warned her that the road to the warehouse was too treacherous to traverse by anyone unfamiliar with driving a wagon … and she was not that accomplished. As a further precaution, two crew members lived there year-round, watching the warehouse and caring for the horses that were used to get to the other side of the island.

Turning to a sailor, he barked, "Take the prisoners to my house! Lock them in the cellar."

"I thought we be hiding them in the cave," the man answered.

Whilst supplies for Windemere were kept in a small warehouse, right behind it was a cave completely hidden by vegetation. It was there that stolen goods were stored until the search for them died down. Then they were loaded back on a ship, taken to a distant port and sold.

"I changed my mind," Captain Silverhill replied. "Now, do as I say!"

Below deck, Noel Stevens and Lady Aileen heard footsteps coming down from the deck above and braced for what was going to happen. They had hoped to be ransomed by their relations whilst still being held in Liverpool, and the idea of being held on some unknown island was disturbing.

"Remember," Noel said, "look around and try to remember everything you see."

Aileen was nodding when the door flew open to reveal two of the ship's crew.

"Come with me, your lordship," one toothless man said to Noel, mocking him with an exaggerated bow and sweep of his hand towards the door.

As Noel headed in that direction, the other miscreant said, "You had best pick up your feet, too, my lady!"

Chilled by the leer on his filthy face, Aileen hurried to catch up with Noel.

Once both were on deck, Captain Silverhill walked over to them. "Welcome to my island! I hope you will find your stay here a pleasant one." As his prisoners looked to the hills where the buildings stood out amongst the trees, he added, "Unfortunately, you will not be able to tour the island. Instead, you will stay in my house until I decide your fate."

With a flick of his hand, they were pushed towards a ladder that led over the side of the ship.

Pemberley

Finding herself alone after the children were put down for a nap, Elizabeth feared the tears that were always close to the surface were about to fall again. It seemed the longer William was away, the more incapable she was of hiding the void his absence created. Not wanting the children to see her upset, or the servants for that matter, she rushed from the house. Clancy faithfully followed.

Once in the garden, she headed straight to the path surrounding the pond. "You may wish to stay here today," she admonished the short-legged little dog. "I fear you may be exhausted by the time I have finished praying."

Though Clancy tilted his head as though listening, he would not forsake his duty and soon was following Elizabeth as she walked and prayed whilst silent tears rolled down her cheeks. She had made two complete laps around the pond with no idea that anyone was nearby until Clancy turned to bark and a familiar voice said, "Do you mind if I join you?"

Quickly brushing away her tears, Elizabeth pasted on a faux smile as she turned to face Mrs. Green. "Not at all, Mimi."

Seeing Elizabeth's expression, Judith Green was clearly not fooled. Instantly embracing Elizabeth, she said, "Oh, my dear, let it go. Cry all you wish. We all miss him."

At those words, Elizabeth began to weep in earnest. The vicar's wife held her, patting her back until there were no more tears. Then she lifted Elizabeth's chin so that she could look her directly in the eye.

"It is evident that I intruded in the middle of your chance to grieve, and for that I am sorry. You must have time alone if you are to remain strong for the children."

Elizabeth wiped her eyes with the handkerchief in her hand. "Usually I am able to cope if I have a good cry whilst they are asleep, but of late I find myself on the brink of tears almost continuously."

"You are one of the strongest women I have ever known, Elizabeth. And, for that reason, I attribute your current state to the fact that you are with child, a condition that heightens all a woman's emotions."

"How did—I have told no one."

"Some might not notice, but to someone who has borne a child it is obvious. Not only has your waist thickened, but you complain of no appetite and, as you have said, you cry easily."

Elizabeth looked down, smoothing her hands over her rounded stomach. "I thought I would have more time before I needed to announce it."

"You do not have to tell anyone until you are ready," Judith Green pronounced with a smile. "That is a woman's prerogative."

Elizabeth smiled. "So even if I get as round as a barrel, it is my secret to keep?"

"Precisely."

At Elizabeth's laugh, Mrs. Green smiled. "I know Fitzwilliam will be thrilled when he hears. He loves being a father."

"And he is such a wonderful one."

"You are fortunate. Some men do not enjoy the company of children."

"Forgive me for not confiding in you sooner. In truth, I wanted to wait until the babe quickened, and that happened only this morning. Moreover, I know the servants will treat me like a delicate piece of china once they know, and I hate being coddled."

"Elizabeth, you owe me no apology or explanation. And as for the servants, I would not be surprised if Mrs. Reynolds and your maid already know."

"I suppose I was foolish to think it was still a secret."

Mrs. Green grasped her hand and gave it a squeeze. "Women who are with child are allowed to be foolish. Now, tell me, have you heard from our dear boy again?"

"Not since he sailed for Ireland, but a letter came today for him. It was from Georgiana and dated a fortnight ago. It must have gone astray somewhere in transit for it to take so long."

"Does Georgiana know William is on his way to Ballyneen?"

"No. He wanted it to be a surprise," Elizabeth replied. "In any case, because he asked me to read his correspondence whilst he is away, I opened it."

"If I may ask, how is Georgiana faring?"

William had shared Georgiana's problems with her in private, so Elizabeth had not revealed to her friend the reason for his trip to Ireland. Without going into detail, she said, "It appeared that she merely wanted to assure William that she is very happy in her marriage. You know how much he always worries about her."

"I do, and I am delighted that when he arrives, he will discover Georgiana is content."

Suddenly, a woman standing on one of the balconies waved at them. Seeing the gesture, Elizabeth said, "I asked the nanny to give me a signal when the children awoke from their naps and, apparently, they have. If the last time you had tea with the children did not frighten you away, would you care to try again today?"

Judith Green laughed. "A little spilt tea could never frighten me away. I would love to join you."

Ballyneen Castle
Four days later

After Georgiana's mare took the fence with room to spare, she guided the animal to where Matthew sat waiting atop his stallion. He smiled proudly.

"Bravo! I know of no man who can best you when it comes to taking fences. You have absolutely no fear!"

"As long as my horse has no fear, why should I? After all, it is she who must do all the work."

In one smooth motion, Matthew threw his leg over his saddle and slid to the ground. Tossing the reins over a low-hanging branch, he walked to where Georgiana waited. Holding up his arms, he caught her as she leaned into him and he guided her to the ground.

"Might I interest you in a picnic, my lady?"

Georgiana chuckled. "How can we have a picnic when we have brought no provisions?"

"That is where you are badly mistaken," Matthew answered, giving her a sly grin.

Securing her horse, he circled Georgiana's waist with one arm and escorted her to the other side of the tree, where a wicker basket had been placed. A blanket lay atop the basket, and Matthew picked it up and spread it on the ground.

Georgiana threw her arms around his neck, kissing him soundly. "How thoughtful you are! You always know just what to do to make me happy."

"I live to make you happy, my love," Matthew replied. "Which is why we sail for England in three days. I shall meet with the man looking for Aileen whilst we are in Liverpool. If he is no closer to locating her, I shall escort you to Pemberley. Your family will be glad to have you visit whilst I continue searching for my sister."

Georgiana's head snapped back. "Are you serious?"

"I am *completely* serious. You have been worried sick about your brother, which makes me worry about you. Therefore, I intend to take you to see him. I have already purchased tickets on a ship leaving Belfast for Liverpool. All that is left for you to do is supervise the packing of your trunks."

Georgiana hugged him tighter, burying her face in his chest. "What did I ever do to deserve such a husband? I love you so much!"

Matthew kissed the top of her head. "It is I who is not deserving of you, sweetheart. Still, if you wish to show your appreciation . . ."

When Georgiana looked up, a smiling Matthew tilted his head towards the blanket on the ground.

The couple did not return to the manor until dusk.

Chapter 11

Belfast
Two days later

Leaving his wife resting in their room at the inn, Viscount Hayworth headed to the office of Watson's Freight Services, the establishment that owned the ship that would take them to Liverpool. Always one for details, he wished to make certain they had been assigned to one of the larger passenger cabins before they boarded the ship in the morning.

Finding the weather fair when he exited the inn, Matthew decided to walk to the office which was located on the docks two streets over and six streets south of the inn. As he proceeded, however, he became aware of a young boy just ahead on the pavement selling newspapers as quickly as he could grab them from his dogcart.

The apparent reason for his success was the headline he was shouting at the top of his lungs: "*Endeavour* sinks with everyone onboard!"

Once Matthew understood what he was saying, chills ran down his spine. "I will take one!" he shouted over the din of those quickly surrounding the boy. When the lad handed him a paper, Matthew tossed him a penny.

Upon unfolding the paper, he began to read the other headlines:

STORM OF THE CENTURY SINKS BELFAST SHIP! REPORTS OTHER SHIPS MAY BE LOST!

REMAINS OF ENDEAVOUR WASHED ASHORE NEAR DONAGHADEE ACCORDING TO LOCALS!

NAMES OF PASSENGERS UNKNOWN!

Realising that was the ship he and Georgiana had been scheduled to sail on, Matthew felt his stomach form knots. Unwilling to let his wife know of the tragedy until he had more facts and trusting she was likely asleep, he hurried to the ship's office. There he found the building teeming with people, and still more were trying to gain entrance. All were shouting questions at one exasperated man behind a counter.

"We will not know the names of all those onboard until our office in Liverpool realises that the *Endeavour* has sunk," the clerk shouted. "At that point, they will send us a passenger manifest, as well as release that information to the newspapers. For now, all sailings are suspended. If you were scheduled to leave in the morning, come back tomorrow afternoon with your tickets and the price you paid will be refunded."

Though annoyed at securing so little information, Matthew recognised that it was not entirely the fault of the shipping company. As he started his trek back to the inn, he began to worry about the effect this disaster might have on Georgiana. Of late it seemed she was very emotional and extremely fatigued—traits that were entirely against his wife's nature. His suggestion that she see a physician before they embarked on their trip had been adamantly refused; however, he was of a mind that if she became too upset when told about the ship, he would send for a physician without asking her permission.

Windemere Manor

Searching for the spot where he had buried the sack he found in the boat, Daniel cautiously weaved his way through the trees and vegetation separating the beach from the manor house on the hill above. As luck would have it, he had spied the sack lying partially beneath the stranger when the boat washed ashore and, upon seeing what was inside, had buried it before informing Mrs. Grubbs about the man. Certain if his employer knew what treasures were in the sack she would take them away, Daniel had no intention of letting that happen.

Finding the three flat rocks in a circle, he removed them and dug in the sandy soil until he felt what he was seeking. Pulling the sack to the surface, he tipped the contents on a grassy area and was once again fascinated by what he beheld. Coins and bank notes of all denominations were mixed with a myriad of necklaces, earrings and bracelets containing clear, sparkling stones interspersed with red, green, purple and blue ones of every shape and size. There were also stick pins like those he had seen Captain Grubbs wear on the few occasions he had dressed for dinner. In addition, numerous silver flasks and pocket watches added variety to the jewels. One watch in particular caught Daniel's fancy—the one he had stolen from the man in the boat.

Picking up that object, he flipped open the case to admire again the beautiful, dark-haired woman inside. He had been searching the stranger's coat for a money pouch when he found the watch. Unfortunately, the pouch, when he found it, held only some papers he could not read. Deciding it not worth losing the watch he most admired, Daniel had secretted the watch, the papers and the pouch with the other items in the sack.

The sound of his name being called penetrated his consciousness, and Daniel jumped at the intrusion. Hiding the watch in his pocket, he tossed everything else back into the sack and began to bury it again. Then, after replacing the rocks, he hurried towards the beach. At length breaking through the undergrowth, he found himself face-to-face with a footman named John.

"Where were you?" John asked irritably. "I have walked the entire length of this beach and all the way to the stables looking for you."

"The pasture. I was checking the sheep."

"How is it that you are always where I do not look?" John replied, shaking his head. "In any case, the mistress wants everyone to know that Captain Silverhill's ship has been seen on the other side of the island, which means it will not be long until he comes to the house. She does not want him to know about the man who washed up in the boat, so if you encounter the captain, keep your mouth shut about him."

"Why?" Daniel asked innocently.

"I imagine because the captain wants to marry Mrs. Grubbs and might be jealous if he knew another man was in the house." John peered over Daniel's shoulder. "It appears that you managed to hide the boat well enough."

Daniel smiled proudly.

"Old Silverhill misses nothing. Are you sure it cannot be seen from the terrace above?"

Daniel nodded.

"Excellent!"

"I do not like Silverhill," Daniel ventured. "I hope she will not marry him."

"None of us want her to," John replied, "but I would not worry if I were you. From what I have witnessed whenever he visits, the mistress does not like him either."

Liverpool

Colonel Fitzwilliam was restless. He had been in Liverpool almost a sennight waiting for Admiral Turlington to reply to the message he had delivered from General Lassiter. Turlington, however, was busy investigating the thefts that had plagued the naval warehouse and had put off addressing the general's concerns until he had more time. This made it necessary for Richard to send a message to the general to explain why he had not yet returned.

In the beginning, he had enjoyed relaxing at the inn and being fed at the army's expense; however, after several days he began to get bored. That morning as he left his room to break his fast, he decided to ask the clerk at the desk if any London newspapers had arrived, and he found himself standing behind a very tall, unhappy blonde-haired woman.

"I do not care to hear why you have no rooms available despite the fact that I sent word I would arrive today! I am tired and wish to rest. Tell me where I might find a comparable room in Liverpool."

"I apologise, Lady Selina. I have no idea why your request was not recorded. I happen to know the only other respectable inn on this street is full as well. Moreover, though there are more inns, none are in areas I would recommend for a lady travelling alone," the clerk replied. "However, should you care to wait, there is supposed to be a room available this afternoon."

Letting go a heavy sigh, she answered, "I believe I have no choice."

"Perhaps you could have something to eat in our dining room and then read for a while in the lobby until I know for certain whether the room will be available. If you agree, I shall gladly hold your trunk in the office until then."

The woman glanced towards the open double doors that led into the dining room. "I do not care to dine alone, for inevitably a man will come to the table and say I remind him of someone he met before or some such nonsense."

"Might I be of assistance?" Richard said, interrupting.

When the lady turned, Richard was instantly captivated by the finest green eyes he had ever beheld, in a face that was utter perfection. Steeling himself to appear indifferent, he removed his hat and bowed.

"Colonel Fitzwilliam, at your service. I could not help but overhear what you said, and because I am in the same predicament—being alone—I wondered if you might agree to share a table with me. I promise not to utter a word unless you speak to me."

To his good fortune, the lady laughed. "Lady Selina Grey. Happy to meet you, Colonel Fitzwilliam. You certainly have a unique approach. I will warrant you that."

"May I assume you agree?"

Eyeing the handsome, red-coated officer thoroughly from head to toe, the lady smiled. "I believe you may."

Windemere Manor
Later that day

Cecile watched from the doorway as Mrs. Kelly wrapped the bandage around the stranger's head and fastened it in place. In the few days he had occupied the guest room at Windemere, she had become consumed with the desire to see him recover. Convinced that so handsome a man must be married, and most likely had children, she fought back the feelings of loneliness that almost overwhelmed her whenever she entered the room. Despite her best efforts, however, her dreams were now interspersed with scenes of him fully recovered, enjoying the sand on the beach with her and David.

"There!" the housekeeper declared. "A clean bandage once more."

Her pronouncement interrupted Cecile's thoughts, and when the servant stood to begin gathering her supplies, Cecile walked over to peer down at the inhabitant of both the bed and her dreams.

"How is he faring?"

Mrs. Kelly stopped what she was doing to give the man a studied look. "There was less blood on the bandage today, which I take as a good sign; however, I am worried that he has not awakened. The truth is, he needs to be seen by a physician."

"You know as well as I the only way he can see a physician is to be transported by ship, and Captain Silverhill has discouraged any ships from docking here. Only Captain Boone is allowed to bring the supplies I order, and I do expect him for another month. Since Silverhill is so secretive about his business, I fear what he may think about a stranger being on the island. I dare not ask him to take our patient to the Isle of Man to see a physician, for I fear he might toss him overboard."

"I agree! Silverhill cannot be trusted."

Cecile sat down on the side of the bed and smoothed a few locks of hair from William's forehead. "My hope is that he will recover and soon be able to return to his family. I know they must be terribly worried about him."

"At least if the captain keeps to his practice of staying at the house above the docks and not insist on staying here, he may remain ignorant of our patient," the housekeeper added.

"I am thankful that I was able to convince him it would not be proper for us to stay under the same roof after my husband died. Let us pray Silverhill keeps to that agreement."

"Do you expect him this evening?" Mrs. Kelly asked.

"His usual practice is to come the day after the ship docks. I see no reason he should not keep to that."

"Well, I am certainly not looking forward to serving him. He is not the gentleman Mr. Grubbs was."

Cecile almost laughed aloud to think Mrs. Kelly thought her husband a gentleman. Still, she would not disparage him to the woman who had served him for so many years. "No. Captain Silverhill certainly is no gentleman."

A moan filled the room, and both women whirled around only to observe no discernible change in the patient. They held their breath and waited for another.

After a while Cecile whispered, "Was I mistaken, or did he moan?"

Her eyes never leaving the patient, Mrs. Kelly nodded. "I heard it."

"Whilst I wish for him to wake, it would be best if he did not make such sounds whilst Captain Silverhill is downstairs."

"Might I suggest we have Mr. Kelly stay with him tonight? If he begins to moan, my husband can give him a small dose of laudanum to quiet him."

"I have to wonder what Captain Silverhill will say about Mr. Kelly being absent."

"We can tell him that Mr. Kelly has a stomach ailment. That would also account for any moans that might be heard downstairs."

"I think that a good plan," Cecile said. "Go tell Mr. Kelly we need him to sit with our patient when Captain Silverhill arrives and stay with him until the captain leaves."

Pemberley

Long after the children's maids had taken them into the house to wash their hands and faces and change their clothes for dinner, Elizabeth sat in the swing with her eyes closed, letting her feet guide it back and forth. It took all her strength to act untroubled whilst her children were present, and having a few minutes reprieve from the pretence was liberating.

Absently stroking Clancy's back as he lay in her lap, when the dog suddenly lifted his head, Elizabeth opened her eyes. Seeing what looked like concern in the dog's expression as he gazed at her, she laughed.

"You, too, Clancy? There is absolutely nothing to worry about. My courage rises with every attempt to intimidate me."

A low growl alerted Elizabeth that a rider was coming towards them from the front of the house. Her heart sank, for visiting every evening had become the habit of their neighbour Gregory Wright. Whilst she tried to be cordial whenever he brought Jonathan to play with Bennet, of late he came alone.

"How are you faring, Mrs. Darcy?" Wright asked, dismounting his stallion in one fluid motion just as William would have.

Why does William look so much more manly when he does the same thing? Elizabeth thought to herself. Aloud she said, "I am well, Mr. Wright. And you?"

"I am fine, as you see."

"And Master Jonathan? Has he returned from his visit with his cousins?"

"His cousins?" Suddenly recalling the lie he had told Elizabeth the last time he was at Pemberley, Wright hurried to recover. "Oh, yes, he has. I did not bring him today because he played with a new hound puppy all morning and was so tired that he fell asleep early."

"Then to what do I owe the pleasure of this visit?"

"Does a good friend need a reason to visit someone he admires?"

Immediately Elizabeth became wary. "Admiration, Mr. Wright?" Elizabeth stood. "If I did not know better, I might think you were trying to flirt with me. Of course, knowing how my husband would react to something of that nature, I am certain you are not that foolish."

She watched his eyes widen as he stuttered, "Of … of course not! I merely meant to say that I admire the way you are overseeing Pemberley in Darcy's absence."

"My husband has set good plans in place and hired excellent managers; all I have to do is follow his instructions. If there are compliments to be paid, they should be paid to him."

"Yes … well, I shall tell him the next time I see him." Still looking unnerved, he added, "I stopped by to ask if you had heard from Darcy after his arrival in Belfast."

"You certainly take an eager interest in my husband's travels."

"In truth, there is a distillery in Belfast that he and I discussed purchasing. I wondered if he had mentioned touring it."

"William told me about the distillery, and to answer your question, I have not heard from him since he sailed from Liverpool. I expect I shall any day now, though."

"Of course." Wright offered her a wan smile. When Elizabeth did not attempt to further the conversation, he added, "It is late. I suppose I should return to Parkleigh."

When Elizabeth did not object, he began to remount his horse. Once in the saddle, he brought his riding crop to the rim of his hat in his usual manner of saying farewell. "Good day, Mrs. Darcy. I shall bring Jonathan over tomorrow to play with Bennet, if that suits."

"It does. I know Bennet will be delighted to play with him again."

Another wan smile, followed by a nod, and he was gone. Elizabeth watched until he rode completely out of sight.

I believe Richard was correct about you, Mr. Wright! You act entirely too familiar now that William is not here.

As Gregory Wright rode back to Parkleigh Manor, he considered how to respond to Lady Catherine's latest missive. That old harridan assailed him almost daily with letters asking what, if anything, he had learned.

Since there is no news to report, I suppose I shall just have to concoct some!

Satisfied with his decision, Wright kicked his horse into a gallop.

Belfast
At the inn

Just as Viscount Hayworth had feared, the instant he informed Georgiana that the ship they were taking to Liverpool had apparently been lost at sea, she had broken down, crying uncontrollably. After he had done everything in his power to calm her, Matthew had sent for the local physician, Dr. Walsh, hoping that he would give her a sedative.

Now as he waited whilst the physician examined Georgiana in the bedroom of their suite, Matthew wondered how he might convince her they should return to Ballyneen for the time being. Suddenly the door opened, and the physician walked out, along with the man's wife, whom he had trained as his nurse. From the serious look on the physician's face, Matthew began to worry if there was more to Georgiana's symptoms than he imagined.

"Viscount Haywood, I must inform you that I will not be able to prescribe anything stronger than herbs such as chamomile tea and valerian, to help calm your wife."

"Why not?"

"Women who are with child should never take anything stronger, and given the fact that she has informed me that she has not had her courses in well over a month, she is likely in that condition. I concocted a draught containing these herbs and have given a dose to Lady Hayworth. I also left the bottle on the table next to the bed. The instructions are written on it."

Matthew's heart began to race. "My wife … Georgiana is pregnant?"

The doctor nodded. "My wife described to Lady Hayworth how the quickening feels, and once that happens, we can settle on a projected date of confinement."

Torn between being thrilled to know he was to be a father and sadness for the circumstances of that morning, Matthew grew quiet.

"I suggest you and Lady Hayworth return to Ballyneen—she mentioned that is the name of your estate. I have an office in Armagh that I visit every month, and I can easily call on Ballyneen from there."

"My wife had her heart set on traveling to Derbyshire to visit her brother, but with what has happened—"

"Yes, my wife and I prayed the ship was not lost, but it looks as though evidence proves that it was. In any case, I would have your wife wait until she is at least five months along and everything is well before giving my consent for travel, and by then perhaps the ships will have returned to normal schedules."

"Thank you, Dr. Walsh. You have eased my mind. I am very appreciative. If you will send a bill to Ballyneen, it will be taken care of immediately."

"There is no need to concern yourself with that now. Just be certain to contact me as soon as Lady Hayworth feels the quickening, and we shall proceed from there."

"You can be certain we will."

With that, the physician and his wife left, and Matthew entered the bedroom to check on Georgiana. To his relief she was asleep. Weary from worry and the events of the day, he undressed and joined her in bed. Sliding his arms around his wife, he pulled her close, and it was not long until he, too, drifted off to sleep.

Chapter 12

Liverpool
The next morning

Richard came downstairs early hoping to meet Lady Selina and perhaps share another meal. Eating with her yesterday had been the most pleasant experience he had had in months, and he was eager to learn more about her. All he knew at present was that she was a single woman from Leicester who had inherited Houghton Park from her late father, Lord Pembroke. She was thirty years old—a fact that came out when she mentioned she was in town to find a cousin who had grown up at her estate. As Richard waited in a chair in the lobby that conversation played through his mind.

"I am afraid my cousin thinks I treat him like a child."

Richard grinned. *"Well, do you?"*

"I suppose I do. You see I am much older than Noel, and I still find it hard not to think of him as my little brother."

"What is the age difference?"

"I just turned thirty, and Noel is but four and twenty."

"That is not a great deal of difference."

"Not now; however, when he came to live with us, he was but five. For years he looked to me for advice."

"That is understandable, but at some point, he had to grow up and make decisions for himself."

"Obviously, that time has come. I fear I reacted very badly to something he decided to do of late. Instead of staying in Leicester to argue with me, he took off for Ireland."

"And you are on your way to stop him?"

"No. I decided that, if he would allow it, I would join him."

"If you do not mind me asking, what was so important that you felt it worth a conflict?"

"Noel came to live with us after his father died and his mother attempted to return to her family; however, they would not allow her to come

back, nor would they take Noel. Apparently, she had married against her father's wishes, so she brought him to us."

"Though Father begged her to stay, too, she declined. It was not long afterwards that we were notified of her death. I did not wish Noel to be hurt again, so I was not in favour of him renewing the acquaintance of his mother's family."

"I can understand why you were opposed, so surely he must as well."

Lady Selina sighed. "Even so, I was too dictatorial. I wish to apologise, and hopefully, we can face them together."

"I pray you are successful."

"Thank you, Colonel."

"Colonel Fitzwilliam! Colonel Fitzwilliam!" Jarred from his reverie, Richard turned to see the desk clerk hurrying towards him holding a newspaper in the air.

"Have you heard the news?" the clerk asked as he reached Richard and shoved the paper into his hands. "The storm sank the ship you asked about when you first arrived."

Shocked, Richard unfolded the paper and began to read. His eyes focused on one headline: ***Remains of ship washed ashore near Donaghadee believed to be Endeavour!***

Heart beating like a drum, Richard recalled Elizabeth's answer when he asked the name of the ship on which William had sailed— *Endeavour.*

He asked the clerk the location of the freight service mentioned in the article.

"The docks are three streets west of here. Once you reach the water, Watson's is approximately four streets to the east."

Once on the street, Richard noted an unusual number of people scurrying this way and that, almost all carrying a copy of the newspaper, and many heading in the same direction as he.

Upon reaching the Watson's Freight Service office, he was only one of a large number gathered at a window where a list of passengers for the *Endeavour* had been posted. Though resigned that William was likely among the passengers, he was determined to see the evidence for himself. Just as a man ahead of him turned away from the window, Richard stepped forwards and right into Lady Selina.

"Colonel Fitzwilliam, I heard the news from my driver this morning and rushed here to see if Noel's name was on the passenger list. Thankfully, it was not." Seeing the anxiety in Richard's face, Lady Selina said, "Do you know someone on that ship?"

"The cousin I mentioned yesterday, Fitzwilliam Darcy, who came to Liverpool just ahead of me, was supposed to have sailed on her. I wanted to see for myself if he is listed."

"Of course." Lady Selina stepped aside. "Please do not let me hinder you."

Richard moved forwards to read the list. Upon seeing William's name, his hands clenched as tears rushed to his eyes. Still, used to controlling his emotions, he swallowed the lump in his throat and walked to the side of the building. He was taking slow, deep breaths when Lady Selina appeared beside him.

"I am so sorry," she whispered.

Unable to speak, Richard merely nodded.

"If there is anything I can do ..."

Richard shook his head absently before murmuring, "I must speak to the manager. I wish to inform my cousin's wife in person instead of having her learn the news from the papers or from an express. If I leave today, I can make Pemberley in a little over a day."

"That would be much kinder. I shall leave you now so you may do what you must. Just know that I will keep you and your cousins in my prayers." She held out a hand. "If we do not encounter one another again, Colonel, I want you to know that I truly enjoyed meeting you and forming a friendship, short as it was. You will always be welcome at Houghton Park."

A sincere look crossed Richard's face as he took her hand. "I shall pray that you have luck in finding your cousin in good health, and I will keep your kind invitation in mind."

Suddenly, the front door of Watson's opened. Touching the tip of his hat, Richard said, "Goodbye, Lady Selina."

Windemere Manor
That evening

Inasmuch as Captain Silverhill had overindulged in brandy at dinner, the night seemed interminably long. Though he talked of the future and how he hoped to work with Cecile to restore the funds lost when her husband's ship sank, what he talked most about was the fact that she needed a husband for protection, and her child needed a father.

As she had in the past, Cecile tried to steer the conversation away from marriage, but Silverhill would not be dissuaded.

"I mean to move to London where shipping is more profitable, and I cannot, in good conscience, leave you here on this lonely island to fend for yourself. You really must make a decision soon. There are ... *circumstances* that may force me to be off without much notice."

"I cannot make a decision quickly, for I wish to speak to my solicitor in Man before making any kind of move. David always told me that there were plenty of funds in the bank to keep the estate solvent should anything happen to him."

"Surely you do not believe that?" Silverhill countered. "If one takes out funds but puts nothing back, even the largest account will eventually run dry."

"David said we were living off the interest on monies he deposited after his great uncle's death. I do not see how that can be gone."

Frustrated, Captain Silverhill stood and threw down his serviette. "Evidently you do not have a head for business! If you will allow me to take you to your solicitor, I am certain he can clear up any misunderstanding."

"I had rather handle my business myself."

"How do you intend to get to Man unless you sail with me?"

"Captain Boone still comes once a month to bring supplies. I can always travel with him."

"I told that old fool not to dock near my warehouses again."

"And *I* told him that he was welcome to dock here whenever he wished," Cecile declared, coming to her feet. "I am still the owner of this island, and I shall allow anyone I wish to dock here."

Silverhill looked as though he was about to explode. Then he forced a smile. "Of course, my dear. I am only trying to keep outsiders from stealing those supplies that your husband and I stored here with intentions of selling in Scotland and Ireland. Seeing that the docks are on the other side of the island, I doubt you would know if anyone stopped here or plundered the warehouses."

"Not to worry, Captain. The shepherds can see the docks from their position on the hills whilst tending the sheep. They keep a watch on that side of the island for me."

The captain did not seem happy to hear that. "You should know then that I am leaving several men here to guard the warehouses when I return to Liverpool. They will occupy the house I normally reside in, so do not be concerned with their presence."

"Thank you for telling me. I will be sure to pass that information along."

A short time later, the captain returned to the docks, leaving Cecile shaken. The housekeeper, who had heard the conversation between her mistress and Silverhill, came into the room to begin clearing the table.

"If you ask me, Cap'n seems bound and determined to force you to marry him or, at the least, to go with him when he sails."

"I shall never give in. I must talk to my solicitor. Perhaps he will have some advice that will help me."

"Let us pray, then, that Captain Boone ignores Cap'n Silverhill's warnings and comes again this month."

Cecile stood. "I heard no sound from our guest, so I assume he is resting well."

"I just checked with Patrick, and he told me the gentleman has not tried to wake since being moved upstairs."

"I pray that he did not give him more laudanum."

"I expressly told Patrick you did not wish him to have more laudanum unless it was absolutely necessary."

"Good." Sighing heavily, Cecile went towards the dining room door. "I mean to check on David and then go straight to bed. I am exhausted."

"Little David is asleep, ma'am. I fed him and put him to bed early."

Nodding, Cecile walked out of the room.

As she watched her mistress leave, Mrs. Kelly murmured, "Mark my words. Cap'n Silverhill means to have you, whether you like it or not."

With that, the housekeeper continued clearing the dishes.

At the docks

"How are the prisoners faring, Jubal?" Captain Silverhill asked one of the men guarding Noel Stevens and Lady Aileen as he reached the house at the docks.

"As well as can be expected. They eat whatever they are fed and have made no attempts to escape." When his employer did not reply, he asked, "How much longer are we going to hold them here?"

"That depends. I sail for Liverpool tomorrow. If the messengers I sent to deliver the ransom notes have returned with favourable replies, the prisoners may be off your hands in less than a sennight."

"What if their relations do not think as well of them as they believe? What if they do not pay the ransom?"

"Then they shall join those who have met their end at the bottom of the sea."

Jubal nodded.

"Make certain the ship is ready to sail in the morning."

"Aye, aye, Captain."

Pemberley
Two days later

As daylight turned to dusk, Colonel Richard Fitzwilliam rode down the long drive towards Pemberley. Whereas normally he would have a word or two with the guards at the gate, today he was so exhausted he did not bother to stop. Instead, he waved and kicked his mount into a gallop again.

Having driven two horses nearly to the breaking point in order to reach Pemberley as soon as possible, he dreaded being the bearer of such horrible news. Still, he could not bear to think of Elizabeth hearing of her husband's fate from anyone but him.

What was more, he was certain that by now the news had reached London.

Thoughts of how his father and mother would react flashed through his mind. William was like a son to them, and he knew they would be stricken by the news. Unbidden, his horrid aunt came to mind.

I suppose Lady Catherine will be delighted to know that if Anne could not have you, Cousin, then Elizabeth would not have you very long.

Stop it! Richard ordered his racing mind.

He had refused to dwell on William's death since learning of the possibility, and the full impact had not sunk in yet. Uncertain how he would cope once it had, he knew at this point he must concentrate on remaining strong for Elizabeth's sake.

Reaching the front steps, a footman came running down to meet him. "Colonel Fitzwilliam, sir. Welcome back to Pemberley."

"Thank you, Sanders," was all Richard managed to say before he began up the steps.

Once in the foyer, Mrs. Reynolds rushed forwards to greet him with a smile.

"Colonel, we were not expecting you back so soon."

Without meeting the housekeeper's eyes, he said, "If possible, Mrs. Reynolds, I would like to speak to Mrs. Darcy straightaway."

Usually a very amiable man, Richard's worried expression and curt manner of address must have alerted the housekeeper that something was amiss.

"Mrs. Darcy is upstairs with Mrs. Green. I shall have a maid fetch—"

Before she could finish, Elizabeth and Mrs. Green appeared at the top of the landing. Laughing and talking as they descended the stairs, upon seeing Richard, Elizabeth exclaimed, "What a surprise! I was not expecting you, Richard!"

Her face glowing with delight, Elizabeth quickly negotiated the rest of the stairs, bringing Mrs. Green along with her.

As they reached the foyer, Mrs. Green said, "I wish you had come sooner. We have visited for far too long, and I fear I must leave now or James will wonder what happened to me when he returns home to find me missing."

As Mrs. Green reached to take the cloak Mr. Walker offered, Richard reached for her hand. "Please stay. You may be needed."

It was as though his words sucked all the air out of the room. Instantly, everyone was silently staring at Richard, who was trying his best not to show any emotion.

At length, it was Elizabeth who spoke first. With an increasingly paler complexion, she pleaded with her eyes as she murmured quietly, "Something has happened to William. That is why you are here."

Clearing his throat, Richard said, "Pray, let us go into the parlour and sit down."

Immediately, Elizabeth became lightheaded, and Richard rushed to catch her before she fell.

"Take her to her bedroom," Mrs. Reynolds ordered.

Richard carried Elizabeth up the stairs. At the landing, Mrs. Green passed a stunned maid. "Ask Mr. Walker to send a footman to fetch my husband."

The maid nodded and disappeared.

At the mistress' bedroom, Richard waited for the pastor's wife to open the door before sweeping inside with his charge and startling Elizabeth's maid, who was coming out of the dressing room. Seeing what was happening, Florence rushed to turn down the counterpane on the bed.

Almost in shock as she stood at the door watching, Mrs. Green was surprised to feel a tug on her skirt. It was Ben.

"I heard noises and then I saw Cousin Richard carrying Mama. Is she hurt?"

Mrs. Green stooped to address the anxious little boy. Smoothing the hair from his worried eyes, she forced herself to don a carefree smile.

"He was carrying your mother, but only because she felt quite tired, and I insisted she rest. You know how comical your cousin can be. He insisted on carrying her up the stairs and depositing her on the bed."

Ben tried to see past her. "May I see Mama?"

Pulling the door closed, the rector's wife said, "I think it would be best if we allow her to rest. That way she may feel up to joining you for dinner."

Suddenly, the nanny rushed up and, seeing Ben, let go a ragged sigh. "I am sorry, Mrs. Green. Master Ben slipped away before I knew it."

"No apology needed, Mrs. Cummings. I know how fast little boys can disappear." To Ben she said, "Trust me. Your mother is well. Return to your classroom and I shall speak to her about having dinner with you and Anne."

"Mimi, you would tell me if my Mama was not well."

On the verge of tears, she clasped the boy to her breast. "Of course, sweetheart."

She felt him pull back. Big blue eyes searched hers for the tiniest hint of subterfuge.

"Cross your heart?"

Her own heart breaking, Judith Green made a cross over it.

Feeling relieved, Ben was about to exit the room, but he stopped abruptly. "I wish Cousin Richard would eat dinner with us."

"He may just do that."

Later

Elizabeth regained her senses when Richard placed her on the bed, and she began asking a myriad of questions. He had had little time to answer before Mrs. Reynolds rushed into the bedroom with a draught to calm her mistress. When the housekeeper asked the maid to help her loosen her mistress' clothes, Richard was relegated to the sitting room and was soon joined by the butler, Mrs. Green and the vicar who had recently arrived. Mrs. Reynolds entered soon afterwards.

After Dr. Camryn examined Elizabeth, he walked into the room to speak to those gathered.

Having already told the others what little he knew about the ship William had sailed on being lost at sea, including that wreckage from the ship had reportedly washed up on a shore in Ireland, Richard was at a loss as to how much he should say to his cousin's wife.

"Is she well enough to hear everything?" Richard asked. "All I managed to say before I left her was that I had seen William's name on a list of those missing."

"Mrs. Darcy and the baby are doing well under the circumstances, so I see no reason to keep the truth from her. No doubt it will be commonly known shortly in any case."

"The baby?" Colonel Fitzwilliam repeated.

"If all goes well, Mrs. Darcy will deliver another child in approximately six months," the physician replied.

"I ... I had no idea," Richard replied, dropping his head in his hands and rubbing his forehead vigorously. "I keep thinking I shall wake, and it shall all be just a bad dream."

Mr. Green walked over to place a hand on Richard's shoulder. "This cannot be easy for you. We are all just grateful to God that you were available to break the news to Elizabeth."

"Mrs. Darcy is awake and requesting your presence, Colonel," the physician added. "I suggest that Mrs. Green go in with you."

Richard nodded.

Then the physician addressed Mrs. Reynolds. "The camomile draught you gave her has taken effect. Please continue with it as needed to keep her calm. I shall return tomorrow afternoon, but you may send for me earlier if you think it necessary."

Dr. Camryn donned his hat and headed towards the door.

"I shall see you out," Mr. Walker said as he escorted the physician from the room.

William's valet, Adams, could not rouse a weary Colonel Fitzwilliam to eat dinner with the Greens and the children; therefore, because Elizabeth was still sleeping, the Greens joined Ben and Anne at a large table in the nursery where their mother often dined with them.

Mrs. Green had hoped that she and James could reassure Ben that their mother was fine and, though it had taken some effort, she felt they had accomplished that by the time they had finished eating. When it came to Bennet Fitzwilliam George Darcy, however, she was badly mistaken.

No sooner had the Greens returned to the vicarage and the children were put to bed than Ben opened the door to the hallway and peered out to see if there were any maids or footmen about. Seeing none, he took the chamber candlestick from the bedside table and set out to find his cousin.

Richard was sleeping so soundly that he did not hear the door to his bedroom open nor did the light the small candlestick provided in the darkness wake him. It was only after Ben had placed the candlestick on a table and climbed onto the bed that Richard became aware he was not alone. Instantly awake, he rolled off the bed and grabbed the sword that he always left propped against the bedside table and braced himself to face the intruder.

Only a small cry of alarm caused him to relax. "Ben, is that you? Good heavens! You frightened me something awful. I might have hurt you had you not cried out. What in the world are you doing in my bed?"

By then Richard's eyes had adjusted to the faint light, and he could see that Ben was sitting on his knees in the middle of the bed with tears rolling down his face.

"I am sorry," the child said, sniffling. "I just wanted to ask you about Papa."

Much preferring to face any enemy than answer his small cousin's questions, Richard laid down the sword and braced himself. He had not had time to tell Elizabeth before she succumbed to all the draughts, but he aimed to return to Liverpool and do whatever it took to find his cousin … no matter the outcome.

Taking a deep breath and letting it go, he sat on the edge of the bed and pulled Ben into his lap, so that the boy sat facing away from him. "What do you wish to know?"

"I overheard a maid say that my Papa may not come back."

Richard swallowed hard. He had never lied to Ben and never would, but he wondered if Elizabeth would fault him for telling her son the truth before she could.

"The ship your father sailed on encountered some … some trouble. It ran into a horrible storm and rumour has it that it wrecked off the shore of Ireland. But I want you to know that I aim to do everything in my power to find your father and bring him home."

Ben sobbed. "Do you promise?"

Richard turned Ben so that he could look into his eyes. They were so large in the darkness that he could clearly see they were awash with tears.

"Yes, I do. Meanwhile, I must ask you to do something for me … something very courageous. Would you like to know what that is?"

"Yes, Cousin Richard."

"Whilst I search for your father, I need you to be brave for your mother and for Anne. Try to keep up their spirits by not letting them see that you are worried. I have learned that when I feel I must cry, if I do it in bed after I retire then no one is the wiser."

"You cry, too?" a shocked Ben asked.

"Of course. Real men cry. They just try to do it when they are alone."

Ben nodded. "I will try not to let Mama or Anne see me cry."

"That is all any man can do ... well, that and pray. Now, would you like me to see you back to your bedroom?"

"I would."

After tucking his cousin's son into bed, Richard did something he rarely did ... he leaned forwards and kissed Ben's forehead. "Try not to worry. Just pray whenever you feel sad and know that I will be praying, too."

"Will I see you before you leave, Cousin Richard?"

"I would not dream of leaving without saying goodbye. Try to get some sleep, and I will see you in the morning."

Richard stood and made to leave, but Ben's voice stopped his progress. "I love you."

Richard's voice broke with his reply, "I love you, too, Ben."

Chapter 13

Pemberley

Having missed dinner the evening before, Richard was the first one in the breakfast room the next day. He had barely eaten since learning of the fate of the *Endeavour* and knew he would likely not eat again until he stopped for the night on his way back to Liverpool.

As a footman poured him another cup of coffee, Elizabeth walked into the room with Clancy close behind. He could tell she had been crying, and by the woeful expression in the pup's eyes and his subdued manner, he could have sworn Clancy was equally affected.

Elizabeth offered Richard a small smile. "Good morning. After your exhausting journey, I hope you were able to get some rest last night."

"I managed to get a little sleep."

Waving away a footman, Elizabeth took the seat next to his and Clancy lay down at her feet.

"Dr. Camryn was here quite early this morning, and the vicar accompanied him. They are such dears to worry about me. I … I asked the vicar what you had to say about the shipwreck, and he told me everything."

Richard dropped his head. "I wanted to tell you last night but—"

"I know." Elizabeth patted his arm gently. "Besides, it was probably best hearing it from Reverend Green, as I know how you hate to be the bearer of bad news."

Greatly affected, Richard barely nodded.

"I have just come from speaking to Ben, and he told me about your talk last night."

"Forgive me if I spoke out of turn, but I was caught unawares. Ben overheard a maid say that William might not come back, and I did not have it in me to lie or to put him off by saying he should ask you."

Taking a deep breath, Elizabeth slowly let it go. "How can I ever be upset with you after you rode so far to break the news to me? And now you are obliged to ride straight back to Liverpool. 'Thank you' will never suffice to express my gratitude."

"I would do anything for you and the children."

Elizabeth said solemnly, "I know." Then she added, "Actually, I am pleased that you told Ben the truth but also gave him hope. Until this morning, I was not in the frame of mind to speak to him about his father. Still, being the inquisitive little boy he is, I feared he would realise something was amiss and learn the truth somehow … and it seems he did."

"Sometimes I fear Ben is too smart for his age."

"In times like this, I cannot disagree. I am pleased, too, that you told him that you intend to look for his father, for in my heart, I know that William is not dead."

"You do?"

"You may not have noticed, but our love has always been a peculiar kind. William and I often know when the other is near before we set eyes on one another. Many times I have known when he was on his way home, though he may have been scheduled to arrive days later." Dabbing at her now teary eyes with one of William's handkerchiefs, she lifted her chin. "And, after much prayer and deep reflection, I know that my William still lives."

Not wishing to contradict his cousin, Richard reached to give her hand a squeeze in solidarity. "I return to Liverpool this morning. Rest assured that I will do everything in my power to find him."

Elizabeth's brows knit. "Will the army allow you the time?"

"My father has great influence with General Lassiter. That will not be a problem," he replied. "Now then, would you do me the honour of breaking your fast with me?"

When she smiled, Richard motioned for a footman. "A plate for Mrs. Darcy and more coffee for me." As the servant rushed to do as asked, Richard continued, "I mean to keep you company whilst having another cup."

"My guess would be that you mean to make certain I eat something," Elizabeth teased.

Richard laughed. "You know me too well!"

"By all means, let me get started then, for I do not wish to keep you from leaving for Liverpool. Ben is certain you will come to the classroom to say your farewells to him and Anne before you go."

"Master Ben is correct." Richard's expression softened. "I admire how you and Darcy have raised him. He is not only a very intelligent little scamp, but he has a tender heart."

"Just like his father."

"Aye. Like his father."

"Before you take your leave," she added, "I have a letter I want you to give William as soon as you find him."

Swallowing against the lump in his throat, Richard said, "Of course."

Liverpool
Silverhill Shipping Company

"Cap'n Silver, sir, the warehouse is almost empty!"

Looking up from his desk, Silverhill addressed the man he had left in charge of emptying the warehouse. "Parton, do you think we can get everything on one ship, or must we make two trips?"

"It will definitely take two."

"Well, get as much onboard as possible."

"Aye, Aye!"

After Parton left, the sailor Silverhill had sent to Houghton Park with a ransom letter regarding Noel Stevens came through the door. "Basil, what took you so long?" he barked.

"Leicester is not that easy to get to from here," the man replied. "Besides, it seems the owner of Houghton Park, a Lady Selina, was not there. She left her steward, Mr. Dobbs, in charge. At first, he did not want to believe the ransom letter was authentic, but after I showed him the items you confiscated from Mr. Stevens' luggage, he began to listen. I explained that not only would Stevens be killed if he brought in the law, but his own life depended on how he handled the ransom."

"Go on."

"Dobbs had the authority to approve the ransom and petition the bank for the funds from his mistress' account. He will be the one to meet you in Liverpool and make the exchange."

"So, when is he to arrive?"

"In ten days' time, he will check into the Crown Inn and await further instructions."

"Ten days! I wanted to be out of Liverpool in a sennight," Silverhill protested.

"Three thousand pounds should not be that hard a sum to raise; that is why I set it so low."

"You forget. Dobbs must make a trip to the bank in London before he travels to Liverpool."

"Do you know if anyone has heard from Morton?"

"Not to my knowledge, but Berkley Hall is farther than Mr. Stevens' family seat."

"If I do not hear back from Lady Davidson's relations in a timely manner, her ransom may have to be paid by Stevens' family," Silverhill huffed. "He suggested they would be happy to do so."

"I could be wrong, but it appeared to me that Dobbs was not eager to part with three thousand pounds for Mr. Stevens, so I do not see him paying a ransom for someone else."

"We shall see about that when the time comes."

Windemere Manor

For days William had drifted in and out of consciousness. The few times he had awakened—such as when he was given water or broth—he had kept his eyes closed, pretending to still be unaware. Everything was foreign to him—the people, the house and the reason for his injury. He could not even recall his name. Confused, he hoped to make sense of things before anyone realised he was conscious.

That morning, however, he was completely unaware that someone was in the room when he opened his eyes and looked around.

"Oh, my!" cried an elderly woman. "You are awake at last!"

Without waiting for a reply, she rushed from the room, quickly returning with a younger, red-haired woman.

"Sir, my housekeeper, Mrs. Kelly, and I are so pleased that you are awake."

"I ... I ... water," William murmured in a raspy voice.

"Of course!" The younger woman poured a glass of water from a pitcher on the table beside the bed. Sitting down beside him, she said, "Help me raise him enough to drink, Mrs. Kelly, just as we have done before."

The housekeeper hurried to William's other side, and between them, they managed to help William to a sitting position. Once he had drunk all that he could, they laid him back against the pillows.

The red-haired woman waited anxiously for him to speak and, when he did not, said, "I am Mrs. Grubbs, and you are at my estate on an island called the Calf of Man. Can you tell me your name?"

Exhausted from the effort to drink, William could only murmur, "I cannot recall. How did I come to be here?"

"During one of the worst storms in many years, you washed ashore in a jollyboat. You had an injury to your head and nothing on your person that would reveal your identity."

William closed his eyes. "How long have I been here?"

"Not too long," Cecile replied. "However, now that you are awake, we hope to have you back on your feet soon."

Suddenly, one of the tallest men William had ever seen rushed into the room. Though his black hair and beard had long since turned grey, his shirt sleeves were rolled up, displaying well-toned arms. That, along with a pair of broad shoulders, made it apparent he was no stranger to hard work.

At the sight of him the housekeeper cried, "Look! Our patient has awakened! Now your work will begin in earnest."

To William she said, "This is my husband. With Mr. Kelly's help we were able to change your clothes and bedsheets and help you to sip some water and broth. He will be the one to help you stand once you get your legs beneath you."

Too weary to reply, William merely nodded.

Mrs. Grubbs interrupted. "Now that our patient is awake, I think he might enjoy a bowl of the soup you made for lunch and a hot cup of tea."

"I should have thought of that!" the housekeeper said as she rushed towards the door. Calling over her shoulder, she added, "Mr. Kelly, find more pillows to prop behind him. He will need to sit up better if he is to eat."

London

As Gregory Wright's coach slowly entered the outskirts of town, he began racking his brain to think of a good excuse to give Catherine de Bourgh regarding why he had not been able to seduce her nephew's wife. Apparently, Darcy's aunt thought Elizabeth Darcy a hoyden because she insisted he seduce her whilst her husband was in Ireland— something he knew would never happen.

Elizabeth Darcy is more of a lady than you will ever hope to be!

All he had concocted thus far was the excuse that Jonathan had been ill, and he had had no opportunity to visit Mrs. Darcy of late.

The old bat will never believe that or, if she does, she will likely not think it a valid excuse.

The last bridge to cross before entering London proper came into sight. Sighing, Wright resigned himself to being browbeaten once again by Lady Catherine. Then, recalling she told him not to come until after dark and to enter through the alley, he decided to direct his driver to White's. There, he could pass the time until darkness cloaked his presence at her house.

The de Bourgh townhouse

Apparently, Catherine de Bourgh's servants were used to their mistress' odd ways, for when Wright arrived after dark at the back gate, the grooms waved his coach through the entrance without a single question. Moreover, they offered his men refuge in the grooms' common room whilst they waited and escorted him to the rear entrance of the manor house without a word.

Once inside the bleak, dark confines of the townhouse, Wright followed the butler to the foyer, where his nemesis stood waiting.

"It took you long enough to get here!" the impressively clothed matron bellowed.

Wright might have thought her a beauty once, but the constant downturn of her mouth proved a vivid reminder of her ugly nature. "I told you I would arrive today," he replied.

"And I said I wanted you here yesterday." When he did not reply, she continued. "In any case, this has changed everything!" With that, she tossed him a newspaper with the headline touting the sinking of the *Endeavour* in bold letters.

"I heard rumours of that along the way." Wright shook his head. "I refused to believe such a tragedy until I saw it in the London papers."

"Well, you can believe it now! Fitzwilliam's name is listed among the missing. That irresponsible nephew of mine most likely died on a trip to save his sister's imprudent marriage. I told Darcy that Viscount Hayworth was nothing but trouble, but he refused to listen to me."

"Why do you think Darcy would get involved in Georgiana's marriage? He might have just wanted to see her. After all, they are very close."

"Humph!" she sputtered. "Georgiana was married only months ago. No, there had to be trouble brewing to pry him away from Pemberley."

"I imagine this will postpone your plans for me to seduce Mrs. Darcy. After all, she will be in mourning for at least a year."

"Nonsense! Women like that are never without a man for long. No doubt she will welcome your attention, now that Darcy is not there to meet her carnal needs."

"I know Mrs. Darcy well, and you are entirely wrong about her."

"I am the one holding your debts, and I expect you to do as I say, so keep your opinions to yourself!"

Wright sighed. "And what is it you want me to do now?"

"The same as before, but instead of seducing her to convince Darcy of her worthless nature, you will convince everyone else, including that horrid housekeeper at Pemberley. Create a scandal large enough that all the servants become aware of the affair, and even Mrs. Reynolds will be eager to tattle to my brother. I want Matlock to take the children away from her and toss that whore into the hedgerows without a penny to her name."

"I have not been successful in gaining her attention whilst Darcy was merely travelling. I do not see how I can gain it now that she will be in mourning."

"That will be your problem, Mr. Wright. I spent thousands of pounds on that ludicrous distillery in Ireland, and I will not let my expenditure be in vain. I want Elizabeth Darcy to lose everything, including her children!" Lady Catherine cried. "Do you hear me?"

"If you do not stop shouting, the whole of England will hear you."

"Your insolence is not appreciated."

"Do you plan to return to Kent now?"

"No. Whilst you are seducing Elizabeth, I intend to try to influence my brother. If I am successful, I can convince him that he needs to think about taking those children under his wing, now that their father is presumed dead. Then, when Elizabeth is exposed as the whore she has always been, the earl will be in the frame of mind to act."

"As I have said before, Mrs. Darcy is a lady, and one who has shown no interest in me. I doubt you will be able to convince Lord Matlock that she is an unfit mother."

"If you do your job successfully, *I* will not have to prove anything. *You* will." When Wright did not reply, she added, "Now leave. I do not wish you to be seen here."

Lady Catherine did not have to say it twice. Wright turned on his heel and left in the same manner he had arrived. As his coach cleared the back gate, he took a deep breath of air and blew it out.

If I am ever to have a chance to win Elizabeth, I must wait until she has grieved her husband properly, which means I must extricate myself from Lady Catherine's control. If she continues to press me, I do not know how, but I will defy her even if it means confessing everything. Wright brightened. *Maybe that is the key. Perhaps Lord Matlock would be interested in buying my debts in exchange for knowing what his sister has been up to.*

With that thought in mind, Wright ordered his driver to take him to his godfather's townhouse on Mayfair Lane.

Lord Grassley will not mind if I stay there.

Chapter 14

Liverpool
Naval Headquarters

Though Richard had been in Liverpool for days, he had uncovered no additional information concerning the sinking of the *Endeavour*. Having questioned everyone he knew to query, he decided to pay a call on Admiral Turlington before retracing William's journey to Belfast aboard another of Watson's Freight Services vessels christened the *Fortune*.

As he sat waiting in the naval headquarters, the door to the admiral's office suddenly opened.

"Colonel Fitzwilliam, the admiral will see you now."

Rising to his feet, Richard walked into the room to find the genial, rotund admiral sitting behind his desk with one leg propped upon a chair and wrapped in bandages. Upon seeing Richard, the flame-haired man smiled broadly.

"Good to see you again, Colonel," he pronounced in his usual, thunderous manner. Motioning to a chair, he added, "Have a seat! Pray excuse me for not rising. My physician said I could not be on my feet for another fortnight." Laughing boisterously, he added, "In fact, Dr. Hammersmith would be livid if he knew my men carried me to and from my office every day."

Richard walked over to shake his hand before occupying the chair in front of the admiral's desk. "No apology necessary, sir. Do you mind if I ask what happened to your leg?"

"Not at all! As usual, I was talking and not looking where I was going. I missed a step and fell going down the stairs in the warehouse. Hammersmith said my leg is broken or, as he explained it, the bone is cracked but not entirely in two. He claims if I stay off it, I could be back on my feet within a month or so." Turlington smiled. "That remains to be seen."

Noting the solemn expression on Richard's face, he said, "Though I am pleased to see you again, it appears your visit is not for the pleasure of my company."

"I fear you are correct. I wish to know if you have heard anything more than what the papers are reporting with regard to the sinking of the *Endeavour*."

"No, but why do you ask."

"My cousin, Fitzwilliam Darcy, was listed as a passenger on that ship."

"My word!" the admiral declared. "You have my condolences for your loss."

"Actually, I am here to determine if he *was* lost." At the admiral's raised brows, Richard added. "I know the odds of his survival are slim, but Elizabeth Darcy is convinced that her husband is still alive. I promised her I would do everything in my power to determine his fate."

"I see." The admiral fixed upon a portrait of one of His Majesty's ships on the wall as he continued. "You do know rumours have the ship breaking apart near the Irish town of Donaghadee. Supposedly, items from the ship washed ashore there."

"Yes. I intend to travel to Donaghadee once I reach Ireland."

"You are sailing there?"

"Yes. I mean to trace my cousin's trip as best I can. Only then can I truthfully tell Mrs. Darcy that her husband likely died in the ship-wreck."

The admiral looked away, his expression growing wistful as though he was recalling something. "I know how difficult it is to tell someone their loved one has died. I had to do that far too often in my younger days. And it is much more difficult when the one involved is family."

"Then you know why I must do all in my power to prove whether he is alive or …" Richard grew silent.

"I do. Let me know if there is anything I can do to assist you."

"There is one thing. In conversing with Lieutenant Donavan, whom I met when last I was in Liverpool, I understand he is still on the trail of those who have been stealing shipments from the navy."

"He is."

"Would you ask him to keep an eye out for any information concerning my cousin. It is not uncommon for a man of Fitzwilliam Darcy's prominence to be waylaid by freebooters[8] pretending to be lawful merchants with legitimate vessels. I would not be surprised to hear that a ransom demand has been received for his release."

"Of course! Knowing Lieutenant Donavan as I do, I know he would be glad to help in any way he can."

"Thank you." With that, Richard came to his feet. "I shall be on my way, for I know you are busy."

"When do you sail?"

"Tomorrow."

"If you will, stop in to see me upon your return. I should like to know what you have learned regarding the *Endeavour*."

"I will, sir."

Armagh, Ireland
Flannery's Inn

As soon as Matthew walked into the inn, he noticed Bert Perkins was already seated at a table, enjoying a glass of ale. Despite his best efforts not to get his hopes up, Matthew's heart began to beat faster as he hurried in that direction.

Soon, he sat directly across from the man who had been relaying messages from his uncle, the detective hired to find Aileen.

"I take it from Mr. Osgood's last express that he has found my sister," Matthew said.

Mr. Perkins' smile disappeared. "In a manner of speaking."

"What does that mean?" Matthew retorted irritably. "I am paying your uncle well to locate Aileen, so please do not speak to me in riddles."

"May I ask if you are aware of the ship that sank during the recent storm?"

Matthew's heart leapt into his throat. "The *Endeavour*? Yes, I am."

"Well, my uncle had located your sister in Liverpool and was about to send an express to you disclosing her whereabouts when, out of the blue, she disappeared."

---

[8] *Freebooter – a person who goes about in search of plunder; pirate; buccaneer. Dictionary. Com.*

Though he feared asking, Matthew had no choice. "What has that to do with the ship that sank?"

"Pray forgive me, but there is no other way to say this without causing you pain. Unfortunately, Uncle believes Lady Aileen Davidson was aboard that ship."

As all colour drained from Matthew's face, Mr. Perkins pulled a paper from inside his coat and offered it to him.

"Not only did Uncle get the clerk at the Crown Inn to admit she was no longer in residence, but the clerk was so angry that he confided she left without settling her bill and was in such a hurry that she left her luggage behind."

As Matthew stared blindly at the paper, Perkins said, "Per Watson's Freight Services, that is a list of all who sailed on the *Endeavour*. Uncle thought you would want to see it for yourself. There is a couple listed as Mr. and Mrs. Arthur Gable and, as you well know, that was the name of your father's steward."

Matthew steeled himself not to show any emotion as he quickly scanned the list of passengers. Nevertheless, halfway down the page he was unable to hide the tears that leapt into his eyes when he saw the names Perkins had pointed out. Still, though his heart was nearly breaking at the thought of losing his sister, it was a name only two lines further down that almost made his heart stop beating altogether: Fitzwilliam Darcy.

Flabbergasted, Matthew closed his eyes and began taking deep breaths in an attempt to regain control.

Mr. Perkins shifted in his chair uncomfortably. "I am sorry, sir. My uncle wanted me to express our condolences on the loss of your sister and to tell you that we regret the search did not end successfully."

"It is even worse than you could imagine," Matthew murmured. "My wife has been expecting her brother to visit, and his name is also on the list. I cannot imagine how Georgiana will be able to face losing him as well as Aileen."

"You have my deepest sympathy. I know Uncle Robert will be equally sad, too, to learn that your wife's brother is among those missing."

Letting go a breath, Matthew stood up woodenly. "I must return to my wife." Then, he began searching his coat pockets. "I brought a cheque with me for I felt certain Mr. Osgood had found Aileen. Even though things did not work out as I had anticipated, your uncle did his part, and I wish to pay him what we agreed upon. Did you happen to bring pen and ink with you as before?"

"I always do. They are in my room."

"Then I shall accompany you upstairs."

"As you wish."

Ballyneen Castle

The moment Matthew walked through the door, he was met by his aunt in the foyer. Needing to enlist her help to keep Georgiana busy while he met with Mr. Osgood's nephew in town, Matthew had finally informed her about his sister's predicament and the Bow Street Runner he had hired to locate Aileen.

"From the look on your face," Aunt Mary declared, "I fear to ask what you learned in Armagh."

"Let us go into the drawing room where we can speak privately."

Once there, Matthew began to explain. "I received a list of the passengers who were on the *Endeavour* when she sank, and not only was my father's steward listed as being on the ship, but he was apparently accompanied by his wife."

"Do you believe Mr. Gable's *wife* is Aileen?"

"I have no reason to think otherwise."

"Heaven help us," Aunt Mary murmured, sinking down in a near-by chair as she fanned her face with her hand.

"What is more, Georgiana has been expecting a visit from her brother, Fitzwilliam Darcy, and he is listed as a passenger as well."

Aunt Mary's hand flew to her heart. "This will be unbearable for poor Georgiana! And it could not have happened at a worse time, what with her being with child."

"No. It could not," Matthew stated. "Where is my wife at present?"

"After she broke her fast, her stomach became upset."

"Again?"

"Yes, but Dr. Walsh said it was to be expected in the first months. In any case, I insisted she lie down, and as far as I know, she is still in her bedroom."

"Pray prepare one of the draughts Walsh prescribed to keep her calm and bring it to our sitting room. I would like you to remain near-by while I speak to her about what I learned."

"Do you think it might be better to say nothing about this until she is further along?"

An expression of deep regret settled on Matthew's face. "I promised her there would be no more secrets between us, and I mean to keep that promise."

"I understand. I shall fix the draught and bring it upstairs as quick-ly as possible."

As his aunt started to walk away, he called, "Aunt, I wish to say that I appreciate the kindness you have shown Georgiana and me, despite the turmoil we brought along with us. I know that your life was much more serene before she and I arrived at Ballyneen."

His aunt smiled. "I was never blessed with children, and you and Georgiana have filled that place in my heart. I assure you that it has been a pleasure to be of service however I could."

"Still, I wish you to know that I am appreciative, for I fear our problems are about to grow much worse. After all, Georgiana has no parents to turn to and Fitzwilliam is her only sibling. Though she came to love Elizabeth Darcy as a sister, and Aileen after we married, my sis-ter's present situation has devastated her. Consequently, I have no idea how Georgiana will cope once she knows both Aileen and Fitzwilliam are lost to her."

"Georgiana may surprise you, Matthew. She still has you, and now that she is expecting a child, there is a new life to consider. We shall just have to pray that she will look to the future and remember the past only as it gives her pleasure."

Matthew smiled wanly. "I think you have heard Georgiana quoting her sister."

"Yes, I have. Still, Mrs. Darcy's advice is good to remember in times like these."

"I agree." Taking a deep breath and letting it go loudly, Matthew said, "Say a prayer for me. I shall need all the help I can get as I try to explain everything to Georgiana."

Watching her nephew walk out of the drawing room, Lady Mary was struck by Matthew's attitude. *I am amazed that you turned out to be such a caring husband. My brother was certainly no example to follow in that quarter. I shall have to credit your mother for your excellent character.*

Then, recalling what she was supposed to do, Aunt Mary hurried towards the kitchen to fix the draught.

Georgiana's bedroom

As Matthew neared the bed, he found Georgiana sleeping so peacefully that his entire being began to throb with the pain of knowing how dreadfully the information he held in confidence would affect the woman he loved. Checking himself before sinking down on the bed, a thought came to mind.

Perhaps I should wait … at least until she awakens.

When he turned to go, however, Georgiana stretched out a hand, murmuring, "Stay."

Taking her hand, he allowed her to direct him to a place beside her on the bed. Then, he leaned over to place a soft kiss on her forehead.

"You startled me, my love. I thought you were asleep."

"I was merely dozing. I do not think I have slept soundly since we returned from Belfast."

"I am sorry to hear that. Perhaps that is why you are so tired of late … other than being with child?"

"I am certain it is, but I can do nothing to alleviate the problem, for I cannot help worrying about Brother. Without any letters and the fact that he never arrived for a visit, my mind keeps whispering that he might have been on that ship." Matthew could not disguise how severely Georgiana's remark upset him.

"What is it? Do you know something you have not told me?"

Unable to look into her eyes, Matthew dropped his head. "While I was picking up the mail in Armagh, I met with the nephew of the man who has been searching for Aileen."

"Why did you not tell me that you were to meet him? I would have accompanied you."

"With the stomach ailments you suffered of late, I feared taking you on those ghastly roads to Armagh. Besides, because of a letter Mr. Osgood sent last week, I surmised he was going to disclose he had found Aileen. I hoped to surprise you with that information when I returned."

"From the look on your face, I can only assume he has not found her."

Matthew took both of her hands in his, kissing first one and then the other. "Sweetheart, before I say anything more, you must find it in yourself to be strong. If not for me, then for our child."

Tears filled Georgiana's eyes, and all she could manage was a nod.

"Mr. Perkins brought me a list of the passengers who were supposed to have sailed on the *Endeavour* the night she sank."

Other than her eyes growing twice as large, Georgiana showed no emotion. Having no choice, Matthew told her everything he had discovered in Armagh. Even after he had finished explaining about her brother, she remained silent as though she were in a trance.

When he could not coax her to speak, he cried, "Georgiana!" Letting go of her hands to frame her face, he turned her head so she faced him. "Sweetheart! Speak to me!"

Aunt Mary heard his cries and rushed into the room. Taking stock of the situation, she rushed back into the sitting room. Pouring a cup of tea she had brought upstairs, she quickly emptied the draught into it and stirred. Once finished, she hurried back into the bedroom.

Holding the cup out to Matthew, she said, "This is not hot. Perhaps drinking it will help her."

Pemberley

The day had seemed to last forever, but now that the children were in bed, the house was too quiet for Elizabeth. She crept out of her bed and onto the chaise on the balcony. She preferred speaking to the Lord about her problems as she lay under the stars; she also felt closer to William there. They often spent nights sleeping under the stars when he was at home, and tonight, as she pulled a soft blanket over her and looked up at the velvety, black sky sparkling with millions of stars, Elizabeth could no longer hold back the tears that threatened every second of every day.

Covering her mouth with one of William's handkerchiefs so no one could hear if a sob escaped, she was crying quietly and praying silently when she felt Ben crawl onto the chaise beside her.

Swallowing hard to squelch her tears, she tried to smile as she wrapped an arm around her son and, pulling him closer, kissed the top of his head.

"What on earth are you doing awake, sweetheart? You should have been asleep hours ago."

From his raspy voice she could tell Ben had been crying when he began to speak. "I … I could not sleep, Mama. I woke up, and for a moment, I thought Papa was home. I slid out of my bed to go find him, and then I remembered he is not here." Ben sniffled. "I miss Papa so much."

"I understand, Son. I miss him very much, too."

"Why are you not in your bed?"

"When your Papa is home, after dark he and I often lie on this chaise discussing you and Anne … or Pemberley. After first asking the Lord to guide us, it seems easier to make important decisions under the enormity of God's magnificent creation. That is why I feel closer to Papa under these stars than anywhere else at Pemberley."

"As I came through the door, I thought I heard crying. Are you afraid that Papa is not coming back?"

Elizabeth knew her faith was being tested. "No, I truly believe he will come home, but that does not keep me from missing him very much until he does."

She heard Ben sniffle again. "I do, too."

"Would you like to lie here with me until I retire?"

"If I do, everyone will think me a baby. Papa asked me to take care of you and Anne while he is away. He said I must be the man of the house until he returns, and I do not wish him to know I failed."

"Ben, no one could ever mistake you for a baby, and I believe that keeping me company is an excellent way of caring for me. And you must believe me when I say that you could never disappoint your father or me."

Ben snuggled even closer. "Then, I shall be glad to stay with you, Mama."

They talked for what seemed an hour before sleep finally overtook Bennet. As Elizabeth carried him back to his bed, she took note of how heavy he was now.

I will not be able to carry you much longer my precious son, but you will always be my baby.

Chapter 15

Windemere Manor

Once he was fully awake and able to eat normally, William quickly progressed from sitting in his bedroom to occupying a chair on the balcony for much of the day. The balcony ran the length of the front of the manor, with each room on that side featuring French doors that opened onto it. To regain his strength, William practised walking the length of the balcony. Though he could barely make one trip down and back the first day, by the fourth, he could easily achieve five rounds. Feeling certain he would be able to go downstairs to the dining room ere long, William was beginning to recover his spirits, although he still could not recall who he was or how he came to be there.

As he was returning to the large chaise situated just outside his bedroom, he noticed movement in the garden below. Scanning the area, he noted that Daniel, a servant who often brought his dinner upstairs, was making his way through a spot almost hidden from sight by dense vegetation. It was only when Daniel stopped that William had a clear view, and he watched as the young man dropped to his knees, removed some rocks, and began digging industriously in the sand. Out of the blue, the sound of Mr. Kelly calling his son broke the silence. Daniel instantly quit what he was doing, recovered the hole, and replaced the rocks. Then, he ran towards his father.

William thought it strange, but from the beginning, he had found Daniel an odd fellow. He seldom spoke and would not meet William's eyes whenever he tried to engage him in conversation. It was obvious that Daniel was slow-witted, but William noted that he did whatever job was assigned to him well and with no complaints.

Sinking into the soft cushions of the chaise once again, William's thoughts flew to more pressing things. For one thing, he felt certain that the clothes he had on were not the kind he would have chosen for himself. He understood they were not his, for Mrs. Grubbs had said he washed ashore with nothing but the clothes on his back, which were cut off to facilitate caring for him. She confessed to fetching items belonging to her late husband—clothes she felt certain would fit him. She had been correct in that assumption, for they were fashioned for a man close to his height and weight; however, catching sight of himself in a mirror, William could not help but believe he would have dressed differently than Mr. Grubbs.

A small voice within spoke. *But since you have no idea who you are, how do you know what you would have worn?*

Before he had time to ponder that, Mrs. Grubbs walked onto the balcony holding her child. She had begun spending more time with him since he was recovering and often brought the boy along. William was beginning to think she was trying to make him feel comfortable around the blond-haired boy, and that day proved no different, for she sat down on a chaise next to his, with the child in her lap.

"Good afternoon, sir. I was hoping you might like to take tea with me today. If you like, we could enjoy it here on the balcony."

Having no reason to refuse, William replied, "Of course."

"Excellent! When I put David down for his nap, I shall inform Mrs. Kelly to serve tea here."

The child climbed from his mother's lap onto the chaise with William, eventually settling in his lap. An image stirred within him, and William recalled another little boy who had sat in his lap, only this one had dark hair.

Could I have children of my own?

Cecile unhurriedly intervened, pulling the child back into her lap, saying, "Come, David. Do not disturb our guest, for he is not fully recovered yet."

When William did not reply, Cecile added, "A penny for your thoughts."

"I… I am sorry. I seem to recall a little boy sitting in my lap, only he had dark hair."

She pasted on an insincere smile. "How wonderful! Have you recalled anything else?"

"No. This is the first I have remembered."

"I am certain you will recall more as time passes." Standing up with David, she added, "I shall leave and return in time for tea."

Once alone again, William tried his best to recall who the dark-haired, little boy might be, but he could not. Frustrated, he closed his eyes and, being tired, was soon nodding off to sleep.

Ballyneen

Worried about his wife, Matthew now spent most of his time close by her side. When Georgiana was not asleep, she could be found walking the garden paths surrounding the manor, crying quietly. Though he often reminded her of the child she was carrying, nothing seemed to reach her, and he was growing more worried with each passing day.

After walking with Georgiana that morning, Matthew had returned his wife to her bedroom and was coming down the grand staircase in search of his aunt just as a footman answered the door. He was totally taken aback when Georgiana's cousin walked into the house.

"Richard!" Matthew said and walked forward to shake his hand. "I would say it is a pleasure to see you again, but with all that has happened, I have to believe your presence here is because you bring more unwelcome news."

"Then evidently you are aware that Darcy is missing and was listed as a passenger on the *Endeavour*."

"I am and, more importantly, so is Georgiana. Moreover, we have reason to suspect my sister was also aboard that ship."

"I am deeply sorry to hear that. How is my cousin faring?"

Cautiously glancing up at the landing, Matthew said, "Let us go into the parlour so that Georgiana cannot hear us."

Once they were inside that room and the door was closed, he continued. "My wife is not well at all. Because she is increasing, she is trying to hold herself together. Still, she is finding it hard not to grieve. She cries continuously."

"Georgie is with child? I had no idea."

"We only learned of it ourselves right before we were set to sail to Liverpool. We had tickets to travel right after the storm, but upon learning of the *Endeavour's* fate, all trips were cancelled. We were advised to return home and await further news. Besides that, the physician in Belfast insisted that Georgiana not sail until she was further along in her pregnancy."

"If I may ask, why were you sailing to Liverpool?"

"We were headed to Pemberley. I thought it would help Georgiana if she saw her family. She had been writing to her brother and when his letters stopped, she was convinced he must be on his way here. When days passed without any sign of Fitzwilliam and no subsequent letters, she began to worry in earnest."

"I see."

"I am surprised, however, that you came so far just to tell us the news."

"Actually, that is not my purpose in coming to Ireland. I promised Elizabeth that I would find Darcy." At Matthew's raised brows, he quickly added, "She believes he is still alive, and I hope to prove her right."

"Will that not just give her false hope?"

"Call it what you may, she believes it, and in my heart, I want to believe it. I told her I would do my best to prove whether he did or did not perish when the ship sank. I decided to trace his intended journey in order to do that. When I got to Belfast, I spoke to the manager of Watson's Freight Service's office there. He told me a Mr. Edgeworth had been placed in charge of categorizing what washed ashore in Donaghadee."

"Yes, I read that the locals there reported items had washed ashore."

"In any case, I travelled to Donaghadee to talk with Edgeworth and discovered something that did give me hope."

"Oh?"

"Yes. It seems the items that washed ashore did not belong to the *Endeavour*, but to another ship, the *Venture*, which was a Scottish freight hauler that sank during the same storm."

Matthew sighed. "I do not see how that could inspire hope."

"I spoke to several old salts who were working the wreckage. They have sailed these seas for years and they speculate that the *Endeavour* may have sunk closer to the Isle of Man, which means that if there were any survivors, they might have been able to ride the tide back to the island. They contend the tide that night was to the east and would have taken any flotsam in that direction."

"But there have been no reports of items washing ashore in that area, have there?"

"Not that I know of, but if someone was to wash ashore on a deserted section of the Isle of Man, or even the Calf of Man, which is nearby, no one would know until—"

"Forgive me for being a naysayer," Matthew interrupted, "but that seems highly unlikely."

"It may be. Still, it is all I have to cling to at present, and I choose to believe it possible."

"What will you tell Georgiana? I do not wish to get her hopes up if …"

"If what?" Georgiana said, making her presence known. She had slipped inside the room and was standing with hands on her hips, glancing from one man to the other.

"Sweetheart," Matthew said, rising and going towards her. "Richard has been telling me of his search for your brother."

"I heard that much." Addressing Richard, she said, "I may be heart-broken, Cousin, but I am a woman, not a child to be protected. Please tell me all that you have discovered about Brother."

Glancing at Matthew to discern his thoughts on the matter, when he nodded, Richard repeated everything he had shared with her husband. Afterwards, Georgiana walked over to a sofa and slowly sank down into the cushions without saying a word. She looked to be deep in thought, and the men were exchanging worried glances when she finally deigned to speak.

"I should like to go with you."

Matthew and Richard simultaneously began to argue why that was not a good idea, with her cousin having the last word. "In your delicate condition, I cannot possibly agree to take you with me. What I will do is promise to keep you informed whilst I pursue every possibility."

Aware she was not going to win the argument, Georgiana finally nodded in agreement, though she was clearly unhappy. "I suppose I have no choice but to trust you to do as you say."

"You have always been able to trust me, and you still can."

"When do you intend to leave Ireland?" Matthew asked.

"I return to Belfast tomorrow morning, and as soon as I can ar-range passage aboard a ship, I intend to sail to the Isle of Man."

Matthew walked over to stand behind his wife. Placing a gentle hand on either shoulder, he said, "Then let us celebrate having your company for tonight. I imagine that with your travels, you have not had much chance to enjoy a hot bath, so I will order one prepared. Then you can rest before dinner is served."

"I would welcome that."

As Richard rose to leave the room, Georgiana called out. "Wait!" When he turned around, she jumped up and ran into his arms crying. "I am sorry. I forgot to say how relieved I am to see you. I love you so much, and I appreciate all you are doing to recover Brother."

As he hugged her, Richard patted her back. "I know, Poppet. I love you, too." Then he pulled back to look into her eyes. "Promise me that you will try not to worry. That will not be good for you or the little one."

"I promise," Georgiana said, sniffling.

Belfast

As Lady Selina Grey walked into the office of Watson's Freight Services, she was surprised to see Colonel Fitzwilliam ahead of her at the counter. He had his back to her, and she listened as he chatted with the manager whilst simultaneously booking a passage on the next ship leaving Belfast.

"I am sorry you were unable to discover anything regarding your cousin in Donaghadee," the man behind the counter stated as he wrote Richard's information on a ticket.

"That may be a blessing in disguise," Richard replied.

"I pray it turns out to be," the man answered. Finished writing, he looked up to address Richard. "You understand that this ship is sailing to the Isle of Man first, do you not? It will dock there for two days to unload freight before sailing on to Liverpool. Will that suit?"

"That will work out perfectly. I wish to follow a hunch on the Isle."

"Excellent." The manager pulled a stamp from a drawer and stamped the ticket paid on front and back before sliding it across the counter. "The ship is set to leave tomorrow morning at seven o'clock. Do not be late, or you may have to wait four or five days for another going in that direction."

"I will be here. You can count on that." As Richard turned to leave, he was placing the ticket inside his coat pocket and did not see Lady Selina until he practically ran into her.

"Excuse me!" Suddenly realising who the beautiful woman was, he smiled. "Lady Selina, what a coincidence! What are you doing in Belfast?"

"The same as you, it seems," she replied. "I came here looking for Noel."

"And did you have any luck?"

Her smile faded, and Richard thought he saw tears shining in her eyes as she replied, "None at all. I travelled all the way to Dungannon, praying that he had made it that far; however, his relations informed me most rudely that he had not. Now, I am here to book passage back to Liverpool via the Isle of Man. I hope to trace my cousin's path elsewhere."

"His relations in Dungannon were not at all upset to learn he is missing?"

"I can say with authority that they were only upset to hear that he was planning on visiting them." She sighed heavily. "I would give anything if I had been wrong about their character, but I was not. They would not have welcomed Noel even had he made it that far." Pulling a handkerchief from a pocket in her gown, she dabbed at her eyes. "Forgive me, Colonel. I told myself I would not cry again over those worthless people."

With two fingers Richard lifted her chin tenderly. "What say you to spending the rest of the day with me? I need to tour a distillery that Darcy's neighbour in Derbyshire wanted him to invest in before all this uproar started. For my own satisfaction, I wish to know if it would have been a good investment or a trap to have Darcy invest in a pig in a poke."

Lady Selina could not suppress a smile at the term.

"Whilst we are out and about, we shall have something to eat and see the local landmarks before we must return. You are staying at the Belfast Inn, are you not?"

"I am, and you have made me an offer I cannot refuse, Colonel. I am certain you will not mind if my maid accompanies us. She is waiting in my carriage."

Disappointed that they would not be entirely alone, he said, "Of course not. She is welcome."

"Excellent! Just let me book a passage, and I shall join you."

"Take all the time you need."

Belfast Distillery

Long before their carriage stopped in front of the distillery, it became obvious from the repairs needed to the outside of the building that this once profitable enterprise had seen better days.

As he helped Lady Selina out of the carriage, Richard jested, "I believe someone has been drinking up the profits instead of taking care of the business."

As she turned to take in the building, Lady Selina agreed. "It does not present as a profitable enterprise. Let us hope the inside is an improvement."

Richard was already turning the knob to the front door, which proved to be locked. "That is bizarre. What business keeps the front door locked during the middle of the day?"

A loud noise from somewhere behind the building prompted him to say, "Wait here whilst I see if anyone is about the premises."

As he rounded the side of the building, Richard found two men unloading a wagon full of apples. They were so busy they did not see him until he spoke.

"Is one of you the manager of the distillery?"

Both men stopped shovelling apples into a bin, and the oldest one said, "Who wants to know?"

"I am Colonel Fitzwilliam, an officer in His Majesty's army. My cousin had been offered a partnership in this distillery, and he asked me to inspect it whilst I was in Belfast."

Both men laughed. Then, the older one continued. "Only a fool would purchase it now that we are near to shutting down due to the blight!"

"I have not heard of a blight," Richard replied.

"Aye, and you will not if some have their way. It would send the public into a panic and plunge many businesses into bankruptcy; therefore, we are not supposed to say anything about it."

"Yet you have."

"Only because it will soon be known far and wide."

"If there is a blight, where did you get those apples?"

"These few apples were shipped in from Scotland. You can tell they are not of the best quality, so they could not be used for cider; however, they will not even be enough to make our usual quota of vinegar. After they are gone, who knows if, or when, we will get another shipment. Whoever bought the distillery just months ago has been shipping in only enough apples to keep the distillery open, but not enough to keep it viable in the long run. I know, for I am the manager, and Sam here is one of only two employees I have left."

"I appreciate your honesty," Richard said. "Many people would not have told me."

"I am not one to lie. Besides, I will be out of a job as soon as the blight becomes common knowledge."

"I hope you find work with someone who appreciates your honesty."

"Thank you, Colonel."

With that, Richard returned to Lady Selina, and they quit the premises. After the carriage turned to head back to the city square, Lady Selina said, "Why would a neighbour try to trick your cousin into making a bad investment?"

"I have no idea, but I intend to discover the truth once I see that villain again. Moreover, I hope to discover who bought the distillery recently. They had to know it was faltering and must have played some part in this sordid game."

"I agree. Who buys a distillery, yet does nothing to make it profitable?"

"Only someone with an ulterior motive."

Lady Selina sighed. "I do hate that the distillery mystery adds another burden to your shoulders. I cannot help but worry that you carry too much already."

Richard smiled. "I could say the same about you. I do not know many women who would take on the task of finding a lost cousin."

Lady Selina returned his smile. "It seems we are birds of a feather, Colonel."

"And what a fine flock we present."

"Indeed!"

Chapter 16

Aboard a ship
One day later

The sea had been mostly calm since leaving Belfast, which was a great relief to Lady Selina. She was neither superstitious nor fearful of sailing, even though the sinking of the *Endeavour* was never far from her thoughts; however, sleep was not to be had. The moon was full, providing enough light to create an ethereal scene that beckoned her on deck.

She hoped that watching the waves and feeling the sway of the ship might lure her into the arms of Morpheus, but by the time she was dressed, the waves had grown fiercer. Catching the watchful eye of the captain, Mr. Gaston, as she approached the railing, she recognised by the piercing look he gave her that he would rather she had stayed in her cabin.

In truth, sleep had evaded her after she left Houghton Park in search of Noel. A particularly hearty spray of seawater suddenly battered the spot where she stood, causing her to catch her breath and quickly back away from the railing. Simultaneously, footsteps behind her announced she was not alone. Turning, she found her travelling companion.

"Colonel, I see you cannot sleep, either."

"No, I cannot."

"Tell me," she said, "do you think that what we desire—to find our loved ones—is a hopeless task?"

"Whether or not it is, I do not think either of us is willing to accept they are gone forever without doing our level best to ascertain the truth."

Lady Selina nodded. "Not knowing is the worst, and I can only imagine how hard it must be for Mrs. Darcy, with two small children asking where their Papa is."

"Did I tell you she is expecting another child in six months?" At the shocked look on the lady's face, Richard added, "I learned of that when I went to Pemberley to tell Elizabeth that Darcy was missing."

"That poor woman!" Seeing the anguish on Richard's face, Lady Selina comforted him by gripping his hand. "And that makes it even harder for you. It is evident that you love your cousin and his family very much."

Richard swallowed hard before he answered. "The only way I can go on is to focus on finding Darcy and believing that I shall." He sighed heavily. "I must."

"I know exactly how you feel."

A sudden dip of the bow of the boat sent Lady Selina reeling, and Richard pulled her into his arms to keep her from falling. Surprisingly, after the ship righted itself, Lady Selina made no move to leave his embrace.

When at last she stepped away, she tried to make light of what had happened. "I believe I should return to my cabin lest I wash overboard!"

"I shall be glad to escort you ... just to be certain that does not happen."

London
Matlock House
A drawing room

Whilst sitting with his foot elevated on a cushioned footstool, Lord Matlock discussed with his wife the latest post they had received from Richard regarding his search for William. Unprepared for visitors, the earl was upset when his butler suddenly entered the room.

"Lady Catherine de Bourgh, my lord."

Lord Matlock groaned aloud. "First gout, and now this!"

"Hush," hissed his wife from where she sat across from him. "Catherine will hear you, and that will result in another argument."

"Frankly, Eleanor, I do not care!"

Not concerned with whether or not she would be received, Lady Catherine was right on the heels of the butler. Aware that she had heard everything, Lady Matlock rose, nodded to her sister, and quit the room without a word. That left his cantankerous sister to focus all her attention on Lord Matlock.

"You do not care about what?" Lady Catherine croaked as she halted in front of her brother, thumping her ever-present cane on the floor. "Speak up!"

"Nothing that concerns you, Catherine," Lord Matlock replied. "You will forgive me for not rising, but the gout in my toe prevents it."

"If you would not drink so heavily, you would not have gout!"

Ignoring her counsel, the earl said, "What brings you here today? I have not heard a word from you since …" He looked as though he was trying to recall. "Since dear Anne's funeral."

"Yes. Well, it seems you are about to attend another funeral."

"I should have known that you would travel all this way just to gloat over what may have happened to Darcy," Lord Matlock said dryly.

"*May* have happened? Are you mad? If one is to believe the ship's passenger list, he was aboard the *Endeavour.*"

"Richard is not certain about that. In fact, he writes that he is investigating further. Not surprisingly, however, you felt it necessary to come here to demean the boy whilst he is not here to defend himself."

"If you ask me, Fitzwilliam demeaned himself and our family by marrying that harlot! And it is my belief that the fool drowned whilst on a mission to settle Georgiana's marital troubles. I tried to warn him that Viscount Hayworth was not what he appeared to be. His family is atrocious, and rumour is that his father has lost control of his own daughter. It appears she has run off with his steward. I am not surprised there is already trouble in Georgiana's marriage."

"If you demean Darcy again, I shall have you tossed from the house." Once Catherine's face had settled into a barely controlled scowl, he continued. "And you have no proof that Georgiana has any marital problems."

"All the proof I need is knowing that Darcy would not run off to Ireland so soon after Georgiana's wedding *unless* there was some problem she could not solve on her own. You and I both know that he would never be parted from *that*—from his *lover* for so long a time unless it was crucial to saving his sister's marriage."

"This is your last warning. Eleanor and I admire Elizabeth, and I will not hear anymore slights against her, either."

"If my hunch is correct, you may not feel that way about her much longer."

"What are you insinuating?"

"Only that I have heard from those who know that she takes lovers whenever Fitzwilliam is not at home. They say the daughter she bore is not even his."

Lord Matlock barked a laugh, though his ire was rising. "You will have to do better than that if you want to cast aspersions on my niece. Both of Fitzwilliam's children are the spitting image of their father."

"I intend to prove everything I say. After that, if you are truly the head of this family, you will take control of Pemberley for the sake of the heir and toss that chit out on the streets." With that, Lady Catherine stomped towards the door, again taking her frustration out on the marble floors with her cane.

"Leaving so soon?" Lord Matlock called after her.

Lady Catherine stopped and turned to face him. "I am, but I shall return soon with irrefutable proof. When I do, you will apologise for your attitude towards me."

"Do not hold your breath," Lord Matlock murmured as she stalked out the door.

Derbyshire
Parkleigh Manor

Upon deciding he would hold his ace—confessing all to Lord Matlock if Lady Catherine continued to press him to ruin Elizabeth Darcy—Gregory Wright returned to his estate several days later. If he were to have any chance of securing Elizabeth as his wife in the future, it was imperative to call and express his sincere condolences regarding her husband's untimely demise.

Whilst he had not wished for Darcy to die, he would not let the chance of making a good impression on Darcy's widow pass. After all, he was in the perfect position to insinuate himself into her life, since Jonathan and Bennet were the best of friends, and he was not above using his son to accomplish his purpose.

As Wright inspected his appearance in the floor-to-ceiling mirror in his dressing room, his valet suddenly appeared at the door.

"Sir, you asked me to tell you when your son was ready to leave. The nanny has Jonathan dressed, and he awaits you in the nursery."

"Thank you, Gaines."

Running a hand through his hair in a bid to make it lie down, he headed to the nursery.

Pemberley

As Adams went through his employer's closet once more, he prayed to find at least one item of clothing that required repair. He needed to keep busy to avoid thinking of what had occupied his mind constantly since the sinking of the *Endeavour*.

Mr. Darcy is dead. NO! There is a possibility that he lives!

Or was there? With each day that passed, Adams' faith waned a little more, and now he was not as certain that Mrs. Darcy was correct that his friend would return.

His friend? In truth, not only was Fitzwilliam Darcy his employer, but through the years, they had truly become friends.

"There you are!" he heard a small voice say. He looked down to find Bennet standing beside him.

Making a concerted effort to smile, Adams squatted down to Bennet's level. "What can I do for you, Master Bennet?"

The boy held out the shirt Adams had given him the night he wished to sleep with something belonging to his father. "I would like you to put more of Papa on this shirt," Ben answered sheepishly.

"Of course!" Adams replied more enthusiastically than he felt. "I can remedy that quite easily."

Crossing to the dresser where a tray with various items stood, he removed the stopper from a bottle of cologne and dashed several drops on the shirt before handing it back to Bennet. "How is that?"

Burying his face in the shirt, Bennet took a deep breath and smiled. "Now it smells like Papa." Then his expression turned pensive. "What makes it smell so good?"

"I believe sandalwood is the main ingredient."

"What is that?"

"As I understand it, it is a tree that grows in India, and the oil from it is used to make cologne, as well as for other purposes."

"I am glad that it reminds me of Papa."

"As am I, Master Bennet."

"Do you think Cousin Richard will find Papa?"

The question made Adams pause, for he did not know how to answer honestly. "I pray every day that Colonel Fitzwilliam finds him soon," he murmured.

Bennet's voice broke as he said, "I miss him."

"I know you do. I miss him, too," Adams replied, gently ruffling Bennet's hair.

Suddenly, the housekeeper opened the bedroom door. "Mrs. Darcy is looking for you, young man," Mrs. Reynolds said, smiling at Bennet. "Come with me, and I shall take you to your mother."

After Bennet followed Mrs. Reynolds from the room, a disheartened Adams sat down on the bed. *How will that child ever recover if his father does not return?*

The thought of William being lost to his children and wife was too painful to dwell on, so Adams forced himself to shake off the thought. *I must believe he will return, for my sake as well as theirs.*

Spying a pair of William's boots beside the wardrobe, he picked them up and headed towards the dressing room to give them another polishing.

Aboard ship

As Richard lay on the narrow bed in his cabin, arms beneath his head, he was lost in the memory of how good it felt to hold Lady Selina in his arms. If he were not mistaken, she had felt something, as well. After all, she had not attempted to break away from his embrace when the boat righted; instead, she had stayed in his arms as though that was where she wished to be.

It had been years since he had even kissed a woman because he was in no position to entertain thoughts of marriage and a family of his own, and he would never raise expectations he could not fulfil.

Nonetheless, there was hope. The steward at the small estate in Derbyshire that he inherited from his grandmother was working to increase its income sufficiently to allow him to retire from the army.

Perhaps in two years' time I shall be able to pursue a wife.

Instead of that thought helping him to relax, his weary mind played it repeatedly until at long last he blew out a deep breath, sat up on the side of the bed and chastised himself.

You cannot focus on getting better acquainted with Lady Selina, no matter how much she appeals to you. Instead, you must keep your wits about you if you intend to find Darcy!

Knowing that her memory would not fade without help, he reached under the bed and pulled out a small satchel. Rifling through the bag, he found what he was looking for: a small bottle of whiskey. Taking several swallows, he placed it back in the bag and pushed it under the bed. Then, falling onto his pillow, he prayed that he might get a few hours of sleep before daylight.

Pemberley

As Judith Green and Elizabeth sat in the swing watching Bennet, Anne and Clancy play near the fishpond, the rector's wife surreptitiously watched her friend for any signs of despondency. It seemed Elizabeth was trying too hard to be the cheerful woman she had always been.

Reaching to take Elizabeth's hand, she leaned close to whisper, "You know that you do not have to pretend with me."

Out of the blue, Elizabeth's smile vanished, and her chin began to quiver. Before Mrs. Green could even react, a handkerchief gripped tightly in Elizabeth's other hand flew up to cover her mouth, stifling a sob.

"I ... I cannot lie," Elizabeth began to say before biting her bottom lip. "I am constantly on the brink of collapse. Oh, I still believe God has kept William safe, and he is alive, but waiting to hear from him is torture. Still, I must stay strong for the children. Ben, especially, looks to me for reassurance that his father will come home, so I cannot let him see me cry. And my sweet Anne is too young to realise anything is amiss; however, when Ben speaks of William, as he often does, she looks to me with those big, innocent eyes and says, 'Papa home?' It is almost more than I can bear."

Elizabeth wept quietly into her handkerchief as Judith slipped an arm around her shoulder. "If it would help, I could stay with the children for a little while to give you a respite. Perhaps if you visited your family—"

Elizabeth shook her head vigorously. "No, I will not leave Pemberley. I will be right here when William returns. Besides, the children are all that keep me from going mad."

Suddenly, a man on horseback came riding around the corner of the house. The women exchanged glances, for both suspected they knew who it was before they could see him properly. Fortunately for Mr. Wright, he had brought Jonathan with him, and the child was a more welcome guest. Bennet had caught sight of his friend and was already running towards the swing, whilst Anne, who was playing with Clancy, was still unaware of the visitors.

Shading her eyes with a hand, Elizabeth looked up at her neighbour. "Mr. Wright, what brings you to Pemberley?"

Gregory Wright dismounted, placing Jonathan on the ground. Bennet instantly asked his playmate to follow him to the fishpond, and Wright watched as his son followed Darcy's. Then, assuming a sombre expression, he removed his hat and turned to answer Elizabeth.

"I came because I heard the news, and I wish to express my condolences on the loss of your husband. I know how hard it is to raise a child without your spouse, and I would not wish that on anyone. I could not have asked for a better friend than Darcy, and I shall miss him and his wise counsel regarding Parkleigh Manor."

"I thank you for all the sentiments, Mr. Wright, but it is too soon to speak as though my husband is lost."

Wright appeared stunned. Looking to Mrs. Green as though expecting her to explain, when she said nothing, he murmured, "I … I apologise if I am mistaken. I heard the news of his death in Town. In fact, it came directly from Mr. Darcy's aunt, Lady Catherine de Bourgh."

Annoyed, Elizabeth looked away. "Of course. She would be eager to come to London and spread the news of his demise to all who would care to hear of it."

"Forgive me if I offended you. I merely meant to express my sincere condolences and to bring Jonathan to play with Bennet. I hoped he might—well, I hoped that playing with Jonathan might raise Bennet's spirits. Have you heard anything from Darcy?"

"Not yet," Elizabeth replied. "But Colonel Fitzwilliam is searching for him."

"I am sure you mean well, Mr. Wright," the rector's wife interjected, "and I am certain that Mrs. Darcy appreciates your kindness."

This prompted Elizabeth to recall her manners. "Yes. Yes, I do. You were kind to think of us. And it is evident that Bennet is glad to have Jonathan here to play with. Will you allow him to stay until this evening? That will give them both time to work off some energy and sleep well tonight." Unsaid was the fact that Jonathan was to stay whilst *he* was to leave.

"If that is your wish, I should be glad to let Jonathan play until dark."

"I would like that very much."

"I suppose I should get back to my estate." Silence reigned. "I have just returned from London, and there is a stack of letters a foot high waiting for me in the study."

"Then, do not let us keep you," Elizabeth replied.

After the gentleman had ridden out of sight, Elizabeth said, "Perhaps I should have been more gracious and asked him to stay for tea, but that man gets on my nerves. I cannot help but feel he is a vulture waiting to step into William's shoes."

"I would argue with you," Mrs. Green replied, "but after observing him since your husband left for Ireland, I feel you may be right. Not that I can blame him for falling in love with someone as wonderful as you … although he should be ashamed of trying to catch the eye of a married woman."

"He is wasting his time," Elizabeth declared. "I have given it a lot of thought. If God were to take William from me, I would never marry again. No man will ever take his place in my heart, and it would be a lie to make vows to another that I cannot keep."

Judith Green squeezed her hand. "You and Fitzwilliam certainly have a fierce kind of love."

"God has blessed us with a forever love," Elizabeth murmured quietly.

Suddenly, interrupted by the children's shouts, they turned to see

Clancy chasing a duck through the fishpond, with Bennet and Jonathan following right behind the little, white terror.

Elizabeth laughed. "William has tried so hard to teach Clancy not to chase the ducks and to teach Bennet not to chase after Clancy when he does."

"Somehow, I think that once Fitzwilliam returns, he will find it hilarious when you tell him how miserably he has failed on both counts."

Elizabeth hugged her dear friend. "That is what I love about you. You know my husband so well!"

Chapter 17

Windemere Manor

After spending the morning on the balcony outside his bedroom, William realised the only people he had seen thus far that day were the housekeeper and a maid. Therefore, when Mrs. Kelly brought up a tray of food around midday, he enquired, "May I ask if Mrs. Grubbs is well? Usually, I see her before this hour each day."

Instantly, the smile on the housekeeper's face disappeared. "Captain Boone, who has always delivered supplies from the big island, arrived early this morning. The mistress had business to conduct in Port Erin with her solicitor; therefore, she decided to sail back to the Isle of Man with him. She should be gone only a few days."

"She left without saying a word to me," William stated irritably. "I wish I had known she was going to the big island, for I would have liked to have accompanied her. Perhaps there, someone would know who I am."

"Mrs. Grubbs feared you would insist on going, and she did not think you well enough to travel. She worried you might suffer a relapse by trying to do too much too soon; consequently, she purposely said nothing before leaving."

"I should have been allowed to decide what is best for me!" he huffed.

Mrs. Kelly quickly began tidying the table that held the tray in a bid to leave. "I am sorry you feel that way, but I must say I agree with Mrs. Grubbs. Even after only a few turns on the balcony, you practically collapse in that chair from exhaustion. You are not in any shape to go on a trip."

William rolled his eyes at her assertion but was too angry to reply. Consequently, Mrs. Kelly soon quit the room.

Once alone, a thought occurred to him. *Daniel mentioned feeding horses, so there should be one I could borrow to explore the island. Perhaps now is as good a time as any since no one is here to stop me.*

The Isle of Man
Port of St. Mary
The next day

Richard stood on deck as the ship approached the harbour at Port of St. Mary[9] in the southern portion of the Isle of Man. Always an early riser, after Darcy's disappearance he felt fortunate to get even three hours of sleep a night, and last night had proven no exception. Though he had been awake since the early morning hours, by the time he decided to go above deck, the sun was rising.

Spying Richard, Captain Gaston walked over to stand beside him. "At dinner last night, Lady Selina mentioned that you were on a quest to find your cousin who may have gone down with the *Endeavour*. I have not made my conjectures widely known, but I believe we may have passed near where that ship sank—if one takes into account their route."

Stunned at the revelation, Richard murmured, "Truly?"

"Yes. At one point that evening, the weather became so grave I thought we might go down as well." The captain looked out on the water as though recalling the event. "I had never experienced a storm of that magnitude in all my years at sea." He shivered before continuing. "In any case, I recall seeing some flotsam in the water—not much, mind you—but it was all we could do to stay afloat, and there was no way we could have retrieved it."

"Do you recall where you saw the flotsam?"

"Keep in mind we were being tossed about and were far off course, but I would conjecture that it was closer to the Isle of Man than the shores of Ireland, as was reported in the newspapers."

"Did you report your observations to anyone in authority?"

"I did, but my employer was certain the *Endeavour* went down near Donaghadee and did not wish to hear otherwise." Glancing to Richard, he added, "I am sorry that I cannot be of more help. I lost my

---

[9] *Port St. Mary is a village district in the southwest of the Isle of Man. The village takes its name from the former Chapel of St. Mary which is thought to have overlooked Chapel Bay in the village. In the 19th century, it was sometimes called Port-le-Murray, but for this story, I shall refer to it as Port of St. Mary. Wikipedia*

youngest brother at sea, and I know how something of that nature can haunt you."

"If it were not for my cousin's wife and children, I might be able to accept that Darcy is gone. Elizabeth Darcy, however, is positive he still lives, so I have pledged myself to make certain one way or the other. After speaking to the man in charge of investigating the items that washed ashore at Donaghadee, I am convinced that wreckage was not part of the *Endeavour*."

"So that is why you are here? You think someone on the Isle of Man might have seen something wash ashore?"

Richard sighed heavily. "If I can say truthfully that I could find no trace of my cousin, then I will have done my duty to my family."

"I understand. Might I suggest that because we will be in Port of St. Mary two days before we sail on to Douglas, you hire a carriage and travel west to Port Erin today. The fishing vessels that sail off the western coast will be more likely to have news regarding anything washing up on this end of the Isle."

"Thank you for the suggestion. I shall head to Port Erin the minute we dock. I can spend the night there, which will give me the rest of today and tomorrow to see what I can find out."

"Think nothing of it." Then, the captain cocked his head. "Do you think Lady Selina will accompany you to Port Erin, seeing that she is looking for her cousin as well?"

"I cannot say, though she and I are both eager for any news of the *Endeavour*. In her case, she feels her relation may have been unlucky enough to have ended up on that ship even though he was not listed as a passenger."

"I think it beneficial that she has someone to escort her about Man, for many in trouble with the law end up on this island. Robberies are commonplace."

"Because we are basically on the same quest, I am glad I can be of service to her."

"Just be sure to return to the ship before we sail to Douglas, or you will be stuck here until you can book passage on another vessel."

"I will try to be punctual."

169

Windemere Manor

As soon as he awoke, William rang for a servant and informed the maid who responded that his stomach was out of sorts and that some buttered toast and tea would be all he would eat until the matter settled itself. After Mrs. Kelly brought up the toast and tea, he told her that he planned to lie in bed all day and asked not to be disturbed until he rang for a servant. The housekeeper hastily retreated from the room as though afraid she might catch whatever illness he had.

William proceeded to eat the toast and drink the tea quickly. Then, grabbing two apples from a bowl of fruit, he stuffed them into his pockets before proceeding to sneak out of the house via the staircase at the end of the hall and the back entrance to the manor. He knew the direction of the stables since Daniel always headed to the left of the manor whenever Mrs. Grubbs suggested he check on the animals.

Feeling weaker the farther he walked, William stopped every so often to rest as he made his way towards the stables. Upon seeing the building in the distance, however, his elation quickly dampened when a thin, older man letting the horses into a paddock spied him. Knowing he must convince the servant to obey his wishes, William instantly assumed an air of authority when he reached the paddock.

"Mrs. Grubbs said I might borrow a horse to ride whilst she is away. Which one do you recommend?"

After eyeing him for a time, the wizened old groom seemed to accept his presence there. "You must be the one what washed up on shore after the storm—the one what cannot recall his name."

"It appears Daniel has told you all about me."

"Daniel talks a lot, but he is harmless," the man replied. "I would choose the bay if I was you. He is not as young or spirited as the black and, from what else Daniel said, you have been mostly off your feet since you got here."

"That is true; however, I wish to resume riding and thought today would be a good day to begin."

"Follow me then, and I will saddle him." As they walked inside the stable, the servant asked, "Did the mistress explain that no one is allowed near the docks on the opposite side of the island?"

Recalling that Mrs. Grubbs mentioned her late husband and Captain Silverhill had constructed warehouses beside the docks and declared them off-limits to anyone else, William nodded in acquiescence. "She did, but I have to wonder how Captain Boone delivers supplies to the docks with no problem."

"Oh, Captain Silverhill bows to Mrs. Grubbs wishes 'bout that. Still, he does not like Captain Boone ignoring his orders, and Silverhill is not someone you want to cross, you know. He has at least two men staying in the house on the cliffs. They watch the warehouses and are dangerous."

"I will keep that in mind."

Never one to be intimidated, once William had ridden as far as the cliffs overlooking the docks, he dismounted and tied his horse to a tree. Walking over to the edge of a rocky formation to examine what was below, he was stunned to catch sight of a woman and a man, both with hands tied behind their backs, being marched into a cave by a man with a rifle.

Stunned, he instantly dropped to the ground, lest he be seen. He was uncertain what to do next. After all, he was not only unarmed, but he knew nothing about what happened on this side of the island. From what he had witnessed, he wondered, too, if Mrs. Grubbs had any idea. No matter the reason, it was obvious the couple was being held against their will.

Troubled, but unable to do anything until he could arm himself, William determined to go back to the manor and find a weapon. Then, God willing, he would work his way down to where the prisoners were being held and learn what he could.

As the passengers departed the ship, Richard guided Lady Selina to one side of the dock so they could speak in private.

"I have decided to go straight to Port Erin. Captain Gaston advised me that if anything washed ashore from the *Endeavour*, it would more likely have been found there."

"I wish to go with you."

Richard smiled. "You are aware that you may be exposing yourself to gossip if our joint trips to unearth information become common knowledge?"

She smiled wryly. "Even though my maid is always at my side?"

"I fear that may carry little weight."

"I am thirty years old. I own my own estate, and I have money enough that I need not depend on a man ever again," she answered saucily. "Should my reputation become fodder for the *ton,* I could not care less."

"Perhaps not, but I had rather not be the source of gossip regarding you."

Seeing that he was serious, Lady Selina instantly became sombre. Grasping his hand, she said, "Richard Fitzwilliam, you are the most kind-hearted and proper gentleman I have ever met, and it was your attitude about your missing cousin that gave me the strength to keep looking for Noel."

Richard stared at his feet. "You are too kind."

"Trust me, I am not being kind; I am merely being honest." She tilted her head, trying to catch his eye. Once she had, she said, "I did not reach thirty without meeting a lot of *so-called* gentlemen. I know a real one when I meet him."

When Richard did not reply, she added, "So, if you will locate a carriage, I shall inform my maid that the three of us are bound for Port Erin."

As she hurried away to fetch her maid, Richard shook his head in wonder. *And you, Lady Selina, are unlike any woman I have ever met.*

Windemere Manor

It was growing dark by the time William crawled back to the treeline where he had left his horse. Beginning to wonder if he could find his way back to the manor once it was completely dark or whether Mrs. Kelly had sent out servants to look for him, he was about to mount the animal when he heard a deep, gravelly voice say, "Well now, what have we here?"

Before he could turn, something hit the back of William's head. Knocked to his knees, as everything turned black, he fell to the ground. Fortunately, this injury was not nearly as grave as his previous one, and he awoke whilst being tugged up some steps by two men. Pretending to be unconscious, once they reached a landing he recognised it as

172

the deck that surrounded the house. Tossed unceremoniously onto his stomach, the men began to argue over his fate.

"Cap'n Silver will be angry that he was snooping around," one man said. "I say we toss him into the water right now!"

The one with the deeper voice appeared to be in charge, for he replied, "Cap'n Silver will have your head if you act without orders. Besides, Mrs. Grubbs knows this man is on the island, for the horse he was riding belongs to her. Cap'n favours that woman, and I just imagine he will not be happy to find out she has another man. He may wonder, too, what else she has been hiding from him. No. We had best wait until the Cap'n returns, and let him deal with the intruder."

The other villain scratched his chin. "Where shall we keep him?"

"With the other hostages. In any event, I do not see any of them being alive in a week or so."

Each grabbed William by an arm to drag him inside the house. Thinking him still unconscious, the youngest said, "You are one lucky bastard! You will be our guest at least until Cap'n Silver returns."

Port Erin
Later that evening

The day had been long and tiring and, even though their trip had proven fruitless, Richard, Lady Selina and her maid were glad to be back in Port Erin. They had driven as far as the road extended on that side of the island and talked to many of the owners of the fishing vessels moored there, though none had reported seeing any debris after the huge storm that sank the *Endeavour*. Nevertheless, several of the captains had suggested the Calf of Man might be a better place to search, as the *Endeavour's* path would have taken it closer to that island.

Having secured rooms at an inn that had a large dining room, as they checked into the inn Richard suggested they all change clothes and meet for dinner in an hour. However, when the time came for dinner, only Lady Selina came downstairs.

As Richard escorted her into the dining room, she said, "My maid is too exhausted to leave the room. I promised to have a tray sent up, so she can eat and rest."

Secretly pleased, Richard replied. "I fear I wore you both out trying to speak to every ship's captain today."

"There is no need to apologise. I did not wish to make another trip tomorrow, either."

Dinner was served promptly, and Lady Selina retired shortly afterwards.

Left on his own, Richard ordered a brandy in the hope that it would help him to sleep. Not long afterwards, he noticed a man who looked familiar sitting alone at another table. His brows furrowed as he tried to recall where he had seen the chap, whilst at the same time the man noticed him and surreptitiously brought a finger to his lips as a sign to be silent. Intrigued, Richard was surprised when the man said something to the maid who brought him a tankard of ale, then rose and walked towards his table.

"Colonel Fitzwilliam," he said, extending a hand, "how good to see you again. Might I join you?"

Richard had stood to shake hands and, after he agreed, both sat down. Glancing about, the stranger said, "You were right to look at me askew. The last time we met I was in uniform."

"Now I recall," Richard replied. "Lieutenant—"

"Please," Lieutenant Donavan motioned with his hands for Richard to speak more quietly. "For now, just call me Donaldson."

"What is this about?"

The lieutenant leaned closer to say, "I am working secretly and do not wish my real name known … at least not yet."

"I see. Do you intend to tell me about your assignment? Otherwise, why acknowledge me?"

"I knew you were too clever not to figure out where you had seen me, and I feared you would call me by name. I felt obligated to explain why I could not respond to that."

"Might I be of service? I am returning to Port of St. Mary tomorrow evening, but I will help however I can until I leave."

"Do you see that table on the left as you enter the dining room—the one with three men and a red-haired lady dressed in blue?"

Richard strained his neck to see over the lieutenant's shoulder. "Yes."

"If my sources are correct, she is Cecile Grubbs, and she owns Windemere Manor, which takes up the better part of the Calf of Man."

"And why is that important?"

"I have reason to believe she is the lover of Captain Silverhill."

"The one who owns the warehouse in Liverpool?" Richard interjected.

"One and the same. Everyone I ask said he brags of having warehouses on the Calf—he was once partners with the redhead's late husband, David Grubbs. Supposedly, Grubbs and Silverhill stored materials there until prices rose and then shipped them to Scotland, Ireland and other ports. They may have had a legitimate business at one time, but the possibility of making more by stealing shipments, even from the navy, was too hard to resist."

"I cannot imagine having the gall to steal from the navy. They will track you until they find you or you die, whichever comes first."

Donavan smiled proudly. "We are persistent. Unfortunately, greed is the downfall of many a man."

"I cannot disagree."

"Would you join me when I introduce myself to the man on her right? Having someone with me may make my presence seem less threatening."

"I shall be glad to. Who is the man you speak of?"

"Captain Boone, an old salt who still sails the waters between here and Liverpool. As I understand it, he was a good friend of David Grubbs' uncle, who left everything to his nephew in his will. Boone continues to ferry supplies to Mrs. Grubbs every month or so. On occasion, she accompanies him back to the Isle to see her solicitor or banker, which I suspect is why she is here now."

"And the other men?"

"Just servants."

Richard nodded. "Whenever you are ready, say the word."

Just remember, I am Mr. Donaldson and, if they ask, we met in Liverpool when you were looking for your cousin who was listed as a passenger on the *Endeavour*. I will let them think I am a merchant interested in having Mr. Boone ship my wares to the Isle of Man."

After introducing himself and Richard to Captain Boone, that gentleman introduced both men to Mrs. Grubbs. Afterward, the lieutenant got straight to the point.

"Mr. Boone, I wished to meet you because I deal in fine leather products, and I am thinking of opening a shop in Port Erin. I will need a ship to deliver my goods from Liverpool to the Isle of Man every two months or so. Your name has been mentioned with excellent references, and I wondered if we might come to an agreement on a price. Naturally, I wish to take a voyage on your vessel before signing any contract."

"I should be glad to discuss the matter, Mr. Donaldson, but right now I am not at my leisure. If you could meet with me after I return Mrs. Grubbs to the Calf of Man, I would be glad to accommodate you."

"Would it be possible for me to sail with you to the Calf and back?"

Mrs. Grubbs instantly interrupted. "I ... I am afraid that is impossible. My late husband's partner in our shipping business does not allow strangers on the island."

"It is not my intent to step foot on the island," Donavan replied. "I only mean to sail to the island and back to test the vessel."

"That is impossible," she replied.

"Very well," the lieutenant declared. "Then, I suppose I shall have to wait and sail with you after you have returned Mrs. Grubbs to her home."

Captain Boone reached into his coat and brought out a card. "This lists the address of my office in the Port of St. Mary. I shall meet you there in a sennight."

Assuming a smile he did not feel, Lieutenant Donavan said, "I look forward to it."

As Richard and the naval officer made their way across the dining room to their table, Donavan whispered, "That did not go as I had hoped. Still, it reinforces my theory that they are hiding something on that island."

"Actually, I am glad that you suggested we meet him," Richard replied stiffly.

Just now comprehending a change in Richard's demeanour, the lieutenant said, "Oh? How so?"

"That young man at the table—the one who seemed oblivious to everyone else—was playing with a very expensive pocket watch in his lap. I could see it simply because he sat directly below me, but I doubt anyone else would have noticed."

"I confess that I did not notice it, but how could a watch make you glad?"

"The watch he kept opening and closing happens to belong to my cousin. I would recognise it anywhere, but most of all because it contains a portrait of his wife Elizabeth. That villain kept opening it to have a look at her."

"I am shocked that you did not snatch it from him!"

"It was all I could do not to take the watch from him and beat him until he confessed how he came to have it; however, like you, I noticed the reluctance of the lady to allow you on the island. No. Though I wish to act swiftly, I must make certain that when I make my move to rescue my cousin, I have enough men along to do the job credibly and still keep him safe."

"Sounds like you need a navy ship to escort you to the island, and men enough to help you search for your cousin."

"I would be eternally grateful for that kind of help, as would my father, the Earl of Matlock. Moreover, I am certain he would reward you handsomely for Darcy's safe return."

Donavan smiled. "The watch alone should be enough evidence to convince Admiral Turlington that I need to invade the island. What say we return to Liverpool as soon as possible and make our case?"

"Tomorrow cannot be too soon."

"Good. My ship is waiting at Port of St. Mary. You can sail back to Liverpool with me, and we can plan an invasion straightaway."

"What about my friend? Lady Selina is looking for her cousin. Together we have been searching for him and Darcy."

"I think it best that she return to Liverpool as previously scheduled. There will be time for you to meet her there before we execute our plan. Hopefully, she will understand that we cannot take a woman along on so dangerous a mission."

Richard shook his head. "You do not know Lady Selina!"

"Then I am glad it will be left to you to tell her."

Chapter 18

London
Matlock House

Lord and Lady Matlock had just finished breaking their fast when their butler entered the breakfast room with a puzzled look on his face. Instantly taking note of his expression, Lord Matlock asked, "What is it, Perkins?"

"One of Lady Catherine's footmen is here, sir." Perkins sniffed haughtily. "He came by way of the alley and says he has some information that he is certain you will want to hear right away."

"Show him to the library, and tell him I will be right there."

With a raised brow, Perkins left to do as ordered, though his expression indicated he considered the matter highly unorthodox.

Even Lady Matlock appeared perplexed at the news of one of Lady Catherine's servants coming to their house. "Since it appears you know, pray tell me why one of Catherine's servants is here to see you?"

"That would be because I had one of our own trusted footmen enquire of one of my sister's footmen if he wished to make an extra schilling by informing me of her comings and goings. I imagine this fellow is here to collect his reward." The earl rose. "Do you wish to join me in hearing what he has to say, my dear?"

"I would not miss it for the world."

The library

Due to the gout in his foot, the earl leaned heavily upon a cane for support as he and Lady Matlock entered the library. They found Lady Catherine's footman, with his hands locked behind his back, staring out one of the floor-to-ceiling windows overlooking Hyde Park. The man was dressed in one of the gaudy uniforms that his sister insisted they wear—black britches beneath red coats with excessive gold trim and epaulets—which made him easily identifiable. However, this one carried a greatcoat which he had apparently tossed over the uniform. With that and his hat pulled low over his forehead, he would be barely recognisable as a servant. Lord Matlock thought it a clever disguise.

"I understand you have some information for me," Lord Matlock declared, causing the man to whirl around and bow clumsily. The earl was not surprised to see he was quite young.

"I-I was told that you wished to know of your sister's travels, especially when she leaves town," the man stuttered.

"Not only when she leaves," Lord Matlock replied, "but I want to know where she is headed."

"She left this morning for Derbyshire, sir."

"And you know she was headed to Derbyshire because—"

"I heard her tell Mr. Sloan—he drives the vehicles. She said that she was off to Derbyshire to right a wrong."

Lord Matlock walked over to a desk and opened a drawer. Retrieving a few coins, he handed them to the footman. "Here is the reward I promised."

The man rocked back on his heels nervously. "Will you wish to know of her whereabouts in the future?"

"Until I tell you to cease, I would be pleased if you continue to keep me informed," Lord Matlock said whilst pulling a cord.

Suddenly, the butler opened the library doors. "Perkins, please show this gentleman out."

As the butler proceeded to do that, the earl added, "Perkins." The servant stopped and waited. "Afterwards, tell Mr. Gibson to prepare the coach for a trip right away, and inform Mr. Nelson to begin packing my trunk. I wish to leave as soon as possible."

"As you wish."

After the others had left the library, Lady Matlock said, "Are you out of your mind? The physician said that until the draught he prescribed causes the gout to recede, you were to rest with your foot upon a stool."

"Dr. Graham has no idea what I must deal with. For now, the gout must rank second in my worries, for if Catherine is going to Derbyshire, I have no doubt she intends to torment Elizabeth. Seeing that Richard has turned up no word on Fitzwilliam yet, she must be out of her mind with worry, and the least I can do is present a united front in support of her. To that end, would you like to accompany me?"

"With enough help, I can be ready to leave in an hour."

"Excellent! I do not want Catherine to get too far ahead of us."

Port of St. Mary

As Richard was preparing to board the naval ship that was to take him to Liverpool, Lady Selina appeared to be forlorn.

Glancing between him and Lieutenant Donavan, she murmured quietly, "I wish I could go with you."

Encouraged, Richard clasped her hands and gave them a soft squeeze. "As do I, but for now I think it best if we do as Donavan asks. It is true that he and I will arrive at Liverpool ahead of you, but that should give me time to convince Admiral Turlington that the navy should help me search the Calf of Man for Darcy before you and I meet again. The admiral might balk if he thought I intended to bring you along, so it is best that you stay out of sight."

Lady Selina looked down. "I know you are right, but I cannot help but feel you have stumbled upon something that may involve more than just your cousin. If they have Mr. Darcy on the island, what is to say they do not have my Noel there."

"Hopefully, we shall know the answer to that question soon. Meanwhile, you can rely on me to let you know what I discover as quickly as possible." When she said nothing, Richard lifted her chin so she had to look him in the eye. "You do believe me."

An errant tear slipped from her eye. "You are the only man I *do* believe." Then, waving a hand in dismissal, she added, "Pay no attention to me. I suppose I am merely melancholy at the thought of splitting up a team as grand as you and I."

Without giving it any thought, Richard said what was in his heart. "If you feel as I do, perhaps once this is over, we might consider remaining a team."

Lady Selina blushed becomingly. "What are you implying, Colonel?"

"I cannot say until this matter is settled, but after I have done my duty to my family, I wish to speak to you about the future."

An expression of adoration crossed her face. "I look forward to hearing what you have to say."

"For now, I need you to take a room at the Crown Inn once you reach Liverpool. I shall meet you there before I leave for the Calf of Man. Just remember. Tell no one—not even your maid—what Lieutenant Donavan and I are planning."

"You may rely on my silence."

"I think that is the first time any woman has ever said that to me," Richard teased.

"I hope it is the first time any woman has had reason to."

He smiled broadly. "It is."

"We need to leave now, Colonel," Lieutenant Donavan declared, interrupting their conversation.

With an awkward glance at the lieutenant, Richard brought one of Lady Selina's hands to his lips for a soft kiss. "We will meet again soon."

"I am counting on that."

Though he wished to seal their understanding with a kiss, Richard knew this was neither the time nor the place, so he turned to follow the lieutenant onboard the ship.

As the vessel began to leave port, he stood on the deck until Port of St. Mary and the woman he had fallen in love with were completely out of sight. A mixture of guilt and joy rushed over him. Guilt that he could feel so happy with his cousin's fate still undetermined, and joy because he had never been in love before. While he hoped discovering Darcy's watch would result in restoring him to his family, a niggling thought kept so simple a solution as that at odds: *Darcy would never have given up his treasured timepiece without a fight.*

Just as he had since the news of Darcy's presence on the ill-fated ship had reached him, Richard instantly pushed that thought to the far recesses of his mind. *I must believe Darcy is alive, else I cannot do this!*

Blinking to keep at bay the tears that almost always filled his eyes at the remembrance of his cousin, Richard drew himself up to his full height, and with sheer willpower, went to find the cabin Lieutenant Donavan had assigned to him.

Calf of Man
On the east side of the island

If not for a window curtain that had been left slightly open, William would have awakened in total darkness. Surprisingly, though he lay on the cold floor with his hands tied in front of him, he did not have to struggle long before managing to sit up.

Once he had, a disembodied male voice spoke out of the darkness. "You have been asleep for so long that we thought you might be near death. Are you well?"

Surveying the room to discover who had spoken, the sliver of light coming through the curtain allowed William to barely make out the form of two people sitting on a sofa across from him.

"Except for being sore from lying on the floor, and stiff from the cold, I imagine I am well enough," William replied. Then, twisting his head and neck to relieve the tight muscles there, he added, "How long have I been in this position?"

A female voice answered, "Since yesterday evening when you were dropped right where you are now. I wish we could have offered you a blanket but, alas, they keep our hands and feet tied when they leave us alone. I am surprised they did not tie your feet as well."

"Might I enquire *who* you are?" William asked.

"I am Noel Stevens of Houghton Park in Leicester," the man answered. "The blackguards who captured you also kidnapped me and Lady Davidson mere days ago in Liverpool. We are being held for ransom."

"Lady Davidson," William repeated.

"Yes. I am Lady Aileen Davidson of Berkley Hall in Southampton," the woman interjected.

"Where have I heard the name Berkley Hall before?" William asked. Searching his mind for an answer, suddenly a memory rushed back. "I have a sister, Georgiana, and she was lately married at Berkley Hall in Southampton."

"Georgiana!" Lady Aileen cried. My brother is Viscount Hayworth, and he recently married Georgiana Darcy. You must be Mr. Darcy, though I would never have known you if I passed you on the street. Your clothes are different, your hair is much longer, and that beard conceals your face!"

William had entirely forgotten about the beard he had neglected during his convalescence. He stroked it unconsciously as he repeated "Darcy." Then, as though accustomed to it, he said authoritatively, "Fitzwilliam Darcy of Pemberley in Derbyshire."

"You said it as though you had no idea of your identity," Lady Aileen offered.

"In truth, I did not. According to Mrs. Grubbs, who owns the manor on the other side of the island, I washed up on this island in a jollyboat right after the great storm a few weeks past. I had nothing on my person that would identify who I was and, furthermore, a hard lick to my head had left me unconscious for a time. Once I awoke, I was unable to remember anything—not even my name. It was only after hearing you say Darcy that I realised who I am."

"Mrs. Darcy must be sick with worry," she stated.

As a scene suddenly took shape in his mind, William looked as though he had been transported to another time and place. There, a beautiful young woman was playing on a beach. For lack of a bonnet, her long dark hair was being whipped about by every breeze. In her arms was a girl of about two, whom she twirled in a circle, while a boy approximately four years of age, ran hither and thither chasing a little white dog. *Elizabeth … Bennet and Anne!*

Dropping his head to his still bound hands, William moaned, "Oh, Lord in Heaven, how could I have forgotten my darling Elizabeth and our children."

"Bennet and Anne," Aileen supplied. "I recall meeting them at the wedding. Such beautiful children."

As William suffered to think he had forgotten them, Mr. Stevens said, "Try not to castigate yourself too meanly. From the injury you described, it is understandable that your memory might be affected, at least for a time."

"You spoke of a Mrs. Grubbs," Lady Aileen continued. "Will she look for you when she realises you are missing?"

"Presently, she is on the Isle of Man. I have no idea what will happen when, or if, she returns to learn I am not at the manor."

"It might be best if we all keep silent about your identity," Noel Stevens offered. "Silverhill is seeking ransom money, and if he suspects you are rich, he will act accordingly." Then, he added more thoughtfully, "Unless, of course, he decides to kill you. Then, telling him who you are might buy you more time."

"I agree. For the present I shall pretend not to know my name," William replied. "Now, tell me about this Captain Silverhill."

"He owns a shipping business in Liverpool. He also apparently owns these docks, the buildings here, and a warehouse that is hidden in a cave behind them. It was he who took us captive in Liverpool and brought us to this dreadful place. And, unless someone pays the ransom he is asking for our return, Lady Aileen and I shall likely be dumped in the ocean before long."

"Let us pray that the ransom is being arranged as we speak," William replied.

Sudden footsteps on the stairs leading up to the house made it known their captors had returned.

"Pretend to be asleep," Noel whispered. "Aileen and I will do the same and perhaps they will let us be for now."

When the footsteps passed the door, William closed his eyes. Remembering the last time he had held Elizabeth in his arms, he dreamed of running his arms around her once more. Filled with yearning, he prayed that God would let him live to see her and his children again.

As the Calf of Man appeared in the distance, Cecile Grubbs' stomach began to tie in knots. She moved to stand beside Captain Boone, who was equally anxious and wary of finding Captain Silverhill had preceded them to the island. Both were relieved to learn the ships they had seen in the distance were merely the remnants of old ships David Grubbs had never restored to a seaworthy state when he inherited them from his uncle.

She grasped her old friend's arm as they grew closer to the docks, saying nervously, "I hope Captain Silverhill will not return until after I have left for the Isle of Man. Mr. Sanderson is arranging for a house where I can stay until he sells Windemere Manor."

"What of the stranger you are entertaining? The one who washed ashore?"

"I cannot abandon him. He will just have to travel with me until he recalls who he is or until he is healthy enough to leave on his own." The captain looked sceptical, so she changed the subject. "You are planning to wait here until I can make arrangements to go with you, are you not?"

"It was I who suggested you take your solicitor's advice. Therefore, I cannot, in good conscience, leave you behind. Still, what if Silverhill were to trail you to the Isle of Man and take you by force?"

"He could, but the house is only a few hundred yards from the constable's office in Port Erin. My solicitor plans to hire one of the officers to watch the house, so Silverhill would be daft to try anything there."

"If you sell Windemere Manor, where will you go?"

"Most of her life, my aunt lived in a village near Mansfield, and I am familiar with the area. With any luck, I can assume my grandmother's maiden name, keep to myself, and be able to avoid that despicable man."

By then the ship had docked, and Captain Boone's men had jumped onto the wooden walk to tie it down. Wary of those men Silverhill left at the house to keep watch over the warehouses, Boone quickly had the supplies for Windemere Manor loaded onto a wagon kept there for just that purpose. Soon, with nary a sight of Silverhill's cohorts, he and Mrs. Grubbs began the slow drive back to the manor house.

Parkleigh Manor
Days later

Gregory Wright was in his study with the windows and the door propped open against the heat when the sound of an argument in the foyer grabbed his attention. His butler, Mr. Norton, had a deep, sonorous voice that carried well, especially when he was asserting his authority; however, the strident voice of an angry woman was proof that he was finding her hard to control.

Suddenly, Wright realised who possessed the angry voice. His patience at an end, Wright threw down his pen, splashing ink across the letter he had been trying to write. He stood and straightened his waistcoat and cravat before striding from the room to confront Lady Catherine.

The moment Lady Catherine caught sight of him, she dismissed the butler and spoke directly to Wright.

"There you are! You worthless excuse for a man! I should have known you were not at Pemberley doing as I instructed!"

"No, I am not," Wright replied. Then, steeling himself to be strong, he said, "You should know that I have no intention of drawing Elizabeth Darcy into a trap or to implicate her in something of which she would never take part. She is not only a lady, but she loves Darcy and is true to him. I should know, for, on occasion, I have tried to turn her head. She never gave me the time of day. You are just an old, spiteful woman who gets enjoyment by seeing others suffer. Well, I will not be a part of it."

"Save your breath! I came here merely to see Parkleigh Manor, since it will soon be mine, *not* to give you another chance. I will enjoy seeing you and that spawn of yours thrown off this property."

"I had rather give up my home than my morals, as you have done."

With that, Lady Catherine marched out the front door without another word. Realising where she was likely going, Wright called to the butler, "Find Mr. Gaines straightaway. Tell him I need my riding attire. Then send a footman to the stables and tell them to saddle my horse."

Pemberley

Elizabeth had just taken tea with her children in the nursery and was returning to William's study to examine the mail when the sound of a large coach stopping in front of her home caught her attention. Heart in her throat, she paused in the foyer and listened for the knocker to sound. Then, she watched the footman closest to the front door open it.

She could not have been more surprised had Satan himself walked into the house, though judging from the scowl on Lady Catherine's face, she felt certain that that demon had accompanied her. Though in no mood to spar with her archenemy, Elizabeth motioned for the footman to fetch Mr. Walker whilst she discovered the reason William's aunt was at Pemberley.

Before she could say a word, that evil woman addressed her. "You can be at no loss, Miss Bennet, to know why I am here!"

Elizabeth almost laughed aloud at Lady Catherine's insistence on using her maiden name.

"I am Mrs. Darcy, whether you like it or not, my lady. You will address me as such, or this conversation is finished."

Suddenly, Mr. Walker rounded the hall to the left, followed by two of Pemberley's largest footmen. They each took a place on either side of Lady Catherine. From another direction, Mrs. Reynolds rushed onto the scene before calmly walking over to stand beside her mistress with her hands folded benignly.

"Do you think I am afraid of these ruffians you have summoned?" Lady Catherine bellowed. "I am of noble birth, and not one of them will lay a finger on me for fear of the consequences."

"I would not count on that, my lady," Mr. Walker replied. "Our servants respect Mrs. Darcy, and they will not take kindly to anyone who would abuse her."

Unperturbed, Lady Catherine continued. "I will never accept you as Mrs. Darcy, and after I am finished no one in the family will, either. Since my nephew has been so foolish as to get himself drowned trying to save his sister's regrettable marriage, I am here to remove Fitzwilliam's heir from the premises. Fitzwilliam George Darcy will be guided by the Fitzwilliam and de Bourgh families until he is of age to manage Pemberley."

"My son's name is Bennet Fitzwilliam George Darcy, and his place is here at Pemberley. He is not going anywhere."

"That boy will never be addressed by that name again! And as for you and that girl who is plainly not a Darcy, you must find another place to reside."

A booming male voice cried, "I fear it is you who will be making changes, Catherine!"

Every head turned to see Lord Matlock standing in the open door with his wife right behind him.

"Walker, will you have these footmen escort my sister to an empty servant's quarters? Force her inside, if need be. I will have my men make sure she cannot escape until we make our return to London the day after tomorrow."

Mr. Walker bowed. "Certainly, my lord."

As Lady Catherine shouted obscenities, the footmen began to escort her towards the kitchen and the servants' quarters. Suddenly, Gregory Wright stepped inside the open front door. Spying him, Lady Catherine directed her ire in that direction.

"You will find yourself out on the streets. Mark my words! Your day is coming! See if anyone helps you then!"

Chapter 19

Liverpool

Richard was halfway up the staircase at the Crown Inn when he heard his name called. Turning, he saw one of Lieutenant Donavan's men waving at him from the lobby. Walking back down the stairs, he waited at the bottom as that man caught up to him.

Looking about cautiously, the sailor said quietly, "I apologise, Colonel Fitzwilliam, but Lieutenant Donavan said to tell you that things have changed. We must be off to the island in the next half hour. He asked that you come to the docks as quickly as possible."

"Tell him I will be there, and he is not to leave without me!"

"Yes, sir!"

As the sailor rushed from the building, Richard again mounted the stairs and headed to Lady Selina's room. Reaching it, he knocked softly and heard footsteps coming towards the door. The maid opened it and, seeing him, stepped aside.

"Good morning," Richard said as Lady Selina entered the room from an adjoining bedroom.

"Good morning, Colonel Fitzwilliam." She turned to her maid. "Sarah, please leave us."

With the maid gone, Lady Selina rushed over to grasp Richard's hands and give him a brilliant smile. "I have missed you."

Richard returned her smile as he gave her hands a gentle squeeze. "I wish I could stay and talk but I was just informed that Lieutenant Donavan is ready to sail and is waiting for me. He was to search Captain Silverhill's warehouse the minute he reached Liverpool, so I assume if we are following Silverhill to the island, the search here was unproductive."

"Captain Silverhill?"

"A captain who owns a warehouse here, as well as one on the island. The navy has long suspected he was involved in the theft of their supplies but needed more proof. Knowing my cousin could be on the island makes it even more imperative that we inspect that site as soon as possible."

Selina's smile faded. "I pray that if Mr. Darcy is being held there, you can rescue him without bloodshed."

"As do I, but I have something more to tell you and I would advise you to take this information with a grain of salt." Richard became sombre, searching her face before continuing. "When a person is being offered for ransom, matters do not always end well. It has been my experience that sometimes the person being held is no longer alive when the ransom is paid."

"Are you speaking of your cousin?"

"No. I am speaking of *your* cousin. The local constable recently told the admiral that a Mr. Dobbs from Leicester reported to him that Silverhill was holding a man named Noel Stevens for ransom. Dobbs is in Liverpool to facilitate the exchange of money, but Silverhill did not produce your cousin when he came for the funds."

Stunned, Lady Selina's hand covered her heart. "Mr. Dobbs is my steward. So, all hope that Noel is alive has been crushed?"

"No, there is still hope. Silverhill told your steward that he would release Stevens at a later date, so we will not know for certain whether your cousin is alive until we search Silverhill's ship and the warehouse on the island."

Lady Selina's eyes filled with tears. "Please, take care. I could not bear it if … if any of you were harmed."

Richard raised one of her hands to place a soft kiss upon it. "Do not worry. I have been in enough battles to know when to duck. I give you my word that I will return unharmed."

Offering a wan smile, she said, "I shall expect you to keep your word, Sir." Then all pretence of composure vanished. "I know you must hurry, so I will not delay you any longer."

Richard nodded and began to leave before suddenly turning around. Pulling Lady Selina close, he framed her face with his hands and kissed her forehead.

"I realise this is not the most opportune time, but I must tell you that I love you."

Without awaiting a reply, he rushed from the room.

Walking to the door, Selina watched the man she loved go down the stairs and out of the hotel without a backwards glance.

After saying a prayer for his safe return, she went to the hotel clerk to enquire where Mr. Dobbs' room could be found.

Pemberley

The farther Lady Catherine was escorted from the foyer, the fainter became her hateful diatribes, though that did not stop her from unleashing them. After she was completely out of hearing, all eyes focused on Mr. Wright.

That gentleman had come to be of service to Elizabeth by confessing all that Lady Catherine had been demanding of him. Instead, now that Wright found himself face to face with Lord Matlock, he was suddenly speechless.

At length, removing his hat, he bowed nervously. "Lord Matlock, I had no idea you would be here. Lady Catherine was at Parkleigh Manor earlier, and when she left, I felt certain she would come straight to Pemberley to confront Mrs. Darcy. That is why I hurried here to intervene. Now it seems my help was not needed."

"We have things to discuss, Mr. Wright, and I am certain Mrs. Darcy will wish to be included," Lord Matlock replied. "Perhaps it would be best if we remove to a place where we can talk privately."

Lady Matlock stepped closer to Elizabeth and placed an arm around her waist. "Come, my dear. Let us all go into the drawing room." To Mrs. Reynolds she said, "I am parched after our trip and would love to have some lemonade."

The housekeeper dropped a curtsey and went to fetch refreshments. Once the drawing room doors were closed, Lady Matlock said, "My dear niece, I apologise for Catherine's shocking behaviour. You should not have had to deal with her vicious words on top of all that has happened. I fear I must conclude from her actions today, that she has finally gone completely mad. I only wish we could have arrived in time to prevent her attack."

"I feel the same way," Elizabeth stated. "She must be mad."

Now that the confrontation was over, Elizabeth could not hold back her tears. Wiping her cheeks with the backs of her hands, she said, "Forgive me. I try so hard not to let anyone see me cry, but I am not always successful."

Just then the door opened, and Mrs. Reynolds came in holding a tray of lemonade and biscuits. As she placed them on a side table, she asked, "Should I stay and pour?"

"No, thank you," the countess replied.

After the housekeeper left, Lady Matlock poured a glass of lemonade for herself and one for Elizabeth whilst both Lord Matlock and Mr. Wright declined. Leading her niece to a large sofa, where they sat together, the countess continued.

"You owe no one an apology, dear girl. I cannot imagine how you have held up under the strain for this long."

Overhearing, Lord Matlock interjected. "I completely agree!"

Elizabeth's anxiety seemed to lessen. "It has been very difficult for all of us, especially the children," she murmured. "We miss Fitzwilliam so very much."

Lady Matlock patted her hand. "We all miss him immeasurably. He is such a dear man. Still, there is hope that Richard will locate him, and many people are praying for that outcome."

Sniffling, Elizabeth nodded.

Lord Matlock turned and addressed Gregory Wright. "Whilst I appreciate your concern for my niece, I have to wonder what business you have with my sister that would bring you here just now. Why was Catherine at your estate, and what did she mean by 'seeing you on the streets?'"

Though ashamed to admit the debts that Lady Catherine had held over his head for months, Wright knew he had no choice but to confess all the failures that had brought him to this hour—including the lies he told Fitzwilliam Darcy about the distillery in Belfast at Lady Catherine's orders. Once he had finished, Lord Matlock was shocked into silence, whilst Elizabeth was livid.

"After everything Fitzwilliam and I did to help you after Emma died, you would try to ruin us? Without my husband's assistance, you would have lost Parkleigh Manor to creditors long before now." She stood and began to pace. "And to think that every time you brought Jonathan to visit Bennet it was merely a ruse to discover if Fitzwilliam had believed your lies about the distillery or to flirt with me in the event that something happened to him!"

She threw up her hands, allowing the shawl she was wrapped in to fall to the floor. "Lady Catherine is evil, but at least she did not try to hide her hatred. You are even more evil, for you pretended to be our friend!"

Elizabeth dropped her head in her hands and wept. This prompted Lady Matlock to examine her niece more closely. Without the shawl, the evidence that Elizabeth was once again increasing became evident. The countess went over to wrap her arms about her.

"Try to remain calm, my dear. A woman in your condition should not get so upset." Giving her husband a pointed look, she said, "I am taking Elizabeth to her suite."

Once his wife and niece had left, Lord Matlock did not hide his anger. "Be advised that I do not take kindly to how you tried to manipulate my nephew and niece, or to the way you succumbed to my sister's orders just to protect yourself."

Contrite, Wright hung his head. "Whatever punishment you mete out, I deserve. My only concern is that my son is not left without anyone to see to his welfare."

"What of Fitzwilliam's children?! You apparently cared nothing for them! And, as for your own son, you should have thought of him before you began to gamble again," Lord Matlock hissed. "As it is, you may rest assured that my sister will *not* be calling in your debts, for I intend to remove her from conducting any business in the future. Henceforth, with the aid of an overseer, I intend to manage Rosings. Thus, in essence, *I* shall own your debts. I will decide what to do about them *and you* once I have had time to consider everything. Is that understood?"

Without a word, Wright nodded.

"As for Catherine, I could send her to Bedlam, but that would reflect badly on the entire family. Instead, until the day she dies, she will be a virtual prisoner at Rosings. All correspondence coming from or going to her will pass through me. No longer will she be allowed to travel outside the confines of the property or entertain company. The only exception is that she will be allowed to attend church services, and only because she needs to hear the sermons even if they do not reach her hard heart."

Suddenly he seemed aware that Wright was still waiting. "Return to your home and pray that Richard locates my nephew alive. Perhaps then I will not be of a mind to punish you as cruelly as I wish to at this minute."

As Wright quit the room, Lord Matlock walked over to a liquor cabinet to avail himself of a glass of brandy. After pouring, he looked to the ceiling, uttering a prayer.

"Lord, you know I am not a righteous man, but I do try to follow the scriptures concerning treating others as I would have them treat me. I rarely ask anything of you, but today I beg you to return Fitzwilliam to his family. Elizabeth and the children need him. So do we all."

Quickly tossing the brandy down, he winced as it burned his throat.

Windemere Manor

Returning to the manor to find her guest missing, Cecile Grubbs was sick with worry. It was obvious from the information the shepherds related to the groom—that the horse William borrowed the day he went missing was now in the paddock next to the warehouses at the docks—he was, in essence, a prisoner of Captain Silverhill.

As Cecile paced the drawing room trying to think of a solution, Captain Boone offered, "Can we not just go to the docks and ask if he is there? Perhaps they will let your guest go if you enquire about him in person?"

Nervously rubbing her arms with her hands, Cecile said, "Surely, they realise that he has been staying with me. If they wished to be civil, they would not have held him in the first place. No. Clearly, they are holding him for Captain Silverhill's return." Seizing a pillow off a chair, she angrily threw it across the room. "I knew that gentleman would not take kindly to being left behind. That is why he escaped the house after learning that I left for Man without telling him."

"You did not tell him? What were you afraid of?"

"I-I suppose I was afraid that once on the Isle of Man he would encounter someone who knew him."

"And he would desert you," Captain Boone interjected.

Cecile nodded. "I know it was foolish of me, but I hoped he would never remember his past and stay with David and me."

"That is understandable. You are still a young woman, and David needs a father, but that is no way to obtain a husband. After all, he may already have a wife and children who must miss him dearly."

"Though I may appear heartless to you, my conscience has not let me forget that possibility."

"Still, because he has made himself known to those miscreants who work for Captain Silverhill, I fear what that blackguard will do, should he return before we leave. Obviously, Silverhill is enamoured of you, and if he learns you have been hiding a man at Windemere Manor, he will believe you were having an affair."

"Even though that is not true," Cecile sighed. "In any case, I cannot leave this island without him. Silverhill has a violent temper and acts as though he owns me. I have no doubt he would kill my nameless guest without reservation if I were not here to explain."

"Then perhaps we should leave tomorrow as though nothing were amiss. I will sail directly to Man and request the help of the navy there to remove your property and the stranger from the island."

"I will not leave him to face those reprobates alone. They are imbeciles, so they will hold him for Silverhill's instructions, and they will not dare lay a hand on me unless given orders to do so."

When Captain Boone tried to protest, she held up a hand. "I owe him that much. If you return with help before Silverhill does, all should be well."

Captain Boone stood. "Then let us get some sleep. I will sail at first light."

Pemberley

Elizabeth's aunt offered encouragement by playing with the children after dinner and sitting with her until she was ready to retire. Once alone in her bedroom, though, Elizabeth was unable to rid her thoughts of Gregory Wright's betrayal. Over and over, she saw him enter one of Pemberley's many gardens, dismount his horse and place Jonathan on the ground to play with Bennet. Then, all the while speaking lies designed to make her think he was there to offer solace, he planned how to take what belonged to William.

At length throwing aside the counterpane, Elizabeth donned her robe and walked out onto the balcony. Looking up at what appeared to be a blue velvet blanket covered by a million stars that lit up the night, she recalled being on the balcony and seeing this same spectacle the night before William left for Ireland. She had been on the verge of tears at the thought of him leaving, and he had been trying to comfort her by teasing her that as soon as he returned, they would try again for another child.

Having no idea she might be pregnant, William wrapped his arms around her and whispered how deeply he loved her. She had almost confessed to him then, but she knew William would never leave her if he suspected she was with child, not even to save Georgiana's marriage.

"Have I told you today that you are the love of my life?" he had murmured, kissing just below her earlobe. "I was made to love none but you, sweetheart. For as long as I live, my heart is yours."

She delivered a soft kiss to his lips. "I feel the same way about you, my darling. I am hopelessly devoted to you for as long as I live."

He kissed her deeply and thoroughly before pulling back to add, "I know how tender your heart is. Please try not to grieve my absence. My plan is to speak with Matthew and Georgiana, determine what is to be done and leave forthwith."

"What if the solution takes more time?"

"That is up to them, not me. My desire is to make my opinion known and depart. It will be up to them to take my advice ... or not."

He had kissed her then with such passion that the thought of it stole her breath even now. "Come home to me, William. I am not complete without you."

For a reason she could not explain, Elizabeth felt William's arms surround her once more, and it gave her hope. On her way to the bed, she opened the top drawer of her dresser and grasped the robe he had inadvertently left in her bedroom just before departing for Liverpool. Taking a deep breath of the soap and sandalwood that still lingered on the robe, she fell asleep with it in her arms and dreamt of being on the beach with her family as she had been only months before.

Chapter 20

Ballyneen Castle
A bedroom

As Viscount Hayworth watched his wife going through every drawer in the chest a second time to make certain nothing had been left behind, he remarked, "I do not know why you feel you must take everything you own with you."

"This is *not* everything I own, Matthew," Georgiana said good-naturedly. "However, after Richard's last letter to me and the one you received from your father yesterday, I have a feeling we may be in England longer than you anticipate. The fact is, I cannot wait to see Brother, but I know he shall be on his way back to Elizabeth and the children the instant Richard locates him; thus, if I wish to see Fitzwilliam, I must go to Pemberley."

"You seem very confident that Richard will find him on the Calf of Man."

Georgiana lifted her chin defiantly. "I am. I know Richard would not have written me about Fitzwilliam's watch unless he was certain he would find him there."

Not wishing to discourage Georgiana's beliefs regarding her brother, Matthew kept silent as she continued. "If you cannot locate Aileen in Liverpool, we will likely have to pay a visit to your father at Berkley Hall. After all, he has information from the man he paid to follow her, so perhaps he can tell you where to begin your search. All of which brings me back to the fact that I shall need every stitch of clothing I have here."

Recalling the letter he received the day before from Berkley Hall, Matthew tensed. In the missive, his father related that a man had arrived at his door, supposedly representing an unknown ship's captain from Liverpool who was demanding a ransom for Lady Aileen. Lord Camden thought it was just an attempt by his former steward to extort money and claimed he would not be surprised to find that his daughter was part of the plot. Moreover, he had bragged about rejecting the man's demand for money.

"I have no desire to see my father since he was the reason Aileen ran away in the first place, and to reject the ransom demand without determining if it was real was not only foolish, but it may prove deadly for my sister."

"I know how worried you are for Aileen—we both are," Georgiana replied, grasping his hand and giving it a comforting squeeze. "I have refrained from even considering it, but do you believe the ransom demand may have been legitimate?"

"I honestly have no idea. Whilst I do not want to think my sister would be a party to something of that nature, she has already done things I would never have believed of her." Matthew shook his head as though he could not make heads or tails of Aileen's actions. "After Richard has recovered your brother, I intend to ask his help in finding Aileen."

"One thing I know for certain is that my cousin will leave no stone unturned until he learns how Fitzwilliam's watch got into the hands of that fellow from the Calf of Man."

"I agree with you there."

"In any case," Georgiana said, as she stopped to examine a pair of short, brown walking boots, "you should be grateful that half of my things are still at Berkley Hall. If you recall, you promised we would not be here very long, so I did not pack everything."

Recalling how he had misled his wife into thinking they were only going to visit his aunt at Ballyneen for a short period of time, Matthew resolved not to complain about an excess of luggage any further.

"Just be certain everything has been packed by noon, for we leave for Belfast soon afterwards."

"Are we still set to sail the day after tomorrow?" Georgiana asked.

"Barring unforeseen circumstances, we are."

◦◦◦◦◦◦

Pemberley

As usual, Mrs. Green and Elizabeth sat in the swing near the fish-pond, each working on projects retrieved from their sewing baskets whilst also keeping an eye on the children as they played. Elizabeth was placing delicate stitches around the collar of a new shirt she was making for William, whilst Judith crocheted mittens that she planned to distribute to the poor at Christmas. Suddenly, Bennet came running towards them holding up something he had found near the fishpond.

"It is an old coin, Mama!" he announced proudly. "I am going to give it to Papa!"

Then he addressed Mrs. Green. "Mimi, Papa taught me to save all the old coins I find. He has been collecting them since he was my age, and his collection shall be mine one day. He said so!" Presenting the coin to his mother, he said, "Will you keep it for me until Papa returns?"

"Of course, I will, sweetheart," Elizabeth replied, taking the coin and examining it closely. "This looks much older than any you have found before." Reaching out to ruffle her son's hair, she smiled. "I am certain Papa will be very interested in it."

"I am going to look for more!" Bennet declared, turning to head back to the pond. Anne and Clancy, who had only just now caught up to Ben, immediately turned around and tried their best to catch up with him again.

As Elizabeth dropped the coin into her sewing basket, Mrs. Green said, "I have not heard you mention your sister of late. Does Jane even know that Fitzwilliam is missing? Or does the rest of your family, for that matter?"

"Papa knows. He reads several newspapers a week, so there was no hiding it from him. And he has been in touch with the Gardiners since the news broke. He writes that he has been keeping William's disappearance a secret from Mama and my younger sisters in the hope that Richard will have good news of William before he must inform them." She heaved a ragged sigh. "As for Jane and Charles, I believe I told you that they have been in Scarborough for the past five months because his aunt was ill."

Judith Green nodded. "I remember now. You did."

"That lady has recently died, leaving Charles as her executor. According to Jane, he has been trying to sort out her finances in order to sell her estate after making some needed repairs. Knowing how distressed Jane is that she cannot be at Ivy Manor when their child is born, I have not said anything to her about the sinking of the *Endeavor*. She would insist on coming here to comfort me, and that would create a hardship for her. I also want to wait on Richard's report before saying anything."

"Tell me again where Ivy Manor is and when the babe is due."

"Their estate is in Alfreton, approximately twenty miles southeast of here, and the child is due in about three months."

"Oh my! The roads from there to Scarborough are so rough I would not advise her to travel them in her condition. She had best stay where she is until after the child is born."

"That is precisely what the physician in Scarborough recommended. In any case, seeing that she and Charles hardly ever read the newspapers, I doubt either is aware of all that has occurred. At least, Jane has not mentioned it in her letters."

"You cannot keep it a secret forever."

Elizabeth sighed. "I know, but I am trusting God that when I do have to explain to her what happened, it will include news of my husband's safe return."

Mrs. Green slid an arm around Elizabeth's shoulders and leaned in to kiss her cheek. "James and I have been praying and trusting God for that as well."

They were interrupted by Anne who, out of breath and talking too quickly to be clearly understood, had reached them just ahead of her brother.

"Mama, look!" the bright-eyed, little girl said as she thrust a small, round rock in her mother's hand. "Papa coin!"

"That is not a coin!" Bennet yelled the instant he caught up to her. "Tell her it is not, Mama!"

Elizabeth reached down to pull a dishevelled Anne into her lap. Brushing several stray curls from her child's forehead, the questioning expression in her daughter's eyes touched her heart. Overcome with love, she placed a kiss on Anne's forehead, saying, "Let me have a good look at your coin, my darling girl."

Taking the rock from Anne, she turned it over several times. "I think your Papa will be very pleased to see the coin you found."

"But, Mama!" Bennet interrupted.

Elizabeth pulled her son forwards, so he stood beside his sister. "Now, Bennet. What do you suppose your Papa will say to Anne when she shows him the coin she found?"

Bennet stood silent for a time, during which his expression changed from annoyance to understanding. Letting go a long sigh, he said, "I think Papa will say that she has done well."

Leaning across Anne, Elizabeth cupped Bennet's cheek tenderly. "You know your Papa very well, and I am so proud that you are proving to be just like him."

Bennet perked up. Smiling, he said, "I am?"

"Yes. Not only are you the image of your father, you are just as intelligent, gentle and kind. I know he will be so proud when I tell him how you reacted to Anne's discovery."

"Papa loves Anne," her daughter stated resolutely with a nod of her head.

Elizabeth tried not to cry as she embraced them both. "Yes, Papa loves you and Bennet so very much, and so do I."

Bennet began to squirm out of her embrace. "Let us find more coins, Anne."

He took his sister's hand, and Anne slipped off Elizabeth's lap. Bennet then led her back down the path towards the pond, with Clancy right on their heels.

"You are a wonderful mother," Mrs. Green said as she watched the siblings leave. "I know I have told you that before, but your children's actions prove that I am not being partial."

"They are so even-tempered it seems unfair for me to take credit for their behaviour."

"Nonsense. Their temperaments are a direct result of how you and Fitzwilliam have reared them. I have met enough spoiled children to say that with conviction."

"I must agree with you in regard to their father, and I am blessed to have him as my husband and the father of my children."

"I think he is blessed to have you as well."

Elizabeth blushed.

Mrs. Green held up the pair of mittens she had just finished. "That makes twelve pairs of mittens and five pairs of gloves."

"How many do you plan to make?"

"I could easily give away fifty pairs, if I include men and women as well as children on my list, but I do not have enough yarn to create that many."

"Before you leave, I shall write a note to Mrs. Benefield at the drapery shop telling her to put whatever you need on our account. Moreover, once I finish this shirt for William, I shall begin crocheting mittens and gloves to help with your project. As we did last year, William and I plan to contribute shoes to the children of our tenants for Christmas, along with other necessities and some toys. We would be glad to donate shoes to those in the parish that you know are in need—whether man, woman, or child."

"How generous of you!"

"William's guiding verse is Proverbs 19:17. 'He that hath pity upon the poor lendeth unto the Lord.' I choose to believe that God will repay William's generous heart by bringing him home to me and the children. God's promises are all I cling to at present."

Patting Elizabeth's hand, Judith Green said, "Oh, my dear, James and I are clinging to them, too."

The Calf of Man

The moment Captain Silverhill arrived at the island, he went straight to the house to check on his captives. Finding William amongst those tied up in a back room, he demanded of his men, "Who is that?"

"He be someone we found on the hill overlooking the warehouses, Cap'n Silver, sir," one of his men explained. "He be spying on us, so we tied him up until you could say what is to be done with him."

Giving William his full attention, the captain walked over to stand directly above the sofa where his newest prisoner sat.

"Who are you, and what are you doing on this island?"

"I am afraid I cannot help you. I do not recall what—" William began to say before Silverhill struck him. The blow sent his head flying back, splitting his lip and causing blood to pour down his chin.

"Perhaps with the proper incentive you will recall," the villain taunted.

Noel Stevens cried out. "He is telling you the truth! He explained to us that he washed up on the island after that huge storm several weeks ago. He had sustained an injury to his head and cannot recall anything from his past."

Silver turned on Noel. "Shut up, or you will be next! He can talk. Let him defend himself!" Then he addressed William again. "Why not make it easy on yourself by starting at the beginning and telling me everything?"

William proceeded to tell the captain just what he had told Noel Stevens and Lady Aileen before she had stirred his memory.

Once he had finished, the captain stared at William for what seemed like an eternity before he asked, "How long have you and Mrs. Grubbs been lovers?"

"I am not her lover," William declared angrily.

"If that is true, why would she hide your presence from me?"

"All I know is that she helped me to recover from my injury and got me back on my feet. Other than that, I cannot claim to know what she thinks or why she acts as she does."

Silverhill huffed, "Likely another lie!" To his man, he said, "Untie his feet. I am taking him to the manor house with me. When he and Cecile are in the same room, I shall see who is lying."

Later

So that Captain Silverhill would not realise that the Royal Navy was about to bring him to justice, Lieutenant Donavan chose to sail to the Calf of Man in a much smaller vessel, one that the navy had captured and which still flew a foreign flag. That vessel was considerably easier to manoeuvre than his regular ship, and rather than just a normal crew, he had requested and been granted command of twenty additional sailors, each battle-hardened, in excellent health and equipped to fight.

From intelligence received from Lieutenant Parton, who had earlier penetrated Captain Silverhill's warehouse crew and had been passing information to Admiral Turlington for weeks, it was known that Silverhill was running with a scaled-back crew, most of whom were old, out-of-shape, heavy drinkers.

Hoping to catch Silverhill unawares, Donavan gave orders to lag behind when they sailed from Liverpool, preferring to dock at the island at least an hour or more after Silverhill did. He figured if he could catch that blackguard on land feeling safe and with many of his crew resting below deck, it would make for a less volatile situation. Though Richard desperately wanted to raid the island as soon as possible, he had agreed.

Everything was falling into place as Donavan's ship carefully approached a dock on the far side of Silverhill's vessel. Once their ship was secure, the sailors slipped silently onto the neighbouring vessel without firing a shot. They discovered no one was topside. In fact, all the crew was below deck, most already asleep or rapidly becoming inebriated. The few that were not, were easily outnumbered. Thus, in a very short time, every one of them had been placed under arrest and were locked up on the navy's vessel.

Whilst this was happening, Lieutenant Donavan, Richard and the elite group of sailors surrounded the house and warehouse. A signal was given, and the doors to both structures were simultaneously pommelled with battering rams. The only resistance encountered was one blackguard guarding the house. Once he caught sight of the number of men at the door and was ordered to drop his weapons, he surrendered without a fight.

Richard took that man's gun and sent him to the floor with a strong right hook. "Tie him up!"

Looking about the room, he hurried to the only door. Opening it, he found a man and a woman sitting on the floor. Their hands and feet were tied, and rags were stuffed in their mouths so they could not speak. Quickly set free, both hostages began thanking their rescuer, especially Lady Aileen who had recognised him.

"Oh, Colonel Fitzwilliam! You may not remember me, but we met briefly at my brother's wedding to your cousin not two months ago. I am Matthew's sister, Aileen."

"Honestly, I met so many people at the wedding that I did not recognise you."

"I can imagine my appearance is much altered, too," she replied. Then she motioned to her companion. "This is Noel Stevens. He was kidnapped in Liverpool alongside me."

"Mr. Stevens," Richard repeated. "How fortunate to have found you. I have been in Lady Selina Grey's company often of late as we searched for our loved ones."

"We owe you our lives," Stevens began to say before Richard brushed aside his gratitude.

"I am glad to have freed you both, but I came here specifically to look for my cousin, Fitzwilliam Darcy. I have reason to believe he is being held on this island against his will."

"Mr. Darcy joined us as a hostage only days ago," Lady Aileen replied. "Until I mentioned who he was, he seemed to have no idea. As we talked, he gradually began to recall more. He had suffered an injury to his head, you see, and had been unable to recall anything of how he ended up injured or on the island."

"He was still here until about an hour ago when Captain Silverhill arrived," Stevens added. "Once that blackguard discovered your cousin, Mr. Darcy acted as though he still could not recall anything. This made the captain angry, and he took him to the manor house where he plans to confront the owner, Mrs. Grubbs. Apparently, he is very possessive of that woman and thinks Mr. Darcy has been having an affair with her. Which would, in his evil mind, explain why she has kept Darcy's presence on the island a secret."

Lieutenant Donavan stood behind Richard, listening silently. Abruptly, he stated, "Colonel, we need to get to the manor before Silverhill harms Mr. Darcy."

Richard had already concluded that and was halfway to the door before he replied, "I spotted a stable beside the warehouse. If we ride, we can get there faster."

Chapter 21

Windemere Manor

As Mrs. Grubbs descended the grand staircase, she was shocked to see the front door fly open and Daniel rush into the foyer, eyes wide with fear.

"He is here!" the young man cried. "He is almost to the door!"

Terrified of Captain Silverhill, Daniel did not bother to close the door. Instead, he ran up the stairs to find his parents. Thinking Daniel might be speaking of the man who had been recovering from his injuries at her home, for a brief moment, Cecile's spirits soared. All hope was quickly dashed, however, when Captain Silverhill and two of his men walked through the still-open front door. Moreover, the captain was gripping the arm of the very gentleman whom Cecile had come to care for. William's hands were tied behind his back, and blood covered his face and shirt.

His alarming appearance shocked Cecile, and her hands flew to her mouth to stifle a cry. Gathering her courage, she declared, "Why did you harm him? He is injured and not able to defend himself!"

The captain shoved William forwards so hard that he lost his footing and fell on the marble floor. "I have brought your lover back to you!"

Cecile, crossing to William, began shouting, "Leave him be! He is nothing more than a stranger who washed ashore after the great storm. Mrs. Kelly and I have worked for weeks to keep him alive, and now you have injured him again!"

"A stranger, indeed! Then why did you keep his presence here a secret from me? Only lovers would keep each other's presence confidential!"

"I did it because I knew you would act exactly as you are! Though you have no right to be, you are jealous, and I feared you would not let him remain here until he had completely recovered. After he had, I planned to have Captain Boone take him to the Isle of Man so that he might discover his identity."

As Cecile bent to help William to his feet, the captain warned, "Keep your hands off him!"

In fear of what Silverhill might do, she stood completely still. "Are you so irate that you cannot see he is unwell? Your mistreatment of him has been horrific, and I fear it may have reversed what progress he has made!"

"If you think I care, you are entirely mistaken!" Nevertheless, Silverhill quickly covered the distance between himself and his nemesis, drew his sword and cut the ropes holding William's hands behind his back. Then he sank just the tip of his sword into his prisoner's back.

"Get up!"

Cecile screamed at the sight of the blood spreading on William's back as he struggled to his feet.

Ignoring her, Captain Silverhill ordered, "Turn around and face me!"

As he turned to face the irate captain, William quickly glanced about the room. His eyes settled on the only thing he might be able to use as a weapon—a letter opener lying atop a silver salver on a nearby table.

Silverhill's next words instantly brought his attention back to that villain. "Inasmuch as Cecile will not admit you are lovers, perhaps you will tell me the truth. That is, if you wish to live."

"What assurance do I have that I will live if the truth is not what you wish to hear?"

This enraged the captain. "You get no assurances! I decide whether you live or die, and it is incumbent upon you to convince me that you are telling the truth."

Reluctantly, William began. "Mrs. Grubbs told you the truth about my presence here and our relationship. I washed ashore in a jolly boat, most likely from a ship that sank during the great storm. I was unconscious for days and just began walking a week or so ago. When Mrs. Kelly told me that Mrs. Grubbs had sailed to the Isle of Man, I decided to chance riding again. That was what I was doing the day your men spied me near the warehouses."

"You expect me to believe you were spying on my warehouses merely by accident?"

"It is the truth. When I happened upon them, curiosity got the better of me, and I dismounted to have a better look. The next thing

I knew, I awakened inside the house beside the docks, tied up like a thief."

Several times during the inquisition Silverhill's eyes shifted from Cecile to William and back again. When William had finished, the captain said, "I believe your tale of washing ashore and having to recover from your injuries; however, in light of the fact that Mrs. Grubbs kept your presence here a secret from me, it is my belief that you became lovers."

Simultaneously both William and Cecile began refuting his claim, but Silverhill would not listen. Tossing his sword aside on the marble floor, he swiftly drew the pistol he always wore on his belt.

He aimed it at William, snarling, "I see no reason to keep you alive."

"Wait!" Cecile cried. "You could hold him hostage for a ransom. He was dressed as a gentleman when he washed ashore. Perhaps he has family who are looking for him and will pay for his return."

"I doubt this fellow has anyone who would care if he lived or died!"

Suddenly, a voice unfamiliar to everyone but William echoed in the foyer, "And that is where you have made a fatal mistake!"

As the captain turned to find Richard pointing a pistol at him, William lunged for the letter opener. He managed to grab it, only to collapse just as a shot rang out.

Cecile screamed, "No!"

Believing William mortally wounded, Cecile's eyes stayed locked on him. It was Captain Silverhill, however, who suddenly fell backwards, hitting the marble floor and exposing a large hole in his forehead.

Having had no time to defend himself, William looked astonished—not only to find himself alive, but to see someone he recognised gripping a smoking pistol. In addition, on either side of his cousin, several sailors had Silverhill's men secured so they would neither interfere nor cry out a warning.

Letting go the breath he had been holding, William cried, "Good heavens, Richard! Am I grateful to see you!"

Richard rushed forwards to clasp his cousin in a robust embrace, his well-regulated emotions seemingly abandoned as tears filled his eyes. Richard's countenance displayed his effort to regain control whilst he held William. Witnessing the cousins' emotional reunion, Lieutenant Donavan ordered his men to gather the captives and follow him from the house.

At long last, despite a large lump now firmly lodged in his throat, Richard loosened his grip enough to speak.

"You are not any more grateful than I am to find you, Darcy! Only God knows the agony those of us who care for you experienced after learning your ship had sunk. In spite of everything, however, Elizabeth was adamant that you were still alive, and her faith strengthened my own."

Deeply moved, William murmured, "My darling Elizabeth! Please tell me she and our children are well."

"Other than missing you every minute of every day, they were all in good health when I last saw them at Pemberley. Moreover, Elizabeth sent you a letter. It is in my bag onboard Lieutenant Donavan's ship."

"Just to read whatever she wrote will be heaven." Taking a deep breath, William closed his eyes. "I cannot imagine what a torment this has been for her."

"I can honestly say she has been the epitome of a loyal wife and mother, taking strength from her faith in God, and keeping the children's spirits high."

A noise on the stairs announced Mrs. Kelly. Seeing the rapidly expanding stain on the back of William's shirt, she declared, "I shall get my bag of medicines and tend to your wound, sir."

Mrs. Grubbs pointed to a nearby door. "If you will go into the drawing room and remove that shirt, I shall provide you with a clean one."

William tried to protest, but Richard whirled him around to have a look at his back. "Good Lord, Darcy! You are bleeding like a butchered hog!"

Grasping his arm, he led Darcy towards the drawing room.

It was not long until Mrs. Kelly rushed back into the room with a small bag, and Mrs. Grubbs followed with some scissors and sheets.

The wound was not long, but it was deep enough to warrant stitches. Since he had learnt to administer stitches whilst in the army, Richard took on that task and finished it quickly, if not painlessly. He had put Mrs. Kelly to work cutting strips from an old sheet, and he wound those strips around William's torso to hold the bandage in place over the injury.

Once satisfied, Richard stood. "There! If you will take care not to pull out those stitches, I predict you will be as good as new in a few days. And if you shave off that beard, perhaps your wife and children will recognise you."

William ran a hand over the beard. "I shall be glad to be rid of this. It itches."

As William stood to don the new shirt Mrs. Grubbs held out, Richard asked, "Do you have any more britches or shirts my cousin might use until he can get home?"

"I already have Mr. Kelly packing a bag with what is left of my husband's best clothes. They are useless packed away, and I thought he—*Mr. Darcy*, I should say—may need them. Daniel will bring them down shortly."

William turned to address her. "I recalled my identity after I was taken captive and met the hostages Captain Silverhill was holding for ransom. As fate would have it, one hostage was Lady Aileen Davidson, sister to Viscount Hayworth of Berkley Hall in Southampton. He married my sister only months ago. Lady Aileen recognised me and mentioned meeting my wife and our children at the wedding. That opened a flood of memories to me."

Mrs. Grubbs smiled wanly. "I am not surprised to learn that you are married and have children. You were so comfortable with my son that I thought you must be someone's father."

Wishing to change the subject, William motioned to Richard. "May I introduce my cousin, Colonel Richard Fitzwilliam. He has been searching for me since news of the *Endeavour's* fate hit the newspapers."

"We have already met," Richard replied, bowing curtly. To William he said, "I shall tell you all about it later, Cousin." Addressing Cecile again, he added, "You have my sincerest gratitude for tending to my cousin. I do not believe he would be here today without your kind assistance."

"No thanks are necessary. Mrs. Kelly is an excellent nurse, and she and I just did what any Godfearing people would."

"Will you be staying on the island?" William asked.

"For now. No doubt the navy will have questions regarding my husband's business dealings with Captain Silverhill. After that is settled, I hope to sell Windemere and move to Mansfield," Cecile replied. After a moment, she added, "I think I should like to live the rest of my life near people who knew my family. Besides, David will have more possibilities in England than on this island."

"I am certain my wife will wish to thank you in person," William added. "You have an open invitation to visit Pemberley to meet my family whenever you are settled and have opportunity."

Lieutenant Donavan returned just as Daniel came into the room carrying a small travelling bag. Seeing Daniel reminded Richard of Darcy's watch.

"You, there! I will take that watch you have in your pocket!"

Daniel blanched and took several steps back. "I-I have no watch."

"What are you referring to, Colonel?" Mrs. Grubbs asked. "As far as I know, Daniel owns no watch."

"When I met with you and Lieutenant Donovan in Port Erin, this man had Darcy's pocket watch in his lap. I recognised it because he kept opening and closing the lid, and I got a good look at the portrait of Mrs. Darcy inside it."

Mrs. Kelly crossed the room. "Daniel, if you have the watch, give it to the man."

He searched his jacket. "Yes, Mama." Retrieving the watch, Daniel held it out to Richard, who briefly looked at it before handing it to William.

"That is a portrait of your wife, is it not, Cousin?"

As William peered at the likeness of Elizabeth inside the watch, he struggled to keep his composure. "It certainly is, but my watch was taken from me by one of two men I caught looting the ship. I must have fallen into the jolly boat after one of them struck me on the back of my head."

"That makes sense," Donavan said. "These thieves were intending to use the jolly boat to escape, but you fell overboard after being struck and hit the boat hard enough to set it free from the ship."

Abruptly, William recalled seeing Daniel digging in the sand. "Lieutenant Donavan, if you will follow me, I think I know where Daniel may have hidden more valuables from the ship."

Directing everyone to the place in the sand where he had seen Daniel digging, William was proven right when beneath the stones in the sand were four pouches containing not only wallets, jewellery boxes, loose jewellery and thousands of pounds belonging to the passengers of the *Endeavour*, but also some personal papers that had Jake's and Drago's names on them. Later they would be identified as hardened criminals who, in trying to execute the perfect theft, died along with their victims.

After all the buried bags were brought into the house, Lieutenant Donavan dumped the entire contents of one on newspapers he had spread on a large table in the foyer.

Picking up a beautiful diamond and emerald necklace, Richard said, "I cannot imagine how you will match this with the right family. I would think a lot of lies will be invented when something of this value is at stake."

"We give weight to portraits that show their ancestor wearing the jewellery, bills that show when they were purchased, and testimony of friends and family. If something cannot be matched without a doubt, I imagine the courts may sell the lot and divide the proceeds amongst the relations of those who were lost."

William spied his wallet and, picking it up, found it still contained a blank bank note he had placed inside it. "I make it a habit to never travel with anything of great value, with the exception of my watch, which I try not to bring out in public."

"If only more people practiced your habit," the lieutenant replied. "Those who tend to display their wealth are often relieved of it whilst they travel."

Placing the items on the table back inside the pouch, Lieutenant Donavan ordered all the pouches placed inside the carriage for transport back to the docks.

The lieutenant joined his men in the wagon, since it would leave for the dock first and he wished to look over the contents of the warehouse before returning to Liverpool. That left William and Richard with exclusive use of the carriage.

William had become unusually quiet, so Richard asked, "What is on your mind, Cousin?"

"After I regained my memory, I tried to picture what I would have done if the circumstances had been reversed—if I thought Elizabeth had been lost at sea."

"And what did you decide?"

"I am incapable of imagining life without her. We are knit together so solidly that, if not for the children, it would be difficult for me to carry on alone for the rest of my life."

"Surely, after a few years you would meet someone else who could be a good mother for the children."

"I *know* I would never marry again. Once you have experienced a perfect love, one cannot simply settle for less. I had rather my children be raised by me and devoted servants than have another woman try to take Elizabeth's place."

Richard smiled. "Might I suggest, then, that you no longer dwell on anything so wretched. Who knows! You may have something wonderful to focus on when you return."

William looked puzzled. "What do you know that I do not?"

"I fear I have overstepped the boundaries between a husband and wife by saying as much as I have; however, I do not wish you to be caught unawares in case your wife is very emotional when she first sees you again. Be gentle with her."

"What are you babbling about?"

"When I went to Pemberley to inform Elizabeth that the *Endeavour* had sunk, she fainted. The local physician was called, and as he reported on her condition to the vicar and Mrs. Green, I overheard him say that your wife will be delivered of another child in approximately six months."

"Another child," William whispered, as though weighing the prospect. "Elizabeth knew but did not tell me before I left for Ireland."

"She probably knew you would never leave had you known."

"This is true, and Elizabeth has always been more concerned about others," William said, shaking his head. "Yet another reason to thank you for finding me, Cousin."

"The only thanks I want is for the child to be named after me if it is a boy!"

"Boy or girl, somehow it will carry your name!"

Later

Just as Lieutenant Donavan returned to the docks to order all the prisoners onboard for transport back to Liverpool, Captain Boone arrived aboard another navy ship that had been stationed at the Port of St. Mary. This ship was under the command of Captain Reginal Shirley.

"Captain Shirley … Captain Boone," Donavan declared, saluting his comrade and shaking each man's hand as they approached him on the dock. "You will be pleased to know that Captain Silverhill is dead, and that everything is under control."

Captain Shirley, a much older man, smiled. "So, we were not needed after all."

"On the contrary," Lieutenant Donavan replied. "Having another vessel here will allow us to transport all the prisoners safely back to Liverpool without being crowded like fish in a barrel in the little ship I commandeered. I plan to sail first thing in the morning."

Boone's eyes twinkled with his reply, "It is good to see you again, *Mr. Donaldson*, or may I call you Lieutenant Donovan now?"

As Donovan laughed, Captain Boone continued, "Now our conversation at Port Erin makes sense. I had to wonder why any gentleman with an ounce of intelligence would want to open a leather goods store in such a remote place as Port Erin."

"I apologise for the lie, but I had to keep my identity a secret at that point."

"No need for apologies. I am just glad I could be of service by bringing more troops with me. Let me say, though, that I am truly relieved that you killed that villain before we arrived. Silverhill was not a man to be taken lightly, and he had been pressing Mrs. Grubbs to marry him. It was only a matter of time until he forced her to comply with his wishes."

"Well, he will not force himself on anyone else or perpetrate any more crimes," the lieutenant declared. "In addition to helping Mrs.

Grubbs, we managed to free two people he had kidnapped in Liverpool and was holding for ransom, as well as Colonel Fitzwilliam's cousin, Mr. Darcy."

"So, Mr. Darcy is the man Mrs. Grubbs has been helping all these weeks?"

"Aye. He is fortunate to be alive, given all he went through," the lieutenant answered.

"Indeed, he is," Captain Boone said. Then, assessing those gathered to board the ships, he added, "I take it Mrs. Grubbs is staying here for now."

"She will be needed to testify in an inquiry into her late husband's business dealings with Captain Silverhill. I will assure her that the navy has found nothing indicating that she participated in their nefarious business dealings; however, her testimony will be needed to close the case."

"I can attest to the fact that she was forbidden to go down to the docks, other than to board my ship whenever she sailed to the big island with me. And she often stated that she had no idea what her husband was doing with the warehouses."

"We found evidence in the warehouses that Silverhill was stealing from the navy, as well as others. But I should like to summon you to the inquisition as well."

"I should be glad to testify."

Shortly, the group was met by Colonel Fitzwilliam and Mr. Darcy, who walked up to them on the docks.

Richard spoke first. "Captain Boone, it is good to see you again and under much pleasanter circumstances than I had anticipated."

"I could say the same about you, Colonel," Boone replied.

Motioning towards William, Richard added, "This is the cousin I have been searching for, Fitzwilliam Darcy of Pemberley in Derbyshire. He had just reclaimed his memory when Silverhill descended on the island."

"So, the man you have been looking for was here all along," Captain Boone said, shaking his head. "Simply amazing!" Turning to William, he added, "I am glad that you not only regained your senses but were able to keep your life after meeting that blackguard."

"I owe my life not only to Mrs. Grubbs and her housekeeper, but also to my cousin and Lieutenant Donavan, who arrived just in time to stop the *good* captain from killing me."

"Good captain, my foot!" the old man cried before adding, "To survive all that you have, there must be an army of people praying for you."

"You have no idea," William answered. "And I have no doubt that my precious wife's prayers alone have touched heaven's throne."

"Then you are a most fortunate man," Captain Boone said.

"Indeed. God has blessed me more than I deserve," William replied.

"I have often told him that very same thing, Captain Boone!" Richard declared. "But it took you to make him finally confess it."

"Only because I do not like you to believe you are always right," William said teasingly. "Your hat barely fits your head as it is!"

That comment brought laughs from all the men standing about.

Chapter 22

Liverpool
The next morning

Once they were assigned a cabin on Lieutenant's Donavan's ship, William immediately asked about Elizabeth's letter.

Retrieving it from his bag, Richard handed it to his cousin, saying, "She wrote this missive the morning after I told her the *Endeavour* had sunk. She was insistent that I give it you as soon as I found you."

Richard looked down sheepishly. "I confess it was not my finest hour. I was out of hope and very despondent. I could not see how anyone could survive a sinking ship, though I said nothing to her of my doubts. Still, Elizabeth was so positive you were still alive that she convinced me of it, too. Darcy, I do not know how a man with your inflated ego and pompous airs accomplished it, but you managed to marry an extraordinary woman."

"First, I thank you for the kind words regarding my character," William said sardonically. "Still, I will admit that securing Elizabeth's love was pure luck on my part; well, *that* and God's grace."

"Now, if you do not mind, I should like to read my letter and then borrow your shaving kit to rid myself of this beard. Except for the clothes, I would like Elizabeth to see the man she sent off to Ireland— not a dishevelled stranger."

"Of course." Locating his shaving kit, Richard laid it on the desk in front of William. Then, no doubt to give his cousin privacy, he crossed to the farthest porthole to take in the view.

As he brought the missive written in Elizabeth's beautiful hand to his nose, the faint scent of rosewater recalled memories of the love notes his wife often left for him in his study. Closing his eyes, William imagined her sitting at her small writing desk and penning the missive. Then he broke the seal and began to read.

My Darling William,
Through steadfast prayer, I know that God, in His infinite

*grace, has kept you alive for my sake and the children's. He knew
we would be utterly destroyed without you.*

    *I cannot convey the depth of my thankfulness to Him, nor
the intensity of my love for you. I lack the words to do either
justice. But, like a fresh breath of air after a rain, the belief that
I shall soon hold you in my arms has renewed my battered soul
and filled my heart with joy.*

    *Come home to us as soon as possible, dearest. We love you so
very much.*

Your devoted wife,
Elizabeth

William had already been planning to return to Pemberley straight-away, and Elizabeth's loving words only reinforced that. As he refolded the letter and placed it inside his coat, he said, "As soon as we reach Liverpool, I plan to set out for Pemberley."

"Surely you cannot mean that?" Richard asked. "It would be best to take a room at the Crown Inn and start for Derbyshire the next day."

"I do mean it. I had rather start for Derbyshire as soon as possible."

"I do not imagine you left your coach and servants in Liverpool to await your return from Ireland."

"Of course not! I hired a coach to take me there with plans to hire another when the time came to return home."

"Then surely you know that, given such short notice, it may take time to find a reputable business with a decent vehicle for hire. Or need I remind you of the coach you hired in Cornwall the summer after your graduation from Cambridge—the one with a wheel that came off during a rainstorm when we were barely a day's journey out of town?"

William sighed loudly. "I need no reminders, thank you. But surely with enough incentive, I should be able to hire something decent without much delay."

"How much incentive?"

"I am willing to pay double the current rate." At Richard's raised brows, William added, "It will be worth every farthing to see my family sooner rather than later."

"I know how much you wish to see them, Darcy, but trust me to find something suitable as quickly as possible."

"We shall discuss it again later," William replied. "For now, I plan to shave and then get some rest. I want to wake as soon as we reach Liverpool."

"I will not argue with you about that."

As Richard crossed the cabin to where his bag was occupying a bed, he stopped beside William to give his shoulder a squeeze. "I am not a very religious man, but in case I have not made myself clear, I thank God that He saw fit to spare your life. Not only would your wife and children be bereft without you, but I would have been, as well."

Too affected to reply, William bit his lip and merely nodded.

The next morning

The sound of shouts above deck and a quick look out the porthole revealed they were nearing the docks of Liverpool.

"It appears we are here," Richard said. "As soon as we land, you and I, along with Mr. Stevens and Lady Aileen, shall head straight to the Crown Inn to procure rooms for tonight. That will allow me to reunite Mr. Stevens with his cousin."

At William's raised brows, Richard added, "Lady Selina and I have been travelling in the same circles, trying to find you and her cousin. Naturally, I know which room she occupies at the inn."

Supressing a smile, William repeated, "Naturally."

"Do not act so smug!" Richard protested. "You do not know everything."

"Then tell me the truth," William stated solemnly. "Do you consider Lady Selina more than a friend?"

Shyly, Richard looked down. "If you must know, I fancy myself in love with her, but since I have not the means to marry presently, I wonder if I should offer for her now or wait until I have the funds in hand."

"You mentioned that she owns Houghton Park and is wealthy in her own right. I assume that means she may marry whomever she chooses. I say if you love her, make her an offer."

Richard smiled. "You make it sound so easy. However, I am not certain she feels the same way about me."

"I have never seen you so affected by any woman, and if I have learned anything from my ordeal, it is that life is short and can change in an instant. Grab whatever happiness you find and hold it tight while you are able."

"That is true. You may have convinced me."

"I hope I have. While you are reuniting Mr. Stevens with his cousin, I shall write a letter to Elizabeth and have an express rider deliver it straightaway. It may only precede my homecoming by a few hours, but I will not have my love wait one minute more than necessary to know I am safe and on my way home to her."

"That is an excellent idea. The clerk at the Crown Inn will send for an express rider, which will leave us more time to handle whatever business might arise before we can leave."

Suddenly, a sailor rapped on their cabin door. "Gentlemen, Lieutenant Donavan would like to see you before you leave the ship."

"Tell him we shall be there shortly," Richard replied. After the sailor left, he addressed William. "Have you made much progress in providing Donavan with your testimony?"

William picked up the piece of paper on which he had been writing. "I have written down everything I recall from being onboard the *Endeavour*, finding myself at Windemere Manor and my short-lived experience with Captain Silverhill. My testimony is not likely to do much towards convicting that blackguard of anything except threatening to kill me and the other hostages. Still, I have pledged to answer any questions that might arise in the future, as long as I can do so from Pemberley. I shall gladly testify under oath with the local constable as my witness."

"I believe Donavan will agree to that, especially because he will already have the testimony of Mrs. Grubbs, Captain Boone, Mr. Stevens and Lady Aileen."

"I am amazed that things have worked out as they have," William continued. "Even if it is true that Lady Aileen ran away with her father's steward, it seems Mr. Stevens is not deterred by her past actions. In fact, he seems quite taken with her."

"She seems quite taken with him, too."

"Let us hope Lord Camden will forgive his daughter. Family is too precious to discard if there is any hope of reconciliation."

"If he will not, should she and young Stevens marry, I feel certain Lady Selina will welcome them at Houghton Park."

"And residing at Houghton Park could possibly provide the gossips with an explanation of where she has been since leaving her father's estate."

"True. Sometimes if something sounds romantic, a complete fabrication will be believed over the truth. At least, that is what Mother maintains."

"And Aunt Eleanor is always right," William said with a grin.

"Yes, she is," Richard replied. "Now, let us join Lieutenant Donavan so that we may be among the first to leave the ship."

The Crown Inn

After securing a room for Lady Aileen and leaving Darcy in the room they would share that night because they could not leave until morning, Richard escorted Noel Stevens to Lady Selina's apartment. Upon opening the door, the maid stepped back to allow them to enter, and just as she did, her mistress walked out of the bedroom.

Hand flying to her heart, Lady Selina cried, "Noel, thank the Lord you are alive!"

Seeing her grab the top of a chair to steady herself, Noel rushed to his cousin's side to embrace her. "Pray sit down."

As soon as they both were occupying a small sofa, he turned to her to say, "The colonel has informed me that you and he have been searching for days for me and his cousin, Mr. Darcy. I apologise for leaving for Ireland without saying anything to you. That was childish of me, as well as foolish. If not for Colonel Fitzwilliam and members of the navy, it would have ended very badly."

"Yes, we followed every lead," she managed to reply, "but I have to credit Colonel Fitzwilliam for inspiring me to keep looking. I had little hope after learning the *Endeavour* had sunk and not finding a trace of you in Liverpool. If not for him, I might have given up and returned to Houghton Park thinking you were dead, instead of travelling to Ireland and the Isle of Man, where the colonel found a lead."

"You went to Ireland? Did you visit my relations in Dungannon?"

"I did," she replied. Unwilling to bring his spirits down by talking of her unpleasant reception, she added, "I shall tell you about that later. Suffice it to say, they were of no help."

"If not for the colonel, I might have died," Noel confessed. "Mr.

Darcy, Lady Aileen and I were close to being killed on that island when he arrived with naval reinforcements."

Richard interrupted. "Excuse me, but I need to return to Darcy. He and I must decide what to do about Lady Aileen, who it turns out is Georgiana Darcy's new sister." At Lady Selina's puzzled look, he added, "Mr. Stevens can inform you of the details of how Lady Aileen came to be a hostage alongside him. If you should need anything, he knows which room Darcy and I are in."

With a melancholy expression, he addressed Lady Selina. "Darcy and I will be heading to Pemberley, in Derbyshire, at first light. Naturally, he wishes to see his family as soon as possible."

She swallowed hard. "Naturally."

It was all Lady Selina could do not to call out when Richard turned to exit the room. Hurrying to the door, a thought came to mind as she watched him until he was completely out of sight. *Will I ever see you again, my love?*

Suddenly, Noel asked a question which brought her thoughts back to the present. "Selina, I wonder if Lady Aileen might share your apartment tonight since you have two bedrooms. I believe she is still too vulnerable to be left alone."

"Of course she may. Perhaps you will consider occupying her present room once she moves in with me. That would keep you from having to crowd into Colonel Fitzwilliam's accommodations."

"That would be wonderful, but I have no money to pay for a room, or anything actually, until I can access the account at my bank."

"Have no fear of that. I have plenty to pay for both our expenses until we get home." She hesitated, then added, "You are planning to return to Houghton Park with me, are you not?"

"I am, but first I must speak to Lady Aileen. I do not want her to think I have abandoned her. I know that she has some problems to work out with her father before we can discuss our future, and Mr. Darcy expressed his desire to have her stay at Pemberley until she can reconcile with Lord Camden. I wish to discuss when we might see each other again."

Lady Selina smiled. "So, it appears that you have fallen in love."

"I have," Noel said, now grinning from ear to ear. "I realise that all I have to offer her presently is Whistledown Farm in Wales. No doubt you recall that Lord Pembroke was kind enough to leave it to me in his will after grandmother's death. It may not be a grand estate, but I shall work hard to make it profitable again if Aileen will have me."

"When is the last time you were at Whistledown Farm?"

"I must have been about seventeen. Your father took me with him when he visited."

"Then you are unaware that I have been improving the estate since you reached your majority—adding tenant homes and acreage to it, increasing the number of sheep and cattle. All of that in addition to having work done on the manor house to bring it up to date. In fact, the current income is presently over two thousand a year with very little oversight, and the proceeds have all gone back into the estate's coffers. Along with the money you inherited from Father, there is nearly fifteen thousand pounds in that account at present. That is not a lot, but it is a start if you are willing to work to see it grow."

Overwhelmed, Noel embraced his cousin again. "You and Uncle Harvey were always so kind to me. I did not deserve his kindness; nor do I deserve yours."

"You are family! And if I learned anything after you left for Ireland, it is that family should be held close to the heart." She hugged him tighter. "I cannot wait until you marry and have children enough to fill the halls of both our estates."

Noel laughed. "What about children of your own?" At Lady Selina's dismayed look, he added, "You are still a young woman. If you would go to London for the Season, you would find there are many good men left who are worthy of you. Then, you could *help* me fill our family with children."

Lady Selina blushed. "I once thought I never wanted to marry or have children, but lately I have been reconsidering my resolution."

"Oh, my! If it was lately, may I assume that means you have developed feelings for Colonel Fitzwilliam? I saw how you looked at one another."

"I am not going to listen to you speculate about my life, young man!" Lady Selina teasingly replied. "I have been like a mother to you, and you should respect your elders."

Noel leaned in to kiss his cousin's forehead. "You cannot order me about, Selina. I shall not stop until I know everything there is to know about you and the colonel."

Having said that, he left to find Lady Aileen.

Left alone, Lady Selina's thoughts returned to Richard. *I hope there is something worth reporting before you leave for Pemberley.*

Later

As it grew time for dinner, Lady Selina, Lady Aileen and Mr. Stevens stopped by the colonel's room to ask if he and William wished to join them in the dining room.

"I have no appetite. I had rather stay here and retire early," William pronounced.

"What about you, Colonel?" Noel Stevens asked Richard.

"That sounds good to me. Unlike my cousin, I believe I could eat a horse."

"I hate to disappoint you," Lady Selina replied playfully. "But I understand beef stew is the featured item tonight."

"I cannot wait," Lady Aileen declared. "Mr. Stevens and I have not had much to eat in days, and none of it was appetising."

After they had all eaten and were preparing to go back to their rooms, Richard took hold of Lady Selina's arm to slow her progress. Glancing to where Noel had begun to escort Lady Aileen up the staircase, he said, "Will you take a brief walk with me in garden? We will not be gone long."

"What about Lady Aileen? She will be alone with my nephew."

"They have been alone with one another for days; one more time will not matter."

Lady Selina laughed. "You are right!"

Richard extended his arm, and she placed her hand upon it. Without another word they crossed the lobby of the inn to a door leading to a small, walled-off garden. Although lanterns had been lit all around the enclosure, making the entire space look magical, at this hour of the evening there was no one else about.

As soon as they stopped walking, Richard pulled Lady Selina into his arms for a gentle kiss. As her hands slid up to lock behind his head, her body seemed to melt into his, and what began tenderly soon became a duel between his lips and hers.

Richard broke the kiss suddenly, gasping for breath as he lay his head atop hers. "Forgive me. I never meant to kiss you so fiercely."

"You did not? What a shame, for I was hoping you would repeat it."

"You were?"

"Yes. Moreover, I hoped you would say you have no intention of sending me back to Houghton Park without an understanding between us."

Richard became flustered. "I *do* want an understanding between us … that is to say, I want you to marry me; however …"

Selina's green eyes twinkled. "However?"

"I have not the funds just yet to resign my position with His Majesty's army and become a gentleman farmer. I cannot ask you to marry me just to watch me leave at the next whim of my superiors. I could be ordered to the Continent with no warning."

"I thought I made it clear that I am wealthy enough for the both of us! And what good is money if life is spent alone? Is it not the second son's lot to find a wealthy woman and marry her? So, what is wrong with marrying me?"

"Nothing is wrong with that. In fact, you are everything I have ever wanted in a wife. It is just … I wanted to take care of you, and not the other way around."

"Oh, Richard. Do you not see? You *will* be taking care of me. And if you care half as much about me as I care about you, we shall be the happiest of couples!"

A fierce kiss ensued before Richard whispered into her hair, "I love you with all my heart, Selina Grey. Will you become my wife?"

"I love you, too," she murmured, "and yes, I will marry you."

Another searing kiss followed before Richard broke away to say, "I must see Darcy home first. Then, I shall come to Houghton Park so we can make plans to wed. If you agree, I would like to keep our good news quiet until after we have set a date."

"I agree. Take your cousin home and, once he is settled, come to me."

After several more kisses, each more passionate than the last, the door to the garden opened and a subtle cough was heard.

"I am sorry, sir," an employee of the inn said, "but the door must be locked by this time each evening."

Taking Lady Selina by the hand, Richard pulled her past the employee and inside the inn, saying, "That is quite alright, my good man. We were just leaving."

Chapter 23

The next morning

William awoke to find himself alone in the room he had shared with his cousin. In the time it took to quickly shave and dress, he became irritated that Richard had failed to wake him as he had requested.

Suddenly, the sound of a key in the lock announced that the colonel had returned. Poised to chastise him, William was taken aback when the door opened, and Georgiana rushed into his arms.

"Oh, Brother!" she cried, beginning to tear up. "Thank the Lord you are safe. I have been so worried about you!"

Richard and the viscount entered the room just as William stuttered, "I-I am well, Georgie," as he kissed the top of her head. "Please do not cry, or you may get me started."

He turned to Matthew. "I do not understand how you got to Liverpool so quickly. Surely, you had not yet heard from Richard that he had found me."

"No, we had not. Only after we ran into Richard downstairs and he explained the extent of your ordeal were we made aware of what you had endured. That he was involved in my sister's rescue, too, had to be an answer to our prayers."

"There have been a lot of prayers answered," William replied. "But if you did not know I had been rescued, why did you set out for England?"

"For weeks, Georgiana has been worried that you had not replied to her letters and thought for certain you must be on your way to Ballyneen. After reading the news of the *Endeavour* being lost, we both feared you might have been on board. In addition, the man I hired to search for Aileen had had no luck finding her, so we decided it was time to sail back to England to get answers to both of our questions." At William's nod, Matthew continued. "I understand Aileen is with Lady Selina, and I am anxious to speak with her."

To Georgiana, he said, "Visit with your brother whilst I talk to my sister; I shall return shortly."

As he went to leave, he held out a hand to William. "Darcy, I am relieved not only to find you alive but, apparently, in good health."

William shook his hand and once the viscount left, pulled Georgiana into another embrace before guiding her to a settee where they both sat down.

"Am I correct to believe that you and the viscount have settled your differences?"

A sob escaped Georgiana. "I am so sorry to have caused this entire ordeal by asking you to come to Ireland. Our problems were caused entirely by a misunderstanding, and now that we have talked about the matter, Matthew and I are as well-suited as ever, whereas you came close to dying whilst trying to help me!"

"Shh!" William hushed. "You are not to blame for the storm or for the circumstances in which I found myself. Only the Lord knows why bad things happen, but He saw fit to bring me through all of it, and, for that I shall always be thankful."

"As will I," she said, kissing his cheek.

"Will you return to Pemberley with Richard and me?"

"No. I do intend to visit, but only after we have settled things with Aileen and Lord Camden. Matthew intends to inform his father that we do not wish to return to Ballyneen, as well as to learn his intentions regarding Aileen."

"You and Matthew will need to speak to Lady Selina's nephew, Noel Stevens. Apparently, he is smitten with your sister and she with him. Richard and I believe they will marry soon."

"If Mr. Stevens is an honourable man and she finds him suitable, *that* would certainly make for a fortunate solution to Aileen's quandary."

"According to Richard, Stevens is not only honourable, but he is wealthy enough to make a good catch."

Amazed, Georgiana shook her head. "It seems all my worries have been for naught. I need to remember to trust in God's love for us."

"I truly believe prayer is the only reason I am still alive, so I heartily agree."

Pulling his sister closer, he kissed the top of her head. "Now, what is this I hear about my becoming an uncle?"

Georgiana seemed taken aback. "Who told you?"

"Who is it who knows everything first?"

She laughed. "Richard!"

Hours Later

In a coach

They were so weary that Richard and William had little conversation after leaving Liverpool. In fact, Admiral Turlington's personal coach, loaned to them at Lieutenant Donavan's request, was so comfortable both fell asleep shortly after their journey to Pemberley began. Consequently, Richard was startled awake when his cousin suddenly spoke.

"If we make the inn at Sutton by dark and rise tomorrow at dawn, I can be home by tomorrow night."

"We will have to change horses more often than usual just to make Sutton," Richard replied grumpily. "Not to mention we need excellent weather. If we run into rain along the way, it could take another entire day to reach Pemberley. Darcy, you must be reasonable."

"Why are you being so pessimistic?"

"I am not trying to be. However, since Admiral Turlington was kind enough to lend us a driver and two footmen along with the coach, I imagine he expects us to return them in the same condition in which they began this journey. Which means we need to allow them to get some rest."

William sighed heavily. "I cannot wait another moment to see Elizabeth and the children. Every fibre of my being aches for them, and part of me wishes to leap out of this coach and take off on horseback."

"I know you miss them terribly, but you need to get home safely. You have not fully recovered from your ordeal during the storm, and I should not have to remind you that you lost a good deal of blood, thanks to that wound on your back."

Frustrated, William took a deep breath and blew it out. "I know you are right, but I—"

Richard interrupted, changing the subject. "What is your opinion of Lady Aileen accompanying her brother and Georgiana back to Berkley Hall? Do you think Lord Camden will welcome her with open arms?"

"Perhaps *not* with open arms. Lord Camden appears to be a harsh man and used to having his own way. One can only hope he learned the importance of family after she ran away." William shrugged. "In any case, I imagine she will not be too disappointed if her father does not change his way of thinking, since Mr. Stevens has proposed marriage."

Richard shook his head. "I would not say this to anyone but you, but I believe Lady Aileen is fortunate that the steward she ran off with died when the ship sank. Had he lived, I have no doubt he would have turned up at some point demanding money to keep silent."

"You may be right about that."

"I know such men. Trust me. I am."

Out of the blue, William smiled widely, causing Richard to ask, "What has suddenly made you happy?"

"I was just imagining Georgiana as a mother."

"She will be a most loving mother; she has had a good example."

"Why do you say that? Mother died soon after she was born."

"True, but she had you. I have never told you this, but I have always admired how you raised Georgiana. Uncle George was absent far too much after Lady Anne died to be a good father, but you made certain your sister had love and guidance. My aunt could not have done a better job of making her feel secure."

"I cannot agree, but I did the best I could under the circumstances."

"Nonsense! You were an excellent mother *and father* to her!"

Shaking his head, William said, "Just think. Georgiana's child and my next will be about the same age. Would it not be wonderful if my children and hers grew up close to one another? And I am not just speaking of merely the distance in our estates, but of a closeness of kinship. I know my life was better for having grown up with you."

"I feel the same," Richard replied with a wry grin. "If not for spending my summers with you, I would have killed Leighton years ago." Pleased to hear William laugh, he continued. "Now that the viscount is determined not to return to Ballyneen, what you desire may come to pass."

"Speaking of living nearby, will you live at Houghton Park after you and Lady Selina marry? I understand it is less than forty miles from Pemberley."

Richard answered warily. "Who said we had plans to marry?"

"No one had to; it was written all over your face this morning."

A smile played at the corners of Richard's lips. "I took your advice and asked her to marry me after dinner last night, and she agreed."

Delighted, William reached across the coach to slap his cousin's knee. "Bravo! When were you going to tell me?"

"We decided to wait until you were settled at Pemberley, and I had joined her at Houghton Park to finalise our plans before making an announcement."

"I will keep it a secret, then."

"We both know you never keep secrets from Elizabeth, so I expect you will tell her straightaway. Just ask her not to mention it to anyone else, especially not my parents. We will announce it once we have our plans in place."

"I know Elizabeth will be overjoyed for you, just as I am, but we will do as you wish." Turning to look out the window, William asked, "How far are we from our next stop?"

"I estimate we have about five miles to go. We can eat at the inn whilst we wait for the horses to be changed. The food is nothing special, but it is edible."

"How do you know this?"

"When you have travelled as many miles as I have in His Majesty's service, you know every place where you might get a decent meal … or a bad one!"

"I shall have to trust you on that."

"Yes, you will. Now I suggest you close your eyes and try to rest. I have a feeling you will need all your strength once you and Elizabeth are reunited."

"Richard!" William said, drawing out his cousin's name in a warning. "What have I said about speaking of my relationship with my wife?"

"I was merely referring to your children demanding all your attention once they learn you have returned. I know how energetic Ben can be, so I wonder at you and Elizabeth having any time to yourselves."

"I suggest you stop explaining whilst you are ahead."

Richard bit his lip to keep from smiling. "Yes, Cousin."

Pemberley
The next day

It was the middle of the morning when an express rider arrived at the portico of Pemberley. After showing him to the kitchen for food and drink, Mr. Walker rushed towards Mrs. Reynolds' office to show her the letter the man had brought. Finding the housekeeper at her desk, he stepped inside the room, shut the door, and quietly handed her the missive.

"This just came by express," he murmured, as though not sure if he should be happy. "If I am not mistaken, it is written in the master's hand."

As the white-haired servant took the letter and examined the handwriting, he watched her shoulders slump with relief. Closing her eyes she whispered, "Thank you, Lord." Then, looking up at the butler, she added, "I feared we might never see his handwriting again."

Mrs. Reynolds stood and smoothed her skirts. "I shall take it to the mistress. Please find Cook and have her send a pot of tea up to Mrs. Darcy's sitting room."

Reaching into a drawer, she removed a small jar. "I will take Dr. Camryn's calming draught along should she become upset. I can mix it in with the tea if it becomes necessary. In any case, please have a footman stand by to fetch the doctor if need be."

As the housekeeper rushed down the hall towards the grand staircase, Mr. Walker hurried to the kitchen.

Elizabeth's sitting room

Though Bennet and Anne were usually in their classroom by this hour, practicing numbers and letters with the assistance of paints on paper or chalk on a blackboard, today they had joined their mother in her sitting room. Elizabeth often supplemented their education by writing short tales that illustrated whatever they were being taught at the time. She would read the stories to them and quiz them on their numbers. Today, as she sat on the settee with Anne in her lap, Bennet sat as close as possible beside her.

Mrs. Reynolds poised just outside the door to peek inside and heard Elizabeth say, "Mrs. Purrser came to visit Mrs. Squiggly, the rabbit who had just given birth to eight babies. She wanted to leave her a basket of baby clothes and a blanket."

Addressing Bennet, Elizabeth asked, "Do you recall how many babies Mrs. Purrser has? She is the barn cat we read about in our last story."

"Six!" Bennet replied. Anne repeated his answer, as she always did.

"That is correct," Elizabeth replied. "Now, who can tell me which one has the most babies, Mrs. Purrser or Mrs. Squiggly?"

"Mrs. Squiggly!" Bennet answered confidently. "She has two more babies than Mrs. Purrser."

"Two more!" Anne proudly repeated.

"You both are right!"

Just then, Elizabeth looked up to see Mrs. Reynolds with a concerned look on her face. Kissing Anne, she set her on her feet and leaned in to give Bennet a kiss on his forehead, saying, "Ben, darling, please take your sister back to the classroom and tell Mrs. Cummings that I said you performed so well with your numbers that you may each have a gingerbread biscuit with tea."

"Yes, Mama!" Eager to get the treat, Bennet and Anne filed out of the room past Mrs. Reynolds without any argument.

The smile on Elizabeth's face faded as soon as the housekeeper stepped into the room. She stood. After so many years working alongside each other, Elizabeth could interpret her expressions easily. "You look worried."

Instead of arguing, Mrs. Reynolds merely held the missive out to Elizabeth.

"This came by express rider just now."

A maid suddenly hurried into the room and set a tray of tea and biscuits on a small table in front of the window seat before exiting as quickly as she had come. Reaching into her pocket to be certain the draught was still in place, the housekeeper's anxiety rose as Elizabeth broke the seal and began to read.

> *My precious Elizabeth,*
> *Richard and I are in Liverpool, and, God willing, I shall hold you in my arms again tomorrow evening. I cannot promise with certainty, but I will do everything in my power to make it happen.*

Wishing you to receive this note before I arrive leaves no time to go into details of all that has happened. What I will say is that I love you and the children with all my heart, and I cannot wait to be reunited.

Your loving husband,
William

Elizabeth sank down on the settee and began to sob. Uncertain what news the letter had brought, Mrs. Reynolds walked over to pat her shoulder gently. "There, there, Mrs. Darcy. Pray remember the babe and try to stay calm."

"I-I am not-not crying because I am sad, but because I am so very happy," Elizabeth managed to stutter at length. "William is on his way home! He and Richard were to leave Liverpool yesterday morning!"

"Thank the good Lord!"

"Yes!" Elizabeth cried, looking up. "Thank you, God, for answering my prayers!" To Mrs. Reynolds she said, "According to this letter, he may be able to make Pemberley this very day."

"Do you intend to tell the children?"

"No. Anne is full young to understand why we will have to wait. And although I sometimes think Bennet is wise beyond his years, he is still just a baby. If William is not home by the time they retire, I had rather they wake up to discover he has returned than have them look for him every minute."

"I brought some of the calming draught Dr. Camryn created for you. Would you like to take it?"

"I had rather not. It makes me sleep far too long, and I have a great deal to do before William arrives."

Elizabeth stood. "Please have hot water brought up for a bath right away. I shall make use of the lavender soap William purchased for me in London, for he loves that fragrance." Reaching for a bellpull, she said, "I will need Florence's help washing my hair. If I wash it now whilst the sun is still out, it should dry quickly if I sit on the balcony."

She hurried about the room, opening drawers and bringing clothes out to lay on the bed. "Oh, and I want the children to have their baths directly after dinner. A bath always makes them sleepy, and if William is not home by then, I wish them to retire early so they will be well-rested tomorrow."

"Yes, Mrs. Darcy."

As Mrs. Reynolds walked out of the mistress' sitting room, it was with a much lighter step than she had entered it. A weight had been lifted from her shoulders. Trying to keep up the appearance of believing the master would return for the sake of Mrs. Darcy and the children had taken a heavy toll—a burden that increased the longer the ordeal lasted. Elated to learn everything would soon be as it should, Mrs. Reynolds smiled at all the maids and footmen she passed.

When she encountered Florence on the grand staircase, Elizabeth's maid stopped her. "Forgive me, but may I assume the express brought good news?"

"It did. The master is on his way home and might even arrive today."

"How wonderful!" Florence replied. "I tried to have faith that he would return, but—"

"I know," Mrs. Reynolds said, patting the maid's arm. "It is surely a miracle!"

On a highway just outside of Lambton

"I have to say your luck is holding, Darcy. We should make Pemberley not long after dark."

Trying not to let his emotions get the better of him, William replied, "I cannot agree entirely. It was not luck, but Providence, that brought me home."

"You may be right. I had believed you were buried at sea, but you have returned from the dead … much like Lazarus."

"I have thought of that a lot since I came to my senses. So many died. Why was I spared? It makes me want to live every day as though it could be my last. I shall never take my family or my position for granted ever again. Whatever good I can do as the head of my family or the master of Pemberley, I intend to do it."

Richard laughed. "Well, I, for one, think you were a pretty good man just as you were. However, if it would make you feel any nobler,

I would love for you to gift me with Uncle George's double-barrelled pistol, which I have long admired."

"I said I intend to become a *better* man," William answered, smiling crookedly. "Not a *foolish* one."

Chapter 24

Pemberley

By the time dinner was served, William still had not returned. Very disappointed, although she tried hard not to let it show, a weary Elizabeth had put the children to bed though she could not bring herself to retire as well.

"Ma'am, may I be of service before I go downstairs?" her maid asked. "Do you wish to change clothes?"

Having donned a light-blue silk nightgown and placed the matching robe at the foot of her bed, Elizabeth replied, "No, thank you, Florence. I am perfectly comfortable as I am."

She held up a book of poems by the Irish poet Thomas Moore. "William and I often read an excerpt from this before we retire. I intend to occupy this chaise and read from it until I cannot keep my eyes open, so there is no need for you to stay awake as well."

Florence smiled. "Very well. Unless you ring for me, I shall see you in the morning."

An hour later, before retiring for the night, Mrs. Reynolds went upstairs to check once more on the mistress. She found Elizabeth asleep on the chaise with the book splayed across her chest. Clancy lay sleeping below her on the floor. The dog stirred when she picked up a blanket and placed it over her mistress, but he made no sound and went right back to sleep before the door to the bedroom closed again.

As she went down the grand staircase, the housekeeper was surprised to see the footman who was posted at the front door open it and walk out on the portico. Hearing the unmistakable sound of a coach on the gravel drive, a flick of her wrist sent another footman after Mr. Walker as she hurriedly followed the first footman outside.

Elizabeth's bedroom

The minute Clancy heard an all-too-familiar sound on the drive below, he was wide awake. Running to the bedroom door, he began to scratch at it and whine. Unable to escape, he hurried back to Elizabeth and began barking.

It took Elizabeth a moment to realise what had roused her. Instantly wide awake, she grabbed her robe and donned it as she hurried towards the bedroom door. The moment she opened it, Clancy sprinted out of the room and down the hall towards the grand staircase as fast as his short legs could carry him. Full of expectation and her heart pounding in her chest, Elizabeth followed.

Suddenly, the dark, moonless night teemed with people. Grooms and footmen appeared seemingly from nowhere to assist the huge, black coach parked at the steps leading to the front door. The vehicle was so resplendent that Mrs. Reynolds knew at once it must have brought the master home. Too dazed to move, she waited for the coach door to open.

Even with the torches that always lit Pemberley's lawn after dark, it was difficult to recognise the face of the man who exited the coach first. It was not until that figure turned and she recognised Colonel Fitzwilliam that her heart began to hammer so forcefully she feared she might faint from sheer happiness.

Mr. Walker, who had joined her on the portico just as Richard stepped out of the coach, was not as dumbfounded. "Saints be praised! Our boy has returned, Mrs. Reynolds!" he pronounced jubilantly.

Too filled with emotion to reply, the housekeeper merely nodded before realising she had forgotten her promise to Mrs. Darcy. "I must inform the mistress that Mr. Darcy is here."

As she hurried back into the foyer, she was shocked to see Clancy bounding down the grand staircase with Elizabeth right behind him.

"Please, Mrs. Darcy, do be careful," was all Mrs. Reynolds managed to say as both Elizabeth and Clancy passed her on their way out the front door.

The housekeeper hurried back to the portico and was surprised to find Mrs. Darcy standing there as motionless as a statue, watching the scene below. The second William alighted from the coach, however, the back of one of Elizabeth's hands flew to her mouth to stop a small sob from escaping, and instantly she darted down the steps.

Having no time to utter another warning, the housekeeper followed as quickly as possible.

William, who had stooped to pet a jubilant Clancy, stood just in time to catch sight of Elizabeth coming towards him. She looked like an angel with her dark hair loose about her shoulders, her silky blue robe sparkling in the light of several lanterns now set along the steps. With no time to react, he braced himself as she flew into his arms. He lifted her off the ground as her arms slid around his neck and she buried her face in his cravat.

"Oh, William! Oh, William," she repeated until another stifled sob escaped, and the words were replaced with a torrent of tears.

Tightening his embrace, William kissed her hair and whispered endearments in her ear. "My dearest love ... my heart."

Placing her back on her feet, he cupped her face and searched her ebony eyes. Evidence of the love that had sustained him throughout his long ordeal shown through her tears and he confessed, "I love you more than life, Elizabeth Darcy," before capturing her lips and kissing her passionately.

After she gained a measure of control, Elizabeth murmured against William's shirt, "Forgive me, darling; I promised I would not make a spectacle of myself in front of the servants, and I fear I have done just that."

"You have nothing to apologise for, sweetheart; however, I pray you will calm yourself for the sake of the child you carry."

She pulled back to look at him. "You-you know about the baby?"

"Richard told me. He was worried for your health."

Elizabeth shivered, prompting William to remove his coat and wrap it around her shoulders. "Let us go inside. It is too cold for you to be outside dressed like this."

As they began up the steps, one strong arm around her waist to support her, William asked, "Are the children asleep?"

"Yes, but if you like, we can wake them."

"Let the poor babies sleep. Tomorrow morning will be early enough to surprise them. All I want at this moment is to look upon their dear faces before I retire."

During the tender scene, Richard had picked up Clancy and headed up the steps. "Come on, my boy. You will have to await your turn for a proper welcome. Mrs. Darcy takes precedence over everyone tonight."

Encountering Mrs. Reynolds, who had stopped half-way down, he glanced back at the lovers below. "I hate to admit it, but at one time, I thought I would never witness their reunion."

"I believe we all had our doubts, even if we never gave voice to them," the housekeeper replied quietly. Then, promptly changing the subject, she asked, "Will you be wanting a hot bath, Colonel? I had water heated earlier, but it is still warm and can easily be reheated."

"No, thank you. Darcy and I both paid extra for a bath at the inn last night."

"Then I shall send up some warm water so you can wash. As for dinner, I fear everything has been returned to the kitchen, but Cook can send up a dinner tray if you like. She fixed Mr. Darcy's favourite venison stew."

"I would like that very much."

Watching the Darcys, Mrs. Reynolds reflected, "I wonder if the master will want to eat now."

Glancing back at his cousins, Richard chuckled. "I wager that Darcy has more on his mind tonight than food."

Endeavouring not to smile, Mrs. Reynolds waved a hand in dismissal. "Go on with you, Colonel, and make certain to take Clancy. Except for the master, you are the only one that dog will mind. If he is allowed to run the halls, he will keep the entire house awake, trying to follow the master."

"Did you hear that, Clancy? You have a reputation for not taking orders. Only an old bloke like me can truly appreciate an independent spirit. Let us prove to Mrs. Reynolds that your wilful reputation is a falsehood of the gravest kind. It is not that you do not take orders; it is simply that you have your own opinion of what needs to be done and when."

The housekeeper waited until Richard disappeared inside the house to let go a small chuckle. William and Elizabeth had reached her by then.

"Will you have something to eat now, sir?" she asked.

Stopping to gaze lovingly at his wife, William pulled Elizabeth close to kiss her forehead. "I appreciate your concern, Mrs. Reynolds, but I have the whole world in my arms right now, and I am in want of nothing."

After placing a tender kiss on each of his still-sleeping children, William allowed Elizabeth to escort him to her bedroom. Once there, she locked the door and turned to look at him with a mixture of unadulterated love and desire.

As he began to unbutton his waistcoat, Elizabeth hurried to assist. With each button loosened, she stood on tiptoes to place a fervent kiss on his lips.

Growing more impassioned with every touch, it was only after she had helped him pull his shirt over his head that Elizabeth noticed the bandages wrapped around his torso.

"You have been hurt!" she exclaimed, stepping back. Then, turning William so that she could examine his back, she asked, "What happened?"

"Nothing serious," William replied as he faced her again, offering a forced smile and small shrug. "I did not move fast enough to avoid a sword, and Richard insisted on sewing me up. You know he worries like an old woman, so I acceded to his wishes to make him happy."

Elizabeth's eyes filled with tears. "Do not humour me, William. My nerves are too raw. I know that if Richard stitched it closed, the wound must have been serious."

Pulling her again into a tight embrace, he placed more kisses just below her ear and moved down her neck. "Even if it were, it is halfway healed already."

When instead of replying she bit her lip, William lifted her chin with two fingers. "Look at me."

When Elizabeth complied, he brushed the tears from her cheeks with his thumbs. "God saw fit to bring me home in reasonably good condition, so instead of contemplating the bad that happened, we should rejoice in His goodness."

Swallowing, she forced a smile. "You are correct. And I do thank God for bringing you home safely."

As William helped her out of her robe and gown, it became clear what would happen next. "Will it affect your wound? I do not wish to cause you still more pain."

"The only thing that would pain me now, my darling, is not being allowed to love you."

With that, William whisked the woman he adored off her feet and laid her on the silky sheets of the bed before joining her.

The next morning

When Elizabeth awoke, she reached out for William, only to discover his side of the bed empty. Confused, she glanced to where a candle on the bedside table had almost burned through. She was about to throw off the counterpane when William entered the bedroom by way of the balcony. As he pushed aside the curtain covering that door, it became clear that dawn was already breaking.

"There you are," she murmured as he walked over to sit beside her on the bed and leaned in to kiss her. "I have no recollection of when you left me. It must have been very early."

"It was. Richard rises with the sun, and I knew he would want to show Adams how to care for my wound before he leaves for Houghton Park tomorrow. My cousin is such a stickler when it comes to training those who must follow his instructions. Moreover, I wished to change clothes before seeing the children."

"Adams was already awake?"

"He was. I suppose the entire household, except for Anne and Bennet, is aware that I arrived last night. I found Adams already laying out my clothes when I entered my bedroom."

"He was a tremendous help with Bennet whilst you were away. Our son often went to him for reassurance when he was despondent, and Adams always knew what to say or do to allay his fears."

"I shall be certain to thank him."

Elizabeth pulled William closer. "I wish we had more time to be alone this morning," she whispered against him.

"I debated waking you before I went to dress, but it was obvious that you were exhausted when I got home, and it did not help that I kept you awake a good portion of the night."

"It was as much my choice as yours," Elizabeth replied, cupping his cheek tenderly. "I was afraid that if I fell asleep, I would wake to find your homecoming was all a dream."

"I know, my love," William replied, kissing the tip of her nose tenderly. "It seems impossible to me to go from despair to heaven in such a short span of time."

Elizabeth leaned in so that their foreheads touched. "I could selfishly keep you in bed all day, but the children deserve to see you as soon as they are awake. They have missed you so sorely."

Bringing her hands to his heart, he said, "Elizabeth, before I left for Ireland, I knew I loved you and the children, but after coming so close to losing everyone dear to me, I have a new appreciation for what constitutes genuine love. Thank you for loving me and for giving me Bennet and Anne. I could not have asked for a better wife or mother for my children."

She stroked her small, rounded belly. "I cannot wait until this little one can join us. He or she will have the best man in all of England for a father."

Leaning down to kiss her stomach, William said, "All you need to know, little one, is that your mother is absolutely perfect. I know, for I spent years avoiding all women because I doubted I could find the perfect one to be my wife. Then Providence slapped me off my high horse, and I landed at Elizabeth Bennet's feet."

She laughed. "I do not recall it happening like that at all!"

"Oh, but I do!" William replied, grinning, "And I have an excellent memory."

William and Elizabeth had barely entered the children's classroom when the side door burst open. Bennet, always the leader, rushed in, leaving Mrs. Cummings to follow leading Anne. Because William had his back to the door, for a moment Bennet stood dumbfounded at the sight. It took barely a second, though, before he realised who was there.

As William turned, Ben rushed forwards, wrapping himself around his father's legs. "Papa!" he shouted.

William stooped to embrace him while Anne struggled to be free of her nanny's grip. Once put on her feet, Anne ran towards William crying, "Papa! Papa!"

Holding both his children left William with no free hands to wipe away the tears streaming down his face. Blinking steadily, William mouthed "Thank you" as Elizabeth removed a handkerchief from her pocket and dabbed at his eyes.

Greatly affected by the scene, Mrs. Cummings slipped out of the room to hide her own tears.

That afternoon

Mrs. Green and Elizabeth sat on the large, white swing in the garden watching their husbands and Colonel Fitzwilliam instruct Bennet on how to ride his new, golden-coloured pony. William was also holding an insistent Anne, who kept asking to ride the pony, too.

"What a pretty animal!" Judith Green observed. "I have never seen one quite that colour. Has Bennet given her a name yet?"

Elizabeth giggled. "Despite the objections of my husband and mortification of the colonel, he wanted to call her Daffodil."

Judith Green laughed. "I thought Bennet wanted to be a soldier. I cannot imagine anyone riding into battle aboard a mount called Daffodil. Daffodil ... Daffodil," Mrs. Green repeated. "There is simply no way to say it without smiling."

"The colonel managed to convince him to change it to Pegasus by telling him that a pony named after that Greek myth would run so fast people would think it had wings."

Suddenly, the rector was walking towards them, holding Anne. "She wanted to speak to her mother," he said, smiling as he placed her in Elizabeth's lap.

Immediately the child pointed towards Pegasus. "Anne's pony!"

Elizabeth tried not to laugh. "No, sweetheart, that is Ben's pony, but with Papa's help, you will be allowed to ride her. And, once you reach your fourth birthday, Papa will buy you a pony of your own."

Clearly not happy, Anne pouted and closed her eyes. Kissing her daughter's head, Elizabeth said, "I fear she is worn out and needs a nap. She and Bennet have not rested since seeing their father this morning."

Eyeing her husband as he walked back towards the others, Judith

Green said, "We really should leave. I fear we have already overstayed our welcome by remaining this long, but the instant James heard that Fitzwilliam had returned, he was resolute that he would see him today. You know James thinks of your husband as a son … we both do."

"And we think of you as our family, too. We are forever indebted to you and the vicar for watching over us whilst William was away. With all my family scattered hither and yon, I could not have endured this ordeal without having you both for support."

"James and I are just happy to be of use." She stood. "I shall corral my husband and point him towards the vicarage so that you and Fitzwilliam may have some time alone."

"We will not be totally alone until Richard leaves for Houghton Park tomorrow morning."

"I heard him mention Lady Selina to James. Do you think he will marry her?"

"Since Richard will be here for dinner, why not stay and ask him yourself. I feel certain he will tell you."

"No, thank you. James needs to be home to prepare Sunday's sermon. In light of Fitzwilliam's return, he mentioned teaching on the Prodigal Son."

Elizabeth laughed. "I hope he does not intend to use William as an example of the prodigal."

"Certainly not!" Mrs. Green said, laughing. "But the idea of welcoming Fitzwilliam home brought to mind the joy of having a beloved son return to his father's bosom." Wiping away a stray tear that slipped from her eye, she added, "God has surely answered all our prayers."

"Yes. He has."

That evening

Despite knowing that William would have to be told about Lady Catherine's pact with Gregory Wright and his aunt's shameful visit to Pemberley, Elizabeth had not wished to ruin her husband's first hours at home by mentioning that subject. Consequently, knowing the colonel needed to be informed as well, she had waited until the evening to broach the subject. As she debated how to begin, luck would have it that Richard and William began a conversation that provided a natural opening for her.

"You are not obligated to lend me a coach for my journey to Houghton Park, Darcy. I was planning on riding Titan."

"After searching so long for me, you must be weary. Lending you the coach is the least I can do to make your trip more comfortable."

"I will not pretend that I had rather travel on horseback, so I shall just acquiesce and say thank you."

"You are most welcome. By the way, have you thought to inform the earl of my recovery?"

"I sent a short express when we first got to Liverpool; however, I am certain he is eagerly awaiting my return to London to acquaint him with the details."

"Speaking of the earl," Elizabeth interrupted, "he and Lady Matlock were here a sennight ago."

Now she had the attention of both men.

"They were here?" William repeated.

Schooling her features to show no evidence of the distress that incident still evoked, Elizabeth answered calmly. "Yes. I did not wish to dampen the joy we all felt at your homecoming, so I purposefully waited to tell you what brought the Matlocks to Pemberley. However, now that Richard is to leave, it is incumbent that I—" Pausing, Elizabeth swallowed hard.

William reached for her hand, saying tenderly, "I am home, sweetheart. No one can harm us now."

Reassured, Elizabeth proceeded to tell them everything. Once she had finished, Richard stood and began to pace.

"I knew you could not trust that snake! I forgot to tell you, Darcy, but whilst I was in Belfast, I went to the distillery Wright wanted you to buy. According to the manager, it is nearly out of business. A blight on the apple crop in Ireland means the only apples they have to work with presently are imported from Scotland. He said they were paid for by an anonymous investor, but the distillery could not long sustain the cost of shipping them in from other countries. After learning of our dear aunt's manipulation of Wright, I imagine she was the anonymous investor."

Suddenly, he turned to Elizabeth. "By the way, what punishment did Father mete out for Lady Catherine and Mr. Wright?"

"Lord Matlock said that, from that point on, all of Mr. Wright's debts held by your aunt belonged to him, and he would decide what to do about him once he had time to consider all the implications. As far as I know, he still resides at Parkleigh Manor."

"And our aunt?"

"Your uncle contended that if he sent her to Bedlam, it would reflect badly on the entire family. Consequently, he vowed to appoint someone to oversee Rosings, and from now until the day she dies, Lady Catherine will be a virtual prisoner there. All correspondence will pass through Lord Matlock, and she will not be allowed to travel outside the confines of the property or to entertain company. The only exception will be to attend church services."

Richard barked a laugh. "As though attending church will do her any good!"

Elizabeth had watched William's jaw tighten as she spoke, though he stayed silent.

"We both know our aunt is capable of great evil, but after all you did to help that sorry Wright—" Richard cried, slamming his hand against the table. "I find it hard to believe he was not only willing to stab you in the back, but the moment he thought you were dead, he was eager to make Elizabeth his wife!"

"He could never have me!" Elizabeth declared. "I never thought of him as anything beyond Jonathan's father. Besides, if anything were to happen to William, I would never marry again."

Roused from his deliberations by that declaration, William brought Elizabeth's hand to his lips for a soft kiss, making her smile.

"Still, if possible, he would have stolen you!" Richard declared. Irritated at his cousin's silence, he added, "Have you nothing to say, Darcy?"

"I will later. For now, what I will say is that I should have paid more attention to my wife's intuition. She cautioned me not to put much trust in Wright again."

Forming a fist, Richard pounded it into his other hand. "Maybe I should put off my trip until after I have a word with that blackguard!"

"You should focus on your future and let me deal with Wright."

"It would be cruel to make Lady Selina wait any longer. Go on to Houghton Park."

Richard smiled wryly. "It seems I am outnumbered."

Chapter 25

Pemberley
Three months later

As Adams walked into his employer's bedroom, he was surprised to find Mr. Darcy examining the contents of a dresser drawer. Certain that he had packed everything needed for the trip, the valet enquired, "May I ask what you are looking for, sir?"

"I just recalled that when I left the island, I placed my pocket watch inside a small pouch for safe keeping and hid it in the bottom of the satchel of clothes Mrs. Grubbs was kind enough to give me. When I arrived here, I dropped that pouch in this drawer until such time as I could take it to my jeweller. It had stopped working after being buried in the sand." He shook his head. "I suppose I have learned not to be a slave to time, for this is the first I have thought about it since."

"I have noticed that you have become more tranquil," Adams replied.

"What do you mean by that?"

"Perhaps I should have said you do not appear to let things disturb you as much as before your ordeal."

"I will take that as a compliment," William replied, before suddenly holding up a pouch. "Ah, here it is!"

Taking the watch from the pouch, he opened the lid and gazed at the portrait of Elizabeth inside. After rubbing his thumb lovingly over her image, he placed the watch in the small pocket of his coat reserved for such items.

"Even if it never works again, I shall always cherish it for holding the likeness of Mrs. Darcy."

"Perhaps her likeness could be placed inside another watch," Adams suggested.

"Perhaps. By the way, have you seen my wife? I assume she is waiting patiently beside our coach."

Because Adams, Elizabeth's maid, and the children's nanny were all accompanying them to London, two coaches had been readied. One for the servants and one for the Darcy family.

"That is why I am here," Adams replied. "Mrs. Darcy has not come down, and I thought I might find the two of you together."

"Go to the coaches and tell the drivers you discovered us, and we shall be down straightaway."

Quickly crossing the sitting room to his wife's bedroom door, William opened it and walked in. It was obvious that her luggage had been taken downstairs, but as he turned to leave, he noticed the curtain covering the door to the balcony was open. Crossing to it, he peered out and found his wife leaning against the rail. A light wind was blowing the curls that always seemed to escape her bonnet, and her eyes were closed.

Going straight to her, he slipped his hands around her waist from behind. "Why are you still here, my love?"

Her body relaxed into him, stirring up a yearning he had no time to quench. Steeling himself not to get carried away, William kissed the top of her head, saying, "Is anything wrong?"

"No … yes! Oh, I do not know!"

"Tell me, sweetheart."

"Since your return, everything has been perfect. I love Pemberley so much, and I suppose I wished to be hidden away here forever."

William pulled her tighter against his frame, kissing her neck just below her bonnet. "I know. I feel the same way. Still, we both knew this day would come, and seeing that Richard did so much for me … for us … I feel I must attend the ball celebrating his engagement."

"Of course, you must," Elizabeth declared. "Pay no attention to me, darling. I am behaving like a child who cannot have what she wants. I suppose being unable to see Jane and Charles' new daughter is another reason I am sad."

William laid protective hands over her belly. "By the time we are to return to Pemberley, the Bingleys should be resettled at Ivy Manor. I promise we will visit them on our way home." Beneath his hand, the baby kicked, the sensation startling William. "He is very strong. That was quite the punch."

"Why do you assume the babe is a boy? Anne probably kicked me much harder and more often than Bennet."

"That sums up what I know about carrying a child." After Elizabeth stopped laughing, William grew solemn. "I wish you had agreed to let me go alone."

"I also owe Richard for your life." She turned in his arms. "Besides, do you recall what we said the night you came home?"

"In the future, where one goes, we both go," William answered.

"Exactly!" Rising on tiptoes, she brushed a kiss across his lips. "Do not worry. Dr. Camryn said I am in excellent health and perfectly able to travel."

"I cannot help worrying about you. It is my nature."

"And I dearly love your nature," she replied, kissing him again—this time more passionately.

Pulling back, he said, "Come! I just imagine Bennet is asking Mrs. Cummings where we are for the thousandth time."

Elizabeth laughed. "No doubt."

In the coach

The children had risen so early that they were asleep before the coach passed through the gates of Pemberley. Anne lay across the seat cushion with her head in Elizabeth's lap. Across the coach, Bennet was in a similar position against his father. William looked lovingly at his son before locking eyes with Elizabeth, who smiled adoringly at him.

"I recall that during the first year of our marriage whenever we travelled in a coach, I would end up asleep, curled against you," she said. "In fact, we always sat so close that if one of us snored, the other would wake."

"Are you insinuating, madam, that I snore?" William teased, his dimples emerging as they always did when he tried not to smile.

"I said if *one* of us snored! It could just as easily have been me … that is, if I am to believe your assertions that I snore."

"You only snore when you have a cold, my love. Besides, in a way I find the sound of your snores quite comforting."

One eyebrow raised in question. "In what way?"

"Your snoring sounds just like the snores my childhood cat made whenever she slept next to my head."

Holding up the novel she had brought to read during their journey,

Elizabeth pretended she might toss it. "If this would not hit Bennet, I would teach you not to compare me to a cat."

"Calm yourself," William said, chuckling quietly. "If you only knew how much I loved that cat, you would not be angry."

"Well, when you put it that way—"

Suddenly Mr. Palmer rode past their coach atop a huge, sorrel stallion, catching Elizabeth's attention. Chalmers Palmer, a retired Bow Street Runner whom William had recently hired to oversee the men who guarded his properties, was quite the phenomenon. Having curly red hair and a bushy beard to match, he was several inches taller than William and broader across the shoulders. In Elizabeth's estimation, this giant of a man not only looked formidable, but most likely weighed twice as much as her husband.

"I have a question regarding Mr. Palmer." When William nodded for her to continue, she asked, "Why is he accompanying us to London when he was hired to improve the safety of Pemberley? I thought Mr. Simmons was merely an assistant."

"I hired Mr. Palmer to be head of *all* security. That means at Pemberley and Darcy House, as well as on the road. He brought on two of his former colleagues from Bow Street—Mr. Simmons, whom you met, is tasked with overseeing Pemberley, and Mr. Roberts, who will be in charge at Darcy House. Roberts is currently in London, and we shall meet him once we arrive."

"How much will it cost to have men watch us twenty-four hours a day, seven days a week?"

"Whatever it costs will be worth it. After all, what good is our fortune if something should happen to you or the children? Once I learned that my aunt walked right past our footmen to accost you, I swore that would never happen again."

"I doubt even you could have stopped Lady Catherine. All the servants know her and, I dare say, were afraid to confront her."

"Mr. Palmer will make certain that does not happen again."

Elizabeth smiled as though an amusing thought had come to mind. Seeing it, William commented, "Do you care to share what you find so funny?"

"I was wondering if Mr. Roberts looks as fearsome as Mr. Palmer or Mr. Simmons? I know that if I were someone up to no good, seeing either of them would disavow me of the notion."

William laughed. "I imagine we will discover that Mr. Roberts is a large fellow as well. There is something to be said for being confronted by someone twice your size."

Elizabeth reached for William's hand, and he leaned forward to clasp hers. "You are so attentive to our needs. I cannot fathom how you manage all your responsibilities."

"Which is why I hired Palmer. It is now *his* responsibility to keep us safe, which leaves me free to concentrate on running the estate."

"Has it crossed your mind that your aunt might try to ruin Richard's engagement ball?"

"I do not see how she could. The overseer for Rosings makes certain she has no visitors nor access to a vehicle."

"Lady Catherine is not easily intimidated, and I fear she may circumvent any restrictions."

"If it will ease your mind, I shall have Palmer correspond with the overseer at Rosings—I believe Uncle called him Mr. Snow—once we reach London. I will send a letter of introduction to make certain he knows that Palmer is legitimate. If my aunt makes any attempt to leave Kent, I will inform him that Palmer should be notified along with my uncle."

"If Mr. Palmer keeps an eye on her, I shall feel better about the situation."

"Please do not let anything worry you, my dear. Just make your feelings known, and I shall respond accordingly. I truly meant what I said to Richard. I should have listened to your worries about Wright's endeavour, and I mean to respect all your concerns from now on."

Elizabeth's heart clenched at the unmistakeable love in his eyes. "Thank you, my darling."

"If you keep looking at me like that, Elizabeth, after we stop to change horses, I will have the children sleep on one side of the coach and have you sit beside me. Then I can kiss you whenever I wish."

"I fear that if you act on your feelings, it may take days longer for us to reach London. We might even miss the ball."

William grinned crookedly, making him appear much younger. "Oh, but what fun we would have in the meantime."

Kent
Rosings Park

The chatelaine at her waist rattled with every step Mrs. Bradford took. As the housekeeper at Rosings made her way to her mistresses' bedroom, for some reason the sound of the keys made her usual anxiety rise even higher.

Lady Catherine has not consulted me since Mr. Snow took over the estate. What could have happened to make her summon me now?

Because the man hired by Lord Matlock oversaw every aspect of Rosings, the lady of the house had kept silent regarding her new situation. The housekeeper knew it could not have been easy for Lady Catherine de Bourgh, for she was not the type of woman to be told what to do.

Reaching the elaborately carved bedroom door, Mrs. Bradford took a deep breath and knocked. The familiar voice sounded as sharp and controlling as ever when it answered. "Come!"

The room was dark, and it took a moment to locate Lady Catherine. She was seated near the only light in the room, close to a small bay window. There, she liked to read the newspaper and take tea every morning. She waved the housekeeper over without speaking.

Once Mrs. Bradford stood in front of her, Lady Catherine ordered, "Sit down."

Not comfortable sitting in her ladyship's presence, the old servant perched on the edge of the nearest chair with her hands folded in her lap.

"How long have you worked for Rosings?"

"This January will be two and thirty years, ma'am."

"I thought as much," her ladyship murmured before going silent.

Just when Mrs. Bradford thought her employer might be waiting for her to say more, Lady Catherine spoke again. "You and I have not always seen eye to eye, but we have managed to work together, am I right?"

"Yes, ma'am."

"I appreciate your candour and your loyalty to my family. You have never disappointed me."

"Thank you, my lady."

"For that reason, I have an offer to make you." The look of surprise on the old servant's face caused her to quickly add, "Mr. Snow and Lord Matlock believe they have confiscated all the funds I had in the house, storing them in the safe in the office and leaving me without a farthing to my name. My own brother keeps me a prisoner and intends to do so until I die. He already has the safe which held all the de Bourgh jewels at his house in London. All he left me is this ring and a pearl necklace, which I had secreted in a corner of my closet."

With that assertion, Lady Catherine held up her left hand to display a large, blue sapphire surrounded by diamonds. "I am surprised that blackguard did not remove this from my finger." She took a deep breath and continued. "In any case, if he believes that by removing all valuables from my reach, he can force me to remain a prisoner here, he is sadly mistaken."

Mrs. Bradford merely blinked self-consciously at that proclamation.

"What if I told you I have been biding my time, waiting until they think they have won before I retaliate? In addition to my ring and pearls, I also have three hundred pounds hidden in this house and, should you agree to help me, that amount and the pearls will be yours. What do you say to that?"

"I-I suppose it would depend on what you ask of me."

"You know as well as I that I am not mad. Still, just because I do not agree with my family on certain issues, they label me as such." When Mrs. Bradford did not reply, she added, "Lord Matlock has spoken of cutting expenses by letting most of the staff go, so I cannot guarantee you will have a job here much longer. This may be your only chance to leave with something of value."

Seeing the frown on the housekeeper's face, Lady Catherine said, "All I need you to do is trade places with me in a sennight. It will only be for a day or so, just long enough to allow me to escape to London. Then you may escape Rosings, too, using the money."

"But we do not look anything alike, madam."

"We are about the same size. If we exchange clothes and you wear one of my wigs, a pair of my thick glasses, and keep yourself sequestered in my bedroom for at least two days, I know we can achieve success. During that time, should Mr. Snow ask to see me, simply have a maid tell him you are indisposed."

"I-I do not wish to do anything against the law."

With the help of her cane, Lady Catherine rose to her feet. She pounded the stick on the floor. "My brother is not the law! He may not like that you helped me to undermine him, but he cannot prosecute you for it. Besides, with three hundred pounds you can quickly disappear without a trace."

"How will you manage to get to London? You cannot walk to the village and catch a post coach. If you try, you will surely be caught."

"That will be the easiest part. We will pretend your father has died, and you must go to London to arrange his burial."

"But-but my parents are long dead."

Frustrated, Lady Catherine cried out. "Mr. Snow is not aware of that!" Glad that her outburst had silenced her housekeeper, she continued. "I will insist that you have been a loyal servant, and the least Rosings can do is supply you with a coach to London."

"And if Mr. Snow does not agree?"

"He will. Believe me." Lady Catherine sighed. "If possible, try to stay a full two days after I leave in the coach before you disappear."

"If I agree to help you, will you promise not to do anything … *unlawful* once you reach London? I do not wish to be accused of helping you in the commission of a crime."

"You should know by now it is not in my nature to take orders from anyone, especially not a servant. You will just have to trust me."

Mrs. Bradford's mind worked furiously. *I am not of a mind to answer for whatever mischief she creates. Still, three hundred pounds and the pearls will serve me well in the future.*

"Well, have you made up your mind?"

Taking a steadying breath, the housekeeper replied, "I will help you."

London
Matlock townhouse

Reluctant to encounter his father, Viscount Leighton had the carriage take him to the back of his family's townhouse. There he emerged from the vehicle and hurried quickly towards the rear door of the manor, hoping to go up the back stairs to his rooms without meeting any member of the family. Just as he reached the door, he happened to glance to the left to see his brother and soon-to-be sister in a passionate embrace behind a clump of tall shrubs.

Although he was not happily married, he was pleased that his brother seemed to have found the perfect match. Smiling, he slipped silently towards the pair until he got close enough to speak without being heard by anyone else.

"You had better find another hiding place, Brother. Mother will have an apoplexy if she finds you like this!"

Instantly, Richard and Lady Selina broke apart, each sighing with relief when they discovered it was only Leighton. Still, a red-faced Richard was irritated that his sibling had bothered to interrupt.

"Have you nothing better to do than spy on me?"

"If I *were* to spy on you, it would be my sole occupation. Even without trying, this is the third time I have caught you kissing. The first two times I never bothered to let on, so I suggest you either find better hiding places or limit your tête-à-têtes to behind locked doors."

Feeling immensely satisfied, Leighton walked away only to hear Richard call out, "You are merely jealous."

The smile left the viscount's face. Richard had spoken the truth. He was.

Once they were alone again, Lady Selina took Richard's hand and led him to a lighted path. As they began to walk, she said, "We should be glad that your brother found us and not your mother. I am still embarrassed by what she said when she found us in the library."

"Well, I am not. We are engaged, and I see no reason we should ask permission of a parent to share a kiss."

"Still, I already fear what your mother thinks of me. After all, we were strangers, and she knows nothing of me or my family."

"She does know, however, that I would only ever love a true lady. Lord knows I have had enough fallen women chase me since I began wearing long pants, and not one of them interested me."

Looking around and seeing no one, Lady Selina leaned in to give Richard a quick kiss. "I am so pleased that none did."

"What about you? You have never mentioned being pursued by another man."

Lady Selina looked pensive. "When I was twenty, there was a young man I thought I would marry. His father, Lord Boykin, and mine were friends. He was a second son who entered the navy when he was only eighteen. When I met him, he was two and twenty and thinking of marrying."

"Lord Boykin? My father mentioned that name often when I was younger. Was his estate in Sussex?"

"Yes. Monticeto Hall in Sussex. The young man I hoped to marry was his son Martin Suddeth but he died during a battle at sea."

"I am sorry to hear that."

She shrugged. "It was long ago, and, in truth, I do not know if I was in love with Martin or in love with the idea of marriage. He was handsome, kind and dashing, and I thought he would be my husband one day. After he died, I never met another who rivalled him … until you."

Now it was Richard's turn to steal a kiss. "I am sorry that he died so young, but I am grateful that you found no one to replace him in your heart before you met me."

Another passionate kiss ensued—a kiss observed by Lady Matlock as she stood at a window overlooking the garden. Instead of being shocked, a smile crossed her face. *I knew it would take a special woman to win your heart, my son. And I am so pleased that you and Lady Selina crossed paths.*

"What are you staring at so intently?" Lord Matlock asked as he looked up from where he sat dealing cards. "I thought you asked me in here to partner you at cards since you could not locate Richard or Lady Selina."

"I was just thinking how beautiful the gardens are and how I might highlight them on the night of the ball by bringing in more benches and tables and stringing lights down every path. In that way our guests may enjoy eating dinner under the stars, if they so wish."

"Come, my dear! Forget about the ball for one night. Every time you mention it, I am reminded of how much it will cost me."

Lady Matlock laughed. "You cannot fool me, Edward! You are just as excited as I to have Richard marry and begin a family. And now that he is giving up his career in the army, you can teach him all he needs to know about running an estate. I know you have wished for that for quite some time."

"You are correct, Eleanor. I shall be pleased to have Richard settled in England with a family of his own. He has always had a better attitude about running an estate than Leighton, and I know he will do well."

"Leighton is not to blame for everything that has happened. Lady Susan has been such a disappointment that I wish I had not championed her when he was searching for a wife. Now I wonder whether she cannot have children or merely refuses to have them."

"We shall likely never know, but if I learn that she simply refuses to give him an heir, I may push him to divorce her."

"You no longer care that it would embarrass the family?"

"When I thought Fitzwilliam was lost at sea, I began to question what was really important in life."

"And what did you decide?"

"In the end, family is more important than society's good opinion. I have always cared about my children's happiness, especially Leighton's, as he does not have Richard's easy temperament; however, after Fitzwilliam's ordeal, I could not care less what scandal a divorce might bring."

Outside the open library door, Viscount Leighton stopped when he heard his name mentioned and stood quietly hoping to hear what was said. After overhearing his father's declaration regarding his happiness, he hurried to his room to contemplate all that signified.

I never thought Father cared about me or my happiness. Could I have been wrong all these years?

For the first time in years, he would ponder that question without downing his usual half-bottle of whiskey before retiring.

Chapter 26

London
Several days later

Upon reaching London, Elizabeth put the children down for a nap before lying down herself. William went directly to his study and began sorting through the mail that had accumulated since Mrs. Barnes had been notified to stop forwarding mail to Pemberley. While he was working, there came a knock on the door.

Assuming it was Mr. Barnes, William called, "Come!"

He was taken aback when his cousin walked into the room. "Richard, I hardly recognised you without the uniform."

Having resigned his position in the army a month previously, Richard agreed. "At times, I do not recognise myself. In every mirror I pass, I expect to see my regimentals."

"I can imagine. How many years did you wear a uniform?"

"Close to fifteen. I did not realise how many clothes a civilian needs to get by these days. I had to order a new wardrobe since I am not permitted to wear my uniform any longer. If Father had not advanced the money my grandmother's property has accumulated, I would certainly be penniless right now."

"Once you marry Lady Selina and take control of Houghton Park, you will have no worries about money."

"I realise that, but until it happens, I do not wish to ask my betrothed for money."

"I completely understand." William changed the subject. "In any case, I had not anticipated being welcomed to Town."

"I am not here to welcome you," Richard replied with a smirk. "I was in the neighbourhood and witnessed two giants leaving your townhouse. Knowing you to be in residence, I stopped to make certain they had done you no harm."

Amused, William answered, "How convenient that you waited until they were out of sight to enquire about my welfare."

"I have encountered a few such men in my service for His Majesty, and I know one cannot be too careful around them. I would be no use to you if I were dead." Whilst William laughed, Richard continued. "Honestly, Cousin, those had to be two of the tallest men I have ever laid eyes on."

"For certain. No one could fail to notice Mr. Palmer, the red-haired one, who is my new chief of security. It was he who brought on board Mr. Roberts to be in charge at Darcy House and Mr. Simmons who is already in place at Pemberley. Wait until you see Simmons. He looks like Palmer except that he is completely bald."

"Father mentioned you intended to increase security, but I have been so busy I had forgotten. Do you really think these men are necessary and, for that matter, other than being shockingly large, what qualifications do they have for the job?"

"They are necessary for my peace of mind and, as I told the earl, they are both former Bow Street Runners. That is where they are headed now—to greet old friends at the Bow Street office and put the word out that Mr. Roberts will be working for me in London."

Richard did not reply so William asked, "May I ask why you are here?"

"What kind of welcome is that?"

"An honest one."

"In truth, I stopped by to enquire after Elizabeth's health. Mother, especially, is so worried that the trip may have been too strenuous for her. I fear her worry has rubbed off on me."

"I thank you for your concern. Elizabeth travelled remarkably well for a woman in her condition. Still, the journey was tiring, and she decided to rest as soon as we arrived."

"And the two little scamps?"

"They have been put down for a nap."

Richard nodded absently, drawing William's attention. "Is something else on your mind, Cousin?"

Taking a deep breath, Richard let it go loudly. "I have some bad news to share." William's brows furrowed, and Richard quickly continued. "Lord Camden has died. I got an express this morning from Matthew. It was dated three days ago. In it he said his father had passed the previous day and therefore he and Georgiana will not be able to attend the ball."

At William's despondent expression, he added, "It is probably for the best, Darcy. Hayworth admitted that he was worried about Georgiana travelling to London in her condition. You recall that their child is due only a month after yours. She has not been feeling well, and he was considering cancelling the trip even before his father's death."

"I know how much Elizabeth wished to see her, and, frankly, I was looking forward to seeing her, too."

"Once both your children are born, you will just have to invite everyone to Pemberley to celebrate the new babies, including the Bingleys' new daughter."

"How did you hear about that?"

"I thought I told you. Bingley's housekeeper in Town is the cousin of Mother's cook. Knowing that I am acquainted with Bingley, Mrs. Patterson often mentions their business to me."

William shook his head. "The paths through which gossip is spread are astounding!" Then he added, "I like your idea of gathering at Pemberley. Perhaps by then, you and your wife will have news of your own to celebrate."

Richard looked wistful. "Selina and I do hope to have children straightaway."

"I think you should. After all, you are no longer a young buck!" William teased as he stood to cross to the liquor cabinet. Pouring two glasses of brandy, he handed one to Richard. "To our children!"

Richard clinked glasses with William. "Present and future!"

Before the ball

Whilst William peered at himself in the floor-to-ceiling mirror in the corner of his dressing room, Adams brushed imaginary lint off the back of his dark blue tailcoat.

"Do you suppose I shall pass muster with the *ton* tonight?" William joked.

"Of course you will, sir. I doubt any gentleman there will be more fashionably attired than you."

William relied on his valet to keep his wardrobe current, as he had no stomach for visiting the shops to view the latest in men's clothing. As he turned to look over his shoulder with the handheld mirror Adams offered, William sighed.

"As long as my wardrobe suits Elizabeth, I am satisfied." Running his hand over the silver-coloured waistcoat embroidered with blue, green and red threads in a criss-cross pattern, he added, "I have to say, however, that I especially like this waistcoat, though I have no recollection of owning it."

"Whilst you were ... *away*, Mrs. Darcy picked that pattern from a magazine to which I subscribe. I thought to allow her something positive to focus on for a time and suggested she might wish to choose something to update your wardrobe. She thought a new waistcoat would be easy to incorporate without having you try it on, and she picked this pattern and colour."

Suddenly, the door to the hall opened and Bennet peeked in. Looking at his child, William said, "You should have been asleep by now, Son."

"I-I think Clancy has missed me. With you and Mama away tonight, I thought I would see if he would like to sleep with me."

As Elizabeth's pregnancy progressed and it became more difficult to keep up her daily morning walks, the little white dog had become her constant companion in the house, just as he had when his mistress was pregnant with Bennet and later, Anne. It was almost as though Clancy knew he should keep an eye on her. And so he had, even sleeping next to her bed.

William smiled at Adams before answering. "I think you may be right." Holding a hand towards his son, he said, "Come! Let us see if we can find that little rascal."

Upon opening the door to Elizabeth's bedroom, Bennet let go of William's hand to enter the dressing room. Upon reaching the doorway, his mouth fell open and he stood in awe for a moment before saying reverently, "Oh, Mama! You look so beautiful!"

Sitting in a chair in front of her dressing table whilst Florence placed pearl hairpins that matched her necklace into her upswept hair, Elizabeth wore a purple, silk-brocade gown embellished with silver-coloured embroidery, sequins and crystal beads across the bodice, sleeves and hem. She had commissioned the dressmaker in Lambton to create the gown to accommodate her ever-expanding waist. Upon hearing Bennet's declaration, she turned to smile at her son and at William, who stood right behind him.

When she opened her arms, Bennet rushed into her embrace. "Oh, sweetheart, I am so glad you think so," she replied, hugging him tightly before kissing the top of his head.

"I think you are beautiful, too," William said. "Where is my kiss?"

Florence, who had just finished with her mistress' hair, left the room to give them privacy. William walked over and leant down to collect his kiss from his wife's soft lips.

"You look very beautiful, my darling. The gown is stunning, and you look gorgeous in that colour."

"I wondered if it was too ostentatious, considering I am almost twice my normal size."

"Nonsense! You will be the most beautiful woman at the ball."

William's proclamation seemed to increase her confidence. Focusing again on Bennet, she asked, "What are you doing up? I thought you were sleeping."

Before the boy could answer, William winked and said, "Ben wishes to know if Clancy wants to sleep with him tonight."

At the sound of his name, Clancy, who was lying on a blanket at the far end of the dressing room, began to wag his tail, thumping it against the wall.

"He looks as though he is eager to join you," Elizabeth said. Ruffling her son's hair, she instructed the dog. "Go with Ben, Clancy." The little dog stood to do as asked. "Now, go back to bed, and try not to get up again tonight."

"Yes, Mama."

Bennet stopped to give William a kiss before heading towards the door to the sitting room with the dog on his heels. Once he was out of sight, William shook his head. "He is growing up far too fast."

Elizabeth sighed. "I know." As she attempted to stand, she said, "Give me your hand."

After William helped her to her feet, she laid one hand on her protruding stomach and sighed deeply.

"Sweetheart, are you certain you feel up to attending?"

"All will be fine. Find me a comfortable chair, and I shall watch all the beautiful people dance the night away ... including those women lucky enough to partner my handsome husband."

"If you cannot dance, I certainly shall not." He held out his foot, revealing a boot. "See, I am not wearing my dancing shoes, and my aunt will not allow me on the dance floor with these."

"You will disappoint so many if you do not dance, not to mention vexing Lady Matlock."

William smiled so widely that both his dimples flashed. "Do I look concerned? You know how fond I am of dancing, and you are the only woman I care to partner."

"Still—"

William held up a hand. "I will not be gainsaid. I intend for us to make an appearance, watch the *ton* exhibit their usual boorish behaviour, partake of supper and leave soon afterwards. That will be enough to tire you completely, and I will not countenance any argument to the contrary."

Knowing there was no reasoning with her husband when he set his mind to something, Elizabeth stood and drew soft fingers down his cheek before rising on tiptoes to brush her lips across his.

"I know all of your decisions are made with my welfare in mind, and I love that about you."

Her kiss was passionately returned. "I am glad that you understand me, my love."

Matlock townhouse

Whilst the Darcy carriage contended with the long line of vehicles delivering the wealthiest occupants of London to the Matlocks' ball, Elizabeth could not help but be impressed with the scene awaiting them. The Matlocks' townhouse took up the span of the entire block and every window inside it was alit with a candle-filled chandelier. Torches lined the entire front of the house and the tiers of steps leading down to the pavement.

Footmen in impressive livery lined the portico and steps, ready to assist guests and to restrain vagrants who often appeared at such soirees to beg for a coin. Occasionally, someone arriving would toss a few coins to the crowd, inciting a squabble. For his part, William always supplied his driver with two small pouches of coins to toss to the group—one for their arrival and one for their departure—hoping that would draw attention away from his wife and their vehicle.

As their carriage came to a stop and a footman jumped down to open the door, William noticed a second footman had followed the first, keeping his back to the other footman whilst surveying the growing crowd. William theorised their actions were initiated by Mr. Palmer, since that gentleman had met with all the footmen the day after he arrived at Darcy House.

William turned to help Elizabeth from the carriage. As she descended onto the pavement, he asked again, "Are you certain you feel well? If you have the slightest doubt, just say as much and we shall return home."

Not caring who might be watching, Elizabeth framed his face with her hands, devouring him with her eyes. "I am well, sweetheart. Let us go in and celebrate Richard's engagement."

Holding out an arm, William patted her hand after she placed it there. "I am your devoted servant, madam."

The night seemed to pass quickly, and Elizabeth found herself enjoying the occasion. She had met Lady Selina when Richard brought her to Darcy House for a small dinner party and was delighted to be in her company again. Viscount Leighton's wife was in attendance and, for once, Susan seemed to be enjoying dancing with her husband, as well as most of the men of their circle.

Lady Matlock had placed several comfortable chairs on a platform at one end of the ballroom, where she and Lady Selina joined Elizabeth from time to time to sit out a set and chat. Their hostess had been annoyed to learn her nephew had not worn dancing shoes, but William's lapse was soon forgotten in the excitement of the ballroom filled to the brim with family, friends, and acquaintances—a few that the Matlocks felt obligated to invite, whether they wished to or not.

For Elizabeth, the most entertaining part of the ball was watching the ladies who, upon noticing that she was large with child, quickly made their way to where she sat simply because William was beside her. It was not obvious from his position behind her chair that he was not dressed to dance. Ignorant of the situation, they fluttered their eyelashes at her husband whilst making comments designed to goad him into asking them to dance. Because of that, William was becoming more irritated as the night progressed, and by the time supper was finished, he was eager to leave.

"I agree Elizabeth needs to go home and rest," Lady Matlock stated as she, Lord Matlock, Richard and Lady Selina walked them to the foyer. "And let me say how appreciative we are that you went to such lengths to attend."

"Mother is right," Richard said. "Your support means everything to Selina and me."

"We would not have missed your engagement ball for anything," Elizabeth replied as she stepped forward to hug Lady Selina and then Lady Matlock.

"We should go, darling," William said as he held out a white, silk cloak with a soft, fur lining, which a maid had retrieved for Elizabeth. She stepped into the cloak, and he brought the hood up and over her head before the maid handed Elizabeth her gloves.

As William donned his own hat and gloves, Lord Matlock said, "I sent a footman to tell your driver to pull forward."

"That is most kind. Thank you, Uncle."

As William was escorting Elizabeth out the door, a footman came rushing in. He went straight to Lord Matlock and handed him an express.

"This was just delivered, my lord! The rider is waiting for a reply, so I directed him to the kitchen. I asked another footman to inform Cook he is here, so he will be given food and drink whilst he waits."

Richard moved closer to Lord Matlock as he broke the seal and read the missive. Suddenly, his father murmured under his breath, "Heaven forbid!"

His expression brought Lady Matlock and Lady Selina forward. "What is it?" Lady Matlock demanded as quietly as possible. "What has happened?"

"Catherine escaped from Rosings two days ago. It is believed she was headed to London."

"Good Lord!" Richard said before remembering to speak quietly. "That means she could already be here. I must warn Darcy."

As Richard raced out the front door, Lord Matlock said, "Eleanor, have Perkins put all the servants on alert. If they see my sister, or anyone who looks suspicious, they are to notify me immediately. After you have done that, you and Lady Selina need to return to the ballroom and try to keep our other guests from suspecting anything could be amiss."

As they stood with mouths agape, he hurried to catch Richard.

Elizabeth was so tired when they left that she leant heavily against William. Anxious to get his wife safely to the carriage, he was concentrating on her every step when something out of the ordinary caught his notice. In the group of vagrants standing behind the ropes that separated them from the Matlocks' guests, one in particular stood out.

Covered from head to toe by a hooded black robe, William thought that if that person had been holding a scythe, they would have looked exactly like a drawing he had seen of death coming to take a soul. He had little time to consider that, however, for Elizabeth's slipper caught on the next step, and he had to catch her to prevent her from falling. He was thrown completely off balance when several things happened simultaneously.

The creature wearing the black robe suddenly burst through the barrier and rushed directly at Elizabeth. William was shocked to see a hand escape the robe, holding a long, thin dagger which was quickly raised overhead. All he could think of was protecting Elizabeth.

Stepping between her and the villain, William pulled his shocked wife firmly to his body, wrapping her in his arms. He manged to completely envelope her against any harm whilst offering the culprit his back.

From out of nowhere, Mr. Palmer appeared. Practically flying through the air, he grabbed the attacker as they both fell to the ground and the dagger dropped to the pavement. Only a loud grunt and the sound of cracking bones made it clear that the blackguard had been injured upon hitting the pavement.

William quickly looked back, eager to see the person Mr. Palmer had wrestled to the ground. Though he was keen to order Palmer to remove the black hood, something told him he should not subject Elizabeth to that information.

"Are-are they dead?" she murmured, shuddering in his arms.

William tightened his grip. "I have no idea."

Concurrently, Richard and Lord Matlock reached them. Grabbing his cousin's arm and propelling him towards the carriage, Richard cried, "We will handle this, Darcy! Take Elizabeth home!"

Meanwhile, Lord Matlock was shouting orders to the footmen, directing one to fetch the constable and another to go for a doctor.

"Never mind the doctor, my lord," Mr. Palmer said from his position on the ground. "She is dead."

Lord Matlock knew instantly who it was. Though his heart ached for the sister he had known as a child, he could not mourn the one who presently lay dead at his feet. Still, not wishing to expose his family in front of witnesses, he ordered two footmen to take the body to the rear of the house where the constable could examine it later.

To Mr. Palmer he said, "'Thank you' does not adequately express how I feel. You saved my niece and nephew from certain injury, if not death."

"I was only doing my job, my lord," Mr. Palmer replied as he brushed off his hands after coming to his feet.

"How did you know to come?"

"I received an express from Rosings Park only minutes ago and came directly here."

"How fortunate that Mr. Snow's warnings arrived in time. I received one as well."

"I plan to wait here until the constable arrives," Mr. Palmer said. "I am sure he will require my testimony."

"Let me know when he does. Meanwhile, if you do not mind, I would appreciate your help in seeing the rest of my guests to their carriages unharmed. Whilst I believe the threat has ended, one can never be too careful."

"Which is exactly what Mr. Roberts and I discussed before I left Darcy House. Since he has that residence secured, I will be glad to assist here until all your guests have departed."

Though he wanted to find out who had tried to kill Elizabeth, a numb William knew that his wife's wellbeing was more important. Guiding a traumatised Elizabeth to their carriage, once he helped her inside, he joined her, pulling her into his arms.

As tears began rolling down her cheeks, she murmured, "Why would anyone want to harm us?"

Though he suspected who the culprit was, William could not say that now. "Until I know more, I cannot answer that. But I promise I shall inform you once I do." When she said nothing else, he added, "I would like to send for Dr. Graham once we are home ... to be certain you are well."

"No!" Elizabeth replied a little too fiercely. Then, more calmly, she added, "Please, do not send for him. I promise you that the baby and I are well."

"Darling, you are shaking like a leaf."

"Only because it frightened me so severely to think you might be harmed, but being in your arms tonight will calm me enough to allow me to sleep. Once I have rested, I will be back to myself. You will see."

"Will you at least agree to take one of the draughts Mrs. Reynolds sent along to help you sleep?"

"If it eases your mind, I will."

The hood of her white cloak had fallen off in the commotion, allowing William to kiss the top of her dark curls. "I love you more than life, Elizabeth Darcy."

Chapter 27

London

The next morning dawned dreary and grey, as well as nearly twenty degrees colder. Though already weeks into autumn, the weather had stayed unseasonably warm and sunny until last night. As William rose from the bed he shared with his wife, he shivered. Conscious that the fire in the hearth was almost out, he proceeded to add coals to it rather than summon a maid.

After allowing Adams to help him dress, he returned to Elizabeth's bedroom. Taking two newly warmed bricks that had been lying on the hearth, he wrapped them in a towel and walked towards the bed. As he pulled back the bedclothes to slide the bricks towards her feet, Elizabeth stirred.

Sitting up and rubbing her eyes, she asked sleepily, "What are you about, my love?"

William sat down on the bed and marvelled at how beautiful she looked this morning with her silky, dark curls down and dishevelled. Immediately, a sharp pain pierced his heart at the thought of how close he had come to losing her. Stunned, it took a moment for him to remember to reply. "I-I was hoping to warm your feet without waking you, sweetheart."

Unable to resist leaning in to kiss his wife, William was captivated when her arms snaked around his neck and their kiss grew passionate. It continued so long that he was almost lost in ecstasy when she broke the kiss, bringing him back to the present.

Now conscious of the warm bricks, she murmured, "Hmm, that feels so good, but I was hoping you would warm … well … everything, just as you usually do in the mornings."

Smiling, William pulled back to say, "We spoke of this last night. I wish to be at my uncle's townhouse as early as possible to learn what happened, and there is no need for you to rise at this ungodly hour."

The mention of William's quest sobered Elizabeth. In the chaos of last night, he had mentioned his fear that the attack might have been a continuation of his aunt's campaign against them. Running fingers gingerly along his shirt collar, she leaned forwards until their foreheads touched. "I pray that last night had nothing to do with your aunt."

William lifted her chin so that he could look directly into her eyes. "Elizabeth, even if Lady Catherine is behind what happened, you must know that it is not your fault. I had no intention of marrying Anne, and my aunt would have hated any woman who happened to become Mrs. Darcy."

Elizabeth tried to smile. "If you think mentioning any other woman might have become Mrs. Darcy is helpful, you are mistaken. I am jealous of all the women who were ever under consideration for your wife. Never forget that."

Laughing, William pulled her into a tight embrace. "Oh, my darling. If only you would believe me when I say that no woman ever met my expectations before I fell madly in love with you!"

Elizabeth turned her head to kiss his cheek. "That statement proves how faulty your memory has become. Still, I am thrilled that you have forgotten all those *debutantes* Lady Matlock was listing to consider for your wife once you graduated university."

"I remember only you," William said, kissing her once more.

Then he stood, keeping hold of one hand. "Please try to sleep until the hour you normally wake. I intend to return as soon as possible and may even be home before you have time to break your fast."

"If I am still in bed, will you join me?"

"I will." He kissed her hand before turning it loose. "I shall see you again soon."

"Soon."

As he was being driven to Lord Matlock's townhouse, William reflected on how fitting the worsening weather was, considering the events of the evening before. In spite of the rug the footman had retrieved for him from underneath the opposing seat after he entered the carriage, William shivered.

I should have taken my great coat as Adams suggested.

Instantly, his thoughts returned to what had happened last night. After their return to Darcy House, he had met with Mr. Roberts and read the express sent by Mr. Snow at Rosings Park. Conscious of the fact that the person who had tried to attack Elizabeth was likely someone hired by Lady Catherine, he still hoped to be proven wrong. Though his aunt had acted more and more irrationally in the years since his marriage, he had held out hope that at some point she would come to her senses and accept the inevitable.

I should not have been surprised at what happened last night. After Gregory Wright confessed what Lady Catherine tried to force him to do, I should have known she would never give up.

Before he could castigate himself further, the carriage came to a stop in front of his uncle's townhouse. Sighing heavily, he exited the vehicle and looked to the portico where the front door was being opened.

Matlock townhouse

As William was shown into his uncle's study, he was not surprised to see Richard and Viscount Leighton already inside. After acknowledging the others with merely a nod, he took a seat beside Richard in front of his uncle's desk. Leighton kept his place beside an open window since he was smoking a cigar, and smoke irritated his father's throat.

"Would you like a drink?" Lord Matlock asked, holding up a glass of brandy. "Or perhaps you would prefer a cup of tea or coffee?"

"No, thank you. I need nothing. I have already had a cup of coffee this morning."

"Then, let us get to the point. First, how is Elizabeth?" his uncle asked.

"She is as well as can be expected. At first, she was very restless and had difficulty sleeping until Mrs. Reynolds' herbal draught took effect. She only woke as I was about to leave, and I suggested she go back to sleep until I return."

Lord Matlock looked down for a moment as though he was trying to decide how to begin, so William asked, "What did you learn of the assailant?"

Richard and Leighton both stirred uncomfortably with the question, as Lord Matlock looked William directly in the eye. "Prepare yourself, Fitzwilliam. The one who tried to kill Elizabeth was my sister!"

"The-the person in black was Lady Catherine?"

"Yes. When she could not force others to do it for her, Catherine decided to take it upon herself to exact revenge."

Shaking his head, William sighed heavily. "So, it *was* my fault that Elizabeth was attacked."

"I was afraid you would blame yourself, but what happened was not your fault. If anyone is to blame, I am! I did not fully recognise the extent of her malice ... *or madness* ... until now. I should have checked Catherine's behaviour when she first started badgering you to propose to your cousin." He shook his head forlornly. "I found it easier not to confront her, and I let her wallow in her fantasy for far too long. I am to blame."

"I doubt anything you said would have stopped her," William interjected angrily, standing up. "My aunt was used to being obeyed, and she found my determination to follow my heart unbearable." Realising that a new plan for confinement must be created, he asked, "Where is she now?"

"Even though she was my sister, I think it is for the best that her neck was broken when Mr. Palmer tackled her to the ground."

"She perished?" William sank back into his seat.

'Yes. After reading the note found on her body," Lord Matlock added, "I think she would never have given up her campaign to make you pay."

At William's puzzled look, he pushed a paper across the table. William took it and began to read the almost illegible handwriting.

> *Brother,*
>
> *If you are reading this, most likely I am dead. I had hoped to live long enough to tell all who would listen why I killed that little tramp Fitzwilliam married. However, if this is not the case, then my death will be a fitting response to Fitzwilliam's betrayal of Anne. Her broken heart at his hands is what hastened her demise.*
>
> *Let Fitzwilliam and the whore he married live with the fact that they have killed us both by polluting the shades of Pemberley.*
>
> *Catherine*

Once William had finished reading the note, he folded it and slid it back to his uncle. "I cannot fathom being filled with so much hate."

"Neither can any of us," Richard replied whilst Leighton nodded.

With the mystery of who had attacked Elizabeth settled, William asked, "What did the constable have to say?"

"After he spoke to Mr. Palmer, Richard and me, he accepted our account of what had occurred and our contention that the woman was obviously mad, since none of us claimed to know her. He had the body transported to the morgue."

"You let him think you did not know her? Are you not afraid he will figure out who she is and wonder why you lied?"

"No. I had already taken the note from her pocket, and Catherine had no other identifying papers on her person except for a receipt for a room at the Rose and Crown Inn that was in her housekeeper's name. We took that as well. She was not wearing any jewellery. In fact, the way she was dressed, she could easily have passed for someone's servant. And, according to Mr. Snow, the coach was merely to drop Mrs. Bradford in Town, so it could not be traced back to Rosings. The three of us decided not to stir up gossip by identifying Catherine."

Lord Matlock took a deep breath and let it go loudly. "I told him that I would have the body buried if no one claimed it ... just to be charitable to an obviously mad individual. In that way, I can bury my sister with no fanfare and leave her grave unmarked for as long as I see fit. Perhaps, if we are fortunate, no one will ever connect Catherine to the insane woman involved in last night's attack."

"If I may change the subject, what did you decide to do about Gregory Wright?" William asked. "Mr. Sturgis tells me that, even though Wright and his son still live at Parkleigh Manor, it is being run by a steward."

"That is true. Moreover, Lord Grassley heard rumours about Wright losing control of the estate and came to visit me last week. I plan to tell him all that has occurred *after* we discussed what to do with Parkleigh Manor."

"And what is your opinion?" William replied.

"Lord Grassley and I have been friends far too long for me to ignore his wishes, even if I would like to punish Wright more severely. With your approval, Fitzwilliam, I will keep Parkleigh Manor and manage it through the steward. Once Jonathan finishes university—with suitable marks—I shall turn it over to him. Hopefully, by then, the boy will have proven more responsible than his father."

"And if he has not?" Richard asked.

"Then the estate will be sold and the proceeds placed in a trust for Jonathan's use, for I fear he will need it."

"I hate to mention it, Father," Viscount Leighton said, "but you may be dead by the time that boy finishes university."

"I plan to leave instructions for the property in my will, which will mean that you and Richard will have to follow through with my wishes. I hope you will."

"Of course," Richard replied.

"As for Gregory, Grassley says Dorothea will be heartbroken to learn he had lost control of the estate and she will likely want him and Jonathan to live at Grassley Manor—at least until Jonathan graduates from university. She has often said she would like Gregory to work alongside Lord Grassley, which she believes would help him to be a more responsible father and man."

"Do you think Wright will agree to that?" Leighton asked. "From what I hear at White's, he is too impulsive to ever be left in charge of an estate. But I suppose you would be more familiar with that, Darcy."

William huffed. "The man would not listen to me. I pray Lord Grassley has better luck."

"If he does not live up to their expectations, I do not doubt that Lord Grassley will leave him to his own devices and take charge of Jonathan."

"Can they do that?" Richard asked.

"I do not think any court in England will refuse them, especially if Lord Grassley informs them of all the gambling debts Gregory Wright accrued against Parkleigh Manor."

"I would have liked to have seen him lose everything," William said, "but I know Elizabeth would not want Jonathan to suffer because of his father; therefore, I have no objections to your plan."

"I am glad to hear it," Lord Matlock replied.

William began to stand. "It seems that everything has been settled, so I shall return to—"

Richard interrupted. "Sit back down, Cousin. I have an announcement to make." Every eye in the room turned to him.

"Selina and I have decided not to wait until the new year to marry. Instead, I intend to procure a special licence, and we will marry by the end of next week."

"Your mother will have an apoplexy!" Lord Matlock declared, pushing back from his desk to stand and pace. "There is no way to prepare for a wedding and a breakfast in so short a period of time."

"We do not want a large affair. Mother got to demonstrate her skills with Leighton's wedding and has nothing left to prove to the *ton*. Selina and I wish only to have a small wedding with as few people as possible."

"Why the rush, Brother?" Leighton asked. "I know you are eager to marry, but this seems very impetuous."

"Selina's cousin, Noel Stevens, wrote that he and Lady Aileen are to be married in less than a month. It seems that Lady Aileen was reconciled with her father, and they were about to announce plans for their wedding when Lord Camden died. Since she has also lost her father, Selina would like to travel to Berkley Hall to offer our support, and it would be easier to do that as a married couple. Moreover, Selina knew Elizabeth would not be able to travel again before your child is born, Darcy. Therefore, if you will extend your stay in London another week, you and she may attend our wedding."

"I am certain Elizabeth would love to attend," William replied. "My concern is your mother. Aunt Eleanor will not be happy when she hears about this."

"When is she ever happy regarding what her children do?" The viscount interjected with a wry smile. A frown from his father elicited another quip. "I am just teasing, Father. You know that I love Mother, but she can rival Lady Catherine when she is dead set on carrying out some plan of hers."

"It is not fair to compare your mother to my sister," Lord Matlock replied. "Your mother would never harm you just to get her way."

"Maybe not, but all the Fitzwilliams choose to marry women who share one terrible trait! They are all as stubborn as Hades!" Having said that, the viscount quit the room, chuckling as he did.

At length, a solemn Richard replied, "Good Lord! He is right."

Southampton
Berkley Hall

The day was sunny and warm, so Georgiana decided to walk in the gardens instead of staying indoors as her husband preferred her to do. She smiled to herself to recall all his warnings.

If Matthew has his way, I will stay indoors and off my feet until our child is born!

Her smile quickly dissipated when she recalled that she had not been able to walk out with her husband since Lord Camden's death. In fact, except to share an occasional meal, it had been impossible for Matthew to find time to join her in much of anything since he began to pour over his father's will and finances. She did not blame him, for although Mr. Porter, Lord Camden's newest steward, reportedly has a good head for business, he had been hired after Mr. Gable left and had not yet had time to acquaint himself with all of Lord Camden's past business dealings.

Pushing thoughts of Matthew from her head, she took stock of the landscaped gardens that stretched as far as the eye could see. Though she supposed they would look prettier once winter turned into spring, her impression upon first visiting Berkley Hall still stood. Despite being laid out in a spectacular fashion, these gardens could not hold a candle to Pemberley's more unstructured ones.

Coming upon a cement bench in the shade of a large tree, Georgiana sat to admire a large pond with a fountain in the centre. The fountain was in the shape of a large fish from which water sprang. She was wondering how Pemberley would look with such a statue in the pond nearest the house, and thus occupied, did not hear the footsteps coming in her direction.

"There you are!" Lady Aileen cried. "I asked Matthew where you were, but he did not know. Then I searched the house, and when I could not find you, I decided you must be out here." Noting that her sister was sitting down, she added, "Are you well, Georgiana? Should I summon Matthew?"

Georgiana smiled, shaking her head. "Please do not become your brother! I am quite well, thank you. I was just enjoying the view. I pray you did not alarm Matthew. I left word with the housekeeper where I would be. I would have spoken directly to him, but I did not want to interrupt his work with Mr. Porter. Matthew thinks they may finish all the paperwork today if they keep at it."

"I knew I should have asked Mrs. Hanover if she had seen you, but I was not ambitious enough to walk all through the house again to find her," Lady Aileen replied with a laugh. She then sat down next to Georgiana. "Besides, I knew you would be eager to get out of the house once the rain abated. I have not seen it rain so hard and so long in years." She took a deep breath, seemingly reflecting on that observation. "It is as though the weather knew my father had died and the clouds were weeping along with me."

At Georgiana's surprised expression, she added, "Though Father and I were often at odds, after what happened with Mr. Gable, I realised he was only trying to protect me. I wish I had come to that conclusion before I decided to leave."

"We all do things we regret," Georgiana said, reaching for her sister's hand and giving it a squeeze. "The real test is in admitting our mistakes and accepting responsibility, which you have. Matthew and I are very happy that you and Mr. Stevens have reached an understanding."

"Noel and I are very appreciative of the forgiveness you and my brother have extended. If he and I had not met, my reputation would be in tatters and, I dare say, my actions would have affected you and Brother more than they already had. I do not think I can ever express how grateful I am that you have accepted me back as though nothing had happened."

"You are family, and that is what family does."

Suddenly there was a shout of 'Georgiana' from the direction of the manor. As they turned to look, Matthew waved a hand as he walked in their direction. Lady Aileen declared, "Oh, no! I must have provoked Matthew to worry, for here he comes. I am sorry if I spoiled his plans to be done with all the financial matters today."

"Even if you did, Matthew needed a break. The walk will do him good."

In short order, the new Lord Camden caught up with his errant wife and sister. Without a word, he walked over to place a kiss on Georgiana's forehead. "May I assume that you are well, my darling?"

"You may."

Addressing them both, he said, "I hope I am not interrupting your conversation. Would you like me to sit with you or perhaps escort you around the pond? Or maybe you would care to return to the house? Mrs. Hanover said tea will be ready in less than an hour."

"I think I would like to walk around the pond before returning to the house," Georgiana replied.

Turning to Aileen, he asked, "Would you care to walk with us?"

"No, thank you. I have things to accomplish before tea is served. I will see you both there."

As Lady Aileen watched her brother and sister walk away, she thought to herself: *If Noel and I should be half as happy, I will be satisfied.*

Chapter 28

London

    Elizabeth was pleased to stay a bit longer in order to attend Richard's wedding. Not only was she delighted to see her cousin happily wed, but she dearly wished to see the Gardiners, as well as her parents and sisters, before returning to Pemberley. Invitations to Darcy House had been sent immediately upon their arrival in Town, but the responses received from her family had been disappointing.

    Mr. Bennet had written that he was suffering with a particularly bad case of gout in his right foot, preventing him from visiting until the malady had sufficiently abated. Mary and her husband, the Meryton vicar, along with their two children, were unable to oblige because their youngest was ill. Moreover, Lydia, who had wed John Lucas the year before, had finally cajoled him into taking a holiday in Bath, whilst Kitty, who was still unmarried, was travelling with the Gardiners. Thus, Elizabeth's desire to see her family soon had been dashed.

    In his reply, Mr. Bennet did suggest the Darcys visit Meryton on their return to Pemberley; however, due to his wife's condition, William was reluctant to add more miles to their journey home. Fortuitously, circumstances changed just before Richard's wedding, with the Gardiners' premature return to London and Mr. Bennet's gout improved sufficiently for him to make the journey. Subsequently, Mr. and Mrs. Bennet, the Gardiners, their four children and Kitty dined at Darcy House the evening before Richard's wedding.

    Since the Fitzwilliams and Darcys had made a pact never to mention the episode involving Lady Catherine to anyone lest it affect the family's reputation, that incident was not discussed at dinner. William's ordeal at sea, however, was fair game since, after William was recovered, Mr. Bennet had informed his entire family of all that had happened.

    Accordingly, as quickly as everyone was seated at the dinner table, Mrs. Bennet brought up the subject. "I cannot believe Mr. Bennet kept from me that you were lost at sea," she declared, addressing William. "I would have immediately travelled to Pemberley to help Elizabeth cope with the situation. I can only imagine how upset she and the children must have been. Those poor darlings!"

William and Elizabeth exchanged quick glances before she replied, "Just knowing that you were willing to come is enough, Mama. Fortunately, Mrs. Green and her husband were on hand to offer their support."

Peeved, Mrs. Bennet repeated that dreaded name. "Mrs. Green? Is that not the vicar's wife who is always at Pemberley whenever we visit?"

"Yes," Elizabeth quickly interjected. "Bennet and Anne love her and the vicar very much, and I can always count on them to comfort me and the children should it become necessary."

"Humph!" her frustrated mother replied. "That is what grandparents are for!"

"I think children need as many grandparents as possible, whether they are actually kin or not," Mrs. Gardiner added brightly. "With Fitzwilliam's parents no longer living, it is wonderful that the Greens have filled the void left by their passing."

Choosing to ignore her, Mrs. Bennet continued. "In any case, we are all so relieved that you returned in good health, Mr. Darcy."

"You are too kind, Mother Bennet," William replied sombrely.

However, the matron was not finished. "What would our family have done had you not returned?" She waved her serviette in the air. "Lord knows we will have to depend on your kindness and that of Mr. Bingley should Mr. Bennet die."

Wishing to steer the conversation in another direction, Mr. Bennet instantly enquired, "When do you expect the newest Darcy to make his appearance, Elizabeth?"

"He, *or she*, should arrive in just over a month," Elizabeth replied.

Seeing a worried look instantly cross his son's face, Mr. Bennet subdued a smile as he teased, "From experience your mother and I have learned that babies can come at the most inopportune times." He winked at his wife. "Remember when Kitty decided to come early, my dear?"

Fanny Bennet did not look amused. "It is easy for you to make light of it. I was the one who almost died."

"Oh, come now, dear. Neither you nor Kitty were ever in danger of dying," her husband reminded her. "It is just that you did not care to give birth at an inn with only a midwife to attend you."

"Had Dr. Wortham only warned me that he thought the baby would come earlier than I expected … well, I assure you, we would not have struck out for Lambton when we did."

Noting that William's complexion had turned pale, Elizabeth gave him a reassuring smile as she changed the subject. "Uncle, did I tell you that Lady Selina purchased all the materials for her wedding gown from your warehouse?"

"This is the first I have heard of it," Edward Gardiner replied, beaming at the news. "I hope she is pleased with her purchases."

"Indeed, she is. She has had a modiste designing the gown, but when she mentioned that Gardiner's Warehouse had the most beautiful fabrics in all of London, I was proud to inform her that my uncle owned the business."

"Oh, Lizzy," Mrs. Gardiner replied animatedly. "If she spreads her opinion amongst her acquaintances, that will be a feather in our cap."

"You can be certain that she will, Aunt. She told me as much."

"Speaking of the wedding," Mrs. Bennet interjected. "If Mr. Bennet will agree to lengthen our stay by one day, we could attend the ceremony with you."

Seeing William roll his eyes discreetly, Elizabeth instantly replied, "I fear that is impossible, Mama. Colonel Fitzwilliam and Lady Selina have only invited close friends and family, as they wish to keep the ceremony as intimate as possible."

Mrs. Bennet would not be deterred. "I do not see how adding two people could—"

Elizabeth's father interrupted. "We are leaving first thing in the morning, Mrs. Bennet, and that is final!"

The rest of the meal progressed with very little input from Mrs. Bennet.

As they were nearing the end of the meal, a maid entered the room. Performing a quick curtsey, she addressed Elizabeth. "Excuse me, Ma'am. You asked to be informed when the children had finished eating."

"Thank you, Susie. Please ask Mrs. Cummings to escort all the children to the music room."

The Gardiners' two youngest, Anna, who was thirteen, and George, age nine, had dined with Bennet and Anne in their schoolroom because they found the adult table dull. Consequently, they were already scheduled to rejoin their siblings, nineteen-year-old Martha and seventeen-year-old Benjamin, after dinner.

Once the maid left, Elizabeth said, "Mama, you wished to see Bennet and Anne again, so I thought that we would gather in the music room to hear all the children exhibit their talents. Whilst I am hardly a proficient on the pianoforte, I play well enough to accompany Bennet and Anne as they sing the Italian songs I have been teaching them. Moreover, I have not had the pleasure of hearing Martha play the pianoforte or Anna sing in ages."

Madeline Gardiner laughed. Glancing at her oldest daughter she said, "I am not certain Martha will be pleased. She had little chance to practise whilst we were travelling; however, Anna will sing for anyone who will listen."

Martha rolled her eyes at her mother's assertions just as Elizabeth said, "Then, let us retire to the music room and see who wishes to exhibit."

The next day

Though the wedding of Colonel Richard Fitzwilliam and Lady Selina Grey was not the grandiose affair Lady Matlock would have chosen, it had everything the couple involved cared about. Having had little time for rumours to spread throughout London, St. George's Church was not filled with the usual number of curious spectators but largely by those who had received hand-delivered invitations earlier that week. Approximately fifty people known to the couple filled the front pews and, afterwards, attended the wedding breakfast at Matlock House.

William and Elizabeth had been asked to stand up for the couple, and, whilst he was proud to be his cousin's best man, he was concerned about his wife being on her feet for the entire ceremony. Thus, whilst being delighted for Richard, William appeared subdued as he kept his eyes on his pregnant wife throughout the wedding.

Afterwards, during the breakfast, he witnessed Elizabeth surreptitiously make a concerned face as she laid a hand on her belly. That sent him instantly to her side. "Sweetheart, are you well?

"Yes. I am merely tired; that is all."

"We should return to Darcy House. You have been on your feet all day, and I insist that you lie down and rest."

"But Richard and Selina will be leaving shortly for their honeymoon," she argued. "We cannot leave until after they have."

"We can, and we shall," William said, trying to soften the blow with a loving look as he cupped her face and ran one thumb softly along her jawline. "They will understand."

Suddenly, Richard was beside them. "What is happening, Darcy? Is it the baby?"

Always amazed at how quickly his cousin could detect when something was wrong, William tried to reassure him. "It is nothing that severe. It is just that I believe Elizabeth needs to rest. To that end, she and I will say our farewells and return to Darcy House."

"Of course. You must," Richard replied. "Let me find Selina, and we shall have a private word before you leave."

As Richard left to find his wife, William guided Elizabeth towards a quiet hallway. Once there, he embraced her. "You have been very strong, my darling, fulfilling all your obligations; however, now it is time to take care of yourself."

It was not long until Richard returned with Selina, and after numerous hugs and well wishes, William and Elizabeth returned to Darcy House.

The next day

Concerned about returning to Pemberley so close to his wife's time, without asking Elizabeth's permission, William sent for Dr. Graham the next morning. Though she was not happy about his actions, Elizabeth understood her husband's reason for being anxious and allowed the examination. Once he had finished the exam, Dr. Graham asked for William to come back into Elizabeth's bedroom. As he sat down next to his wife on the bed, Dr. Graham addressed them both.

"Whilst I can see no reason for alarm at present, since the babe is due in so short a period, I suggest you decide now whether to stay in London until the child is born or return to Pemberley as soon as possible."

"Can you guarantee the child will not be born on the road?" a worried William asked.

The doctor smiled. "Only God could do that." Seeing the anxiety written on William's face, he added, "I shall leave that decision to you, but please advise me if you do intend to stay in town so that I may arrange to see Mrs. Darcy regularly until she gives birth."

Once the doctor had left, William tried to talk Elizabeth into staying in London until after the birth; however, she was not of a mind to listen.

"Our child should be born at Pemberley, just as his brother and sister were," she pleaded. "Now, to that end, I suggest we order our trunks packed and leave early in the morning."

"What of your plan to stop at the Bingleys' estate on our way home?"

"Jane will understand if we do not. Besides, we talked of inviting them to Pemberley after the baby arrives. By then, Georgiana's child should already have been born and may be old enough to travel. Therefore, we can host the entire family before Christmas and get to know all the new additions."

Though Elizabeth's cheerful attitude was not convincing, William did not wish to pressure her into staying. "I cannot find the strength to force you to comply, sweetheart. Consequently, since you are the one most affected, I shall allow your opinion to carry the day."

Elizabeth leaned in to cup his face with both hands. Giving him an unusually enthusiastic kiss, she cried, "You are so good to me, my darling!"

Suddenly, the door flew open, and Bennet ran straight to the bed where he proceeded to climb onto it. "Is everything all right, Mama? I-I saw the doctor leaving and I feared—"

Bennet went silent and William pulled his son into his lap. "All is well, Ben. I just wanted Dr. Graham to examine your mother before we leave for Pemberley."

Ben's forehead creased in the same manner as his own, causing a mixture of pride and sadness to fill William's heart. *He is far too young to carry such heavy burdens.*

"What did the doctor say?" Bennet asked solemnly.

"Dr. Graham believes your mother is well enough to travel," William replied.

Bennet's entire bearing changed. It was as though he had returned to being merely a four-year-old boy. "I am glad, for I cannot wait to get home! I have missed riding my pony. I just hope Pegasus has not forgotten me."

Elizabeth opened her arms, and Bennet slid across the bed to be collected within them. "Oh, my darling boy, Pegasus could never forget you."

"I hope you are right, for I do not wish to start training her all over again," he replied gravely.

"I can assure you that will not be the case," William replied, ruffling his son's dark hair. "Now, what say you to letting your mother rest whilst you and I take Anne to the park to feed the ducks? It will likely be the last time she will get to feed them before we leave London."

Bennet kissed his mother on the cheek. "I am so happy that you are well, Mama." Then he slid off the bed and ran towards the door, shouting as he went, "I shall fetch Anne, Papa!"

When he focused on Elizabeth again William's expression was sombre. "If I have not said it today, sweetheart, I love you with all my being—heart, soul and body."

Elizabeth grasped his hands, bringing them to her heart. "I know you do, because I love you just as ardently."

Kissing her gently but firmly, William said, "I shall bring the children in to see you as soon as we return from the park and they have changed clothes. I know Anne will be eager to see you."

"Try not to get distracted by all the women vying to catch your eye when they discover I am not at the park with you," she teased. "Else you will be away for far too long."

William laughed out loud. "What makes you think any woman would be interested in an old married man like me?"

"I have it on good authority that some do not care if you are married, for they are married as well."

"What authority told you that?"

"Your aunt. Moreover, Lady Matlock said outright that there is not one gentleman available to this year's group of debutantes anywhere near as handsome as you."

William, who had begun walking towards the door, stopped in the doorway. He appeared to be pondering what she had said. "To be totally honest, Elizabeth, women of my society never held any allure for me. That is why I had no idea what love was until we met. You can be certain of one thing, my darling, I will never love another woman. You are my first, last, only and forever love."

Having said that, he exited the room, leaving Elizabeth's eyes full of tears. *Just as you are mine.*

The next morning

As Elizabeth walked out of her bedroom, dressed to begin their journey home, she was met with the sight of Ben and Clancy running down the hall towards her.

"Mama!" Ben cried. "Someone is going home with us."

Elizabeth squatted down to Ben's level, grasping his shoulders to still him. "Calm down, sweetheart. Take a deep breath and let it go."

Ben made a show of doing as she asked. Once he had, she said, "Now, tell me *who* is going home with us."

"The man talking to Papa. I heard Papa say, 'Thank you for accepting my offer to travel with us.'"

At that very moment, Mrs. Cummings rushed into the hall, looking for her charge. "There you are, Master Bennet! I apologise for losing track of him, Mrs. Darcy. One moment I was helping him get dressed, and the next he was nowhere to be found."

"Do not worry, Mrs. Cummings. I know how easily my son can disappear." To Bennet she said, "Go back to your rooms and make certain you have packed the things you brought from Pemberley. Once we are on the road, we will not turn around to retrieve any of your toys. Do you understand?"

"Yes, Mama," a more subdued Ben replied.

As her son accompanied Mrs. Cummings back down the hall, Elizabeth pondered the information he had shared. Curiosity got the better of her, and she walked to the top of the grand staircase to peer down into the foyer. Surprised to see a young man she recognised as Dr. Graham's associate, Dr. Colpack, she tried to calm her indignation. *Surely, William would not—*

The man and William were deep in conversation when she began to step quietly down the stairs, and they did not notice her until she was practically upon them. Both appeared unsettled when they noticed her and instantly quieted.

Her wonderful, overly fretful and protective husband tried hard to look completely innocent when he acknowledged her. "Elizabeth, I believe you have already met Dr. Colpack."

The only sign that William was not as calm as he appeared was the fact that he blinked repeatedly whenever he was anxious—such as now. "He-he is headed to Sheffield and has accepted my offer to ride with us as far as Lambton."

William looked so much like a child caught with his hand in the biscuit jar that Elizabeth's anger at his officiousness instantly disappeared. After all, it was hard to stay angry with someone who loved you so much that he constantly looked for ways to keep you safe.

Smiling wryly, Elizabeth got straight to the point. "Dr. Colpack, there is really no need for you to accompany us back to Derbyshire … at least, not for my sake." As he started to protest, she held up a hand. "I fear I know my husband too well to think this is all coincidental."

Apparently, William had instructed the man well, for instantly he replied. "Oh no, Mrs. Darcy! I had already planned to visit my parents in Sheffield and when your husband informed Dr. Graham that you were returning to Pemberley, it seemed he thought it logical for me to travel with you. Your coach is much finer than any I might hire, and I could be of service if needed. I hope you do not mind."

Cutting her eyes to where William stood intently examining his boots, she replied, "If it will make your journey more comfortable, then why should I mind?"

Relieved at the way Elizabeth handled the revelation regarding Dr. Colpack, William let go of the breath he had unwittingly been holding. Reaching for his wife's hand, he said, "Now that that is settled, shall we be on our way? Dr. Colpack's trunk is already aboard our coach, and Adams has my trunk ready. May I assume yours and the children's trunks are packed?"

"Mine is, and as soon as Mrs. Cummings sends word that the children's things are packed, we will be set."

"Let us go upstairs and see how she is faring with the little scamps.

Dr. Colpack, you may go on to the coach; we shall be right behind you."

After watching the Darcys go back upstairs, it was with a great sense of relief Dr. Colpack hurried to the Darcys' vehicle which waited at the stables.

I am relieved that Mrs. Darcy was easier to convince than her husband anticipated.

Chapter 29

On the road

Since William did not wish to tire his wife any more than necessary, the trip back to Pemberley was undertaken as unhurriedly as the
trip to London had been a few weeks earlier. By taking more breaks to
change horses—allowing Elizabeth to stretch her legs—and travelling
fewer miles per day, the usual three-day trip had stretched to four, with
today being the last.

Knowing they would reach Pemberley that evening William could
not hold back a smile as he began the day. The reality that, thus far, Dr.
Colpack's services had not been needed had a great impact on lessening
the anxiety that had dogged his steps since the incident with his aunt
in London—though he was always anxious when facing the birth of
another child. Given his mother's history, the birth of his children had
been his Achilles' heel as he struggled with the fact that many women
did not survive childbirth.

After spending a comfortable evening at his favourite inn in Derby,
William rose early to go downstairs and speak to the drivers of both
coaches and to settle the bill with the innkeeper, Mr. Gamble. He left
Florence to wake her mistress and help Elizabeth dress. Food had been
ordered the previous night and would be sent up shortly. Once Elizabeth, the children, and all the various servants were dressed and ready,
everyone would eat in the private dining room that was part of the accommodations William had rented—an apartment which took up the
entire top floor of the inn and that was reserved only for those wealthy
enough to afford it.

As he was going downstairs, William came to a stop behind a
white-haired couple. When the gentleman turned to see who was behind him, William was surprised to recognise Lord Perkins of Beaufort
Manor. He and Lady Perkins were old friends of the family and had
often visited Pemberley when Darcy's parents were alive.

Immediately, he remembered how disappointed they were that he
did not offer for their daughter, Lady Marigold, when they put her

forth as a candidate for Mrs. Darcy years earlier. As far as he recalled, Lady Marigold had since married and lived in Richmond. Still, had her parents forgiven him for rejecting her?

"Fitzwilliam," Lord Perkins declared so civilly that William's entire body relaxed. "How odd meeting you here after so long a time. My wife and I were returning from Manchester yesterday when one of our horses threw a shoe. We decided to stay the night here and travel home this morning."

"Yes, it is odd," William agreed. "My family and I are on our way back to Pemberley from London."

"Your wife is with you?" Lady Perkins asked worriedly.

"Yes, she is."

"I am surprised to find you on the road, then," Lady Perkins said, her expression full of concern. "We were under the impression that Mrs. Darcy is on the verge of delivering your third child. That is, if the rumours my daughter passes along from the *ton* are to be believed."

Not pleased with being the object of gossip, much less with the hint of censure, William replied with more information than he normally would share. "Since it is at least a month until the child is expected, my wife insisted on accompanying me. Also, one of her doctors travelling to Sheffield, agreed to accompany us as far as Lambton."

Out of the blue, aforesaid doctor appeared directly behind William on the stairway. Without taking note of the man's worried expression, William said, "In fact, here is Dr. Colpack now."

After introductions, the doctor quickly turned his attention back to William. "Excuse me for interrupting, sir, but I fear we cannot leave the inn now."

William's bearing immediately stiffened. "Whyever not?"

"Florence just summoned me to Mrs. Darcy's room. It appears that the child has decided not to wait until we arrive at Pemberley to be born."

Mind racing as he imagined the worst possible consequences, William turned pale. "I-I must attend Elizabeth. Dr. Colpack, please inform Mr. Gamble that we will need the apartment for at least another week … perhaps longer. In fact, I will be glad to rent the entire floor below ours too if our presence here will interrupt other travellers' need for rest. Inform him of everything you will need for the birth—hot water, towels, extra bed sheet—and tell him I shall be glad to cover whatever it costs."

As he turned to go back upstairs, Lady Perkins grabbed William's arm. "You cannot possibly expect Mrs. Darcy to give birth in this inn. Our estate is only a few miles to the east, and we would be glad to host your entire party for as long as necessary."

"Exactly how far is your estate?" Dr. Colpack enquired.

"A little less than three miles," Lord Perkins declared. "Fitzwilliam visited Beaufort Manor when he was just a boy, but he may not recall that now."

Dr. Colpack addressed William. "That short a distance should present no problem in moving Mrs. Darcy if we leave straightaway."

"I shall gladly take you up on your kind offer," William declared to the elderly couple "We are already packed and shall be pleased to follow your coach to Beaufort Manor."

"Excellent!" Lord Perkins declared. "I will send a footman on to the estate to tell my housekeeper to begin preparing accommodations for all of you. How many are travelling with you?"

"Our two children, their nanny and maid, Elizabeth's maid and my valet, my security chief, and, of course, Dr. Colpack. Our groomsmen, footmen and drivers will be happy to stay in the stables if you have room."

"Between the stables, vacant servants' apartments and guest rooms we have plenty of room for everyone. Do not concern yourself in that regard," Lord Perkins replied.

As William and Dr. Colpack rushed back to Elizabeth, Lord and Lady Perkins hurried downstairs to set the footman in motion and to make certain their coach was ready to leave.

Beaufort Manor

Though but a boy the last time he had visited Lord Perkins' estate, it was just as William remembered—a very grand manor house, reminiscent of Matlock Manor, with gardens that rivalled some of the best in England. Still, he had little time to consider his surroundings upon their arrival as he spent the morning trying to calm Elizabeth. She blamed herself for not staying in London until the child was born, and he kept repeating Dr. Colpack's opinion that the date selected for her *lying in* might have been incorrect by a month.

"After all," William said, "You had just gotten word that I was missing and, in your disquiet, you may have miscalculated."

Nothing seemed to console Elizabeth, however, and the next time Dr. Colpack came in the room to examine her, William stepped into the sitting room next door to gather his thoughts. Instantly, a maid pressed a hot cup of tea into his hands and once he had taken a few sips of the warm liquid, he was able to think more clearly.

At that moment, his valet, Mr. Adams, stepped into the room and addressed him. "Sir, young master Bennet wishes to see his mother." Before William could answer, he held up a hand to silence him. "Forgive me. I am aware that I am overstepping my bounds by even bringing up the matter. This cannot be a good time, but I promised him I would present his petition."

Though weary to the point of exhaustion, William knew that his valet was very attentive to his son, and he was appreciative of that. Besides, he still recalled how frightened he had been as a boy whenever his mother had been kept from him as she birthed his brothers and sisters, though none but Georgiana had survived.

"I shall see if Elizabeth feels well enough to have him come in now."

Elizabeth had washed her face, dried her eyes and was smiling as Bennet ran past his father into the room. Once at the bed, William picked him up and sat him as close to his mother as was prudent.

"May I kiss you, Mama?"

"Of course, you may, my darling boy."

Bennet got on his knees and leaned in to kiss Elizabeth on the cheek. "Papa says you will have another brother or sister for me today."

"That is true." Another contraction caused Elizabeth to grimace in pain, though she turned her head, trying not to let Bennet see.

Nonetheless, he noticed. "Are you in pain, Mama?"

After she had recovered, Elizabeth cupped her son's cheek lovingly. "Only a little. Besides, as you grow you will learn that pain is just a part of bringing babies into the world. It may hurt for a little while, but the blessing of having a child is well worth it."

William reached out to clasp Bennet's shoulder and give it a soft squeeze. "Tell you mother what you wish to say, Son, for Lady Perkins is waiting to show you and Anne the special children's garden."

Bennet's forehead wrinkled just like his father's did whenever he was being sincere. "I wish to tell you that I love you very much, Mama."

"Thank you, sweetheart," Elizabeth replied, wincing with the next contraction. "I love you, too. In truth, more than words can say. Now, promise me that you will go to the garden with Lady Perkins and keep your sister occupied by playing with her."

"I promise." With that Bennet was off the bed. At the door, he hesitated a moment, threw his mother a kiss and went out.

With the next contraction—this one much worse than the last—Elizabeth covered her mouth to prevent Bennet form hearing her moan.

Later

Mr. Adams had been inhabiting the sitting room adjacent to the birthing room since the master had taken Bennet in to see his mother. Adams was not in a mood to be there, but his presence could be easily explained. He wanted to be on hand in case his master was ejected by the good doctor and needed someone with whom to commiserate. Darcy had crossed swords with both doctors who had supervised the births of his other children and since neither Colonel Fitzwilliam nor Charles Bingley was present to calm him, the only other man available if something similar happened, was the elderly Lord Perkins. Unfortunately, that gentleman kept nodding off where he sat, despite the mournful cries of Mrs. Darcy.

From the window, Adams occupied himself by watching the Darcy children play in the garden especially constructed for Lord and Lady Perkins' grandchildren. To say he had been astounded when Darcys' security manager appeared from out of nowhere to join those racing after Bennet, Anne and Clancy would be an understatement. Adams noted that, though a man of Mr. Palmer's size looked ridiculous in the chase, he moved with the agility of a much smaller man. The sight of him made the valet smile.

Just like Palmer to find a way to protect the children under the guise of playing with them.

Fortunately, Bennet had found the garden fascinating, and, for a short time, it took his mind off his mother. Not only was there a fishpond, but it was full of large, gold-coloured fish. The pond had a bridge across it that featured a place in the middle where one could safely sit and dangle his feet whilst feeding bread to the fish.

The garden also contained several shrubs trimmed in the likenesses of animals such as dogs, cats, horses, giraffes and elephants. Moreover, several types of swings were hung in tall trees, including double, wooden swings that he and Anne could occupy at the same time, as well as large ropes with enormous knots at the bottom for one to sit on whilst flying through the air. Anne was too small to appreciate the ropes, but Bennet found them exhilarating,

In addition, an enormous boulder had been placed in the middle of the garden. On one side steps had been chiselled clear to the top where a flat area, marked by chains on either side, acted as a fort for children to defend against pirates. On the opposite side of the boulder, a channel had been carved and polished so smoothly that one could slide down it all the way to the ground. Indeed, it was a veritable wonderland for children.

Suddenly, the door to the birthing room flew open and the robust cry of a new-born filled the air as Florence appeared, red-faced, but exhilarated. "He is here! Mother and son are both doing well!" she declared, before hurrying back inside the room and closing the door.

Adams was so relieved that, as he sank into the nearest chair, his entire body relaxed. Lowering his face into his hands to massage his forehead, he was shocked when Lord Perkins seemed to come back to life.

"Wha-what was that?" his lordship sputtered.

"The Darcys have a new son, and the child and Mrs. Darcy are both doing well," Adams replied.

"Excellent!" Lord Perkins replied, dropping his head and closing his eyes again. In mere seconds, he appeared to be asleep once more.

Determined not to be thrown out of the birthing room this time, William had kept most of his opinions to himself throughout Elizabeth's ordeal, though he often had to bite his tongue in order to do so.

It appeared that this child's arrival was taking a heavy toll on Elizabeth; consequently, he vowed not to leave her side. He coped by constantly dipping a washcloth in cool water and mopping her brow whilst repeatedly expressing his love and admiration. This continued until the child was finally held aloft and proclaimed a boy.

Drained, William went silent as he watched the local midwife—summoned soon after their arrival at Beaufort Manor—take the infant and lay him on a table lined with towels. The babe barely made a noise until the strenuous washing brought out his temper, and he howled at the intrusion.

"He certainly has a pair of lungs," Dr. Colpack said, smiling, as he continued to tend to Elizabeth.

The doctor's declaration brought William's attention back to one of his primary concerns. Leaning towards the doctor, he asked quietly, "How is my wife?"

"In light of her struggle to birth your son, Mrs. Darcy is doing quite well."

Closing his eyes, William murmured, "Thank you, God."

Once the doctor had finished with Elizabeth, he said to the midwife, "If you are finished, let Mr. Darcy take the child to his mother."

The instant the babe was laid in his arms, he stopped whimpering. William stammered, "Is he …"

Realising what was on his mind, Dr. Colpack replied, "In my opinion, your son is in good health for what he has been through. He appears to be full-term, which means Mrs. Darcy must have been mistaken about when he was due."

Glancing towards his patient who had her eyes closed, he added more quietly, "Not wishing to put undue stress on you or your wife, I purposely did not inform you that, at the beginning, the child was not in the proper position to be born. I had to manipulate him into position, which is one reason his birth was protracted."

"Had I known that—" William's voice caught, and he shook his head, unable to continue.

"He was not entirely breech, so it was not as bad as it could have been, which is why I decided not to say anything unless I could not get the child turned."

Deeply touched, William lifted his son to kiss his forehead before taking him to his mother. As he held the babe close to Elizabeth, she pulled aside the blanket to count his toes and fingers, at length saying with a weary smile, "He is perfect." Instantly, the baby fixed his gaze on her and appeared to smile.

"He is certainly familiar with your voice," William declared.

"Of course he is. He has listened to me talk and sing to him all these many months. Hand him to me, please."

After William laid the babe in her arms, Elizabeth placed kisses all over his face before saying, "My son, you are fortunate that you are not a girl since your Papa promised to name you Richard."

"And I always keep my promises," William replied as he sank down on the bed beside her. "However, I am certain that should my cousin father a boy he will wish to name him Richard; therefore, to lessen confusion, I thought we would make our son's middle name Richard. What say you to Anthony Richard Fitzwilliam Darcy? Anthony was my grandfather Darcy's middle name."

"I think it suits him perfectly."

Chapter 30

Days later

Lord and Lady Perkins would have been pleased for the Darcys to remain—after all, Beaufort Manor had been too quiet since Lady Marigold had married and moved away. Moreover, their grandchildren only came to visit twice a year, at most. Still, William and Elizbeth were exceedingly happy to be going home eight days after Anthony's birth.

As word of their homecoming was made public, it seemed that all of Lambton was eager to welcome the newest little Darcy home. In fact, many residents lined the streets of the town to wave as the Darcy coach drove through on its way to Pemberley. The vicar and Mrs. Green were waiting at Pemberley to help with Anne and Bennet so that Elizabeth could focus on the new baby whilst also having a chance to recuperate. William was glad for their presence, since neither Jane Bingley nor Madeline Gardiner was there to help, having only recently been informed of Anthony's birth. In addition, their local physician, Dr. Camryn, was planning to take over Mrs. Darcy's care that afternoon, which meant Dr. Colpack was free to travel on to Sheffield in the morning.

Immediately upon arrival, Bennet had begged to ride Pegasus, which prompted Anne to declare that she wanted to ride, too. Though the temperature was brisker than William would have liked, the Greens stated they would be glad to accompany the children to the stables, so he agreed. Bennet was thrilled to discover that his pony had remembered her training—mainly because, unbeknownst to him, the stablemaster had kept up her lessons using large bags of sand in the saddle in lieu of an actual rider. Shortly after being helped to mount, Bennet was riding as proficiently as before.

Moreover, before they left Beaufort Manor, Lord and Lady Perkins had gifted Anne a pony of her own. She was a black and white creature, even smaller than Pegasus, that their stablemaster had named Domino after a game involving black and white tiles he had seen played in London. Domino arrived with a special saddle created to keep small children from losing their seat, and because Anne was used to riding with her brother, she was soon slowly circling the paddock with confidence. She even tried to wave off Mrs. Green, for she wished to imitate her brother and ride alone; however, William had declared that Anne could not ride without supervision until she was at least Bennet's age. Consequently, much to her consternation, Mrs. Green stayed close by her.

Despite the sunshine, after an hour the temperature fell dramatically, and, over the children's protests, their father determined it was time for them to come inside. William did promise, however, that they could ride again tomorrow if the weather cooperated.

Though the trip from Beaufort Manor was undertaken with the utmost care, it had wearied Elizabeth. Consequently, she had slept most of their first day at home, only waking that afternoon when Anthony decided it was past time to eat. His wails of hunger seemed to awaken the entire household, as everyone raced to the sitting room next to Elizabeth's bedroom. Seeing Mrs. Cummings, Mrs. Reynolds and Florence gathered for the same reason as he, William tried not to gloat as he took charge.

"I shall see to Elizabeth," he declared. "Mrs. Reynolds will you have Cook send up a tray of sandwiches, hot soup and some fresh tea? I hope to persuade my wife to eat when she has finished feeding Anthony."

As she rushed out to do his bidding, he addressed Mrs. Cummings. "Please stay nearby in case we need you to take Anthony." Then he addressed Florence. "You know that Anthony always dribbles milk on her gown when he suckles. Please have warm water and a clean gown ready in her dressing room."

Florence curtseyed and went to do as asked. Soon everyone had disappeared except Mrs. Cummings, who had settled in the window seat to await her duties.

✦

Inside Elizabeth's bedroom, William hurried to the windows and threw open the curtains. That allowed him to see that his son, who had apparently been sleeping on his mother's chest. was already feeding.

The sight gave him pause. Elizabeth looked so beautiful that he found himself unwittingly holding his breath.

"Your son has a temper," she murmured, breaking William's contemplation. "Furthermore, he is not very patient … like someone else I know."

"A boy has a right to be upset if he is starving," William replied cheekily, gently running a hand over his son's dark curls as he sat down on the bed.

"Anthony was nowhere close to starving."

"We should leave that up to him to decide, and surely you are not referencing me when you speak of patience," William teased, smoothing a stray curl behind Elizabeth's ear.

His heart sang when she laughed. "Of course not! One could never accuse you of being impatient!"

William smiled wryly. "One could, but I daresay they would be exaggerating."

"I thought you abhorred deceit of any kind," she teased.

"I do, but what has that to do with Anthony?"

Elizabeth laughed again, and he leaned in to give her a quick kiss. "Tell me. How do you feel, sweetheart?"

"I have absolutely no energy, and I feel as though I could eat a pony," Elizabeth replied dryly. Then she quickly added, "Please do not tell Pegasus or Domino I said that."

"It shall be our secret," William said, grinning. "In any case, you will be glad to know I have sent for refreshments. You cannot regain your strength unless you eat."

Once Anthony had stopped suckling and was close to falling asleep, William lifted him from Elizabeth's arms. "I hope to keep him awake more during the day so that he will begin sleeping through the night," he said.

Darcy walked over to a window where he could see his son better. "Anthony looks much like Bennet did at this age. His hair is the same colour, though I believe his eyes are darker."

"I agree. Bennet's eyes were dark blue when he was born and became as light as yours within months. Anthony's eyes are almost as dark as mine already."

William held Anthony out as though trying to gauge his length. "I would be surprised if he is not as long as Bennet was at birth, either. Remind me to ask Dr. Camryn how long Anthony is when he returns. He wrote down his height and weight but neglected to mention it."

Elizabeth sighed. "I pray he is at least six feet tall when he is full grown."

"I do not think that will be a problem. Anthony will likely be as least as tall as my father, who was exactly six feet."

"In any case, he will be handsome, for he favours you."

"I could say the same; he favours you, as well," William replied as he sat down in a large, upholstered chair, resting Anthony in the crook of his arm.

Suddenly, the door burst open, and Bennet, Anne and Clancy rushed into the room, followed by Mrs. Green. "I am so sorry for the intrusion," she declared. "I thought I made it clear that they were to wait in the sitting room until summoned, but they got ahead of me."

"No apologies are necessary," Elizabeth replied as Bennet climbed onto the bed, Anne headed towards William, and Clancy took his usual place on the hearth. "Children, I know you are anxious to see your brother, but you must obey Mimi, Mrs. Cummings and your nannies."

"We will, Mama!" Bennet replied excitedly.

Meanwhile, Anne declared, "See Brother!" So Mrs. Green helped her onto William's knee for a closer look at Anthony.

"Gently," William cautioned as Anne patted her brother's head and leaned in to place a kiss there.

After hugging Bennet and bestowing a kiss on his face, Elizabeth asked him, "What are your plans for today? From the smocks you are wearing, I assume you will be painting."

"Me paint!" Anne cried from where she sat.

Rolling his eyes at his sister's response, Bennet said, "Mimi is going to teach us how to paint flowers."

"How wonderful!" Elizabeth replied. "I hope to see the results of your efforts once you are finished."

"We were going to surprise you with the outcome, but now the secret is out," Mrs. Green replied with a smile. "It is too cold to go outside, so Mrs. Cummings suggested we paint in the conservatory."

"An excellent idea," William replied. "Come, Bennet. If you wish to give your brother a kiss before you begin, you should do so now."

Bennet kissed his mother and slid off the bed instantly. He was tall enough to see Anthony without help and placed a gentle kiss on his sibling's cheek, saying, "I will be glad when he is old enough to ride Pegasus, for I intend to teach him how."

William tried not to smile. "I am certain you will be an excellent teacher."

Meanwhile Anne was holding up her arms to be lifted onto the bed. Mrs. Green did the honours, which gave Elizabeth a chance to cuddle with her daughter.

"My goodness, Anne!" Elizabeth said as she embraced the child. "You are getting so big. You shall be as tall as Bennet before we know it."

"I big girl!" Anne agreed, nodding her head.

"You certainly are!" Elizabeth replied, kissing her.

"Children, if we are to paint something for your mother, we must begin," Mrs. Green announced. Soon afterwards the children were shuffled from the room.

Clancy had curled up on the blanket near the hearth instead of following the children. William chuckled. "It appears Clancy needs a rest from the children, too."

Elizabeth's brows knit with concern. "You have waited on me hand and foot for weeks now. I would not be shocked to learn that you are exhausted. Perhaps it is you who needs to spend today resting to restore your strength."

"I admit that I am tired, but not nearly as exhausted as you. I was only teasing about Clancy, and I could not be in greater humour. I never dreamed that having children could bring such joy. If I had known this, I would have married years ago." Then, considering what he had said, he added, "That is, only if I could have married you back then."

Elizabeth laughed. "Thank you for amending your remark to include me, my love."

William sat down on the bed and leaned in to kiss his wife ardently. "I could never leave you out of any discussion of my happiness, my darling."

Then nodding to a tray of refreshments a maid was placing on a nearby table, he said, "Now that the children are occupied, you and I should have something to eat."

That afternoon, completely unexpectedly, a coach rolled down the long drive and came to a stop in front of Pemberley. As Mr. and Mrs. Bingley stepped out, along with their children, only a few footmen were present to greet them.

Suddenly, Mrs. Reynolds flew out the door, only to encounter Jane coming up the steps. "Welcome to Pemberley, Mrs. Bingley! I fear that the master and mistress may not have been expecting you, for they are both currently occupied. Come in and I shall notify them of your arrival."

"I apologise for not telling Lizzy I was coming. I hope our presence will not create too much of a problem."

"Not at all. Your usual rooms are always ready."

As Jane, holding Rebecca Jane who was now almost two months old, followed the housekeeper into the hall, William joined them. He had heard the coach's approach whilst in his study and stepped out in time to see Charles Bingley walk in holding Thomas Charles, who at almost three years of age was the image of his father.

"Charles!" William declared. "How good to see all of you." He tickled Thomas under the chin, which made the boy giggle, and then turned his attention to his sister. "And this beauty must be Rebecca."

Jane beamed as he moved aside the blanket to admire their daughter. "With her blonde locks and blue eyes, she looks exactly like her mother."

"I cannot deny that she is mine," Jane said, laughing. "Just as Charles cannot deny Thomas is his."

"Elizabeth will be delighted to see you and to finally meet Rebecca."

Charles interjected, "I am sorry if our unannounced visit is inconvenient but—"

"Blame it on me! It is my fault!" Jane interrupted. "I know we are invited for Christmas, but, after I read about Anthony's birth, I just had to come and see for myself that he and Lizzy are well. I have been so concerned about them."

"Do not worry. You and Charles are welcome anytime." Then he added, "I believe Elizabeth is feeding Anthony at present, but we shall let her know you have arrived." To Mrs. Reynolds, he added, "Please see that my brother and sister are settled in their rooms and notify Mrs. Darcy of their arrival."

"Please, follow me," Mrs. Reynolds stated, as she began up the grand staircase.

Pemberley's conservatory
Two days later

Amongst a variety of exotic flowers and plants, Jane sat beside her sister on a large sofa. They each had their feet propped upon matching ottomans as Jane let her head sink into the plush upholstery, sighing, "Oh, Lizzy, I cannot say how pleased I was to find you and Anthony both healthy. After William wrote to say that Anthony's birth was difficult, I was so worried that I had to see for myself that you were well."

"It could have been worse. Dr. Colpack said Anthony was not in the proper position to be born, but he was not entirely breech. Fortunately, he was able to turn the baby, and everything ended well. I do wish, however, that William had not mentioned it in his letter to you. If Mama should hear of it, she will hold me responsible just because I was not at home when Anthony was born."

"Never fear. I shall speak to Charles, and we shall never mention it again. I know how exasperating Mama can be when she settles on something to criticise. She still has not forgiven me for not naming Rebecca after her even after I explained that she was named for Charles' late mother."

"Mama felt the same way when Anne was born. Just ignore her, and she will eventually find something else to complain about."

"Let us talk of more agreeable things," said Jane. "For instance, in my opinion, you have the most attentive husband I have ever seen. I believe Fitzwilliam Darcy would spoon-feed you if you would allow it."

Elizabeth smiled. "He cannot help that he is such a tender-hearted man and that he loves me and the children beyond measure."

"Do you hear yourself?" Jane asked, laughing. "I can recall when you thought him the most overbearing, controlling and rude man of your acquaintance."

"Please do not remind me how foolish I was when we married. My ignorance almost cost me the best man I have ever known."

Elizabeth glanced out the conservatory windows where her husband and Charles were occupied helping Anne, Bennet and Thomas ride the ponies. They had purposefully chosen an area that was in full view of the conservatory windows. "I am grateful that God was able to change my mind about William before I tossed it all away."

"I recall being so pleased when you wrote that William had forgiven you and allowed you to take your rightful place as mistress of Pemberley."

"Believe me, it was not as simple as that. Still, everything worked out for the best." Knowing she needed to raise the topic of William's trials at sea, just as William had pledged to do with Charles, Elizabeth said, "Jane, there is something I must tell you before you hear it from Mama." When Jane did not answer, she continued. "Do you recall when you were in Scarborough, and I wrote that William was off to visit Georgiana and her husband in Ireland?"

"I do, but to tell the truth, with all the turmoil regarding the illness and death of Charles' aunt, I had completely put it out of my mind until I received your letter saying he had returned."

"When I wrote that letter, I purposefully did not tell you what occurred between his departure and his return."

"Whyever not?"

Elizabeth began to share all that had happened—including being told that William had died and Colonel Fitzwilliam's part in proving her belief that he was alive.

Once she finished, Jane sat with her mouth agape before murmuring quietly, "Oh, Lizzy. How horrible this must have been for you. Had you confided in me, I would have rushed here to comfort you."

"I know you would have, which was why I did not tell you at the time. You were in your last months of pregnancy in a strange place, and, by your own admission, Charles was overwhelmed with attending to his aunt during her sickness and subsequent death. At the time, he needed you more than I did."

"But William has been home for weeks now; why have you said nothing?"

"There was too much to relate in a letter. Besides, I wished to tell you in person, and we have not been in each other's company until now. Please do not think I did not wish to confide in you. On the contrary, I knew you would worry yourself sick, and I was trying to avoid that. You must understand that I not only believed William was still alive, but I had to trust that he would return to me, else I could not have survived. Thus, I was trying to think positively."

"I-I believe I understand. Still, I always want to be here for you whenever you need me."

Elizabeth reached for Jane's hand and squeezed it. "That is one thing I love most about our relationship. We have each other for support."

Suddenly Jane pointed to what was happening outside. "Look! Thomas is riding behind Bennet."

"I hope you know what that means," Elizabeth replied wryly. "From now until *forever* Thomas will beg for a pony ... or until you and Charles give in."

Jane sighed. "I am fearful of him riding at his age ... at least, riding alone."

"I understand, for I was, too. Moreover, I still cringe at times when I see Bennet riding too fast; however, William assured me that our son would be a more competent horseman if he learned about riding whilst he was full young. Bennet has been riding with his father since he could sit up, and once his fourth birthday drew near, William began looking for a pony."

"I suppose it is inevitable."

"It is. Just something else a mother must accept as she watches her children grow up. Let us pray that Rebecca is not as competitive with Thomas as Anne is with Bennet, for that creates another set of problems. My daughter thinks she is old enough to do anything her brother does."

"Whilst I love Anne's spirit, I have to agree with you."

Suddenly, the ponies came to stop in front of the conservatory windows, allowing the children to wave to their mothers before they began the long trek back to the stables. As she and Jane threw air kisses at their offspring, Elizabeth said, "It appears that they are done riding and will be inside before we know it. Since the children will be joining us for tea or perhaps some hot chocolate to warm them, I would like to feed Anthony now. I shall go upstairs and see if my son is awake."

Jane stood. "I need to check on Rebecca, too." As they walked up the grand staircase, Elizabeth said, "Would Charles be willing to return to Ivy Manor alone, leaving you and the children here until our family arrives for Christmas? In that way, you will not have to travel there and back again in such a short period of time."

"Honestly, I fear my poor husband could not do without me that long. He is much like William when it comes to family."

"Which is an excellent trait, I think. Whilst many see William as always in command, he needs my support more than most could imagine."

"Is it not strange how much husbands who love their wives need them close by? I have never seen that in our parents' marriage. Papa is always so glad to be rid of Mama when she is visiting family, not to mention he keeps to his study whenever she is home."

Elizabeth sighed. "I do not think either of us could testify that our parents are a happy match. Still, they have managed to stay together."

Once they reached the landing, Jane stopped and turned towards Elizabeth. "At least you and I managed to achieve our girlish dreams." At her sister's quizzical look, she added, "We both married for the deepest love."

Elizabeth smiled wryly. "In spite of doing my best to fail, we certainly did."

Suddenly, an infant's cry broke the silence.

"My son has awakened right on time," Elizabeth declared, smiling. "I shall see you at tea."

"At tea," Jane replied.

After watching Elizabeth enter her sitting room, Jane hurried on to her own rooms.

The rectory
Several weeks later

As Pemberley's footmen unloaded the carriage filled with bags, baskets and boxes of items destined for the villagers of Lambton attending the annual Christmas party given by the vicar and his wife, Judith

Green exclaimed with delight, "Oh, Elizabeth! You and Fitzwilliam have outdone yourselves this year. There must be enough coats and shoes for all of Derbyshire, not to mention enough food to feed everyone who attends."

"If there are any shoes and coats left, just pass them along to those in need. We are not opposed to helping those in the outlying areas of Derbyshire as well as Lambton village."

"God will surely bless you for it."

Elizabeth smiled. "He already has. I do regret, though, that I shall not be available to help you with the party tomorrow."

"You have your hands full with the baby and preparing for most of your family to descend upon Pemberley. Moreover, I regret not being able to help as much with Bennet and Anne after Jane returned to Ivy Manor because I had to focus on the party."

"No need to apologise. We are well-served by Mrs. Cummings, who keeps the nannies assisting her under good regulation. And though I missed Jane very much after she left, her absence was just the incentive I needed to help Mrs. Reynolds finish the Christmas baskets for Pemberley's tenants and to add more gloves, scarves and coats to the gifts for your party."

"I cannot thank you enough; however, I am almost afraid to ask," Mrs. Green continued. "With your family on the cusp of arriving, was your cook able to bake the two-dozen ginger biscuits I requested?"

"Actually, Mrs. Lantrip informed me that she had prepared four dozen biscuits, two dozen lemon tarts and enough bread to make sandwiches using the ham and corned beef she included. In addition to the meat, there are jams and pickles."

"What a relief," Mrs. Green replied. "So many adults have come to depend upon the meal we serve almost as much as they depend upon the gifts for their children. I intend to have a large pot of soup as well, so your contributions will make for a grand meal."

"If you think of anything more you need, just send word," Elizabeth said, giving her friend a hug. "Now, I must return in case Anthony wakes early and thinks I intend for him to starve." She laughed. "Much like his father, Anthony is inconsolable if I am not instantly available to fulfil his every need."

"We both know that you love being there for your family."

Elizabeth grinned. "I cannot deny it."

"Kiss sweet Anthony, Anne and Bennet for me," Judith Green said. "And remember, these days will fly by very quickly, so try to enjoy them. Babies grow up way too fast."

"I tell myself that whenever I begin to feel overwhelmed."

Chapter 31

Pemberley

Richard and Lady Selina arrived on the fifteenth of December, just days ahead of Elizabeth's family, who were slated to arrive on the twentieth. As the coach from Houghton Park, emblazoned with the Grey family crest, made its way up the drive, William, who was in his study, was the first to be alerted. Rushing upstairs, he reached his wife's bedroom just as Mrs. Cummings was taking Anthony from her arms.

"Please hand my son to me, Mrs. Cummings!" William declared as he hurried towards her. "My cousin Richard has just arrived, and I would like him to meet Anthony whilst he is still awake. If you will follow me, you may take the baby to the nursery once Richard has been introduced to his namesake."

The servant, trying not to smile, turned to hand the master his son. William lifted Anthony to place a kiss on his forehead before settling him in the crook of his arm. "I hope you can stay awake long enough to meet your cousin, Son."

Elizabeth rose from the chair she had occupied whilst feeding Anthony. "I shall ring for Florence to help me don another gown and put my hair up. Please greet them whilst I make myself presentable."

"I shall be glad to, my love," William answered. "But I think you look lovely just as you are. Adding a robe and leaving your hair down will suit me."

By then Elizabeth, who had already rung for Florence, had crossed to where William stood holding their son. She stood on tiptoes to give him a kiss. "Thank you for always making me feel beautiful."

"I speak only the truth, my darling."

Suddenly, Mrs. Reynolds stuck her head in the door. "The Fitzwilliams' coach is at the door."

"Lead the way, Mrs. Reynolds," William said as he followed her from the room, carrying Anthony.

310

Richard and Lady Selina were waylaid on the landing to admire the newest little Darcy. Both were properly impressed with the babe, with the colonel declaring Anthony Richard the spitting image of Ben at that age.

Having not known Bennet when he was an infant, Lady Selina pronounced him a beautiful baby who looked very much like his father. This statement made William blush.

"Are you saying my cousin is beautiful, my dear?" Richard teased.

A bit embarrassed at how her compliment was perceived, Lady Selina tried to explain. "I meant only that Anthony is a beautiful baby and that he favours his father—which is just a fact. In truth, both Bennet and Anthony look remarkably like Fitzwilliam, as does Anne, for that matter, though I do think I see some of Elizabeth's features in Anne."

"I am satisfied with how our children have turned out," Elizabeth replied with a chuckle as she suddenly appeared behind them in the hall.

William kissed his son again before handing him to Mrs. Cummings, who had stopped behind Elizabeth. As the servant walked towards the nursery with the babe, Lady Selina tried to make amends.

"I hope I have not offended you, Elizabeth."

"Not at all," Elixabeth replied. "If all our children look like William, I shall be very pleased."

"I do not agree. Anne is practically a miniature of you," William protested. "Moreover, Bennet has your inquisitive nature and intellect, and it is already apparent that Anthony has inherited your dark eyes."

Just at that moment, the door to a bedroom further down the hall opened and Ben rushed out. Seeing Richard, he ran straight towards him exclaiming, "Cousin Richard! I thought I heard you! I have been looking forward to seeing you again!"

Stooping, Richard gave Bennet a hug. "Just as I have been eager to see you, my boy."

"Bennet," Elizabeth said. "Is there someone else you wish to greet?"

Bennet pulled away from Richard and bobbed towards Lady Selina. "I am pleased to see you again, too, Cousin Selina."

"I am so pleased that you are, Master Bennet," Lady Selina said as she stepped forward to accept a hug.

"You were supposed to be taking a nap," Elizabeth reminded her son.

"I was trying to, Mama," Bennet protested, "but, when I heard Cousin Richard talking, I could not help myself."

"If your parents agree, perhaps you may accompany me until time for tea," Richard said, looking towards Elizabeth and William. "That way Bennet and I can catch up on each other's news whilst I wash off the dust of the road and change clothes."

William glanced to Elizabeth, who smiled and nodded. To Bennet he said, "You may skip your nap, Son, but only this time."

"Thank you, Papa."

Bennet grabbed Richard's hand, and as they followed a waiting maid down the hall, she stopped to open the door to one of the larger suites. Richard turned to ask, "What is this? Have my usual accommodations changed?"

"Of course," Elizabeth declared. "Now that you are married, you and Lady Selina will need a suite."

Dutifully, Richard and Bennet walked past the maid and into the room. The maid hurriedly followed, opening the drapes to let in the light.

Lady Selina chuckled, saying quietly, "It appears I am easily forgotten."

Elizabeth replied conspiratorially, "Let us see how long it takes for him to realise his mistake."

Suddenly, Richard's head poked out the door. "Mrs. Fitzwilliam, will you be joining us anytime soon?"

"He has redeemed himself," Lady Selina murmured as she hurried towards her husband.

Watching them go, Elizabeth took hold of William's hand. "I am so glad that we are beyond the games newlyweds play."

Wiliam brought her hand to his lips for a kiss. "I agree." Then, cupping her cheek, he smirked. "I much prefer the games couples who have been married as long as we have play."

Elizabeth playfully swatted his arm. "Shh. They may hear you."

"Let them!" he teased. "They should be aware of the joy they have to look forward to."

With one hand on her back, William began guiding his wife towards their sitting room. "At this moment, I can think of nothing I would rather do than sit in the window seat with you in my arms, stealing kisses and pretending the rest of our family is not about to descend upon us like a flock of birds."

"At least we may enjoy the quiet until the bell is rung for tea."

Two days later

Lady Selina followed Elizabeth to the mistress' study, which was down a separate hall on the family floor. Elizabeth explained that it was one of the rooms she most enjoyed occupying whilst feeding Anthony, as it was isolated from the high traffic areas and the view from there was extraordinary. Mrs. Cummings came, too, carrying a basket of things she felt necessary to keep her mistress and the babe clean during and after Anthony's meal.

Once inside the elegantly appointed space, Lady Selina turned in a circle on the pale green carpet, admiring the coral, teal and lavender wallpaper. "Oh, Elizabeth! I can understand why you love this room. The colours are so relaxing, and the floor-to-ceiling windows provide the perfect panoramic view of Pemberley!"

"The windows are so large that often I will catch sight of William galloping across the pastures in the distance as he returns home. When I see that handsome man sitting a horse the way all gentlemen should—as though he was born to the saddle—I am so proud and grateful that he is mine."

"I will not argue with you about that. He and my Richard are excellent horsemen, and it shows. I am filled with awe whenever Richard gallops across Houghton Park, so I know exactly what you mean."

By then Elizabeth had taken a seat on a lovely sofa upholstered in coral. After Mrs. Cummings spread a small towel across her lap and shoulder, Elizabeth brought the infant to her chest, pulled aside her gown and offered him a nipple before draping her shawl over the child.

Considering how much noise the baby was making whilst suckling, Lady Selina chuckled. "He appears to be an excellent eater."

"He is," Elizabeth replied. "I would even venture to say that he appears to gain weight from one day to the next. Whenever I mention that to William, however, he disagrees."

Lady Selina laughed. "Normally it is the mother who thinks their child is still a baby."

"William is very sentimental. I fear he does not want this child to grow up as fast as Bennet and Anne have."

"That is understandable. Babies do seem to grow so fast."

"You will get no argument from me." Then Elizabeth continued. "I hope you do not mind, but I asked you here so that we could talk privately. It upsets William whenever I bring up Georgiana. He was looking forward to seeing her, Matthew, and their new baby this Christmas."

"As were we all," Selina replied. "At dinner last night you mentioned receiving a letter from Matthew just before we arrived, so I assume you know everything."

"Unfortunately, Matthew is a man of few words. All he said in the letter was that my sister and the baby were both well and that they had named him Colin Matthew Walter Davidson after him and his grandfather. Still, after the difficulty I had in giving birth to Anthony, I wondered if Georgiana is truly well. After all, Colin is her first child."

"First, given what William wrote after Anthony's birth, let me say that Richard and I were so relieved to find you in good health."

"I wish William had not been so forthcoming about how difficult Anthony's birth was—at least in his letters to my family; but, in his defence, he had gone through many rough days before and after the baby was born and was too weary to be anything but honest."

"It was obvious from his letter how much he loves you and how proud he is of you and Anthony."

"Yet sometimes I fear he has no idea how much his love and support mean to me and the children. I am the woman I am because of him. He is truly one of a kind."

"After we have children, if Richard and I are as content as you and William, I shall feel blessed."

"Matthew mentioned that the baby looks like Georgiana. What do you think?"

"I believe he looks more like his father," Lady Selina stated. "Still, he is a handsome little fellow with blond hair and blue eyes, which basically means he favours both his parents. In addition, he can be quite vocal if he does not get his way immediately."

Elizabeth smiled. "From my husband's description of Georgiana as a child, that could describe her."

"Richard said that, too!"

"I am disappointed that they could not travel until after the new year, but I understand that the baby took so long to make his appearance that it precluded Georgiana coming for Christmas."

"Yes. If you believe William is inflexible when it comes to your welfare, you may be interested to know that Matthew is following in his footsteps."

"Georgiana may not be happy about that, but my husband will be."

As Elizabeth lifted Anthony to her shoulder and began patting his back to induce a burp, Lady Selina cried, "Look! William and Richard are galloping across the pasture."

Catching sight of two riders heading towards the stables, Elizabeth said, "It must not have taken long to inspect the hay barn."

"What happened to it?"

"A storm blew a tree across one corner of the building. William has had men working to repair it for a week. He hoped to get it finished before it begins to snow again in earnest."

"Richard was disappointed that not enough snow had accumulated to allow for taking out the sleds."

"William thinks it will be deep enough by Christmas. Let us hope he is right, for that is one activity I was counting on to entertain the children … that and skating on the pond next to the stables."

"I wish I had thought to bring my skates."

"Do not worry. We have plenty of skates in good repair just in case anyone needs to borrow them. I am certain some will fit you."

"Wonderful! I look forward to seeing if I can still skate."

Days later

If Mrs. Reynolds or Mr. Walker felt overwhelmed by the number of guests accumulating at Pemberley in the days preceding Christmas, they were too professional to show it.

The Bennets were next to arrive, bringing Kitty, Lydia and John Lucas with them, whilst Mr. and Mrs. Gardiner and their children arrived the day after. Mary and her family did not arrive until two days before Christmas, given that her husband was the vicar at Meryton and did not wish to shirk his duties during the Christmas season. Since they had visited only weeks before, the Bingleys did not arrive until Christmas Eve, which disappointed Mrs. Bennet so much that she vowed to return with them to Ivy Manor once they departed Pemberley.

William was too in love with Elizabeth to let the behaviour of her relations override his usual tolerant nature; however, he was not above allowing Mrs. Reynolds to caution Kitty and Lydia about running through the house whilst playing hide-and-seek with the younger children. His only solace was in the fact that Bennet and Anne never had to be chastised about such conduct, as they knew better than to behave in such a manner.

On the first full day that he was in residence, Mr. Bennet abdicated any responsibility for his family's behaviour by retreating to the library, whilst Mrs. Bennet, Kitty and Lydia whined about being trapped inside because of the icy weather. To Mrs. Gardiner's credit, she volunteered her husband to escort her, and all who wished to join them, into Lambton, saying they could see the gaily-decorated shops and purchase last-minute Christmas gifts. William insisted they make use of two of his largest carriages—pleased that they could accommodate all of Elizabeth's relations who wished to go.

A heavy snow that night provided enough powder to hitch sleighs to draft horses and pull everyone—old and young alike—around the estate the next day. Leaving the infants to Mrs. Cummings and her assistants, Elizabeth talked Jane into joining her, Bennet, Anne, Thomas and their husbands in one sleigh, whilst the Gardiners, their children, Mary and her family occupied another. This left Mrs. Bennet, Kitty, Lydia and John Lucas to ride in a smaller sleigh—which also happened to be the newest—and which was the only reason Elizabeth's mother agreed to the arrangement.

After hours of gliding over the stark, white landscape dotted with scenes of frozen ponds and lakes and trees that appeared to be sculpted from ice, everyone was ready to return to the manor and partake of the hot chocolate, coffee and refreshments Mrs. Lantrip had promised would be waiting. Plenty of warm ginger biscuits and lemon tarts were sufficient to satisfy everyone's appetites until the dinner bell was rung.

Other days were filled with the entire party painting pictures using the view from the conservatory, choosing sides for snowball fights or ice skating on the small pond nearest the stables. Those who knew how to skate were kept busy instructing those who had never learned the art.

Though Bennet and Anne begged to ride their ponies, William declared that the frozen ground made that too dangerous, not only for the ponies but also for the children. Instead, he had some child-sized sleds fetched from the hayloft in the stables and the men pulled the smaller children around the lawn in them. Clancy tried his best to monitor the welfare of his charges, Anne and Bennet, by circling their sleds and barking his disapproval whenever he thought they were in danger, but even he was growing tired by the time everyone went back into the manor.

Christmas Day proved the perfect opportunity to showcase Pemberley's excellent fare. Even considering the large number of guests in residence, Mrs. Lantrip outdid herself by preparing enough food for a buffet that lasted several days. The Darcys' hospitality included placing a basket containing several types of biscuits, along with individually wrapped caramel candy, in each guests' room to be discovered on Christmas morning.

After assembling in the dining room to break their fast, everyone gathered in the largest drawing room, where a yule log was burning, to sing their favourite Christmas carols and listen to Mr. Gardiner read the Christmas story from the Bible. Then, as they exchanged gifts, they were urged to reveal something they were especially thankful for, which was very moving given how William had survived his ordeal at sea. After the younger children were ushered upstairs to the playroom with their toys, the adults and older children were free to do whatever they wished until tea was served later that day.

Mrs. Bennet cajoled Kitty, Lydia and John Lucas into playing cards with the new deck she had received for Christmas, whilst Mr. Bennet hurried to a quiet corner of the library to read one of several books given to him. A good many of the party ended up in the music room, listening to the new music that had been gifted to various persons. As the Gardiners' children attempted to become familiar with one of the compositions, Richard and Selina sat in the back of the room quietly discussing their future plans with William and Elizabeth.

"So, you intend to leave in the morning," William stated. "Are you not fearful of the roads with all the snow?"

"My coach holds well in the snow and one reason we arrived so early is so that we could leave early as well," Richard replied. "As you are likely aware, my parents stayed in London for Christmas, as did Leighton and Lady Susan. We promised to join them after spending Christmas Day at Pemberley and stopping at Houghton Park on our way to Town. We wish to make certain our steward, Mr. Dobbs, handled the presents for our servants and tenants according to our instructions and that there are no pressing problems."

"You cannot trust him to handle such things efficiently?" William continued.

"It is not a matter of trust," Lady Selina interrupted. "Mr. Dobbs is honest, but he is becoming forgetful in his old age." She sighed. "I fear I will soon have to retire him and hire a younger man."

"In any case, our departure should still leave you with plenty of company," Richard remarked.

"Elizabeth thinks all her relations will soon follow the Bingleys to Ivy Manor, except for Mary's family," William said. "Her husband feels obligated to resume his duties at his parish, so they will also leave tomorrow."

"My mother is determined to see Jane's estate and, knowing how little Papa likes to travel, she thinks this may be her only opportunity," Elizabeth added. "And my aunt and uncle feel they must not forsake their business for too long. I think they plan to leave tomorrow or the day after."

"Ah, so you will soon be rid of all your relations," Richard said, chuckling. "I imagine it will be a long time before you wish to host company again."

"On the contrary, Georgiana and her family are due to visit in January," Elizabeth said. "We will be delighted to see them and the new baby. For my part, it is always good to have another new mother to compare notes with."

"I pray they will visit us once they leave here," Lady Selina said. "We should be settled at Houghton Park by then."

"I cannot imagine why they would not," William added.

Later, as evening approached, William followed Elizabeth to her bedroom where she slipped off her day gown and donned a robe, preparing to feed Anthony. She took her son from Mrs. Cummings, and as the nursemaid exited the room, Elizabeth sank into one of the gifts her husband had surprised her with for Christmas—a plush, upholstered chair made especially to fit her so that her feet reached the floor instead of dangling in mid-air.

As she guided Anthony to a breast, Elizabeth sighed. "This chair is marvellous! It is so comfortable I believe I could sleep in it. Thank you, darling, for thinking of me."

"I always think of you, my love," William replied. "Moreover, I wish to say again that I treasure the shirts you made for me. If you only knew how difficult it is to purchase a decent shirt. Ask Adams! He recalls how often I complained about the ones he had made in London. Those you create fit me perfectly, and I know how many hours it takes to make just one."

She beamed. "Nothing makes me happier than to see you wear something I made especially for you."

By then Anthony was keeping a steady cadence as he suckled and William realised it was the perfect time to present Elizabeth with a special gift he had had made whilst they were in London—one which he wanted to present in private.

Kneeling beside the chair, he held out a black, velvet box. "Darling, I have one more gift for you. I pray this gift illustrates my love, devotion and gratitude for your love and for the children you have borne me."

Because her arms were full, William opened the box, revealing a gold chain featuring a gold heart surrounded by diamonds. In the middle was a heart-shaped ruby—Elizabeth's birthstone.

"The date of birth of each of our children is engraved on the back, along with a small birthstone representing their birth month. Of course, Anthony's birth date and stone will have to be added."

Shocked into silence, at first all Elizabeth could do was stare. At length she reached out to take the heart. Examining it carefully, she murmured "Oh, William, it is lovely. How thoughtful."

"You will note that the engraver left room for more dates on the back."

Elizabeth chuckled. "It appears he expects us to have a lot more children."

"I have given that a lot of thought, sweetheart, and if you must suffer as you did when giving birth to Anthony, I had rather not have more children."

Laying the necklace back in the box, Elizabeth reached out to cup William's face tenderly. "Please do not say that. I had rather die than live as companions, never to feel your loving touch again. Besides, has God not been faithful? He has safely brought us through every torment we have faced thus far. Surely, we can trust Him to take us through whatever we face in the future."

"As usual, you make a good point," William replied, leaning in to kiss her, softly at first, and then more passionately. Anthony began to complain of being crushed between his parents, making his father chuckle. "Thank you for reminding me, Son. There are weeks to go before we can resume marital relations."

"Dr. Camryn said we should wait until the middle of January, but I thought I would ask him again when next he examines Anthony."

"I am sure the good doctor knows what is best; besides, I can wait however long it takes for you to fully recover."

"You truly are the best man I have ever known."

"If I am, it is because you bring out the best in me."

Anthony soon fell asleep and William pulled the sash to summon Mrs. Cummings. Not long after she returned the baby to the nursery, William began to remove his boots.

"We have an hour or so until time to dress for dinner, and I intend to spend it with you."

After he lay down beside Elizabeth and pulled her into his arms, they instantly fell asleep. It was only when a maid knocked on the door to notify her mistress that dinner was about to be served that they awoke.

Chapter 32

New Year's Eve

As it turned out, William and Elizabeth did find themselves entirely without company on the eve of the new year. Other than the grumbling coming from the children about not having their cousins to play with, it seemed almost too tranquil now that all their guests had left. Still, aware that Georgiana and her family would arrive in the next few weeks, they were both ready for the respite.

Elizabeth had fed Anthony and Mrs. Cummings had settled him in the nursery as midnight neared. Therefore, when William came to her, his eyes twinkling as he held out her robe, she could not resist agreeing when he said, "Come, darling, I wish to show you something."

Rising, Elizabeth found herself being guided out of her bedroom and down another hall by William's strong hand on the small of her back. At length they arrived at the door of her study. He took a key out of his pocket and opened it before directing her inside and straight to the windows. They had often sat on the sofa in here, enjoying the view whilst sipping tea and discussing important matters, but tonight the view itself was what he wanted to show her.

It had been snowing all day, but the clouds had departed leaving an enormous silver moon hanging just above the treeline in the distance. The light emanating from it revealed that Pemberley was covered in a thick blanket of snow, shrouding trees and buildings and burying all but the tops of fences. Moreover, in the gardens the smaller statues could scarcely be seen peeking out from the glittering snow. Other than a few flakes of snow floating lazily from the roof whenever the wind blew, nothing was stirring.

William moved to stand behind Elizabeth, wrapping his arms around her whilst pulling her back against his chest as she exclaimed, "Oh, William, it is simply gorgeous!" Sinking into his embrace, she added, "It takes my breath away."

Placing a kiss atop her head, William said, "I knew you would love it."

"I wish an artist could capture this scene," Elizabeth murmured reverently.

"Would that it were possible," William replied. "I have seen paintings of many snow-covered landscapes, but never anything that captured such tranquillity as this."

"You mentioned having a portrait done after Anthony was born," she said. "Perhaps we could discuss such a painting with whomever you choose to do our portrait."

"Perhaps," William murmured, leaning down to place a soft kiss below his wife's ear. Then, taking her hand, he drew her to the sofa where he sat down and pulled her onto his lap.

After sharing a fervent kiss, he said, "I was writing in my journal earlier, adding my thoughts about Anthony's birth, when I happened to remember what I had written shortly after Bennet was born. Perhaps you will recall. We were sitting in the swing in the garden, and I had taken him from your arms to let him rest upon my chest when you suddenly declared him an angel."

Elizabeth chuckled. "Now that you mention it, I do remember. I said Bennet was an angel, and you said I should write that down in my journal so that I could make him read it if he did not act so angelic in the future."

William smiled. "Well, today I learned that you were right all along. It appears that no matter how old he is, Bennet will always act like an angel."

"Oh? How did you come to that conclusion?"

"I was going through the clothes in my chest today, and Adams informed me that Bennet recently asked for another of my older shirts. Moreover, he insisted Adams put a little of my cologne on it, just as he had when I was missing."

"But I was under the impression that Bennet gave that up once Richard brought you home. What would make him want to resume that habit?"

"Adams wondered that, too, so he asked him."

"And?"

"It seems our son believes if Anthony sleeps with one of my shirts, he may not cry so hard every morning."

Elizabeth laughed. "I hope Adams explained that the reason Anthony cries is to alert us that he is hungry."

"He suggested that, but Bennet is convinced that a shirt with my cologne on it will work wonders. Of course, Adams did not have the heart to argue against his opinion."

Elizabeth smiled proudly. "I am pleased that Bennet is such a caring person. I do not recall ever being that solicitous of any of my sisters."

"I might have been with Georgiana, since she was so much younger than I; however, I cannot recall ever being that considerate of Richard, who was like a brother to me," William added. "In any case, I wanted you to know that we have done well with Bennet. He is not only intelligent, but he has a kind and caring soul."

"Which is all we can ask, is it not?" Elizabeth replied. Then she smiled. "Now, if only we can convince Anne to be so generous with her brothers."

William laughed aloud. "Anne has an entirely different temperament. After all, she inherited her mother's spirit and boldness."

"And spirit and boldness do not translate into kindness and caring?" Elizabeth asked, punching his arm. "So, this is your opinion of me."

"You are putting words in my mouth, for surely you know that I think you are all that is good and kind."

Elizabeth made to continue the debate, but William stopped her with a sound kiss. Once finished, he added, "All I am saying is that a family notable for producing reticent men should strive to produce women with lively personalities to counterbalance them."

Giving William a fierce kiss, Elizabeth said, "I am not certain I follow your reasoning, but I choose to believe you have redeemed yourself."

"Thank heavens!"

After sharing more kisses, each more passionate than the last, he said, "I also recall wondering at that time how I could have been blessed with so much happiness when other men were not nearly as fortunate."

Elizabeth ran a teasing finger lightly over his lips. "And have you figured that out?"

"I cannot claim to be an expert, but I have come to two conclusions. One is that parents who try to instil their children with good principals provide them an advantage over those who do not. By the time we met, I may have given pride too much influence over my conduct, but my parents never encouraged me in that. And two, it is essential to listen to God's urgings, especially when it comes to important decisions. If He had not brought you into my life and spoken to me about acting like a gentleman regarding your circumstances, I cannot imagine how my life would have turned out."

"I have thanked Him repeatedly for showing me your good character before it was too late," Elizabeth interjected. "I acted foolishly for far too long."

William smiled broadly. "I think God had his hands full with both of us before we admitted we were perfect for one another."

"I could not agree more."

One tender kiss led to another before William helped Elizabeth to her feet. Embracing her tightly, he whispered in her ear, "Here is to another year filled with unending love and the joy derived from having three wonderful children. I love you with every fibre of my being, Elizabeth Darcy."

"I love you just as deeply, my darling, and I look forward to another year with you and all those I hold dear."

An all-consuming kiss sealed their confessions before William pulled back to murmur, "I could hold you like this all night, my love, but I fear it is time we retire. Anthony may enjoy the smell of the cologne on my shirt, but I expect it will not soothe his belly once he is awake."

"That is because he is a Darcy," Elizabeth replied huskily, rising on tiptoes to rub her nose against his. "And I have found that Darcys are hard to satisfy when it comes to certain hungers."

"Why do I think you are not speaking about food?"

"Perhaps, because it is true?"

Another passionate kiss followed before they took one last lingering look at the landscape and walked back to their bedroom, hand in hand.

Finis

Thank You For Reading!

I hope you enjoyed *Journey of Love – A Pemberley Tale*. I enjoyed writing this story as a sequel to Proof of Love though it did take me longer than I expected.

As always, I would love to hear from you. You can send me an email at DarcyandLizzy@earthlink.net or you can always find me on my forum DarcyandLizzy.com/forum. If you join the forum, you'll find stories posted by a host of JAFF writers whose names I'm sure you'll recognize. Prior to publishing, I always post my latest book there.

If you would like notifications when my books are published or when I begin posting them on the forum, please send an email to this address and tell me you wish to be added to the 'Notifications' email list: Brendabigbee@earthlink. net. I will never share your information, and I promise you will not be inundated with emails.

Finally, if you are so inclined, I would appreciate it very much if you would review this book where you purchase or read books. You, the reader, have the power to make a book more visible by leaving a review.

Again, thank you so much for reading *Journey of Love – A Pemberley Tale*.

With gratitude,
Brenda Webb

Made in the USA
Las Vegas, NV
30 January 2024

85109600R00179